I0634058

The Amber Chalice

Table of Contents

The Amber Chalice

Bounders, Book 2
Saoirse Temple

Published by Saoirse Temple, 2025

This is a work of fiction. Similarities to real people, places, or events are entirely coincidental.

THE AMBER CHALICE

First edition. September, 2025

Copyright ©2025 Saoirse Temple

ISBN: 978-0697505-5-6

Written by Saoirse Temple

Also by Saoirse Temple
<u>Bounders Series</u>
The Fire of Orhowyn (Book 1)
<u>Dear Diary Style Files</u>
Dear Diary; Punctuation Can't Save the World
(But It Did Save Grandma)
Dear Diary; I have 99 Problems and All of Them
Are Numbers
Dear Diary; I Think the Alphabet is Gaslighting
Me
Dear Diary; I've Committed a Capital Offence
Dear Diary; I Don't Think That Word Means
What I Think It Means

For Nolan, Robbin, Gavin and Karis

Prologue

Harpur Diggins sat next to his hoard, crunching on a deer that had wandered into the meadow outside his lair. He was exhausted and the nourishment that the dragon-fire blackened venison provided was reviving his strength. He hoped it would be enough to get him to his next destination; a mountain ledge on the western border between the kingdoms of Epoh and Rednow. There he was going to meet Khol the Black, ruling dragon of Rednow.

The three-day hike through Braydon Wood from Colwygshire was uneventful and had provided him with time to make his plan. After King Arthur and Queen Alex had announced that they were expecting a child, he had felt compelled to take action to ensure that they remained safe should his waning strength become known and another dragon challenge him for rulership over Epoh. it was only a matter of time and with his magic failing and his ability to transform from his human to his dragon form having become almost too excruciating to execute, he had to find a way to look after Arthur and his growing family.

He had spent too much time in human form. It was taking its toll on his magic and with the injuries he'd sustained when he lured three wraiths into a Boundary several moon cycles earlier, he was rapidly growing too weak to rule as the great purple dragon he had once been.

When he'd finished eating the deer, Harpur crawled out of the lair and moved to the edge of the meadow from where he leapt into the sky. His deformed right wing protested against the weight of his body by sending shocking waves of pain through his shoulder and down his back. But he forced himself to carry on, getting as much altitude as he could so he might be able to glide for a few miles before he had to pump his wings again. The distance to the mountain peak was only a hundred miles and when he was fit and strong, he could have done it in a matter of fifteen or twenty minutes. But in his current condition, it was unlikely that he would be able to do it in one shot. Staying close to the mountains so he could land if he needed to, Harpur floundered through the night sky. It was imperative that he arrive before Khol and though it would be a long night on the mountain, his pride would not allow him to let Khol see him struggling so severely.

He arrived a few hours before dawn, even more exhausted than he'd been at his lair, and settled himself on the wide ledge a couple hundred feet below the peak where Khol was going to join him for their meeting. Keeping his right wing toward the mountain side, he strategically placed his left wing to cover the missing scales on his leg where contact with the edge of the Boundary had burned them with frostbite. As for the missing scale over his heart that he'd torn off to save Arthur's life before he'd become king, there was not much he could do to hide it. Even if he could have kept Khol from noticing his injuries, the stout black dragon would sense his weaknesses anyway. Harpur lowered his head to rest on an outcropping of rock and fell asleep.

He was woken at dawn by the sound of wings flapping in the sky above him. Harpur, stiff and sore after his flight from the lair, winced against the pain that shot through his shoulder as he stood to meet the other dragon.

Khol landed a short distance away from Harpur and was instantly struck by the weakness he sensed in the great purple dragon. "Hale, Harpur Diggins," he said as he approached.

"Hale, Khol. Thank you for coming."

"It appears that it is I who should thank you." Khol stared at the spot where the scale was missing from Harpur's chest. "You have confirmed the rumors that you are... not well?"

Harpur scowled at the smaller, black dragon and released a puff of purple-grey smoke from his nostrils. "I'm not done for yet, but it's good to know that I am still a worthy topic of discussion in the Sands of Sancheera."

Khol chuckled. "That you are. As you always have been. To what do I owe the honour of your invitation to meet?"

"I want you to agree to be my witness if I am challenged," Harpur said.

"If?" Khol snorted. "I think you mean when."

Harpur took a deep breath to calm himself. "Don't test me, Khol. Will you do it?"

"Yes, yes, of course. I owe you that much." The black dragon backed away from Harpur. He could sense the weakness in the purple dragon, but he was also aware of Harpur's power.

"You owe me nothing," Harpur said honestly. "What happened was a long time ago. And I never held it against you."

"Revenge was never your way," Khol said.

"No matter who challenges me, you will keep your word and accept the position of witness?"

"I will," Khol said.

"Have you heard of any who might be thinking of challenging me?" Harpur wasn't going to ask this question, but he couldn't help himself.

"Oh, there are a few who have talked about it. But it's all just been posturing. No one of significance has spoken out. Would you like me to tell them I've seen you and that you are not nearly as weak as they may think?"

Harpur was surprised by Khol's gesture. It might buy him some more time. *To grow weaker...* "Do as you think best," Harpur said. "But as I said, you owe me nothing."

Khol turned away from Harpur and moved to the edge of the ledge. "Take care, Harpur Diggins. The next time we meet may be the last." With that, the black dragon launched into the air and flew back to Rednow, leaving Harpur to find the strength to return to Colwygshire on his own.

Chapter One

"You better have it right this time. I could be a father any minute."

A bundle of nervous energy, King Arthur of the Dragon Fire entered the council chambers and glared at the four people sitting at the round table in the center of the room. He did not take a seat. Instead, he rested his hands on the polished oak and leaned heavily in exhaustion upon them. The queen was in labour, about to deliver their first child and he'd been up all-night pacing back and forth outside her rooms while a mid-wife and several servants coached her through what sounded more like a torture session than the joyous beginning of a new life.

He'd been forbidden to attend the birth by the mid-wife, a formidable woman named Alma, who had made it quite clear that his crown did not include a free pass to the event. To his utter amazement, Alex, his queen and the love of his life, had agreed with Alma and Arthur had been summarily banished to the corridor. Various people, including each of the four men seated at the council chamber table had tried to distract him with invitations to eat, to walk, to talk, to get some sleep, but Arthur had stubbornly remained outside Alex's rooms waiting to know if he was the father of a prince or a princess.

Until, that is, a servant delivered a note shortly before dawn that read: *Hiro figured it out!*

Arthur read the note and then looked at the closed door to Alex's rooms. He beat on the door with his fist until it opened and a tired lady in waiting peeked out. "I'm needed in the council chambers. You are to send someone to get me the moment the baby is born."

"Yes, sire." The lady in waiting yawned and closed the door again.

"The very moment!" Arthur shouted at the solid oak barrier. "Do you hear me?"

When he got no answer, he turned and started toward the stairs that led to the main floor where the council chambers were located. He passed a kitchen maid on her way to Queen Alex's rooms with a tray of food for the birth attendants and was reminded of his own unattended hunger. He snatched three sausage links from the tray, which he ate on the way down the stairs. The kitchen maid curtsied and sighed. Then she stopped and rearranged the tray to hide the fact that three sausage links were missing. *Hopefully,* she thought, *I can drop the tray and leave before anyone notices and accuses me of eating them.*

"So, no news yet?" Sok, the elf and senior advisor to the king asked, ignoring Arthur's surly entrance.

"If there was, Sok," Arthur scoffed, "I would have said so. Now tell me what you've figured out so I can get back to my wife and child."

Harpur Diggins sat across the table from where Arthur stood. He was wearing an elegant, black coat and his signature top hat. A cravat of cream-coloured silk was expertly tied around his neck and a large, round amethyst sparkled in the center of it. His once jet-black beard was now an iridescent mauve-white. Being in human form was taking its toll on the dragon and his beard was the most obvious evidence of it. Arthur saw the weariness in Harpur's lavender eyes and another worry was refreshed. *How much longer will you be with us, my friend?* Arthur wondered.

Hiro, a Krist that they had imported from Mysturna, giggled to indicate that he wished to speak. "I have perfected the transporter that will get Anayah safely off Mysturna and bring her here."

Arthur looked at the small being standing, as he usually did, in his telepathically controlled hover gilly. It had been almost a year and half since their friend, Anayah, had escaped from her aunt Analeetah and taken refuge in a sacred place called the Sphere on her home world of Mysturna. With her own magic suppressed by her aunt, Anayah had no way of getting away and coming to Thraeh. Everyone around the table felt some measure of responsibility for what had happened, though it was Harpur Diggins who bore the greatest weight of it. Arthur wanted to rejoice, but he knew better than to get too excited too soon. Inevitably, this announcement would be followed by some thorny caveat, a complication that they would have to overcome before the deed could be done.

"But?" Arthur braced himself for the bad news.

"But Bon wishes to come with Anayah," Hiro said.

Arthur looked, first at Harpur, and then at Sir Davynn Willhart, the other man at the table, to gauge their feelings on the matter. Harpur's face was impassive. Sir Davynn, however, appeared to have reservations.

"What is it, Davynn? Do you object to having an android in Colwygshire?" Arthur asked the knight.

"I find it difficult to imagine a machine that looks and behaves like a man," Davynn said. He reached for an apple and began paring slices off it with his dagger.

Bon, indeed a machine that looked and behaved like a human – mostly – had once saved Sok's and Arthur's lives. He'd had to kill them both first, but in the end, he'd staved off the Entanglement that threatened to transfer their souls and, thus, their personalities from one to the other. Arthur hadn't had much time to interact with Bon, but he was grateful for his skill. He had no problem with Bon coming to live in Colwygshire. If a Krist and a witch from a different world were welcome, why not an android as well?

Arthur, himself, was from Earth. As the king of Epoh, he had the last say. But he had come to rely on the council of Harpur, Sok, Davynn and Hiro since his coronation sixteen months earlier. There was an unspoken agreement between them that on matters such as this, he would not sanction an action without the consensus of the group. It had always been agreed amongst them that they would do everything in their power to rescue Anayah from her prison on Mysturna, but bringing Bon with her had never been part of the bargain.

Since their own collective banishment from Mysturna, Harpur, Sok and Arthur had relied on Hiro for information on Anayah. He was free to come and go between Thraeh and Mysturna and had regularly returned to the underground cavern that was his home on that world. From there he was able to communicate with Anayah and Bon and get assistance from the technologically savvy android in creating a transporter using Arthur's old cell phone, which he had smuggled with him when he had left Earth to become the king of Epoh. The Krist and the android had bonded just as the witch and the android had bonded. It seemed natural – at least to Arthur – that he should join their group.

Arthur turned to Sok. "What do you think?"

"I think that as long as the transporter can handle bringing both of them, that Bon should be allowed to come." The elf stated his opinion and then returned his attention to his never-ending paperwork.

"Harpur?"

The dragon-wizard pursed his lips and, inspired by Davynn, reached for an apple of his own. "The android could be useful." He took a bite of the apple.

"Well, you are all more familiar with it than I am," Davynn conceded. "Let's add a mechanical man to our company."

Hiro giggled with typical Krist glee. "That's wonderful! I will begin making the arrangements." He floated out of the council chambers on his hover gilly.

Arthur eyed the tray of pastries on the table. They looked far more appetizing than the small sausage links he'd pilfered, but it was too far away for him to reach and he didn't have the energy to walk around the table. He could have asked Harpur to move it closer to him, but he decided that this was a good opportunity to practice his magic. Since learning that he actually did possess magical abilities, Harpur had been trying to teach him how to use them. To date, his efforts had been somewhat less than stellar. Still, if he was ever going to develop his skills, he had to practice. How hard could it be to get a pastry to move a few feet?

He concentrated on the confection that he wanted and willed it to float from the tray to his hand. At first the small, fruit-filled pie merely wiggled and jumped on the tray. Harpur and Davynn noticed the movement and leaned away from it, prepared to duck if they needed to. They'd both been witness to Arthur's attempts at magically moving objects and the level of unpredictability was high. It was as likely that it would explode as it was that it would do Arthur's bidding and travel safely to his outstretched hand. Sok remained absorbed in his paperwork and paid no attention.

The pastry continued to vibrate for several seconds. Harpur and Davynn held their breath and watched intently. Finally, it rose into the air and hovered above its companions much like a UFO in an early science fiction B movie. Arthur kept his focus. Just as it began to float toward its summoner, the lady in waiting that Arthur had ordered to come and get him the moment the queen gave birth burst into the room.

"The queen awaits you, sire," she announced. The excitement in her voice crackled like a lit sparkler.

Arthur instantly forgot about the pastry and wheeled around to face her. The pastry, however, did not forget that it was being summoned and picked up momentum. Arthur felt it whiz past his head and watched helplessly as it flew across the room and smashed squarely into the lady in waiting's face.

Without looking up from his paper work, Sok sighed. "We will help the lady. You should go meet your son or daughter."

Davynn, being the gallant and chivalrous knight that he was, was already on his feet and on his way to help the shocked and sputtering victim of her king's inept attempt at magic. As he approached the repentant king, he propelled Arthur toward the door.

Arthur muttered a brief and mildly apologetic apology to the lady in waiting as he passed her on his way out of the council chambers. He took the stairs two at a time, his feet barely touching the treads as he sprinted toward his long-awaited fatherhood. He couldn't wait to meet his son or daughter and count his or her fingers and toes. It sounded ridiculous, but he believed that was what parents of brand-new babies were expected to do.

The door to Queen Alex's rooms was open when he arrived a little out of breath and he rushed into the bizarrely tidy space. He had expected disarray, but found a testament to Alma's efficiency instead. No one would ever have suspected that a child had just been born there. Even his adorably cute hippie girl wife looked as if she had just woken up from a refreshing nap.

Alex's unruly curls were brushed and pinned back with jeweled combs. Her cheeks bore a faint blush of pink and her eyes sparkled with unfettered joy. She wore a lace-trimmed, lavender night gown under a creamy, satin robe. In her arms, she held a tiny bundle, swaddled in a mint-green blanket. From where Arthur stood at the door, he could see a patina of soft, blonde hair poking out of the blanket.

Alex looked up and smiled at her husband. "Arthur, come meet our daughter," she said softly.

"Hello, Princess," Arthur cooed as he took the baby from the queen and cradled her in his arms. His heart swelled, bursting with a powerful love for his child. All at once he was overwhelmed with more emotion than he knew what to do with and it spilled out in a torrent of tears. He couldn't take his eyes off this little girl.

"Arthur," Alex said softly from her bed.

"Hmm?" Arthur replied, barely registering his name. He was entirely enchanted by his new daughter.

"Would you like to meet our son?"

"Yes, dear," Arthur said. He continued to stare at the baby in his arms for a few seconds. "What did you say?"

Arthur finally tore his eyes away from his baby daughter and looked at his wife. She was holding another bundle, this one swaddled in a turquoise blanket. "Where did that come from?" Arthur was almost positive that his fatigue was playing tricks on him. He shook his head to clear the fog. But the second baby remained in Alex's arms.

"The same place that one came from," Alma said over Alex's delighted chuckling. "Where did you think he came from?" The midwife stood on the opposite side of the bed with her hands clasped in front of herself and gave Arthur a pinched look of disapproval.

"Did you know this was going to happen?" Arthur addressed his wife. Alma scared him to death.

"Alma suspected," Alex said, "but we weren't sure until this one made his appearance." She kissed the prince's forehead.

Arthur approached the bed and sat down slowly. He wanted to be as close to the prince as he could get, but wasn't sure Alma would approve of him doing so. When all she did was tsk at him, he allowed the bed to accept his full weight. "This is amazing!" He beamed at his queen, who beamed right back at him.

A noise at the door caused them all to turn. Sok strutted brazenly into the room and toward the bed where Arthur, Alex and the new prince and princess were. Behind him, Harpur and Sir Davynn followed, but stayed a more polite and unassuming distance from the royal family. Alma, of course, rushed to shoo them all out.

"It's okay, Alma," Alex said. "Let them come in."

The stern midwife complied, but couldn't help letting her disapproval show on her unyielding face. "For a few minutes then." She wasn't about to relinquish all of the control she believed she possessed.

"Orhowyn's silvery scales!" Sok shouted as he approached the bed and realized that there were two babies instead of only one. "There're two of them!"

Neither Harpur, nor Sir Davynn could resist this bit of information. They both moved to the end of the bed to confirm for themselves Sok's unexpected assertion. Harpur, the more taciturn of the two, simply nodded. Davynn openly congratulated the royal couple and, as the good and dutiful knight that he was, swore to protect the new prince and princes with his life.

Alex, still somewhat in awe of living in a magical kingdom, smiled at Sir Davynn's declaration and thanked him for his loyalty.

"What are their names?" Sok asked as he lifted the princess out of Arthur's arms and started rocking her gently back and forth as if holding babies was a common occurrence in his life. Every eyebrow in the room was elevated in response to the elf's natural ease with the baby.

Alex filled Arthur's empty arms with his son and adjusted her position against the pillows that propped her up. "The princess is Marian Elizabeth Grace and the prince is Harpur Earl Lancelot Luther."

Sok raised and squinted his eyes in thought. "Then I shall call the princess Meg, but I cannot go around calling the prince Hell. You will need to change his name."

Four brows furrowed in confusion.

"What are you talking about?" Harpur asked.

"It's an elven tradition. My name is Silkhar Ornathan Kluupentarajhar; Sok. So, Marian Elizabeth Grace becomes Meg and Harpur Earl Lancelot Luther becomes Hell. You see? That will never do." Sok began to softly hum an elven lullaby to little Meg.

"You forget that they are not elves," Harpur said to the humming elf.

"I kind of like Meg," Alex said as she tried to reassemble an appropriate acronym for her son.

The long and tedious debates that she and Arthur had had over possible names for their children had led to a few arguments in the weeks leading up to the twins' births. Arthur had insisted on names from the legend of King Arthur and had managed to convince her that Lancelot and Luther could be buried in a boy's moniker as middle names. She had conceded as long as whatever names they chose honoured Arthur's parents. Future children would be named after her own. The only name they agreed on from the start was Harpur for a boy. Once they had settled on Harpur Earl Lancelot

Luther, they agreed that they would not change it. Now, however, Alex was enchanted by the elven naming tradition and wanted her son to have a name within a name.

"We thought we'd just call the prince Harpur, if you don't mind," Arthur said, seeing the look on his wife's face and hoping to stop her from taking this any further.

"I think Harpur is a good choice," Harpur said. He was more pleased than he wanted to show that Arthur and Alex had named their son after him.

"Silkhar Ornathan Kluupentarajhar?" Davynn was still digesting Sok's proper name.

"What if we called him Harpur Arthur Reginald Tristan? Hart!" Alex suggested.

"Ooh!" Sok exclaimed. "I like that. Hart is a great name for a prince. Hart is another name for a stag and stags are sacred forest creatures. They represent leadership and protection."

Alex smiled. She had found a name that met all of the requirements. Reginald was Arthur's father's middle name and Tristan was a knight of the Round Table in some versions of the legend. Then she registered the look of disappointment on Arthur's face. He forced a smile in return, but did not answer. "We will keep the name we chose," she said quietly.

"No," Arthur said just as quietly. "Luther wasn't a very good guy and Lancelot betrayed Arthur. I think our son should be known as Prince Hart."

"You should have consulted me in the first place," Sok said. "I'm good at these things."

Harpur rolled his eyes at the elf. "You didn't choose the name."

"But I inspired it!"

"Harpur Arthur Reginald Tristan it is then," Alex said reaching for her son again. "I could really use a pastry. Are there any left on the tray?"

Davynn turned to retrieve the tray from a table near the window for his queen. "It appears that your attendants have eaten everything." He held up the empty platter.

"I will send for more," Sok said and started toward the door.

"Uh, Sok?" Arthur said.

"Hmm?"

"Leave the baby here." Arthur stood up and walked across the room to take the princess from the elf.

Sok looked at Arthur and sighed. "Very well." Reluctantly, he handed Meg to her father.

"Thank you," Arthur said, shaking his head at the elf's audacity.

With Sok off on a mission and the infants safely in their parents' arms, Harpur and Davynn excused themselves as well.

"You're going to have to set limits with that one," Harpur said. "Establish visiting hours or something. Otherwise, he'll be up here all the time."

Alex laughed. "They could have worse admirers, but I think you are right. If we give him free reign, he'll have them swinging from the trees before they can walk."

Alma returned with a yawning lady in waiting and announced that it was time for the babies to get some rest. Arthur looked at the midwife and was about to tell her that he and Alex were the babies' parents and they would decide when twins needed to rest, but Alex spoke up first. "Thank you, Alma. I'm feeling a little tired, myself. Arthur, don't you have court soon?"

Arthur scowled. The last thing he wanted to do was sit in the throne room and listen to complaints and accusations. But it was court day and it was his duty. And in all fairness, Alex deserved a bit of rest. He passed little Meg to the lady in waiting and then went to Alex's side. "Thank you," he whispered as he leaned down to kiss her. "They are perfect. And so are you."

Alex smiled. "I love you."

"I love you too."

As Arthur followed Harpur and Davynn out of the queen's rooms, he heard the knight mutter, "Silkhar Ornathan Kluupentarajhar?"

"The weirdest part of that," Harpur said, "is that Kluupentarajhar is a Fae name."

Arthur, a few steps behind his friends, perked up. "Fae?"

Harpur and Davynn stopped to allow the king to catch up to them. "It's obscure, but it is definitely Fae in origin," Harpur explained.

"Fae, as in fairies?" In all the time he'd been on Thraeh and living in the Kingdom of Epoh, he'd never heard of fairies outside of a few songs the minstrels sang in the pubs and markets.

"I wouldn't call them fairies to their faces," Harpur cautioned, "but, yes, Fae as in fairies."

"There are Fae in Epoh?" Arthur was curious. He had visions of tiny, winged beings that flew around sprinkling fairy dust behind them.

The threesome reached the top of the stairs and began to descend on their way to the throne room. Sok, it appeared, had accomplished his mission. They met a kitchen maid on her way up with a tray of pastries and cakes for the queen. As she stopped to awkwardly curtsy in deference to the king, each of them removed a tart from the platter and continued on their way. She waited until they were out of sight to put down the tray and rearrange the pastries. This was a common occurrence and she was thankful that the kitchen staff had learned to put extra on the trays for the queen just for these eventualities.

"There are a few living in the southern-most portion of Braydon Wood," Harpur said around a mouthful of delicious tart. "They have been granted the right to live there. As long as they don't bother any of the other races in Epoh and keep the peace, they can stay."

"Why would they bother any of the other races?" Arthur was wondering why this had never come up before. *Shouldn't I know about Fae living in my kingdom?*

"It's always best to leave the Fae to themselves," Davynn contributed. "They are not the most trustworthy of creatures."

Arthur felt a jolt of alarm. "Should we be concerned?"

"The elves will let us know if there is anything to worry about. So far, the Fae have behaved themselves." Harpur popped the last bite of his tart into his mouth and jogged down the steps ahead of Davynn and Arthur to open the door to the throne room.

Arthur made a mental note to bring this up again later.

Chapter Two

Court was Arthur's least favourite royal duty. Listening to people complain about and accuse others of petty infractions was tedious and often boring. It was as if half of the kingdom's subjects were disinclined to think for themselves and preferred to let their king decide for them. Arthur was appalled at the bizarre petitions he was required to make judgements on. His very first case when he became king was that of a local tradesman whose daughter refused to marry the man he'd chosen for her. The sixteen-year-old girl wanted to apply to the weaving guild, but her father insisted that she marry a man nearly three times her age, an unappealing and rather creepy chap to whom the father, it eventually came out, owed a considerable sum of money. When Arthur clued in to the fact that he was, essentially, selling his daughter, he became quite furious. Much to the father's chagrin, Arthur decreed that he was to find some other way of paying his debts and instantly offered to let the young girl live in the castle under his protection while she apprenticed at the guild of her choice. He was setting a dangerous precedent, but he stood by his decision and dismissed the father with a warning not to come before the court with such an unconscionable petition ever again.

Soon after that, Arthur reduced the court days to every fourth day. There were no days and weeks on Thraeh. Months were measured by the moon and the seasons. About as specific as it got was to arrange for a meeting on, for example, the third day after the second moon in the Dark Season at midday. Needless to say, a lot of people were kept waiting – sometimes for days. With specific court days established, Arthur found it easier to pinpoint appointments and meeting times, but there remained a significant margin for error. Functioning without clocks and calendars was one of the hardest things Arthur and Alex had to adjust to. Except for the loosely scheduled bells that rang in the market, there was no way to tell time. To them it was like every day was a Saturday, except court days, which were always like Mondays.

That particular day, the docket contained only eleven petitions. *With any luck*, Arthur thought as he donned his crown and fur-trimmed royal robe, *we'll be done before lunch and I can spend the afternoon with Meg and Hart.* He frowned slightly when he heard those names in his head, but he knew he would warm to them. He glanced at Sok and nodded to signal that he was ready to hear the first petition.

The first petitioners were a butcher and a shoemaker. The pair owned and operated permanent shops next door to each other and were at constant odds. This was the third time in the past moon cycle that Arthur had had to listen to them complain about one another. Before either of them spoke, he was already bored.

"Is this about Dun throwing the blood and offal from the butcher shop in the gutter again?" Arthur asked.

"No, sire," Dun, the butcher quickly answered. "It's about Jacko's stitching machine."

Arthur's brow furrowed. "His *stitching* machine?"

"Yes, sire," Dun continued. "Jacko has installed a machine for stitching leather in his shop and it makes a terrible racket. I can't hear my customers' orders over the noise. Yesterday, I gave the good widow Treen two pounds of fish instead of one pound of ham."

"Two pounds of fish doesn't even sound a little bit like one pound of ham," Jacko interjected. "It's not my stitching machine that is the problem; it's this..." Jacko checked himself before he called his business neighbour a name he would be fined for using in court. "...it's Dun not paying attention. He's all over smitten with that Morgaine Fayle woman who's lodging at the Shire Bend Inn. He's so busy gawking out the window hoping to catch a glimpse of her, he doesn't know what his customers are asking him for."

Arthur silently asked Orhowyn for strength. "Tell me about this stitching machine," he said to Jacko as he beckoned Sok to come closer for a word.

"Well, sire," Jacko said with pride in his voice, "it's quite remarkable. There's a hand crank, you see..."

But Arthur didn't care about the stitching machine. He'd only asked to keep Jacko talking for a minute while he conferred with Sok. "What do you know about this Morgaine Fayle?" he whispered to his senior advisor.

"Not a thing. Except that she is the last petition on the docket today. She's seeking a private audience with you," Sok replied.

"Get her in here now," Arthur said. "I want to see just how distracting this woman is."

Sok left the dais to summon Morgaine Fayle into the throne room.

"...and while it does make a clicking sound when it operating, it's not very loud and it most definitely doesn't prevent old Dun here from hearing orders." Jacko completed his description of the stitching machine.

"Right," Arthur said as if he'd heard every word. "Sounds like a perfectly wonderful invention."

Jacko bowed to Arthur and then shot Dun a condescending look. "Thank you, sire. It is."

Behind the two petitioners, the doors to the throne room opened. All eyes turned to see who was interrupting Dun and Jacko's audience with the king. And all eyes widened as a raven-haired beauty entered the hall and sauntered toward the dais. She smiled as she approached Jacko and Dun. Jacko bowed his head slightly while Dun blushed and giggled like a schoolboy.

Arthur could see why Dun was so smitten. From her gleaming black locks to the shimmering blue-green gown that fitted her curves like a second skin, Morgaine Fayle was most definitely a distraction. As much as he adored Queen Alex, even Arthur had to admit that he would be hard-pressed not to give this woman a second glance.

A motion on Arthur's left caught his eye and he managed to tear his gaze away from the vision in front of him to see Harpur slip out the door. *That is odd*, Arthur thought. He also noticed that Morgaine Fayle noticed the dragon-wizard's departure. She glanced furtively over her shoulder as Harpur literally snuck out of the room. A small smile played across her ruby lips and then she turned her whole attention on Arthur.

Having returned to the dais, Sok announced the newcomer. "The Lady Morgaine Fayle of Andonsheer."

Morgaine curtsied as deeply as her tight gown would permit. "It's just Morgaine Fayle, your majesty. I have no title." Her voice was deep and as sultry as her curvaceous figure.

But you have plenty of wealth. "My apologies... May I call you Morgaine?" Arthur asked, not sure how he should address her.

"Of course."

"Thank you. Again, I apologize. My advisor assumed incorrectly." Arthur cleared his throat and adjusted his position on the throne. "You are a long way from home, Morgaine. What brings you to Colwygshire?"

"I am hoping to acquire some property in your charming kingdom. Perhaps in the north-west?" Morgaine said.

She flipped her long, black hair over her shoulder and Arthur saw that, unlike her other finger nails, which were painted a rich sapphire that matched her eyes, the nail on her index finger was the colour of old bone with a black streak marbling its length from tip to cuticle. She wore no rings. In fact, she wore no jewelry at all. Arthur found this disturbing somehow. Almost as disturbing as the way she made her last statement a question, as if she was challenging him in some way. *Or testing me?*

"I see," he said, unwilling to acknowledge the challenge. "I wish you good luck in your search."

Sok, who was taking notes looked at Arthur, puzzled by this peculiar exchange, but said nothing.

"May I inquire as to why I was asked to join the good butcher and shoemaker? I had requested a private audience with you, your majesty."

Beside her, Dun and Jacko shuffled uncomfortably. Even Arthur had to squirm a little. *How do I tell her I wanted to see how alluring she is?*

"It appears that you are something of a distraction for the businessmen around the Shire Bend. Your presence was required to settle these good merchants' petition." Arthur settled on the truth. He doubted that she was unaware of the effect she had on men.

Morgaine looked at the squat, balding butcher and the stooped, shaggy shoemaker with what Arthur could only interpret as amusement. "Then it seems that I need to hasten my acquisition and remove myself from your fair city as soon as possible."

Dun was so red in the face, Arthur feared he would have a heart attack. "I'm sure that these fine men are sufficiently mature enough to conduct themselves in a more appropriate manner?" Arthur looked pointedly at Dun, who nodded. "Good," he continued. "Jacko, I wish you well with your new stitching machine. Dun, pay closer attention to your customers from now on. And, for the love of Orhowyn, stop bringing your petty differences into my court. I've had quite enough of the both of you."

The two men bowed and scuttled out of the throne room.

"I apologize yet again," Arthur said to Morgaine. "Thank you for coming in. Perhaps you would like to join me for lunch after court is done. You can have your private audience over a good meal."

Sok cleared his throat to get Arthur's attention. "Sire, you are to lunch with the queen today. She is expecting you right after court."

"Of course," Arthur said. He wanted to get back upstairs and see Alex and the prince and princess more than anything, but he was feeling anxious about Morgaine Fayle and wanted also to find out what her business with him was. "Will you agree to postpone the private audience until after lunch? We can meet in the council chambers and there will be no need to rush."

Morgaine tilted her head and looked sideways at Sok for a moment. "That is more than agreeable. I will return at the first bell after the midday chime." She repeated her restricted, yet amazingly graceful curtsy and left the throne room.

As soon as the door closed behind her, Sok approached Arthur and stood next to the throne. "That was interesting."

"Indeed." Arthur rested his elbow on the arm of the throne and gripped his chin as he stared at the closed door. "Do you know why Harpur left so suddenly?"

"I didn't realize he had left," Sok said, looking across the room to where Harpur had been sitting against the wall. "When did he leave?"

"When Morgaine Fayle came in," Arthur said. "As soon as he saw her, he bolted for the door."

"That's even more interesting," Sok said, joining Arthur in staring at the door. After a moment he continued, "Shall I bring in the next petitioner?"

Arthur sighed. "I suppose so. I'd like to get out of here as quickly as I can."

When court finally ended, Arthur dropped his royal cloak on the throne and tossed his crown to Sok to have it put away in the vault. He hated the heavy thing and only wore it when he had to. He wasn't even sure that he ever *had* to, though Sok insisted that it was protocol for court. "It's a symbol of your authority. No one is going to respect a king without a crown," he repeated every time they were preparing for court and had to listen to Arthur grumble about it.

"I'm going up to Alex's rooms. See if you can find Harpur and ask him to join us there. And when Morgaine returns, make her comfortable in the council chambers. I'll be down as soon as I can," he said to Sok, who glared at his back as he left the throne room.

"And I don't get an invitation to lunch?" Sok mumbled to himself as he gathered up the royal cloak and folded it reverently.

As he had earlier that morning, Arthur took the stairs two at a time from the throne room to the third floor where his beloved wife's rooms were. He opened the door and entered to find her sitting up in her bed holding Hart in her arms. He could hear Meg crying in an adjoining room that was serving as the nursery for the twins.

"Is everything alright?" Arthur asked, tossing his head toward the bawling.

"Alma is changing her," Alex explained. "Apparently, it's not her favourite activity."

Arthur nodded, but he still felt like he should go and check on his daughter. He entered the nursery just as the midwife was bundling Meg snuggly into a blanket. The moment she was lifted up off the table, her crying stopped.

"May I?" Arthur asked, holding out his arms to take the baby.

"You may," Alma said in her typically snappish tone and placed Meg in her father's arms.

Arthur instinctively started bouncing Meg. She was wide awake and kept puckering up her lips and frowning as if she was quite disgusted by what had just happened to her. Arthur couldn't help but laugh. This tiny human, only a few hours old, was already asserting herself.

"This one's going to be a handful," he said, sitting down on the edge of the bed next to his wife. He leaned over and kissed Alex, sneaking a peak at Hart, who was sleeping soundly.

"They are quite amazing already," Alex said. "I think that Hart is going to be a scientist."

"A scientist! What makes you think that?" Arthur asked, perplexed.

"He just seems to be a thinker," Alex said, tilting her head and looking at her son.

"Well, I suppose time will tell," Arthur said. "How are you? Everything okay?"

Alex laughed. "As far as I know," she said. "Time will tell in that regard as well."

Arthur blushed.

Two maids came in with lunch trays for the king and queen. Alex's consisted of a thin broth and some steamed vegetables, while Arthur's was heaped with sandwiches and cakes and ale.

"This doesn't seem fair," Alex complained as the babies were replaced by the trays.

"You will eat lightly for a day or two," Alma instructed.

Alex took a piece of cake from Arthur's tray and stuffed it into her mouth as soon as Alma's back was turned. Arthur wisely busied his own mouth with one of the sandwiches.

"How was court?" Alex asked while she glowered at the broth on her tray.

"Interesting," Arthur said.

"That's a switch. Usually when I ask, you say, 'Tedious as always.' What was so interesting about it?" She slurped broth from her spoon and was delighted that it at least tasted good.

"A woman named Morgaine Fayle appeared today. She's rather... disturbing." Arthur lifted a piece of cheese to his mouth, but when he saw Alex's open mouth, he popped it into hers instead.

"Disturbing how?"

"I can't quite put my finger on it. She says she intends to acquire land in the north-west of the kingdom."

"There's nothing up there except forest and mountains," Alex said. "Why would she want land there? What does she intend to do with it?"

"That's just it. I can't imagine." Arthur took another bite of sandwich and chewed thoughtfully. "I guess I will find out later. She's requested a private audience with me and we will be meeting after lunch."

"I expect a full report," Alex said.

Arthur didn't mention Harpur sneaking out of the throne room. Neither did he describe Morgaine to Alex, deciding to leave that out unless Alex asked directly. There was no point in stirring the green-eyed monster that had taken up residence in Alex over the last few months of her pregnancy. He did tell her about Jacko's new stitching machine, though, and that provided a safe segue away from the troubling Morgaine Fayle.

Sok arrived bearing a lunch tray of his own and settled himself on a chair he pulled close to the bed to join them for the remainder of the meal. His intrusions into their private life had become a matter of course. They had long-since given up trying to convince him that he could not just come and go as he pleased. Instead, they came to think of him more like the elven son they would never have. And who would never leave home.

"Did you find Harpur?" Arthur asked.

"Not yet." Sok dipped a piece of bread into a pool of gravy and took a bite.

"He isn't in his room?"

"He is not. Nor is he in Hiro's laboratory, the kitchens, the guard towers, the dungeons or the water closet."

"You checked the water closets?"

"It seemed prudent when I couldn't locate him anywhere else. Just trying to be thorough." Sok licked some gravy off his fingers.

"I wonder where he got to." Arthur did not like not knowing where the dragon-wizard was at the best of times.

"The market, maybe?" Alex offered.

Sok and Arthur both shrugged. It was possible.

"I'm sure he will turn up." Arthur said, trying to convince himself that there was nothing to worry about.

They finished their meals and chatted about Meg and Hart. Sok, much to Arthur's surprise and relief, said nothing about Morgaine Fayle or anything that had happened at court. He seemed to sense Arthur's concern and, in light of happier things to talk about, namely Meg and Hart, kept the conversation light and cheerful. But as soon as he had sated his hunger, Sok wandered into the nursery to see the twins. From Alex's bed, she and Arthur could hear Alma lecturing the elf on proper etiquette and admonishing him for being in the queen's room uninvited.

"I'm their uncle!" Sok exclaimed. "And I'm Arthur's senior advisor. I have just as much right to be here as you do."

Arthur and Alex chuckled.

"He truly is incorrigible," Alex said.

"Maybe he'll drive Alma crazy and she'll quit," Arthur suggested.

"Oh, she's not that bad." Alex rolled her eyes.

"No," Arthur agreed, "she's worse. Couldn't you have found a more friendly midwife?"

"Well, she knows her stuff. And she's only going to be around for a few weeks. Once they are a little older, we'll find a permanent governess for them."

"Thank Orhowyn for that!" Arthur said, standing up to go see his children before he had to leave for his meeting with Morgaine. He bent down and kissed his wife. "I'll just go say good bye to Meg and Hart and then I'll get Sok out of Alma's hair."

"I'll take another of those cakes before you go." Alex pointed at the tray that still held a few of the rich confections.

Arthur handed her a piece of cake, kissed her again and went to save Alma. Or Sok. Arthur wasn't sure who would win if it came to blows between the two of them.

As they reluctantly descended the stairs on their way to the council chambers, Sok reminded Arthur that he wasn't wearing his crown. Arthur sighed. "Have someone fetch the silver circlet from my chambers. I'll wear that."

Sok sighed in turn. "How many times do I have to tell you...?"

"How many times have you told me already?" Arthur cut his senior advisor off before he could go on about the symbol of authority.

"Dozens! Hundreds probably."

"And how's that working out for you?" Arthur jogged ahead down the last few stairs and pushed the door to the throne room open. He held it for his long-suffering senior advisor who swept past him and barked an order to a guard to fetch the circlet and bring it to the council chambers.

"If Morgaine is here, let her in. And then keep looking for Harpur. I was hoping to talk to him before I met with the extraordinary Morgaine Fayle, but I guess I will have to do this cold." Arthur pulled a chair out from the round table and sat down. "He might be at Skull's Keep. Check there."

"Don't you want me to take notes?" Sok seemed disappointed.

"She asked for a private audience. I can write down any notes I think I might need."

Sok frowned. But he did as Arthur asked. Besides, Skull's Keep had the best ale in the kingdom and if Arthur was going to exclude him from the meeting with Morgaine, he'd just expense a pint or two to the royal account!

Arthur sat at the table and pondered the events of the morning. Harpur's abrupt departure when Morgaine had entered the room was disconcerting. Harpur had looked genuinely shaken by her appearance. And the surreptitious glance she had given him had not gone unnoticed. *Do they know each other?* Arthur wondered. *She said she was from*

Andonsheer. That's on the border of the Sands of Sancheera, which is where Harpur was born. And why would she want to acquire land in the north west?

All of the workable land occupied by humans in the Kingdom of Epoh belonged to the king essentially. There were no land owners, per se. Knights acted as Lords over different territories and were granted rights to manage the villages and farms within their territory. In exchange, they collected taxes for the king and paid – and were paid – a portion of the profits from crops, livestock and any industry that was conducted inside their borders. The peasants and workers were thus provided protection, housing and a fair wage in exchange for their taxes and tithes. It was a well-managed system, and one that existed only because Harpur allowed it, for in fact, Harpur owned the kingdom.

This is where things got muddy for Arthur. Dragons on Thraeh owned the world and divided it up amongst themselves into territories. At their whim, they either permitted humans, elves, dwarves and Fae to occupy the land and manage their affairs, or not. So, while Arthur was the king of the Kingdom of Epoh and ruled the people who lived within its borders, Epoh itself belonged to the dragon, Harpur Diggins. And he chose who could or could not live there.

For the most part, Harpur tended to let the peoples of Epoh live as they chose. Humans and elves dominated the populace and lived in relatively peaceful accord. Their treaties enabled the elves to manage Braydon Wood while the humans worked the land. A clan of dwarves mined the mountains in the far south and a colony of Fae occupied the southern-most portion of Braydon Wood and governed the great river that transected the kingdom where it flowed through that vast forest. As far as Arthur knew, the river had no name, though he had heard it referred to as the Fae Waters, which he had just assumed was an Epohian reference to some myth or legend. Arthur had never seen any of the Faefolk, but he so very recently had been assured that they were there and that it was best that they be left alone. He had met a couple of dwarves who had come to Colwygshire to sell the gems their clan had mined, but that had been a brief and altogether uneventful encounter. Each race was responsible for themselves and it was expected that each race respect the others under Harpur's overarching rule. He had no doubt that if a conflict were to arise between any of the races, Harpur would put an end to it in a flash.

The problem that kept nagging at him now was that just prior to his coming to Thraeh from Earth and being crowned king, Harpur had been badly injured while luring three wraiths into a Boundary to the world of Mysturna. He had never fully recovered and in recent months his condition had deteriorated alarmingly. This was attributed to the fact that he had spent eight Earth years in human form, which had caused him to lose much of his regenerative dragon powers. And now that he was so weakened by his injuries, he was vulnerable to other dragons coming to challenge him for ownership of Epoh. It was an eventuality, Harpur had assured Arthur, that was unavoidable. "Pray Orhowyn, when the time comes, that the dragon who inherits Epoh from me looks kindly on the people here," Harpur had warned him. Though he didn't want to believe it, he was sure that Morgaine was referring to Harpur's lair as the *lands* she wished to acquire when she mentioned the north-west, for that was where it was located.

Arthur desperately wished he could talk to the dragon-wizard now.

When the door opened again, Arthur stood up and came around the table to greet his guest. She was wearing a hooded cloak this time that covered her modestly from head to toe. Arthur suppressed his amusement and held out a chair for her. He waited until she had removed the cloak and was seated before returning to his own. "Thank you, Sok. If you could see to that little errand we talked about, I would really like to receive the package as soon as I am done with Miss Fayle."

"And where would you like me to deliver it to once I locate it, sire?" Sok asked, not missing a beat.

"If you could take it to my chambers, and watch over it until I get there, that would be great." Arthur smiled at the elf.

Sok smiled back, relieved he was not being shut out. He was dying to know what had set Harpur off. "Very good, sire."

"Can I get you anything?" Arthur turned his attention to Morgaine. "Wine? Water? Ale?"

"No, thank you. I'm fine." Morgaine replied. "But do have something yourself if you like."

Arthur would have liked a cup of ale, but he decided that it might be best not to have servants walking in on anything sensitive that might come up. "I'm fine too," Arthur said. "Now what did you want to see me about?"

"As I mentioned earlier, I am hoping to acquire some land in the north-west beyond Braydon Wood. I wished to meet with you to determine exactly how I should go about that." Morgaine's face remained passive.

Arthur's hands were clasped on the table top. He leaned forward a little, putting more weight onto his elbows. "As I'm sure you are aware, it is not within my purview to grant lands to anyone. I still don't know why you are here or what you want from me."

Morgaine leaned back in her seat, resting her forearms on the arms of the chair and allowing her long hands to dangle over the ends. Once again, Arthur noticed the unpainted nail on her left hand. This close it looked more like a claw or a talon than a fingernail. "I am well aware of the terms of land ownership, your majesty. I simply wanted to..." she paused, watching Arthur closely, "...understand the people in this kingdom before I move forward with my plans."

"I'm confused," Arthur said. "Are you saying that you want to know if we will be good neighbours?"

Morgaine actually smiled. "That is an excellent way of phrasing it."

"And how are we measuring up so far?" Arthur was not feeling good about any of this, but he, too, kept his expression passive.

"So far," Morgaine said, "I find your people quite likeable."

"I'm pleased to hear it." *More than you realize.* "But I'm still unsure of how it is that I can help you determine how you should put your plans into action. I don't even know what your plans are."

Morgaine thought about her response. "All in good time, your majesty," she said rising from her seat. "I'm afraid that I have taken up more of your valuable time than I intended. I can assure you, however, that you have exceeded my expectations."

Arthur remained sitting. "Miss Fayle?" he said, staring at his clasped hands.

"I do wish you would call me Morgaine." She put her cloak back on and pushed the chair back under the table.

"Miss Fayle," Arthur repeated, "the peoples of Epoh are extremely loyal to Harpur Diggins."

"And that is a good thing."

Just as Morgaine Fayle left the council chambers, the guard Sok had dispatched to retrieve Arthur's circlet appeared. He handed the silver diadem to his king and bowed.

"Thank you... Waldorn, is it?" Arthur took the circlet and placed it on the table.

"Wildorn, sire," the guard corrected.

"Thank you, Wildorn. That will be all."

Chapter Three

Hiro floated into the council chambers expecting Arthur, Harpur, Sok and Davynn to be there. When he found it deserted, he also found himself at a bit of a loss. There was always at least one of them hanging around in the council chambers. He had expected them all to be eagerly anticipating the event they had been planning for over a year and he was more than a little surprised by the fact that they were not. *What could be more important than rescuing Anayah and Bon?* Hiro thought to himself as he turned the hover gilly and prepared to go back to his laboratory. Having missed court altogether, he knew nothing of Harpur's disappearance or the arrival of Morgaine Fayle, and no one had seen fit to relay the news about the births of Meg and Hart to him. But he was savvy enough to know that something must be going on for all four of his friends to be absent at the same time.

Ever the optimist, though, Hiro decided to rescue Anayah and Bon on his own. The others would all be so surprised when the witch and the android appeared later at supper. With a signature giggle, Hiro urged his faithful hover gilly forward through the doors and back to this laboratory, which was situated, rather conveniently next to the kitchens.

Upon arrival, Hiro parked his hover gilly in the corner of the spacious room and set to inspecting the transporter he had constructed using Arthur's cell phone from his life back on Earth. With the help of Bon, Hiro had figured out how to use it to send messages through Boundaries from one world to another. The process had not been particularly stable and he had not been able to get it to accommodate two-way communication, but the transporter only had to work one way and, so far, the tests had proven it to be altogether promising. To date, they had been successful in transporting several animals from Mysturna to Thraeh, only one of which had died. There were always risks with transporting live creatures, but Anayah, Bon and Hiro all deemed them worth it. Anayah, especially, longed to be reunited with Harpur, Arthur, Sok and Hiro, even if it meant leaving her home world forever.

Because they had to transport through a Boundary from one world to another without actually leaving the Sphere first, the system Hiro and Bon had devised was rather more complicated than a regular transporter would be. Essentially, it was a matter of timing and that was the trickiest part of the whole operation. Bon had to transport himself and Anayah to the nearest Boundary to Thraeh at the precise moment that Hiro transported them from the same Boundary to his laboratory. The biggest problem – after the timing issue – was that virtually every Boundary to Thraeh on the Mysturna side was being guarded by Anayah's aunt's supporters. During their test runs, they transported the objects and animals right into the Boundary and then Hiro pulled them through from the Thraeh side to his laboratory at Colwygshire so that the guards at the Boundary had no opportunity to intercept them. Their ability to time the transports and Bounds was an ingenious trick that Bon had devised in which a signal was sent by Bon from the Sphere in much the same way they had sent the messages to the cell phone. Bon had contrived a relay system so that he did not have to be at the Boundary when the signal was transmitted.

When the signal was received, Hiro had to count to ten to activate the transporter. In order to coordinate this step, Hiro had to Bound to Mysturna and communicate with Bon, which he had done that morning after making his announcement to Arthur, Harpur, Sok and Davynn that the transporter was ready. With the hover gilly's ability to bend time, it was a matter of minutes for Hiro to get to a Boundary, make the Bound, contact Bon, make the arrangements and return.

Now he just had to wait for the signal. And that was due within the hour (based on Bon's calculations of the differences in how time passed on their respective worlds). Not that Hiro really understood what an hour was; Bon had constructed an hour glass to compensate for that lack of timekeeping in Epoh and he had coached the Krist on the precise speed and tempo he had to use to count the seconds.

Hiro was disappointed that the others would not be there to greet and welcome Anayah and Bon to Colwygshire. He had so hoped, after all the time that had passed, that the five of them would be there when Anayah and Bon finally arrived. *Oh, well*, Hiro thought with a giggle, *at least our dear friend will be free again.*

Hiro made himself comfortable on a small, Krist-sized stool next to the transporter to watch for the signal from Bon indicating that he and Anayah were ready. He instantly regretted leaving his satchel on the other side of the laboratory. He'd not had a chance to eat since before he had gone to Mysturna and his stomach was growling in protest. It was by pure chance that Davynn arrived only a few minutes into his vigil and Hiro was never happier to see the handsome young knight.

"Do you know where Harpur, Arthur and Sok are?" Davynn asked as he entered the bright and disorderly laboratory.

"I haven't seen them since before court," Hiro answered. "I don't suppose you could pop over to the kitchen and get something for me to eat?"

"I'll see what I can do. Anything in particular?"

"Whatever you can pilfer from under Finch's nose." Hiro was in no position to be fussy. And pretty much anything made under the head housekeeper's supervision was delicious anyway.

Davynn retreated from the laboratory and returned a few minutes later with a plate of freshly baked buns, some cheese and six apples. He brought two large mugs of ale as well and set it all down on a cluttered table near where Hiro was perched on his stool.

"What are you doing?" Davynn asked as he shifted some books and papers from a human-sized chair and dragged it closer to the food.

"Waiting for Anayah and Bon," Hiro said.

"Shouldn't you also wait for Arthur, Harpur and Sok?" Davynn handed a warm bun and some cheese to Hiro and helped himself to some of the same.

"I don't know where to find them and I don't know exactly when Bon will signal to let me know when he and Anayah are ready. I expected the others to be in the council chambers, but apparently there are more important things going on than this long-awaited rescue." Hiro was not petulant by nature, but he couldn't disguise his disappointment.

"Like Meg and Hart, for instance?" Davynn suggested.

"Who or what are Meg and Hart?" Hiro looked up at the grinning knight.

"Arthur's son and daughter. They were born this morning just before court began."

"Twins!" Hiro said with a delighted giggle. "Well, I suppose that does excuse Arthur from being here. How are they doing? How is Alex?"

"Everyone seems to have come through hale and hearty." Davynn reached for an apple. "I expected Arthur to be with them, but when I checked, he wasn't there and Alex said she hadn't seen him since lunch."

"That is strange." Hiro frowned. Then he giggled and jumped off of his stool. "It's time!"

Davynn looked at the complicated mess of wires and devices that Hiro had been staring at. A light was flashing from the corner of the cell phone, which was attached to an easel on one side of a large circle that Hiro had marked out on the floor with chalk. Hiro walked around to stand behind it and reached up to the cell phone, holding a tiny finger over the home button on the bottom. He counted down from ten and when he reached zero, he pressed and held the button.

The flashing light became a steady, blue beam that widened and lengthened over the next three or four seconds, taking on the vague shape of two people standing side by side.

"Come on," Hiro muttered encouragement to the slowly forming forms of Anayah and Bon. "Come on."

Davynn watched, fascinated, if a little alarmed. He had next to no experience with technology and to see two people appear inside a blue beam of light was nothing short of miraculous. He held his breath, enthralled by the spectacle unfolding before him.

"Come on. Come on." Hiro chanted.

The blue beam flickered and danced as the figures within it took on a more solid shape and form. The seconds stretched into a full minute and Davynn could see that Hiro was looking increasingly anxious. Sweat was beading on his forehead and he was pressing the button on the cell phone so hard, his finger tip had turned white.

"Come on!" he shouted in panic.

Then, just when Davynn thought the little Krist was going to give up, the blue beam stabilized and a second later Anayah and Bon were standing in the laboratory large as life.

"That went much better than I anticipated," Bon said, examining his body for wholeness. "I've only lost two fingers." He held up his right hand to show that, indeed, he was missing his pinky and ring fingers. "Anayah, how did you do?"

Anayah looked at Bon and held up her own hands. "I believe I was able to retain all ten digits." Then she hugged the android. "We did it!"

Hiro mopped the sweat from his brow and came back around to face the new arrivals. "Welcome! Welcome!"

There followed more hugging and handshaking. Davynn kept staring at Bon, looking for any sign that he was a machine. He hadn't known what to expect, but he didn't expect the android to look *that* human. Other than his slightly mechanical movements at times, there was no discernable indications that Bon was not a flesh and blood person. Not even Anayah's beauty could distract Davynn from his awe and disbelief.

Bon, on the other hand, took Davynn at face value. "Sir Davynn, I understand that you are interested in developing hover gillies for your men at arms."

Davynn glanced at Hiro and then back at the android. "How does a machine grow a beard?" he blurted out before he had time to think better of it.

"I can appear in a variety of ways," Bon explained, unphased by Davynn's curiosity. He cocked his head to one side and within a few seconds, his beard disappeared, his gray hair darkened to a lustrous chestnut brown and his grey robes changed to a deep burgundy.

Davynn, completely nonplussed, gasped and sputtered for a moment. "You must be a powerful wizard, indeed."

"Not at all," Bon said, changing back to his normal look. "I possess no magic whatsoever. My ability to change how I look is part of the technology that was used in creating me. I have no less than twenty-one guises that I can convert to at will. This is the one that I prefer."

Davynn could only shake his head in wonder.

"Does this mean that you are not interested in developing hover gillies, then?" Bon asked.

"No. No. I apologize," Davynn said, recovering somewhat. "It was rude of me to say anything. I would very much like to have hover gillies for my men."

"Then we shall set to work on that straight away," Bon said, then turned to Hiro. "I will need a few components. Where shall I set up to work?"

Anayah laughed. "Relax, Bon. You don't need to make them right this instant." She patted the android's arm and then asked a few questions of her own. "Where are Harpur, Arthur and Sok? Why aren't they here? Harpur's okay, isn't he?"

"Harpur is Harpur. His condition is..." Hiro hesitated. "...about as good as can be expected. As for where they are and why they are not here, I can only guess."

"I assumed Arthur would be with Alex and the twins..." Davynn began.

"Twins?" Anayah shouted. "As in two babies?"

"That is what twins means," Hiro said. "Meg and Hart."

"A boy and a girl!" Anayah couldn't contain her surprise. "When did this happen?"

"Just this morning," Davynn supplied.

"Well, I suppose Arthur can be forgiven then," Anayah said with a laugh. "But Sok and Harpur should be here. What did you mean by you assumed Arthur would be with Alex and the twins?"

"He's not there." Davynn shrugged. "And no one seems to know where he, Harpur and Sok are."

Anayah frowned. She'd been so looking forward to seeing everyone again and while the birth of the prince and princess would certainly trump her and Bon's rescue, it was odd that Sok and Harpur were absent. More so Harpur than Sok, but her disappointment was palpable.

"Something urgent must have waylaid them," Hiro said.

"Coop, the baker, did say he was revealing a new pastry at market today," Davynn deadpanned perfectly.

Hiro laughed, but Bon and Anayah just stared at the knight utterly unsure whether he was serious or not.

"Come on," Davynn said with a chuckle, "I'll take you to your rooms so you can freshen up. You'll be in the East Tower."

Davynn turned to the door and led Anayah and Bon out of Hiro's laboratory.

"I'll just put all this stuff away myself, then!" Hiro called after them with a giggle.

Arthur had sat in the council chambers for a while after Morgaine Fayle had left. Instinct told him that there was more to the woman than met the eye, but he couldn't put his finger on what that was. He was certain, however, that her appearance had been the catalyst to Harpur's disappearance and that she was a threat to his friend. *Who are you, really, Morgaine Fayle?* he wondered. The only way he was going to find out was to find Harpur. So, he plonked his circlet onto his head and headed to Skull's Keep to see if Sok had had any luck.

As he wandered through the market square, he wondered if he should have checked his own rooms before setting out. He had instructed Sok to bring Harpur there if he found the dragon, but surely Sok would have sent word. He stopped at Coop's stall to purchase one of the baker's new pastries, a fluffy delicacy filled with nuts and dates and drizzled with something Arthur decided could only be chocolate. He was just about to carry on when he felt a tug on his sleeve.

Arthur looked down into the face of a small girl with straggly, blond hair wearing a patched, green pinafore. She held up a rag doll that looked remarkably like her. "This is for the new babies, sire," she said. Behind her, her mother poked her shoulder and she belatedly curtsied before her king. "I didn't know people could have two babies at one time, so I only made one. I will make another, though."

Arthur took the rag doll from the little girl. "It's lovely!" he gushed. "Thank you... What is your name?"

"Lissa, sire," the little girl said and curtsied again.

"Well, Lissa, this is just wonderful. Did you make it yourself?"

"Yes, sire," Lissa said. "My mama helped me a little."

Arthur knelt down so he was at eye-level with Lissa. "It was very nice of your mama to help you. And it was very kind of you to make such a thoughtful gift for the prince and princess. This is the first present they've received."

"It is?" Lissa asked with pride. "I can make a boy doll for the prince."

"That would be great!" Arthur assured her. "Or you could make him a dragon or a horse."

"Ooh!" Lissa's eyes lit up as she turned to her mother. "Can we make a dragon for the prince? A purple one, just like Harpur Diggins?"

Lissa's mother smiled. "Of course. Whatever the king thinks is best."

Arthur felt a slight pang of guilt at having made the suggestion. "I'm sure that whatever you make will be perfect. And Hart will love it."

"The prince's name is Hart?" Lissa asked.

"Yes, and the princess's name is Meg."

"Those are nice names."

"Thank you," Arthur said. He was still not used to them, but he was pleased by Lissa's approval. "When we present them, I want you to be there and I will make sure that you get to meet them personally."

Lissa's eyes grew even brighter. "Oh, Mama, can we go to the presentation? Can we?"

Lissa's mother looked pensive. "I don't know..."

Arthur stood up. "I will make sure you receive a personal invitation. Where shall I send it and to whom should it be addressed?"

Lissa's mother stuttered in awe. "Magnus and Jenna Evern at the tailor's shop on Weary Lane."

"I shall see to it personally," Arthur assured the flattered woman. "Thank you, again, Lissa. Is it okay if we name the doll after you?"

"My whole name is Lissa Olive Valentina Evern. Will you be able to remember all that?"

Arthur laughed. "I will try my best. You might have to remind me at the presentation, though."

"I will," Lissa assured him. She curtsied one more time and then allowed her slightly embarrassed mother to lead her away by the hand.

Arthur watched the pair as they melded into the crowd in the market. He took a moment to sweep the square for any sign of Harpur or Sok and finding none, turned to continue his journey to Skull's Keep.

When he arrived, the few afternoon customers all stood and bowed or curtsied as he entered and walked past. He slipped into a chair at a table where his senior advisor was about half way through a large bowl of savory stew. "As you were," he called over his shoulder when Sok nodded toward the room of genuflecting customers. A shuffle of relieved release rippled through the tavern as they returned to their meals and ales.

Sok shook his head at Arthur. "Are you ever going to get the hang of this king business?"

Arthur squinted and thought about it. "Nope. No sign of Harpur?"

"Nope." Sok shoveled a spoonful of stew into his mouth. "What in Orhowyn's name is that thing?" He pointed at the rag doll.

Arthur looked at the hand-stitched toy. "It's a doll. A little girl named Lissa Olive Valentina Evern made it for Meg."

"I can dispose of it for you, if you like," Sok offered.

Arthur frowned at the elf. "Why would I want you to dispose of it?"

"It's hideous."

"It's delightful."

Sok prevented himself from making an even more derogatory comment by spooning more stew into his mouth.

"I will need you to send an invitation to the presentation to her and her family, by the way. I promised Lissa that she could meet the prince and princess personally. She's making Hart a dragon doll."

"Remind me again after we've found Harpur," Sok said with another shake of his head.

"Oh, don't be such a snob," Arthur admonished.

"What?" Sok grew defensive. "You're the king of Epoh. You should start behaving like one."

"Says the senior advisor to the King of Epoh who is eating stew in a tavern."

"It's good stew!"

"And this is a perfectly lovely gesture from a loyal subject." Arthur held up the rag doll.

"Very well," Sok said with resignation. "Any ideas of where we should look for Harpur next?"

"He's not in the market," Arthur said. "I just came through there."

"How did things go with Morgaine Fayle?"

Arthur shrugged. "I'm not sure. She said she was hoping to acquire land in the North-west beyond Braydon Wood."

Sok paled. "You mean the mountains where Harpur's lair is?"

Arthur nodded. "Can't think of anything else in the North-west beyond Braydon Wood."

"You don't think...."

"I don't know what to think." Arthur interrupted. "But whoever Morgaine Fayle is, she's not who she seems to be."

Sok's brows furrowed as he processed Arthur's words. "We need to find Harpur."

"Indeed."

Sok and Arthur stood up just as a serving woman approached their table to take Arthur's order. "Forgive me, your majesty." She bobbed a harried curtsey. "I didn't see you come in."

"No problem. We're just leaving." Arthur said congenially.

The server bobbed again and stepped out of Arthur's path.

"Put the stew and the ale on the account," Sok directed her.

"What account?" Arthur asked.

"The castle account," Sok said matter-of-factly.

"What castle account?"

The serving woman was wedged between the king and his senior advisor and a table and couldn't escape.

"The one for when I come here on castle business," Sok explained as if he was talking to a two-year-old.

"You came here looking for Harpur."

"At your request," Sok reasoned. "That is castle business."

Arthur took a deep breath. "How often do you come here on castle business?"

Sok tipped his head back and forth, calculating. "It depends."

"On what?"

"On how you phrase your requests." Sok smiled and then marched toward the door.

Arthur turned to the serving woman and handed her four coins. "Will this cover his meal?"

"Oh, yes, your majesty. It most definitely will." She bobbed several times in a row as the coins fell into her hands.

"Good. Keep the change!" Arthur followed the senior advisor out onto the street.

The pair walked in silence for a while. Passers-by who recognized Arthur, bowed as he passed and he did his best to acknowledge them with a smile, but his thoughts were on other things. Harpur for one. Morgaine Fayle for another. But what was really dominating his attention was the castle business account.

"So, why haven't I ever seen this castle business account on the treasury reports?"

Sok shrugged. "It mostly comes out of general revenues."

"Mostly?"

Sok saw the trap that he'd set for himself. "I meant all of it. It all comes out of general revenue."

"I see." Arthur walked on for another minute or so. "I would like it listed separately from now on."

Sok swallowed. "As you wish."

Arthur had expected more resistance. "Do I not pay you enough?"

"Well, I could use a little extra. Yna has expensive tastes." Sok started whistling nervously.

"Are you still pursuing that? I thought she was a thing of the past."

Yna was a warrior elf that Sok had been in love with since before Arthur had met him. He had said he had planned on asking her to marry him, but he would have to best her in a fight in order to secure her betrothal. Sok could hold his own if he had to. But Yna was a daunting opponent. She had accidentally chopped off her own sister's head in a sparring match once and Arthur was sure that that was a mitigating factor in the prolonged proposal procrastination.

"I haven't given up hope," Sok said.

Arthur smiled to himself. "What are you saving up for?"

"If you must know, I'm building a house."

"A house!? Where?"

"In Braydon Wood. Where else would I build a house?" Sok sounded disgusted at having to explain.

"Why?"

The elf took a deep breath. "For Yna."

"You're building Yna a house because...?"

"Because if she accepts it, she might forego the betrothal bout."

"I see." They walked another short way in silence. "Does this mean that you will be leaving the castle if she does accept the house?"

"I'm not sure," Sok admitted. "Yna doesn't approve of my choice of profession, but that would have to be addressed in the negotiations."

"The negotiations?"

"Once the proposal is accepted, then we have to negotiate the terms of our marriage. This is standard stuff, Arthur. You're married. You should know this."

"What sort of stuff do you negotiate?" Arthur couldn't help himself.

"What sort of stuff did you negotiate with Queen Alex?"

"We didn't. We just got married."

"That's insane. How do you know how when to... you know?"

Arthur looked at his friend and was shocked to see how red the elf's face was. "You negotiate *that*?"

"Doesn't everyone?"

"No. That just happens when it happens."

"Huh! You humans are a strange bunch."

"We're a strange bunch? How do you schedule passion?"

Both Sok's and Arthur's thoughts drifted back to their time on Mysturna when they were accompanied by Arthur's guardians, Ralph and Holly, a nearly naked couple that couldn't keep their hands off each other.

"Would you prefer me and Yna were like Ralph and Holly?"

"No. No, I would not. But come on, Sok, what about spontaneity? What happens when you... have the urge and you're not scheduled to do it for like three days? Wait! Don't answer that. I don't want to know."

Sok was happy not to get into the details of the intimate side of elven marriages with Arthur. But the conversation had inspired another thought. "Do you think Harpur went to Braydon Wood?"

Arthur smiled again. "Well, maybe we should go and find out!" he said, slapping his friend on the back. "And you can see Yna while we're there."

Arthur thought it would be prudent to stop in and see Alex and the babies before he and Sok set out for Braydon Wood. Though any excuse to be with them was more than welcome. Harpur's strange behavior and subsequent vanishing act were exigent, if badly timed. And now he had to worry about Sok's unrequited love for a large and terrifying warrior elf. *Do kings get vacation time?* he wondered. *Maybe Alex, me and the babies could sneak away somewhere for a while. No! Not until Alma has moved on!* He shook his head clear of the images of Alma on vacation. *And not until I know what's going on with Harpur. Orhowyn's dusty bones, but this king business can be annoying sometimes.*

They arrived to find Alex's chamber doors open. Voices and laughter drifted out into the corridor and Sok and Arthur both stopped in their tracks.

"Anayah!" they said in unison.

Sure enough, the beautiful, red-headed witch was sitting in a chair next to Alex's bed holding little Hart in her arms. Davynn and Bon were standing at the end of the queen's bed and Hiro was floating in his hover gilly next to Anayah. Little Meg was snuggling with her mom in the big bed. And Alma was glowering from the nursery door, just waiting for the first opportunity to dismiss the invaders and re-establish her authority over the twins. When she saw Arthur and Sok walk in with big smiles and no consideration whatsoever for her duty to the queen and the royal twins, she threw her hands up in the air and retreated into the nursery to sulk. *And possibly plot!* Arthur thought.

The reunion between the friends was a noisy and boisterous affair punctuated with hugs and happiness. Meg and Hart slept through it all, unaware and uncaring about the catching up that was taking place around them. Eventually, Harpur's conspicuous absence could no longer be ignored and Arthur found himself sitting on the bed with his arm around Alex, telling them all about his encounter with the alluring Morgaine Fayle and the odd disappearance of the dragon-wizard.

This generated much speculation among the group about who Morgaine Fayle might be, why Harpur had snuck out of court when she arrived, whether or not they knew each other and where Harpur might have gone. Finally, Sok circled back to his and Arthur's plan to go to Braydon Wood to see if the dragon-wizard had gone to the elves for some reason.

"It's getting late," Sok said. "I think if we're going to go to Braydon Wood, we should go now."

Arthur, having grown comfortable and feeling the lack of sleep from the previous night, shook his head. "You know what?" He paused and everyone looked at him. "Harpur's a big boy. He can take care of himself. Alex and I are tired, so I'm going to ask you all to give us some alone time to rest. If any of you want to go looking for Harpur, go ahead. But I'm going to spend some quality time with my family."

"Even if that is only napping," Alex said with a yawn.

"Of course," Anayah said. "Forgive us. We'll leave you two to your beautiful babies. Congratulations, again." She began ushering Sok, Davynn, Bon and Hiro toward the door.

"Um, Sok?" Alex called out. "Hart needs to stay with us."

Sok, who was holding the prince he'd appropriated from Anayah, turned and reluctantly handed the baby to Arthur. "I'm perfectly capable of looking after an infant."

"I'm sure you are. But for now, Hart and Meg both stay here with us." Arthur held his son out in front of himself and beamed at his angelic sleeping face. "Right, little man?"

"Hmph!" Sok snorted. "They'd have already been introduced to the trees if they were elves."

"But they are not elves," Alex said, lifting Meg up onto her shoulder.

"Hmph!" Sok reiterated before leaving with the others.

The moment that the room fell silent again, Alma emerged from the nursery. "Shall I put the children in their cradle?"

"If you don't mind," Alex said.

"And will his majesty be leaving now as well?" Alma asked as she scooped Hart out of Arthur's hands.

"His majesty will be staying for a while," Arthur said.

"Hmph!" Alma repeated Sok's derisive snort as she watched Arthur remove his boots and settle even more comfortably on the bed next to Alex. She took Hart into the nursery and then returned for Meg. "This is highly inappropriate!"

"We will decide what is appropriate and what is not, Alma," Arthur said. "Now if we could have some privacy...?"

Alma marched away with Meg and closed the nursery door behind herself while Alex and Arthur snuggled closer together.

"It's going to be a long four weeks with that one around," Arthur said, kissing Alex's head.

"It will fly by before you know it," Alex yawned. "Do you think Harpur is okay?"

"I have to believe that he is," Arthur said, though he didn't sound all that confident.

Alex fell asleep almost instantly. But, in spite of his fatigue, Arthur remained awake worrying about the dragon-wizard and what Morgaine Fayle's appearance might mean. He was certain that Morgaine represented a threat to Harpur, but he couldn't fathom what it was or how it might play out. *Why would a woman like Morgaine Fayle want land in Epoh?* he wondered. Eventually, sleep found the worried king and he slept fitfully until a baby's cry woke him up two hours later.

The business of nappy-changing and baby feeding prompted Arthur to leave it all to the women. Feeling somewhat refreshed, he kissed his wife and children and informed Alma that he would return for supper with the queen. This garnered a tight-lipped nod from the midwife, but she thankfully refrained from commenting.

"Arthur?" Alex called as he was about to walk out the door.

"Yes, dear?"

"Your crown." She held up the silver diadem that she had pulled out from under the covers.

Arthur trudged back to retrieve it. "Must have fallen off while I was sleeping."

Alex smiled at her crown-hating husband-king. "Perhaps we need to glue it to your head."

"Don't you dare suggest that to Sok!" Arthur plunked the crown on over his sleep-mussed hair and blew Alex a final kiss. Her laughter followed him out into the corridor.

Arthur entered the council chambers and found them as deserted as Hiro had earlier in the day. A large tray sat on the round table, but all it contained were three apple cores, a half-eaten pastry and a few crumbs. Arthur examined the pastry and decided that it would be a shame to waste it. He took it with him and walked to the double doors that led out into the main entrance hall of the castle. Two guards stood on either side of the doorway and immediately snapped to attention when their king emerged.

"At ease," Arthur said, smiling at the guards. "Do either of you know where I might find Sok?"

The guard on the left stepped forward. "Sok asked us to inform you that he and Sir Davynn have gone to Braydon Wood along with a woman whose name he did not provide. Hiro and a tall, bearded gentleman went to Hiro's laboratory, your majesty."

Arthur nodded. "Thanks. Has there been any word from Harpur?"

The guard on the right stepped forward. "Harpur Diggins is in your private chambers, your majesty."

"Is he now? How long has he been there?" Arthur wanted to sprint to and up the stairs, but he didn't want to appear overly concerned.

"Not long, your majesty," said the guard on the left. "He and an elf woman went up there shortly after the fourth chime. He said to tell you that he was waiting for you, sire."

"An elven woman was with him, you say?"

"Indeed, sire," said the guard on the right. "She had bright red hair and was barefoot."

"Ah! Well, thank you both very much. If Sok returns, send him and whoever is with him up to my rooms."

"As you wish, your majesty," the guard on the left said, but Arthur was already jogging toward the stairs.

"You forgot to tell him that Hiro wanted to see him," the guard on the right said.

"So did you," the guard on the left said.

"Should we send a messenger?"

"If one comes by."

The two guards slumped back against the wall on either side of the council chamber doors and continued their vigil.

Arthur arrived at his private chambers a little out of breath after climbing four flights of stairs to find both of the guards that were posted outside standing at attention. Like their counterparts outside the council chambers, they usually affected a more casual stance. Clearly, Harpur's presence inside was a good influence over them. He nodded at them and waited for the one on the right to open the door. He'd have done it himself, but Sok was adamant that this was their duty.

A cheerful fire was burning in the grate of the massive fireplace and candles had been lit to stave off the growing late afternoon gloom. The large sitting room, however, was otherwise unoccupied. Voices drifted out from Arthur's sleeping chamber and he followed them with a measure of annoyance at having his bedroom invaded without his permission. He entered to find Harpur and Elder Dhonna, the master elf of the Healing Guild, sitting on the floor at the end of his bed reading a very large book.

The book was one that Harpur had entrusted to Arthur shortly after he'd first arrived in Epoh. it magically chronicled Harpur's life and contained the history of the kingdom of Epoh since Harpur had inherited it from Orhowyn Bravvenshyn over two millennia before. The book had always been stored in Harpur's lair, but Arthur had concluded that Harpur had transferred it to the castle in Colwygshire for safer keeping due to his declining well-being. He could not deny the dragon-wizard access to it, but it still rankled that Harpur would assume that access was entirely unconditional.

"Doing a little light reading?" Arthur asked sarcastically.

Harpur looked up from the page he'd been studying and relegated the question to the realm of the rhetorical with a withering look. "I need you to go to the Fae lands and retrieve an item for me."

"Elder Dhonna," Arthur said, buying time to process Harpur's demand, "it's good to see you again."

The elven Guild Master rose from the floor in a smooth and agile motion as if her upper body was levitating. "It's good to see you as well. I'm sorry we invaded your private rooms like this."

Harpur stood up too, though not nearly as gracefully as Elder Dhonna had. He placed the heavy book on the bed and folded his arms. "You can leave tonight."

Elder Dhonna took a deep breath. "Do you not think that Arthur might benefit from some explanation?"

Harpur shot her an exasperated glance. "And what do you propose we tell him?"

"Everything!" Elder Dhonna walked over to Arthur and hooked her arm through his to lead him back into the sitting room. "Bring the book, dragon!"

Harpur grimaced, but did as he was told.

Arthur had grown used to Harpur's surly demeanor and he knew that whatever was going on was important. But go to the Fae lands? Arthur didn't even know exactly where that was. He felt that his best plan of attack was to stay quiet and follow Elder Dhonna's lead. He and the Guild Master sat on a sofa while Harpur poured ale for the three of them after he laid the book down on a low table in front of the sofa where Arthur and Elder Dhonna sat.

They settled into their seats and sipped their ale. Arthur's eyes darted back and forth between the elf and the dragon-wizard, waiting for one of them to say something. Harpur kept his own eyes firmly focused on the book and Elder Dhonna kept hers on Harpur.

"Orhowyn's flaming farts! Will one of you tell me what's going on?" Arthur blurted out after several silent minutes had passed. "Harpur why did you leave court today when Morgaine Fayle came in? And who is she to you anyway? Everyone was worried about you. We looked for you all over the place. Sok, Davynn and Anayah are still out looking for you!"

"So, she made it through the Krist's contraption in one piece?" Harpur deflected. "And Bon? Did he make it too?"

"Yes! And Anayah was a little disappointed that you weren't there to greet her." Arthur threw some guilt at Harpur and took another swig of ale.

"Couldn't be helped," Harpur muttered. He, too, took a long drink from his cup.

"I gathered that!" Arthur said. "But why?"

Elder Dhonna placed a calming hand on Arthur's arm. "Let me explain..."

"I'll do it!" Harpur cut her off. He sat forward in his chair and rested his elbows on his knees, holding his cup with both hands. "Arthur, I'm going to be challenged."

Arthur's cup hovered midway to his mouth. "Challenged? As in another dragon is going to challenge you?"

"That's right. And it's likely going to happen within the next few days."

Arthur had known this could happen, but he had hoped that it wouldn't happen until he was long dead. "What are you going to do?"

"I'm going to accept the challenge, of course."

Arthur stared at Harpur. "But..."

"There is no but; I'm going to accept and fight to keep Epoh."

"But..."

"There's always a chance that I will win, Arthur. It may be slim, but there is a chance."

"Well, why don't we just hide you somewhere until this other dragon gives up and goes away?"

"It doesn't work that way, Arthur. If I don't accept the challenge and at least try, I forfeit the kingdom anyway."

"But you're in no shape to fight another dragon!" Arthur shouted. "He'll kill you."

"And I will die a noble death."

Arthur turned to Elder Dhonna with a pleading look in his eye. "Can't you do something? Can't you stop this? Can't you give him a potion or something so he can at least have a better chance?"

"Arthur, I will do everything in my power to help Harpur. But no one can interfere with the challenge." Elder Dhonna said. "Do you understand?"

"No!" Arthur shouted again. "I don't understand! We can't just stand by and let Harpur die!"

"Thanks for the vote of confidence." Harpur stood up and helped himself to another cup of ale.

Arthur watched his friend drinking ale like it was a normal day and they were just hanging out in the king's private chambers. "You can't seriously be okay with this?"

"I am, actually," Harpur said. "It is the way of dragons and if it's my time, it's my time."

"But what about Epoh? What about all the people who live here? What will happen to them?" Arthur saw his fledgling kingship coming to an abrupt end. He was all too well-aware that a conquering dragon had carte blanche over the occupancy of its kingdom.

"That is up to the dragon who inherits it. I intend to bargain for safe passage out of Epoh if it comes to that."

"Sok is going to flip his roots," Arthur said, suddenly realizing that this news was not going to be taken sitting down by his senior advisor.

"You can't tell Sok," Harpur said.

"And just how do you suppose I'm going to keep it from him?" Arthur abandoned his own seat and walked to the fireplace.

"You can't tell anyone," Harpur said.

Arthur stared into the flames. He sipped his ale. This was a heavy secret. Too heavy. "Don't you think that Sok and Anayah and Davynn and Hiro have a right to know?"

"If I did, I would tell them myself." Harpur let that hang in the air between them.

"Harpur?" Arthur spoke quietly after a prolonged silence.

"Yes, Arthur?" Harpur replied.

"You don't really expect me to keep this to myself, do you? You don't really expect any of us not to do what we can to save you?"

Harpur sighed. "Not really, no," he admitted. "I'm asking you all the same."

Arthur nodded and then finished off the last of his ale. He turned around to face the doomed dragon-wizard. "What is this item you wish me to retrieve for you?"

Elder Dhonna decided it was time to intervene again. "The nature of the item will be revealed to you in time. Harpur needs you to get it, though. And keep it safe. Will you do this for him?"

"If it will help save Harpur, of course I will get it," Arthur stared at Harpur.

"If you don't get it, and I don't win the challenge, I am truly doomed." Harpur's penetrating violet gaze told Arthur how vitally important this thing in the Fae Lands was.

As enigmatic as that statement was, Arthur chose to see a glimmer of hope in it. "So, this item can save your life?"

Harpur and Elder Dhonna exchanged looks. "Let's just say that it could be Harpur's only chance for survival," Elder Dhonna said.

"Very well," Arthur conceded, hoping himself that he wasn't being sent on a wild goose chase just so he couldn't interfere with the challenge. "How do I get to the Fae lands? And where do I find this item?"

A kerfuffle outside the door stopped either Harpur or Elder Dhonna from answering. "Let us in or I'll have you both publicly flogged," Sok's raised, but muffled voice filtered through the thick oak portal.

Arthur rolled his eyes and went to open the door. Sok, closely followed by Anayah, Davynn, Hiro and Bon marched into the room. "Cheeky sods!" Sok grumbled as he passed Arthur and then came to an abrupt stop. Anayah and Davynn, not expecting him to stop walking slammed into the elf's back and sent him flailing further into the room. Sok barely managed to keep from tumbling head over heels across the low table and into Elder Dhonna's lap.

Davynn and Anayah were struggling to keep their own balance as they registered the reason for Sok's sudden halt. None of them had expected to find Harpur in Arthur's rooms.

Hiro and Bon both entered with a good deal more decorum than their companions. While Hiro parked his hover gilly next to the wall by the door, Bon strode over to Harpur. "I believe our search is over!" the android announced.

Anayah detached herself from Davynn's chivalrous grip and walked to where Harpur was standing next to Bon. Without hesitation, she slapped his face. "Thanks for being there to meet me and Bon when we arrived."

A collective gasp rose from the stunned group of witnesses behind her.

"I see a year and a half in the Sphere hasn't tamed your sense of the dramatic," Harpur said with a grin. He refused to rub his cheek.

Anayah's hand came up for another slap, but Harpur caught her wrist and then pulled her into his arms for a long, welcoming hug. Another collective gasp filled the room. This time Anayah contributed to it. Harpur voluntarily hugging anyone was a rare event indeed.

"I'm glad you made it here safely, witch," Harpur said, still holding Anayah close. "And I know you know that if I could have been there to meet you, I would have been." He finally let her go.

"Alrighty, then!" Arthur filled the dumbfounded silence. "Guys, now that we all know Harpur is okay, let's just call it a night, okay?"

"I don't' think so!" Sok said. "I just spent the better part of the day combing half of Epoh looking for the big galoot; I want to know where he's been."

"Mind your manners, elf," Harpur snarled. "If it was any of your business, you'd be told."

Sok crossed his arms and tapped his toe in agitation.

"Galoot?" Davynn asked.

"He means dumbass," Anayah said over her shoulder. "Sok was just being polite." She wasn't ready to let all of her disappointment in Harpur go.

Davynn wondered if he was going to need to draw his sword. No one called Harpur a dumbass. Not even his friends.

But Harpur surprised them all again by smiling. "You will regret that," he said far too congenially to both Sok and Anayah. "But Arthur is right. It's been a rather long and trying day. And I'm sure our king would like to spend what is left of it with his wife and children."

Silence, pregnant with suspicion, filled the room. Everyone knew that something big was going on, but Sok noticed Arthur's weird attempt to telepathically get the elf's attention. The king's eyes were bugging out of his head with the effort of letting the elf know that he needed to talk to him. Sok nodded to let Arthur know he'd received the message and then turned quickly away, lest Harpur see the exchange.

As soon as Sok turned around, Arthur aimed his bulging eyeballs at Harpur. *Don't you dare leave without telling me what I need to know!* was the message.

Harpur glanced over his shoulder as if Arthur's eyes had physically touched him. He, too, nodded at the king.

"Right, then!" Sok said, cheerily. "Let's all convene in the council chambers. I think a snack is in order." He marched back to the door and opened it. When no one moved, he clapped his hands. "Chop, chop! Arthur needs to get to Alex. And we need to properly welcome Anayah and Bon to Colwygshire!"

"I will join you there shortly," Harpur said, holding his arm out for the Guild Master. "I'm going to escort Elder Dhonna back to Braydon Wood."

Reluctantly, the others left Arthur's private chambers, full of questions, but not knowing who to direct them to.

When Sok pulled the door closed, Arthur collapsed onto the sofa and stared at the book Harpur had left on the table. He'd never been able to decipher the archaic script it was written in, but he opened it anyway and turned to the last page. As Harpur's life unfolded, events were magically recorded in the book. Sometimes, they were illustrated and, sure enough, there on the last page was a picture of Anayah and Bon. It was a very good likeness, almost photographic in composition. But what caught Arthur's eye was another illustration. On the bottom right-hand corner was a drawing of a simple, handleless cup, and beneath it, in plain English, were written the words: Amber Chalice.

Chapter Four

Out in the hallway, the questions everyone had were let loose like arrows from long bows aimed, more or less, at Harpur. The dragon-wizard, however, refused to answer, instead reiterating his intention to see Elder Dhonna safely back to Braydon Wood, an intention he had no intention of following through on. With his patented violet glare, he herded the motley group toward the council chambers where he actually intended to leave them while he and Elder Dhonna circled back and continued their conversation with Arthur. A tray full of sandwiches and pastries from the kitchen would keep them busy long enough for him to get Arthur up to speed and, hopefully, away to the Fae Lands before any of them got a chance to interfere.

Sending Arthur off on his own was, in itself, problematic. Arthur was not what one would call a gifted horseman and it was a good three day's ride to the Fae Lands during which he would have to camp at night. Alone. In the woods. Basically, a city boy from Earth, Arthur's survival skills were limited at best. Had his magic been a little more reliable, there would have been more options. As it was, however, the safest bet was to keep things simple and send Arthur off on his own, on a horse and hope he didn't get lost in the forest.

Then there was the matter of Alex. Now that the twins were born, the idea of Arthur going off on an adventure – alone or otherwise – was not likely to go over well. The Queen, diminutive as she was, was a force to be reckoned with when she put her mind to it and Harpur suspected that sending Arthur to the Fae Lands on an errand would be the key that opened the door and let that force out. Granted, it would be limited to a lot of yelling and, quite possibly, a few improvised projectiles being hurtled toward him, but still Harpur dreaded facing Arthur's wife and the mother of his children to tell her that he had sent her husband off alone and unprotected through Braydon Wood. The fact that the biggest threat to his safety was himself would have Alex in a complete dither and while he could stave off much of her fear by sending Sok or Davynn along with Arthur, he wanted to at least try to keep them from getting involved for as long as possible.

"I don't understand why you don't send Sok or Davynn with Arthur. I know you don't want them to interfere, but they are going to anyway. You know Arthur won't keep quiet about this," Elder Dhonna said after they left the others in the council chambers and began climbing back up the stairs.

Harpur sighed. He had seen the bug-eyed exchange between Arthur and Sok, and he knew that Arthur was going to spill everything the first chance he got. All Harpur could hope for was that Arthur didn't get the chance. "If this plan is going to work, Arthur has to be the one to do the deed. The faster we can send him on his way and the fewer people who know about it, the less likely it is that anything will go wrong." Harpur knew all too well how even the best laid plans so often go awry!

"And you really have that much faith in Arthur?" Elder Dhonna asked.

"I do."

They reached the top of the stairs and Elder Dhonna had to wonder who Harpur was really trying to convince.

The guards outside Arthur's door, having heard their footsteps, had snapped to attention. They had never seen so much activity in the king's private chambers. Usually, after the king left in the morning, no one except the maid came in until Arthur returned to retire for the night. It was not the most exciting post and they both knew that they were there because this assignment was one that even they would be hard pressed to screw up. If there were ever any real threat to the king, they would be replaced in a heartbeat. And they were okay with that. They received three meals a day and lodgings, plus a modest stipend for their service. It was enough.

The guard on the left lifted his hand to knock before opening the door for Harpur and Elder Dhonna, but the dragon-wizard stopped him. They could hear voices on the other side. "Who's in there?" Harpur asked in a whisper so as not to alert the occupants to his arrival.

"Sok, the elf, sir," the guard on the right said.

Harpur rolled his violet eyes and grabbed the knob. He pushed the heavy oak door inward and entered to find Arthur and Sok hunched over the book he had left on the low table. "What are you doing here?" he growled at the elf.

The elf and the king both nearly jumped out of their own skins. Reflexively, Arthur snapped the book shut and stared wide-eyed at the looming, and clearly displeased, dragon-wizard. "We were just... um... reminiscing," Arthur stammered.

Harpur cocked his head to the side and raised his eyebrows in disbelief.

Sok, much less cowed by Harpur than most people, stood up and crossed his arms. "You can't seriously expect Arthur to go to the Fae Lands alone." The challenge in his voice was unmistakable.

The punch that Arthur landed on Sok's leg was hard enough to elicit a startled cry of pain that erased the defiance from the elf's face. "Ouch!"

"How did you get up here so fast?" Elder Dhonna asked, stepping in front of Harpur, whose fists were balled at his sides.

"We thought you two were on your way back to Braydon Wood." Arthur's own expression was riddled with guilt.

"I said that for the benefit of the others. I should have guessed that the elf would beetle it back up here as soon as he thought I was out of the way." Harpur relaxed his fists and walked over to the table by the window where the ale jug was. He poured himself a large cupful and made his way to the chair across from Arthur and Sok.

Elder Dhonna decided to ignore the ill-mannered behavior and reached for the book. If Arthur or Sok wanted ale, they could pour their own. Satisfied that her three companions were not going to kill each other, she settled into her own chair and opened the book to see if anything had been added since she'd last looked at it earlier in the afternoon. She would let the boys work out their differences on their own.

Harpur was wise enough to allow the awkward silence to play itself out. Arthur was wise enough to know that he should stay under the radar, so to speak. Harpur had asked him not to tell Sok anything and he wasn't in a rush to face the music on that score. Sok, on the other hand, was wise enough to know that the awkward silence would just grow more awkward the longer it was allowed to go on. And so, he decided to poke the bear, knowing that it might growl, might even roar, but it would not bite or claw him.

"Well?"

Harpur raised his cup to his lips and took a drink of his ale. "I have my reasons," he said after he swallowed the bitter beverage. He was not about to offer any information. So far, all he knew Sok knew was that he wanted Arthur to go to the Fae Lands.

"You have your reasons?" Sok prompted, but when Harpur failed to fill in the gaps, he continued. "And what might those be?"

Harpur looked at Arthur, who was diligently avoiding looking at him. Then he looked at Elder Dhonna, who was absorbed in looking at the book. Sensing she was being looked at, she lifted the page and tapped the drawing of the cup to indicate that it had been added and was now in play. Whether Harpur was ready for it to be or not.

Orhowyn's blood and bones! Harpur thought. *Change of plans.*

"Sok, would you be so kind as to accompany Arthur to the Fae Lands to do a small errand for me?" Harpur's smile belied his fury.

"Not on your life!" Sok exclaimed, unaware that Harpur's life actually depended on someone going to the Fae Lands.

From its place under the radar, Arthur's head snapped up. "Why not?"

Sok turned to Arthur. "I want nothing to do with those filthy elementals! And if you are smart, you won't go either."

"And now you both know why I didn't want Sok to know about this," Harpur growled.

The animosity between the elves and the Fae was deep and eternal. Only the threat of expulsion from Epoh kept the two races from all-out war with each other. Which was another reason that Harpur's plan had to work. If the elves and the Fae ever went to war, the humans and the dwarves would very likely be destroyed along with most of the kingdom.

"I don't understand," Arthur said. "What's wrong with the fairies?"

"Don't call them fairies!" Harpur, Sok and Elder Dhonna all said in unison.

"Sorry. What's wrong with the Fae?" Arthur corrected himself.

"They are disgusting, vile creatures," Sok snapped. "They should be exterminated from every corner of the world. Instead, they are allowed to defile a vast portion of Braydon Wood. And we have to put up with it."

Arthur had never heard such passionate disdain for anything from Sok before. It frightened him more than a little to have the two people he trusted more than anything at complete odds over any topic. He looked to Elder Dhonna for support only to find her looking just as conflicted as he felt.

"They are not vile or disgusting," Harpur said eerily calmly. "Nor are they defiling any portion, vast or otherwise, of Braydon Wood."

"Have you seen what they're doing to the trees down there?" Sok nearly screeched.

"Have you?"

Sok opened and closed his mouth a few times before any sound came out. "Well, no," he admitted, "but I've heard about it from the border patrols."

"Accounts that are grossly over-exaggerated, no doubt," Harpur said. "Do you actually believe I would allow the Fae to cause any harm to any part of Epoh?"

"What are they doing to the trees?" Arthur asked, though he was unsure he wanted to know.

Elder Dhonna took the book over to Arthur and sat down beside him on the sofa. She flipped the pages until she came to one with illustrations of different beings.

"Arthur, the Fae are not natural beings. They are elementals." She pointed to one of the illustrations. It was of a vaguely man-like creature with the body of a tree trunk. "They are created from stolen magic and stolen consciousness. For the most part they are benign..."

From across the room Arthur heard Sok snort in derision.

"...but they are quite feral and when they acquire magic and consciousness, they use it to make more Fae. And they don't care that they are altering the natural world to do it."

"So, they make their kind out of plants and trees?" Arthur didn't understand what was so bad about that.

"Yes. Or rocks, or mud. Occasionally a dead animal. Here in Epoh, though, they are forbidden to make Fae from living trees."

Arthur grimaced at the mention of a dead animal, but chose not to give it too much thought. "What is the harm in making Fae out of living trees? Aren't they kind of like Ents?"

Sok gasped! "What is the harm!? What is the harm?"

Elder Dhonna shushed the elf. "I have no idea what Ents are, but the harm is that living trees are living creatures in their own right. They are sacred to the elves and when one is turned into Fae, it loses its natural essence. It ceases to be a tree. When Harpur inherited Epoh, he welcomed all the races to live here. The elves, as is good and right, were given governance over Braydon Wood. The Fae were given governance over the river and were granted asylum in the southern part of Braydon Wood below the river."

"But they had to agree not to turn any living trees from the wood into Fae."

"That's right."

"Yeah, well, they broke that agreement at least a dozen times," Sok snarled.

Throughout this exchange, Harpur had remained silent. The Fae anthropology lesson was slowing things down, but he hoped that it would also move things along once Arthur was brought up to speed. At the same time, he felt compelled to set Sok straight. "They have only turned five trees into Fae and I have dealt with them."

Sok snorted again. "Is that what they told you? The Fae are masters at lying."

"That's what I know." Harpur glared at Sok.

"Why am I only learning about this now?" Arthur asked.

"Ask your senior advisor," Harpur said. "He was in charge of educating you about this world."

Arthur looked at Sok. "Well?"

"I couldn't bring myself to discuss the evil things," Sok answered defensively.

"How bad can they be?" Arthur wondered out loud.

"They are very bad," Sok said with a shudder.

"The Fae are no worse or better than any other race," Harpur said. "Many dragons will not allow them to live within their kingdoms..."

"For good reason!" Sok spat.

Harpur shot him a second warning glare. "I allow them because they are useful."

"Useful, how?" Arthur asked.

"Useful in that they will keep valuables left in their charge safe," Harpur explained.

"Valuables? Such as?" Arthur prompted.

"Such as the item I need you to retrieve for me." Harpur said. He still wasn't willing to give Sok any more information than necessary.

"You're talking about the Amber Chalice?" Arthur said. When the others all looked at him in surprise, he explained himself. "I saw it in the book on the last page. What is it?"

"The Amber Chalice is a myth!" Sok said matter-of-factly.

"The myth is that the Amber Chalice is a myth," Harpur said, watching Sok with amusement as the elf processed this new information.

Sok couldn't help himself; this was interesting. "It's really real?"

"As real as you and me, my friend." Harpur rose from his chair and refilled his cup of ale.

"Wasn't the Amber Chalice supposed to be the cup that Orhowyn Bravvenshyn drank your blood from in the myth where Orhowyn was a knight and you were the dragon that got killed?" Arthur asked.

"Obviously, that never happened," Harpur said, "but that is how the legend goes."

"So, it is a myth?" Arthur was confused.

"No," Harpur said. "The Amber Chalice is real. It just got woven into the myth about Orhowyn and me."

"Ah," Arthur said. "Then what is the real story?"

A wistful smile passed over Harpur's face. "That, lad, is a story for later. Aren't you supposed to be having supper with Alex and the twins right about now?"

"Crap!" Arthur jumped up and ran to the door. "I'm late, aren't I?"

No one said a word.

"I'll be back as soon as I can. Don't tell the story until I get here."

And with that, Arthur dashed into the hallway and down the stairs to his wife and son and daughter.

When Arthur had left, Harpur drained his ale cup and turned to Elder Dhonna. "Shall we?" he asked, gesturing toward the door.

Elder Dhonna closed the book. "First we need to put this away."

Harpur turned to Sok. "Since you aren't going to stay out of this, meet us back here after supper so we can make arrangements to get Arthur to the Fae Lands." It was a temporary dismissal delivered in in a tone that made it clear no arguments would be entertained.

"The eight chime?" Sok asked.

"Sure," Harpur agreed. "And Sok?"

"Yes, Harpur?

"Leave the others out of this." Again, with the tone.

"I can't guarantee that," Sok informed him. "Anayah is expecting you to come to the council chambers. What am I supposed to tell her?"

"You'll think of something."

"Great!" Sok mumbled as he left the room. "Leave me to deal with the witch. That will be fun!"

The heavy oak door swung shut, leaving Harpur and Elder Dhonna alone again.

Harpur returned the book to the secret vault in Arthur's bed chamber. Before he closed the vault door, he opened the book to the last page and looked at the drawing of the Amber Chalice. It really was an ugly thing. Roughly forged out of iron, it was not functional as a cup. The lip was jagged and sharp and the bottom was uneven. Harpur had always assumed that it was never finished, that the cup the Fae were guarding for him was a project abandoned by its maker and he wondered what the blacksmith had intended for it. Handles? A stem? Perhaps some intricate pattern etched into it. Likely a silver or gold coating, polished to a shine. *I may never know.*

The chalice was old when he had found it; its creator long dead. Rust had already begun to eat away the iron from which it was forged when he had picked it up at the edge of the marsh just north of the Fae Waters in Braydon Wood. He had been drawn to it by the glint of sunlight reflecting off the large amber nugget embedded into its side. He had thought to free the amber from the iron and toss the cup away. But fate had other plans for the relic. And now, it was about to fulfill its purpose.

If that infernal elf doesn't muck things up!

Harpur closed the book and sealed the vault. Then he returned to Elder Dhonna, who was waiting patiently for him in the outer room.

"You know I can see myself home," Elder Dhonna said as they left Arthur's private chambers. "Why don't you go spend some time with Anayah? Your presence might keep Sok from revealing anything."

Harpur sighed. The Guild Master was right. "Are you sure? I don't mind seeing you safely back to the Wood."

"I'm sure," Elder Dhonna patted the dragon-wizard's arm. "I will be perfectly safe."

"I can send a guard with you," Harpur offered.

"That won't be necessary," Elder Dhonna said, "but thank you."

"It is I who must thank you," Harpur replied. "And I am sorry for putting this burden on you."

They reached the bottom of the stairs and stopped to face each other.

"You are not a burden, Harpur Diggins." Elder Dhonna smiled up at her life-long friend. "You're a stubborn old fool at times, but I am honoured that you trust me to help you."

Harpur smiled at the lovely elf. "I will see you at the lair in a few days?"

"Wild Fae folk couldn't keep me away!"

Harpur watched Elder Dhonna drift away on bare feet toward the castle entrance. She stopped a few feet away from the open doors and turned back to him. "By the way, dragon, when this is all over, that chalice is mine."

"And you will be welcome to it, elf!" It was a lie and Harpur hated himself for uttering it. But if it kept his dear friend from veering off course, it was a lie he could live with. *I hope.*

Harpur entered the council chambers expecting a barrage of questions and, possibly, a few accusations. Instead, the group of people gathered around the round table were laughing at a story Sir Davynn was telling about one of his men getting his hair singed off while trying to keep a crowd from getting too close to a burning dragonfoil tree.

"...and he was running around in circles, screaming and beating his own head with his cap. Which was also on fire!"

"Oh, hey, there, Harpur. You're back," Sok chirped over the gales of laughter.

Slowly, the others composed themselves while Harpur tried to decide if Sok was playing along or if he was warning the others. The dragon-wizard sat down and reached for the last pastry on the tray in the middle of the table.

"I am." He took a bite of his pastry.

"Did Elder Dhonna get home okay, then?" Davynn asked sincerely.

"She did." Harpur took another bite.

"Well, I'm glad you could finally join us," Anayah said. She was sitting across the table.

"Me too."

"So, where did you disappear to today?" Davynn asked.

Harpur shot Sok a questioning glance, but the elf was busy munching on a pastry of his own. "I just had a few errands to attend to."

"Well, next time tell someone so Arthur doesn't have a fit and send us all over Epoh looking for you." Sok smiled around a mouthful of pastry.

"Sorry," the dragon-wizard grunted. "It never occurred to me that I would be missed. Court must have ended early."

"There were only a handful of petitions. We were done by noon," Sok said.

"Anything exciting happen in court today?" Hiro asked.

Harpur turned to Sok with narrowed eyes and bated breath.

"Not really. The shoemaker has a new stitching machine," Sok said.

Harpur exhaled in relief.

"A stitching machine?" Bon said, instantly intrigued. "I should like to see that!"

"His shop is right across from the Shire Bend Inn," Sok said. "I will take you there tomorrow if you like."

"I would like that very much." The android looked thoughtful. "A stitching machine? I wish I had thought of that."

For the next hour, the group of friends reminisced and got caught up. Harpur began to relax - as much as a dragon who was about to be challenged for his kingdom could relax. His contribution to the conversation was minimal, but everyone at the table expected this and no one seemed to think his behavior was anything out of the ordinary. Thankfully, none of them pressed him for more information on his disappearance from court, though he suspected that would come sooner or later. He was relieved when a servant entered asking about supper arrangements.

"The king and queen will not be in the great hall for supper tonight," Sok informed the liveried footman. "But we will be having two special guests at the head table. And I will be making an announcement prior to supper being served."

"Very good, sir," the servant said, bowing his way back out of the room.

"I suppose we should all get changed for supper, then," Sok said, standing up from his chair.

"I hope I can remember how to get back to my room," Anayah said, standing up as well.

"I can show you the way," Davynn offered as he dashed to her chair to pull it out for her.

"No need," Bon said. "I know the way."

Davynn frowned at the android.

"Bon, why don't you go with Hiro to his laboratory instead?" Anayah said coyly. "You don't need to change and I'm sure Hiro has some more fascinating things for you to look at while the rest of us prepare for supper."

"Of course, I do!" Hiro giggled. "Come with me, Bon." He aimed his hover gilly toward the door and waited for Bon to join him. "You can hop on if you like."

As the Krist and the android floated away, Anayah took Davynn's arm and the two of them all but floated out of the room themselves.

"Someone's... What's that word Arthur uses?" Sok asked when he and Harpur were alone.

"Twitterpated," Harpur said.

"That's it. Someone's twitterpated."

"Someone doesn't know what he's getting himself into."

"I thought Anayah was in love with you."

"She thought she was too. Once. I dare say that my present condition has encouraged her to move on."

"You okay with that?"

"If things go the way I expect them to, moving on will be her only option."

"What does that mean?"

Harpur stood up and walked over to where Sok was standing next to his chair. "You will find out soon enough, elf."

Before Sok could say anything else, Harpur stuffed the last bite of his pastry into the elf's mouth and walked away.

Chapter Five

Arthur and Alex ate their supper in Alex's chambers sitting at a small table next to a window that looked over the castle gardens. They chatted happily about Hart and Meg, imagining what the future might hold for them. Being a new mother, Alex was easily distracted by the topic of her babies. And Arthur was happy to oblige. It kept him from having to explain to her that Harpur wanted him to go to the Fae Lands. Before he broached that subject, he needed to know a lot more than he did about the challenge for the kingdom and the Amber Chalice. Anything he told her now would only make her worry and, if she was going to worry about anything just then, he'd rather she worried about Hart and Meg.

Supper consisted of roast mutton and steamed vegetables piled into a gravy-soaked trencher. A tray filled with fruit and pastries waited for them to finish the savory main course. They shared a large jug of crisp mead with which they merrily toasted the new lives sleeping in the nursery next door under the watchful eye of Alma.

"Doesn't she ever take a break?" Arthur asked after Alma poked her head into the room for the fourth time.

"Not since Meg and Hart were born. I'm beginning to wonder if she's human." Alex giggled at the alarmed expression on Arthur's face. "Don't worry, my love, Alma is totally human. I was just teasing you."

Arthur scowled from behind his cup of mead. "Not funny," he mumbled.

Alex laughed out loud. "Oh, Arthur, you live among elves and dragons. Does she look like an elf or a dragon?"

"There are other races," Arthur said.

"Such as?" Alex prompted.

Arthur realized a little too late the dangerous turn the conversation was about to take. "Um... Dwarves. There are dwarves in Epoh."

"Alma is a bit too tall to be a dwarf, I think."

"She could be a mutant dwarf."

Alex rolled her eyes. "Will you be staying here with us this evening?"

Arthur looked at his cute hippie girl wife with her halo of golden curls and smiled ruefully. "I have to meet with Harpur in a while," he said.

"Good!" Alex announced, reaching for a pastry. "I'm exhausted. I just want to turn in early and get as much sleep as I can tonight."

Arthur leaned over and kissed Alex. "Of course. Do you want me to stay until you fall asleep?"

Alex placed her hand on her husband's cheek. "Go to your dragon. I'm going to have a quick bath first."

Arthur kissed her again. "I love you so much."

"I know you do." Alex smiled. "I love you too."

Alex's yawn was Arthur's signal to leave. He took the tray of pastries and fruit and headed back up to his own chambers to meet with Harpur and, presumably, Sok.

Harpur, Sok, Davynn, Anayah, Hiro and Bon all strode into the great hall and took their places at the head table. Arthur and Alex's chairs remained empty while the footmen seated the guests and the serving girls placed trays of food and carafes of wine and ale on the tables.

Murmurs filled the room as the guests speculated about the reason for the two empty seats at the head table. Gossip passed on by servants from the castle that the queen had delivered twins dominated the conversations that rippled through the hall. For the most part, they were correct, though a few with more vivid imaginations conjured up more sinister explanations for the king and queen's obvious absence. Sok, however, was about to end any notions of nefarious goings-on and he signaled a footman waiting at the end of the head table, who blew three sharp blasts from a horn to let the guests know an official announcement was about to be made.

Sok stood up and cleared his throat. "Welcome, everyone! As you can see, King Arthur and Queen Alex are not with us tonight. They are otherwise occupied adjusting to being parents!"

A loud cheer rose from the crowd. From somewhere near the back of the hall someone called out asking if it was a boy or a girl.

Sok smiled broadly. "Both!" He gave the guests a moment to absorb that. "Harpur Arthur Reginald Tristan, henceforth to be known as Prince Hart, and Marian Elizabeth Grace, henceforth to be known as Princess Meg, were born early this morning." More clapping and cheering accompanied Sok's official announcement, confirming the gossip that had circulated throughout the city all day. "They are all doing well and are healthy and hale. There will be a presentation of the twins sometime soon and invitations to the event will be sent out in advance. Now, please join me in raising your cups to the new prince and princess of Epoh."

The guests all stood.

"To Prince Hart and Princess Meg," Sok said. "May they know only happiness throughout long and prosperous lives."

"To Prince Hart and Princess Meg," the guests all echoed before clinking their cups with their neighbours and drinking to the birth of the twins.

"Before we eat," Sok continued, "I would like to introduce two more new-comers to Colwygshire. Please welcome Anayah and Bon, both of whom will be making our fair city their home from now on."

"Welcome Anayah and Bon," the guests called out and raised their cups again to them as well.

The formalities over, Sok signaled that it was time to eat by sitting down and reaching for the platter of roast mutton that dominated the center of the head table. He filled his plate and passed the platter on to Hiro, who was sitting on his left. Since Bon, who was sitting next to Hiro, didn't eat, the platter then made its way back to Sok and then on to Harpur, who was sitting to Sok's right on the other side of Arthur and Alex's empty seats.

Chatter from the guests once again filled the room as they then began to speculate about who would and who would not receive invitations to the twin's presentation. Now that they knew there was both a boy and a girl to buy gifts for, much of the conversation involved out-doing each other with ideas for presents for the prince and princess. Bits and snatches of the discussions drifted up to the head table, eliciting raised eyebrows and barely concealed eye rolls.

"Do people really think that gold and jewels are appropriate gifts for the children of the king and queen?" Anayah, sitting between Harpur and Davynn, asked.

"What do people on Mysturna present when babies are born?" Harpur asked in return.

Anayah's face scrunched up as if she was trying to squeeze out a memory. "I don't know," she said at last.

"You don't know?"

"I really don't. Women don't stay in Danaleedh to give birth and I don't recall ever being involved in welcoming a new baby before I moved to Wildwood."

Danaleedh was the city of witches on Mysturna where Anayah had lived and Wildwood was a palace of sorts that served as the centre of governance for the city.

"So, maybe gold and jewels are appropriate." Harpur suggested.

Anayah felt a little foolish at her judgementalism. "What are you going to give them?" She deflected.

"My protection," Harpur said. *Hopefully.*

Anayah smiled. "That is a wonderful gift."

"And you?" Harpur asked.

Anayah sighed. "If I had my magic, I would make them each a moonstone amulet. But that's not happening."

"Are you sure you don't have your magic? You're not on Mysturna anymore." Harpur gave the witch a sideways glance and reached for another helping of roast mutton.

It had been a long time since Anayah had been able to use her magic. After the witch, Anabettah had been killed while helping Harpur destroy three malevolent wraiths from Thraeh, Anayah's aunt Analeetah had taken her grief out by binding Anayah's magic and imprisoning her in Wildwood to keep her from having any further contact with Harpur, in particular, and Thraeh in general. Anayah had escaped to the Sphere, a holy place on Mysturna, where she found sanctuary with the android, Bon. It hadn't occurred to her, now that she was no longer on Mysturna, that Analeetah's binding might be lifted.

She stared at Harpur, hardly daring to hope that she could use her magic again. "Do you think it's possible?"

"I think that even Analeetah's magic isn't strong enough to cross worlds." Harpur forked a chunk of mutton into his mouth.

With growing excitement, Anayah looked around for something to practice her magic on. Her cup was nearly empty, so she focused on the wine jug sitting on the table in front of Davynn. With a gesture of her hand, she bade it rise up and drew it toward her cup. Davynn, instinctively wary after Arthur's frequent failures at magic, put his fork down and leaned as far away from the wobbling jug as he could. His sudden movement was enough to distract Anayah, and when she turned to see what he was doing, the jug turned as well and poured itself out right onto the startled knight's lap.

Davynn yelped, jumping up out of his chair, and Anayah gasped in horror. All chatter in the hall stopped as the guests turned to see what the fuss was about. A footman rushed to Davynn's aid with a cloth to blot wine all over the front of his pants. It was Davynn's turn to gasp in horror as he snatched the cloth away from the footman and hopped behind his chair to blot the wine himself.

"Orhowyn's withered wings, man! What do you think you are doing?" Davynn shouted at the red-faced footman.

"Oh, Davynn! I'm so, so sorry!" Anayah, as red-faced as the footman, stood up to try to help.

Doing his best to remain calm and maintain his dignity, Davynn assured Anayah that he did not require any assistance. "It's no problem, Anayah," he said gallantly. "I'm pleased to see you have regained your magic."

Beside them, Harpur was laughing so hard, tears were pouring from his eyes. Making no effort to compose himself, he blurted between guffaws, "You and Arthur make a fine pair! You two should hang out together."

Anayah smacked the dragon-wizard on the back of the head. That only made Harpur laugh all the harder and soon, though not a single person could explain why, the entire hall was filled with sympathetic hilarity!

Davynn excused himself to go and change his pants and Anayah dropped, mortified, back into her chair. At the other end of the table, Sok and Hiro were processing Harpur's hysterics through filters of abject alarm. Next to them, Bon nonchalantly fake-sipped an imaginary beverage from an empty wine goblet while he observed and recorded the theatrical tableau unfolding around him.

"Enough already!" Anayah snapped at Harpur, which only served to unleash a fresh wave of uncontrollable laughter.

"I think we need to get him out of here," Sok said to Hiro.

"I'm not sure he's capable of walking," Hiro said.

"He's going to hurt himself!" Sok's apprehension grew as Harpur's laughter began to include wheezing.

"Did someone put something in his ale?" Hiro wondered aloud.

Neither he nor Sok had actually witnessed the failed attempt at magic by Anayah and, though they realized that Davynn had somehow ended up with a jug full of wine in his lap, they remained ignorant of the cause. Neither of them could fathom why Harpur would find spilled wine so funny.

"Who would do that?" Sok asked. "Hiro, we really have to try to get him out of here."

"That's it!" Anayah hissed. "I'm leaving!"

Anayah stood up and marched out of the great hall. Mixed emotions of embarrassment, anger and elation coursed through her as she made her way down the hallway toward the stairs she hoped led to the east tower where her room was. She never should have tested her magic in such a public place. *What must Davynn think of me?* she worried as she began to climb the stone steps. This was not the reunion day she had imagined during all those months she was imprisoned in the Sphere.

Sok watched helplessly as Anayah stormed away. Part of him wanted to join in on the laughter, but a bigger, more practical part knew that he had to get Harpur under control. The great dragon-wizard was doubled over, holding his gut and turning an alarming shade of purple-red.

The elf leaned over Hiro and asked Bon to assist in getting Harpur to the council chambers. The android was at least as strong as Harpur and the most likely to be able to guide him safely. For added measure, Sok signaled a stricken-looking footman to help Bon while Hiro snatched a tray of desserts off the table and floated toward the council chambers ahead of Harpur, Bon and the footman.

Orhowyn's cold, dead heart! Sok thought. *The dragon's gone mad!*

When Bon and the footman had maneuvered Harpur out of the great hall, Sok had another footman blow the horn to get the guests' attention. It took several seconds for the crowd to compose themselves, but eventually it was quiet enough for Sok to speak and be heard.

"My apologies, everyone. Our beloved Harpur Diggins appears to have been taken over by an unprecedented case of hysterics. We are getting him help now and I am sure he will be just fine. Please continue your meals. There will be... more appropriate entertainment beginning soon." Sok bowed and then hustled out of the great hall to help tend to the dragon-wizard.

"What in the holy name of Orhowyn is going on?" Sok shouted as he entered the council chambers.

Harpur was sitting in a chair at the round table and appeared to be regaining some measure of decorum. His fits of laughter had receded to minor bouts of the giggles, but he couldn't talk without another outburst threatening to manifest. At least he could breathe again. And his colour was returning to its normal polished poisonwood hue. Harpur waved a helpless hand at Sok and fought to keep from laughing again.

Bon and Hiro could only shrug in answer to Sok's question.

To stave off his vexation, Sok reached for a bowl of pudding from the tray that Hiro had pilfered from the head table and plopped himself down in a chair across from Harpur to eat it. All he could do was wait until Harpur recovered from whatever bizarre affliction he was suffering from. And pudding seemed to him the best way to do that.

The minutes passed and Harpur finally wiped the last of his tears from his eyes and reached for a pudding for himself. He still didn't trust himself to speak, so he spooned pudding into his mouth and thought about how he was going to explain himself. It's not like he could threaten anyone if they spoke about the incident. Half of Colwygshire nobility had witnessed his temporary descent into insanity.

"Well, that was interesting," Sok said. "What happened back there?"

Harpur pushed his pudding bowl away and leaned back in his chair. "I'm a little stressed."

"Stressed?" Sok repeated.

"A little." Harpur nodded.

"Does this have anything to do with..." Sok began, but before he could finish Harpur shot him a warning glare that confirmed his hysterical mirth was indeed concluded. "...that attempt to break into the Boundary house last week?" Sok improvised. "Because if it does, we really should head up to Arthur's chambers to bring him up to speed on the investigation."

Harpur was impressed with Sok's lamely ingenious save.

"What is a Boundary house?" Bon asked.

"When did someone try to break into the Boundary house?" Hiro asked.

"Oh, yeah. I forgot we told Arthur that we would fill him in on that," Harpur said, standing up. "We should go do that right now."

"Hiro, why don't you fill Bon in on the Boundary house situation while Harpur and I go up and talk to Arthur? And maybe someone should go and check on Anayah. She looked a little stressed herself." Sok joined Harpur at the door leading out of the council chambers.

"What situation with the Boundary House?" Hiro was altogether nonplussed.

"Just explain to him what the Boundary house is, then," Harpur said as he and Sok vanished in a cloud of weirdness.

The Krist looked at the android. The android looked at the Krist.

"So, tell me about Boundary houses," Bon said, utterly unphased by anything that had just happened.

Arthur was waiting in the main room of his chambers when Sok and Harpur entered. He had retrieved the heavy book of Harpur's life from the vault and was staring blankly at the new entry about the Amber Chalice. The language and the writing were just too archaic and small for him to decipher and every time he opened the book, he wondered why he bothered to try. But he wanted to look at the picture. It really was an ugly thing!

"It's about time you guys got here," Arthur said, looking up from the book. "What took you so long?"

Sok and Harpur thought they were early, but Arthur wasn't known for his patience when it came to adventures into the unknown and they chalked it up to accumulating anxiety.

"Harpur had to process some stuff," Sok said cryptically, earning a thump in the shoulder from Harpur for his effort.

"Right. Well, let's get to this," Arthur said, glossing over the bait the disappointed elf was dangling in front of him. "You were going to tell me about the Amber Chalice."

Harpur, once again his old taciturn self, did what he always did when visiting Arthur in his private chambers; he helped himself to a cup of ale and sat down. "You seem rather enthusiastic about this," the dragon-wizard observed.

"Is there any way I can get out of it?" Arthur said, accepting a cup of ale from Sok.

"No." Harpur sipped his drink.

"Then let's get on with it," Arthur said.

"For the record," Sok began, taking a seat next to Arthur on the sofa, "my objection to him going alone to the Fae Lands still stands."

"Duly noted," Harpur said, neither agreeing nor disagreeing with the elf.

"I'm not all that keen on going there alone myself," Arthur added. "Why can't Sok come with me?"

"I already told you, I'm not going anywhere near that place!" Sok exclaimed.

"Fine. I'll take Davynn with me then." Arthur looked at Sok with bemused confusion.

"I'll think about it," Harpur said.

Sok and Arthur exchanged bewildered looks.

"I don't see what the big deal is," Arthur argued. "Do you really trust me to find my way there by myself?"

"You follow the Colwygshire Road until it ends and turn right. I'm sure you can handle it," Harpur said.

Arthur had been to the end of the Colwygshire Road. There was nothing there but trees and mountains. "I'm not worried about the road," he said. "I'm worried about the turning right part."

"We can circle back to that later," Sok said, seeing Harpur's growing exasperation with their directionally-challenged king. "Tell us about the chalice."

Harpur took a moment to think about what he wanted to say. "The Amber Chalice is old. It was old when I found it in the mud in the marshes north of the Fae Waters not long after I inherited Epoh."

Sok frowned. "No one lived in Epoh before you inherited it, so where did it come from?"

"That's not entirely true. Orhowyn permitted small settlements to occupy the most southern areas of the kingdom. He just discouraged them from getting too comfortable and expanding their numbers. When a village grew too large, Orhowyn... shall we say took measures to keep their populations in check?"

"Genocide?" Arthur was horrified.

"Not all dragons are as benevolent as I am," Harpur said.

"Clearly," Sok said. "Let's just focus on the chalice."

Harpur nodded. Arthur was looking a little green around the gills and he didn't want to get any farther off track. "At the time I found the chalice,

I was settling a dispute between the elves and the Fae. I won't go into detail. Suffice it to say that both races were pushing the limits of my conditions for their occupancy in my kingdom and I was forced to..."

"Go a little Orhowyn Bravvenshyn on their asses?" Sok suggested.

"Believe me, I took no pleasure in it." Harpur sipped his ale.

"You didn't?" Arthur was even more horrified to think that Harpur could do such a thing, whether it was pleasant or not.

"I did what I had to do to keep the peace, Arthur. I am a dragon. And Epoh is my kingdom. If people don't want to live here by my rules, they are welcome to leave."

"Moving on," Sok prompted. "Did any of them leave after you... you know."

"A good many of the elves did leave Epoh. They refused to live peacefully with the Fae and when I refused to accept their terms, they migrated to Ecaep. But we are getting ahead of the story. Before that happened, an even worse tragedy occurred." Harpur's gaze drifted off into the distance as he recalled the sad story he was about to tell to Arthur and Sok.

"I believed that I had settled the matter between the Fae and the elves. I was unhappy with what I had had to do to stop the fighting between them, and I was taking some time to make peace with myself over it. I had transformed into my human form and was walking through Braydon Wood when I happened across a rusty old cup with a stunning amber nugget embedded into it. I happen to be rather fond of amber and so I picked up the cup and took it back to my lair. I had planned on prying the amber out of the iron and throwing the cup away.

"When I got back to my lair, I discovered the mutilated bodies of three Fae folk lying by the entrance. Their bodies had been hacked to pieces with axes and pierced with arrows. Elven arrows." Harpur let that sink in. "Two were quite dead, but the third, an incredibly beautiful Faeling named Willow was barely hanging on to life.

"I carried her inside and laid her on a bed of gold, hoping that she would absorb some of its healing powers. She had been woven from fallen willow branches – which is where she got her name – with such exquisite and intricate detail that she looked almost human. She was the gentlest and kindest Fae I have ever met and I was sure that she would mature into a great leader of her people. Until a group of elves cut off both her legs, cleaved her head with an axe and shot her with nine hunting arrows."

Sok and Arthur both swallowed; Sok in shame for his people and Arthur in horror of such an atrocity.

"The gold had revived Willow enough for her to tell me who had done this to her. She and her companions had braved crossing Braydon Wood to ask for my help with the marauding elves that were attacking the Fae Lands. They weren't aware that I already knew and had gone to deal with the problem. A group of elves had discovered them in the Wood and had hunted them down and killed them. For some reason that I cannot fathom, they dumped their bodies outside my lair and left them for dead. I assume the elves thought that leaving the bodies of the Fae at my door would serve as proof of the Fae's breech of conditions and that I would punish the Fae for allowing any of their kind to trespass in the elven territory north of the Fae Waters. But I will never know. I hunted each of them down and burned them alive. I didn't bother to stop and ask questions; such was the depth of my wrath."

"What does this have to do with the chalice?" Sok asked softly.

Harpur grunted. "Before Willow died in my lair, she noticed the iron cup with the amber nugget and asked me to bring it to her."

"I thought fairies... I mean Fae were like allergic to iron," Arthur interjected.

Harpur was impressed. "You know your Fae lore!" he said. "They are not allergic to iron. Iron interferes with their magic. Too much or close contact with it can kill them. It's like a poison of sorts. It destroys their magic and since magic is what they are made of, they tend to avoid it."

"So, why did she ask for the cup?" Sok was curious.

"She was dying and she was in pain. She wanted to be released and the iron in the cup gave her a swift end."

Sok looked contrite. "I didn't know the Fae could feel pain."

Harpur just stared at Sok.

"They *are* living creatures, Sok," Arthur said. "Why wouldn't they feel pain?"

The elf's face reddened. "I don't know. It just never occurred to me. Elves don't really see them as living creatures."

"Well, they are," Harpur growled.

"Sorry," Sok mumbled.

"What I don't understand is why the Fae agreed to keep it safe for you if it is harmful to them. And what do you need it for now?" Arthur asked, hoping to deflect the attention away from Sok's callous assessment of the Fae.

"The chalice contains Willow's essence. Her magic and her consciousness were drawn out of her by the iron. But it is stored in the amber," Harpur explained. "The Fae queen is keeping it safe for me because she is being paid in gold to do so. It is hidden in such a way that the Fae can watch over it without it causing them any harm.

"So, you want to bring Willow back to life somehow?" Sok reasoned.

"Not exactly," Harpur said hesitantly.

"Oh, I get it!" Sok shouted in excitement. "You are going to take Willow's magic out of the amber to replace yours!"

Harpur drew a hand across his mouth to mask his growing impatience. "No."

"What then?" Sok asked. He couldn't think of any other reason for Harpur to want to get the cup back from the Fae.

"That, as they say on Earth, is above your pay grade, my friend," Harpur said.

"Ha-ha!" Arthur chided. "You don't have the proper clearance."

"Neither do you, I'm afraid," Harpur said.

"What?" Arthur blurted. "You want me to go to the Fae Lands to get it for you, but you won't tell me why?"

"That's right."

"That's not fair!" Arthur whined.

"Life's not fair," Harpur said. *Look at me. I've lost my magic. I can't even transform back into a dragon anymore. I'm the Orhowyn damned poster boy for not fair!*

A tense silence hung between them. Until Sok decided to end it. "Fair enough," he said without it dripping with sarcasm. "If Arthur is to retrieve the Amber Chalice... for whatever purpose... then he should do so forthwith."

Arthur and Harpur stared at the elf,

"Forthwith?" Arthur said.

"Sorry. It just popped into my head. As meant to say, if Arthur is to retrieve the cup, he really does need someone to go with him. Please, Harpur, let him take Davynn with him. You know that Davynn will keep him safe and he won't cause any trouble for you."

The dragon-wizard looked at Arthur and saw a helpless puppy looking balefully back at him. "Very well. But I swear, Arthur, if you so much as breathe a word to him about anything that I've told you, I'll..."

"I promise!" Arthur interrupted. There was no point in letting Harpur make threats he was incapable of carrying out. "Not a word."

"Why can't Davynn know about the real history of the Amber Chalice?" Sok asked, believing that was what Harpur was referring to.

Arthur suddenly remembered that Sok didn't know about the challenge. "I think Harpur just wants people to keep thinking of it as they have been. You know, as part of the legend of Orhowyn and Xzynthyrius. Right, Harpur?"

"Right. Let's go find Davynn and tell him the good news." Harpur drained his cup and abandoned it on the table by the sofa.

Suddenly Sok knew how Hiro must have felt when he and Harpur left the council chambers. Something truly was amiss. "You do that. I have some paperwork I need to do," he said.

Arthur put the book back in the vault and the three of them left Arthur's private chambers.

It had been a long and eventful day. In spite of the nap he had taken, Arthur was worn out and in need of a proper night's sleep. He forced himself to accompany Harpur to the council chambers, which they found empty, and suggested that they turn in and look for Davynn in the morning. He slumped into a chair and put his head down on the table. Within seconds he was snoring softly.

Harpur considered waking him up, but opted to leave him where he was for the time being. The human part of him sympathized. The dragon part of him was mildly annoyed.

He crossed the expansive castle foyer and poked his head in the door to the great hall where the guests were still enjoying the evening's entertainment. The head table was empty, so he closed the door and headed up the hallway that passed the kitchens to Hiro's laboratory. There he found Hiro and Bon deep in discussion about how best to construct hover gillies for Davynn's guards.

"Have you seen Davynn?" Harpur asked, entering the laboratory and helping himself to an apple from a bowl on the cluttered table where the android and the Krist were seated.

"He was here a while ago. But he went to check on Anayah," Hiro said. "I see you have recovered from your... affliction. Did you and Sok bring Arthur up to speed about the Boundary house?"

"Yes," Harpur said with a slight smirk. "He now has all the information he needs."

"I can't believe that an attempt to break into the Boundary house escaped my attention," Hiro pried. "Davynn didn't seem to know anything about it either. When did this happen?"

There had, of course, been no attempt to break into the Boundary house. The Boundary house was, to all intents and purposes, impenetrable. It had been built by the elves to protect the portal that led from Braydon Wood to Earth. The fact that it was against the law for people from Thraeh to use it to Bound didn't stop some from trying. And dying! After Arthur had been crowned king of Epoh, he had successfully negotiated with the elves to have a building constructed around it to prevent anyone from Bounding without a proper permit. The elves had been reluctant at first, but had acquiesced when Arthur suggested that they both design and build the structure and granted them governance over its use. Only Harpur could get into it without the aid of the elves.

"It was a minor offence. The elves are taking care of it," Harpur brushed off Hiro's inquiry. "I'll see if Davynn is in Anayah's rooms." He turned to leave.

"What do you need Davynn for?" Hiro asked. "Perhaps I can help you."

Harpur looked at the nosy Krist and shook his head. "I just want to tell him that Finch knows how to get wine stains out of clothes. Wouldn't want his fine pants to be ruined." He grabbed another apple and left the open-mouthed Krist to untangle such un-dragon-like concern.

"Orhowyn's ample arse, he's worried about ruined pants!" Hiro said after the dragon-wizard was gone. "Something very odd is going on here, Bon. Something very odd, indeed."

Harpur circled back around the council chambers, peeking in quickly to ensure Davynn wasn't there before carrying on up the hallway to the stairs that led to the east tower. As he passed the hall leading to an adjunct to the castle proper where the guild offices were housed, he saw Sok turning a corner toward the archives. *What's he up to?* Harpur wondered, but kept going as he wanted to connect with Davynn before the knight retired for the night.

There were too many secrets being kept and he realized that he was the reason for most of them. He had to keep the challenge that he knew was coming from becoming public knowledge. The last thing he wanted was to face his challenger in front of an audience. Especially this particular challenger. He was thankful that Elder Dhonna was so willing to help him with it all. As fond as he was of Arthur, Sok, Anayah and the others, Elder Dhonna held a special place in his old dragon heart. He wouldn't go so far as to say he loved the Guild Master, but his feeling toward her were about as close as a dragon could ever hope to come to it.

He climbed the stairs to the second floor where Anayah's rooms were and knocked. He'd seen Anayah in every state of dress a woman could attain during the years she had shared his makeshift lair on Earth, and he wasn't bothered by any of them. But time had reinstated the need for a respect for her privacy and since he had managed to find his way into her bad book twice that day already, he dared not go for the hat trick.

When the door opened, he was surprised to see a pretty brunette instead of the ginger-haired witch. "Who are you?" he asked.

The pretty brunette curtsied. "I am Mara, sir. Can I help you?"

"I'm looking for Anayah. I thought these were her rooms."

"They are, sir. I've just come to turn down her bed."

"Ah! Is Anayah here?"

"No, sir. She's gone for a walk in the gardens with Sir Davynn. I expect she will return shortly." Mara did not invite him in to wait.

"Thank you, Mara. I will go and look for her there." Harpur smiled at the maid and left. He was almost back at the top of the stairs before he heard the door click shut again.

Down the stairs, down the hall, across the foyer and out through the castle doors he went. His dragon eyes scanned the gardens that spread out in front of the castle on the opposite side of a wide courtyard that opened to the road that led down to the city gates. The gardens were softly illuminated by lanterns that hung from posts along a winding pathway. At the far end, next to a fountain, he spotted Davynn and Anayah standing close together. *A little too close?* Harpur watched them for a minute before descending the wide steps to the courtyard and on to the gardens. *Definitely twitterpated,* he thought. Even from this distance, he could sense how nervous Davynn was.

"Ahem," Harpur cleared his throat to alert them to his presence. "I'm not interrupting anything, am I?"

Davynn looked toward the throat-clearing and, seeing Harpur standing there, took a long step away from Anayah.

"As a matter of fact..." Anayah began.

"Not at all, Harpur. I'm glad to see you are back to your usual self," the knight said, trying not to look like an errant teenager whose date's father had just showed up.

"Yes," Harpur said. "I am too. Do you mind if I borrow Davynn for a minute, Anayah? I won't keep him long."

"As a matter of fact..." Anayah began again.

"We will only be a minute, m' lady," Davynn said with such formality, Anayah was too taken aback to protest.

Harpur led Davynn a short distance away and talked to him for the minute he and Davynn had promised to be. Then they shook hands and Harpur returned to the castle.

"What was that about?" Anayah asked when Davynn approached her again.

"He needs me to accompany Arthur on an errand tomorrow," Davynn explained.

"What kind of an errand?"

"Arthur needs to get something that the Fae folk are keeping for Harpur and he wants me to go along to keep Arthur safe."

"Why doesn't the old coot go and get it himself?" Anayah was still annoyed with the dragon-wizard. Even more so for interrupting her and Davynn.

"He didn't say," Davynn said. "Coot?"

"Never mind," Anayah said, slipping her arm around Davynn's elbow. "Let's not allow him to ruin our evening."

"Indeed," Davynn said with a nervous smile.

They continued walking slowly farther along the pathway away from the castle in silence.

Something is going on, Anayah thought to herself.

Something is going on, Davynn thought to himself.

They hadn't gone far when Anayah stopped. "It's getting a little chilly out here. Maybe we should head back to the castle."

"As you wish," Davynn said a little too quickly. He barely contained a sigh of relief. Not that he wanted his time with Anayah to end. He was just too distracted by Harpur's cryptic request to enjoy her company the way he would have liked to.

He escorted Anayah back to her rooms and then ran back down the stairs to the council chambers where he found Arthur sleeping in a chair with his head on the table. No one else was around. He briefly considered leaving Arthur where he was, but he couldn't bring himself to let the poor guy spend the night with his head on a table. So, after failing to rouse him, Davynn lifted the comatose king out of the chair and carried him over his shoulder up the stairs to his private chambers.

By the time he had dumped Arthur onto the bed, the castle had all but wound down for the night. The guests from the great hall had all gone home. The kitchens were dark and the lights in Hiro's laboratory had been extinguished. The only signs of life that Davynn could find were the guards posted throughout the castle. He decided to call it a night and retreated to his own rooms in the guard house. Answers to his questions would have to wait until the morning.

A few minutes after Davynn had gone to the guard house, Sok blew out the candle he had been using to find his way around the archives. When he had first come to work in the castle, he had spent a lot of time in the archives and he knew every book and every scroll within it. It had taken him a while to find the book he had gone there for, an ancient spell book that was kept under lock and key among the forbidden texts. It was not where it was supposed to be and when he finally found it tucked behind some other books on a top shelf, he was not surprised to discover that one page had been torn out of it.

"Gotcha now, dragon!" the elf said.

Chapter Six

"She's going to kill me, Harpur!" Arthur said angrily as he mounted his horse the following morning just before dawn.

"She's not going to kill you. I will talk to her," Harpur assured the miserable king. "Once she realizes how important this is, she will forgive us both."

"You're not the one leaving your wife and day-old twins to go off on some cockamamy quest for a rusty old cup without saying good-bye." Arthur glared down at the dragon-wizard standing on the ground.

And you're not the one who is about to be challenged. "It will be okay. Trust me. Just go get the chalice and bring it to my lair." Harpur stood as far away from the horses as he could. To them, he still smelled like a dragon. And horses were not keen on dragons at the best of times. Arthur's mount was already prancing nervously underneath him and Harpur worried that Arthur might not get out of the stables before being thrown to the ground. "Take care of him, Davynn."

"I will." Davynn spurred his horse forward. *If his whining doesn't drive me insane.*

Harpur watched them ride away toward the city gates. When they reached the corner and turned onto the main road from the castle, he turned in the opposite direction and headed to Skull's Keep. He wanted some time to himself before he returned to the castle and had to face Alex.

The city was only just beginning to wake up. A few merchants were pulling carts filled with goods toward the market, while a few others were already there setting up their stalls. The permanent shops on Shire's Bend were still closed, but the inn was starting to stir as guests, eager to continue their travels, collected their belongings and made their way to the stables from which Harpur had just come.

As Harpur made his way past the inn, he felt eyes upon him from above. Glancing up, he saw Morgaine Fayle looking down at him from her window. Their eyes met and Harpur saw a small smile tug at the corner of her lips. He simply nodded in return and kept walking. He had too much to do before he could deal with her. Morgaine Fayle would have to wait.

Skull's Keep was empty at that hour, save for a handful of old men gossiping over mugs of jamba at a central table near the bar. Harpur motioned for the barmaid to bring him a cup of the same aromatic elixir and settled himself at a table next to a window. In a small niche above his table, the skull of a long-dead citizen of the kingdom stared down at him. Before it was a public house, Skull's Keep had been the entrance to a series of catacombs that snaked beneath the city. When the catacombs had been sealed, some of the skulls of the dead that rested there had been removed and were now, like the one above Harpur's table, dispersed throughout the pub in similar niches. It was customary to leave a coin or two in the niche as an offering to honour these long-forgotten souls, which is what Harpur did just as the barmaid delivered his jamba.

"You're up and about early," she said as she placed his cup on the table.

"Busy day ahead," Harpur replied, handing her another coin in payment for the much-welcome beverage. "Thought I would get a jump on it."

"I hear the queen gave birth to twins," the barmaid continued. "Is it true?"

"It is," Harpur said. "A boy and a girl."

"The king and queen must be so happy!"

"That they are," Harpur said.

Sensing that Harpur did not want to chat, the barmaid smiled. "I'll leave you to your jamba, then. Holler if you want anything else."

"Thank you," Harpur said to her retreating back.

A few minutes passed in blessed solitude before the pub door opened again and Harpur watched a cloaked figure enter. He'd been half expecting it, but he couldn't hide his disappointment when a hand pulled back the hood of the cloak and Morgaine Fayle stood scanning the room searching for him. When she spotted him, the smile that had started in the window at Shire's Bend Inn broadened.

"There you are," Morgaine Fayle said, making her way toward his table and taking a seat, uninvited, across from him.

"What do you want, Morgaine?" Harpur kept his expression neutral.

"You know what I want, Xzynthyrius," the raven-haired beauty said. "What I need is to know why you are still here."

Harpur took a sip of jamba and stared out the window into the street. Being called by his true name stirred some unwelcome emotions he wasn't prepared to deal with. He took a minute to compose himself before answering. "There are some things I need to take care of first."

"Well, I advise you not to take too long." Morgaine rose from her chair. "I wish to get this over with."

Harpur sipped his jamba. Still looking out the window, he said with more confidence than he felt, "And I advise you, Morgaine Fayle, be careful what you wish for."

Morgaine's eyes narrowed slightly. She leaned over the table, bringing her lips close to Harpur's ear. "You are weak, Xzynthyrius Dreamfinder. It is time for you to accept your fate," she whispered.

Harpur turned his head slowly toward Morgaine. His eyes were blazing violet-red and dragon fire glowed in his chest. Morgaine could feel the heat and she backed away. "My name is Harpur Diggins."

They stared at each other for several long seconds, each of them taking measure of the other until Morgaine finally took a step back. "I will wait for you, Harpur Diggins," she said quietly in a tone of respect and reverence. Harpur only nodded in reply and watched as Morgaine drew her hood back over her head and left Skull's Keep.

When the door closed behind her, Harpur breathed a sigh of relief. The fire in his chest cooled and his eyes returned to their normal deep violet. *Well, that went better than I thought it would,* he thought as he drained his cup and left the pub as well.

An hour later, Harpur strode into the council chambers to find Sok, Hiro, Anayah and Bon breaking their fast at the round table with stacks of pancakes, eggs and bacon that Hiro had produced from his magic satchel. They could have waited for the kitchens to make their meals, but Finch, the head housekeeper, had decreed that porridge was on the menu that morning and so they had opted for something a little less bland from Hiro's satchel.

He had just come from Alex's rooms where he had broken the news of Arthur's departure to the Fae Lands to her. To his utter amazement, she had accepted it with what he could only describe as relief, if not outright joy.

"Oh, thank Orhowyn!" Alex had exclaimed. "It will be good to have him out of my hair for a few days."

Harpur, having braced himself for quite a different reaction, didn't know how to respond.

"You're sure he's going to be okay, though, right?" Alex continued as she rocked the sleeping Meg in her arms.

"Davynn is with him. I'm sure he will keep Arthur safe," Harpur assured her.

"Good!" Alex handed Meg to a maid and sat down at her table to eat the porridge that had just arrived. "I won't have to listen to him complain about Alma and I won't have to listen to Alma complain about him. When do you expect them back?"

"Oh, nine or ten days. No more than that, I think." Harpur watched her spoon the gruel into her mouth with surprising relish.

"Is that all? You can't keep him busy for a bit longer? Three or four weeks would be perfect."

Harpur was beginning to get a too-good-to-be-true feeling and wanted to escape before something went wrong. "I doubt his errand will take much longer than that, but I will let you know if things change." He couldn't bring himself to make promises he didn't know if he would be able to keep.

"Well, do your best," Alex chirped.

Harpur took that for a dismissal and retreated from the queen's chambers. *Orhowyn's teeth and talons! That was too easy.*

In the council chambers, he sat down and helped himself to a plateful of food and another cup of jamba. Anayah, Hiro and Sok were all staring at him as he loaded his plate and started to eat.

"What?" he finally said when the glares failed to cease.

"Where are Arthur and Davynn?" Hiro asked.

"Sok and Anayah didn't tell you?" Harpur said. "They've gone to the Fae Lands to retrieve something the Fae are keeping for me."

Now that Arthur and Davynn were safely on their way, there was no reason to keep that part of the plan a secret anymore.

"They left earlier than I expected," Anayah said accusingly.

"They left when I needed them to." Harpur speared a piece of pancake and put it in his mouth.

"Actually," Sok began, placing on the table a tattered old book that had been stashed behind him on his chair, "I did tell them. I told them everything."

Harpur looked at the book and then up at the elf. "What's that?" he asked casually.

"I know what you're up to. I know what you're going to do with the Amber Chalice." He had a smug look on his face.

"Oh, really?" Harpur said. "And what do you think I am going to do with it?" He picked up a slice of bacon and bit it in half.

Sok flipped the book open to the place where the page had been torn out. "Last night you told Arthur and me that the amber in the chalice contains the magic and consciousness of the dead Fae girl, Willow, did you not?"

Harpur looked at the book again. "I did. What of it?"

"You also told us that you are not planning on using Willow's magic to restore your own, nor are you going to attempt to reincarnate Willow herself. Correct?"

"More or less." Harpur was both amused and curious.

"Then the only other possible explanation for you needing the Amber Chalice is that you are planning on using Willow's essence to give Arthur the power to transmute into a dragon!" Sok delivered his indictment with deadpan confidence.

Harpur didn't know what he had been expecting, but it wasn't that. "Why in Orhowyn's good name would I want Arthur to transmute into a dragon?"

"It's obvious," Sok said. "You have lost your magic. You are unable to maintain dragon form and Arthur has your blood inside him. So, before another dragon comes along to challenge you, you are going to give Arthur the power to take on dragon form so you can give him the kingdom and we don't have to worry about being expelled from Epoh if another dragon inherits."

Harpur pinched the bridge of his nose. *That's actually rather ingenious. I wish I had thought of it.*

His silence gave Sok even more confidence. "I did some research last night after we left Arthur's chambers. If you aren't going to bring Willow back and you aren't going to use her magic to restore your own, this is the only other thing Fae essence could be used for. The missing spell from this book," Sok tapped the open page, "is exactly the spell you need to make this happen."

Harpur pushed his plate back and rested his elbows on the table. He clasped his hands together and looked at Sok. "Well, Sherlock, you are forgetting one thing."

"What's that?" Sok's confidence began to crack.

"You just said that I have lost my magic. I couldn't cast that spell even if I wanted to. And I assure you I am not planning on turning Arthur into a dragon." Harpur watched the crack widen.

"You could get someone else to do it for you," Sok said desperately.

"Anayah could do it!" Hiro blurted out. "She has her magic back now."

All eyes shifted to Anayah, who was sputtering in embarrassment over her spectacular failure when using her magic for the first time in the great hall the night before.

"That won't be necessary," Harpur said. "I have no intention of using that – or any – spell to turn Arthur into a dragon. Besides, I think Anayah needs some time to reacquaint herself with her powers. Give the lady an opportunity to adjust."

Anayah appreciated the rescue and her heart softened toward Harpur. "Thank you," she said.

Hiro apologized. He had gotten swept up in the excitement.

"Now that we are done with that nonsense," Harpur said, looking pointedly at Sok, "I will be returning to my lair for a few days. It's been some time since I've been there and I would like to... do some spring cleaning now that the weather is improving."

"We can go with you," Sok offered, not quite ready to be done with the *nonsense.*

"No," Harpur said sharply. Then realized just how sharp he sounded. "Thank you, but I would prefer to handle it myself. Besides, with Arthur away, you will need to look after castle business. And I imagine that Hiro and Bon are eager to get working on the hover gillies."

"What about Anayah?" Sok said, hoping to keep at least one of them close to Harpur.

"What about her?" Harpur asked just before a forkful of egg disappeared into his mouth.

"What's she going to do?"

"Whatever she wants," Harpur said. "As long as it's here in Colwygshire," he added when Sok seemed to see a loophole in the dragon-wizard's answer.

The elf scowled. "May I ask a question?" Sok said. When no one objected he continued. "Who is Sherlock?"

Arthur and Davynn made good time down the Colwygshire Road. For the first half hour, Arthur droned on about Alex's reaction to his leaving, telling Davynn repeatedly how badly he was going to pay for this and he never should have agreed to it. Davynn, loyal knight that he was, listened patiently for as long as he could before he had to put a stop to it.

He spurred his horse to a trot, forcing Arthur to do the same to keep up. Arthur couldn't bounce, balance and talk at the same time, so Davynn kept this pace for a time, while he reveled in the silence from his companion. When he figured Arthur's bones had been jarred enough, he slowed his horse back down to a walk and, before Arthur could find his tongue, he introduced a new subject. "You missed some excitement in the great hall last night."

"Oh?" Arthur said. "What happened?"

Davynn, too enamored with Anayah, chose to find the entire incident amusing. He shook his head and smiled as he recalled Harpur guffawing loudly in front of the Colwygshire nobility. "You should have been there!" he said. "Harpur fell into a fit of hysterics after Anayah tried to use her magic to pour wine and ended up dumping it all over me instead."

Arthur had a difficult time deciding which part of that statement he wanted more detail on first. The hysterical Harpur won. "What sort of fit?"

"He started laughing and he couldn't control himself," Davynn explained. "It was a sight to behold."

"I can't imagine," Arthur said as he tried to conjure an image of Harpur laughing uncontrollably. "Did you say Anayah used magic to pour wine?"

"I did. She tried to fill her cup, but something went wrong and the wine ended up in my lap. That's what set Harpur off in the first place." Davynn started to chuckle at the memory of the dragon-wizard writhing in his chair.

"But I thought Anayah's magic was..."

"Apparently, now that she's not on Mysturna anymore, Analeetah's spell no longer works." Davynn adjusted his seat in the saddle.

"That's wonderful!" he said. "But how did the wine end up on you instead of in the cup? Anayah is a highly skilled witch."

"She's out of practice. It seems that magic is a use it or lose it proposition." Davynn kicked his horse into an easy canter.

Arthur gave his own mount more rein and held on tightly to the saddlebow. He wanted to ask more about Harpur's fit, but staying on his horse took all of his concentration. Davynn, on the other hand, was pleased to have found an effective way to keep Arthur from focusing on Alex.

Not wanting to push the horses too hard, Davynn slowed the pace back to a walk a short time later. He was relatively sure that Arthur had been sufficiently distracted from his worries, but to be certain, he launched into another subject before Arthur had a chance to bring it up again. "What is this object we are retrieving for Harpur anyway?"

Arthur took a few seconds to consider his answer. "From what I can tell, it's a rusty old cup."

Davynn looked at his king. He was expecting it to be something like a magical sword or something of that nature. "A rusty old cup?"

"Pretty much, yep," Arthur confirmed. He wasn't sure how much he should say about it.

"What does the dragon want with a rusty old cup?"

"That I do not know. Harpur wouldn't tell me."

"He sends you off to the Fae Lands to get a rusty old cup and he doesn't tell you why?"

Arthur shrugged. "It's Harpur. He must have a good reason."

Arthur understood that the Amber Chalice had something to do with the challenge Harpur said was imminent, but he had no clue what that might be. He looked over at the knight and made a decision.

"I'm not supposed to tell you this," Arthur said.

"Tell me what?" Davynn asked.

"Harpur is going to be challenged."

They rode on for a minute while before Davynn replied. "Eventually."

"No. Any day now."

Davynn reined in his horse and stopped. "What?"

"Harpur is going to be challenged. Soon." Arthur's horse stopped a few feet ahead of Davynn's and he turned it around so they were facing each other.

"Sire, did it ever occur to you that Harpur is sending you to the Fae Lands to get this supposed rusty cup so that you are not around when the challenge goes down?" Davynn was looking at Arthur like he was a complete fool. "There probably isn't even a rusty old cup to get!"

"It occurred to me," Arthur said. "But there's more."

Davynn remained silent, waiting for Arthur to go on.

"The rusty old cup is the Amber Chalice."

"Ha!" Davynn scoffed. "The Amber Chalice is a myth. A myth, Arthur!" He turned his horse and started riding back the way they had come.

"Where are you going?" Arthur called after him.

"Back to Colwygshire. This is a waste of time!"

Arthur rolled his eyes. *Orhowyn's fiery breath! I shouldn't have told him.* He kicked his horse into another bone-jarring trot to catch up to Davynn.

When he caught up to the knight, he slowed his horse. "The chalice is real. And Harpur needs us to get it for him. I don't know what he needs it for, but I trust him."

Davynn, though it went against his loyal knightly grain, kept going. And kept silent. He was seething with anger at the dragon-wizard for sending Arthur on this pointless errand, and at Arthur for being suckered into doing it.

"Davynn, are you listening to me?"

More silence.

"Sir Davynn, I order you to stop your horse right now!" Arthur shouted.

Unable to disobey a direct order, Davynn stopped. But he refused to look at his king. It was the most defiance he could muster.

Arthur cleared his throat. He had never issued an order to Davynn, nor had he ever shouted at him like that. He felt terrible. "I'm sorry," he said. "I know you think that this is all a ruse, but I'm telling you it's not. The chalice is real. And Harpur needs it. Now, let's turn around and go to the Fae Lands."

Davynn heard the conviction in Arthur's voice and felt torn. He had promised Harpur that he would watch out for Arthur and, whether the Amber Chalice was real or not, he did have a duty to his king. "Fine," he said at last. "But if we get to the Fae Lands and there is no chalice, I'm going to kill Harpur myself!"

"Fair enough," Arthur said. *But you'll probably have to stand in line behind another dragon.*

Davynn tabled his anger for the time being. Before long, he and Arthur were chatting amiably about Hart and Meg, Anayah and Bon's safe arrival on Thraeh and even, eventually, about the Amber Chalice and what it might have to do with the challenge. They both instinctively avoided talking about the challenge itself, or what might happen if Harpur lost. They were careful to use the word 'if', but every time one of them did, they amended it to 'when' in their minds. The idea of another dragon ruling Epoh was just too terrifying for either of them to think about. The very idea of a future without Harpur, no matter how infuriating he could be at times, was simply unfathomable. Whenever the conversation veered too close to the danger zone, they circled back to the twins or the witch and the android. And whenever Arthur started to fret about Alex, Davynn just spurred his horse into a trot, which effectively ended the king's ability to talk at all.

By the time they stopped to make camp for the night, Arthur's legs and backside were aching miserably. He could barely get off his horse and, once he did, he wasn't sure he'd be able to get back on again in the morning. Davynn instructed him to walk it off and gather some firewood while he unsaddled the horses and built a fire ring with stones. He had chosen a spot near a creek that ran parallel to the Colwygshire Road where they could water the horses and fill their waterskins.

They were protected by a copse of trees, one of which was a dragonfoil that was just starting to bud with silvery, purple-blue leaves. This one was quite small, only a few inches taller than Arthur. Still, he marveled at the fact that only a few weeks earlier, it wasn't there at all. It would probably triple in size by the fall, and then, when the last leaf fell to the ground, it would burst into flames and burn to ash in a matter of minutes. Arthur shivered at the memory of having walked into the flames of a dragonfoil tree to fulfill an elven prophecy, which made him king of Epoh. It had been a spectacular moment in his life, but one he hoped he would never have to repeat.

Davynn lit the fire and Arthur parceled out a share of the jerked venison, hard cheese and flat bread for each of them. If Hiro had been there, they would have been dining on something a little more interesting, like succulent roast chicken smothered in gravy. But Hiro and his magic satchel were far behind them at the castle and they would have to make do with what they had for the next several days.

"I expected more travelers to be on the road today," Davynn said as he settled next to the fire to eat his supper. They had only passed about a dozen or so people on the road, half of which were guards returning from patrols.

Arthur hadn't thought about it. "Is it unusual for so few people to be moving around the kingdom?"

Davynn shrugged. "It is springtime. I suppose most folks are busy tending to their fields. The road will get busier in the summer when the crops start to grow. I just thought there would be more people travelling now that the weather is so fair."

Not for the first time, Arthur wondered why he didn't know more about the way things worked in Epoh. "Davynn, do you think I'm a good king?"

The knight looked at Arthur and saw the doubt on his face. "I think you are a fine king, sire."

"But I don't do much," Arthur said. "I mean I preside over court and I sit at the head table in the great hall, but that's about all I do."

Davynn appeared to be thinking. "What else do you think you should do?"

"I don't know," Arthur said. "I'm supposed to be the king of Epoh, but I don't have any real authority."

"You know that Harpur is the actual ruler of the kingdom, right?" Davynn was confused.

"I know that. But what is the point of being king when all I really am is a figurehead?"

"I see," said Davynn, nodding. "Don't underestimate your importance to the humans of this realm, Arthur. Harpur has been a great ruler here. He's kept the peace for centuries. But humans like to feel like they are being led by one of their own. You are more than just a figurehead in their eyes; you are the liaison between them and Harpur. You represent them and look out for their interests. They need to know that someone will stand up for them. And Harpur needs someone to keep them in check. He has no desire to have to deal with the day-to-day problems of our race. You rule your people, Arthur."

Arthur let this new perspective wash over him. "What about the other races? Who rules them?"

"Well, the elves are governed by a Council of Elders, as you know. The dwarves have a king. King Röggenar, I believe he is called. The only other race in Epoh is the Fae, and they are basically anarchists. They have a queen of sorts, but doesn't rule so much as she incites riotous behavior among her kind." Davynn took a drink from his waterskin and wished it was ale.

Arthur looked alarmed. "She incites riotous behavior among her kind? What does that mean?"

"The Fae have their own system. I can't pretend to understand it, but it's how they do things." Davynn shrugged again.

"Are the Fae dangerous?" Arthur asked. He was having trouble accepting a queen that incited riotous behavior in her kind.

"They can be," Davynn answered calmly. "But only if they are threatened. Then they can be quite vicious. Generally, they tend to be more mischievous than dangerous."

"Mischievous how?"

Davynn scrunched up his face as he searched for a good example of Fae mischief. "Dangling people by the ankles over an open fire."

"How is that not dangerous?" Arthur was flabbergasted.

"I'm not saying accidents don't happen. Don't worry, sire, I won't let the Fae dangle you by your ankles over a fire." Davynn couldn't help but laugh at Arthur's expression.

"I can't believe Harpur wanted me to do this alone," Arthur said. "What was he thinking?"

"He was probably thinking you would be safer by yourself."

"What?" Arthur was incredulous. "How could he possibly think I'd be safer facing a race of anarchists who think dangling people over open fires is mere mischief alone?"

"You are what the Fae call an Innocent. When an Innocent wanders into their lands, they simply watch them for a while and when they are sure they aren't a threat, they ask them what they want and then escort them out again. I, on the other hand, am a knight. They might not be too happy to have an armed guard, much less a knight, encroach on their territory." Davynn laid down and rested his head on his hands. "Get some rest, Arthur. And try not to worry. If all goes well, we'll be in and out in an hour. Then we can head north to the lair."

Arthur stared at the flames of the fire. There was so much going on in his head, he couldn't think straight. He knew he wouldn't be able to sleep, but he laid down with his head against his saddle and tried to sort through the jumble of thoughts that were knotted up behind his eyeballs, causing a headache.

He knew that Harpur was going to be challenged by another dragon soon. But he didn't know when. He knew that Morgaine Fayle was somehow involved. But he didn't know how. He believed that the Amber Chalice containing the essence of a dead Fae girl could help Harpur. But he didn't know why. He could see all the dots; he just couldn't connect them.

It occurred to him that Harpur had not explained who Morgaine Fayle was. He remembered asking Harpur about her, but thinking back, Harpur had ignored the question and asked about Anayah and Bon's arrival through the transporter. *Did the wily old dragon-wizard simply distract me with other issues?* He had been too tired after staying up all night waiting for the twins' arrival to have noticed at the time. Now, though, he was convinced that Harpur had deliberately avoided talking about Morgaine.

Across the fire, Davynn started snoring, which evoked a wide yawn from Arthur. The last thing he thought was that he was glad that Davynn was with him on this weird quest, but he was going to need more help to get through the next several days. At least!

Harpur left the castle shortly after breakfast. On foot, it would take him three days to get to his lair. If he'd been able to transform into his true dragon form, he could have flown there in no time, but this way bought Arthur and Davynn more time to get to the Fae Lands and retrieve the Amber Chalice. He knew that the Fae would be glad to have it out of their territory and would give it to Arthur without much trouble. Unbeknownst to anyone else, the Fae queen had been at Arthur's coronation ceremony and would recognize him as Harpur's emissary. Davynn's presence may cause some suspicion, but he trusted the knight to conduct himself appropriately and see the deed done. Ideally, Arthur would have gone alone. But Harpur always knew the likelihood of that had been slim from the beginning.

Before he began his journey, Harpur stopped by Alex's chambers to say good bye. He had told Anayah that his gift to the twins was his protection and he intended to make good on that, no matter how things unfolded in the coming days. He might not have been able to wield his magic, but his magic still existed. And it was potent and powerful. All he had to do was transfer some of it from himself to Hart and Meg.

Alex received him with surprise and a smile. "I thought you were going to your lair for a few days," she said.

A maid was brushing her curly, blond hair and Alex spoke to Harpur's reflection in the mirror above her vanity.

"I am," Harpur confirmed. "I will be off as soon as I have said good bye to the twins. Would you mind if I went in and saw them for a minute?"

"Aw," Alex crooned, touched by Harpur's affection for her newborn babies. "Of course, you can. You couldn't have come at a better time. Alma is finally taking a break and shouldn't be back for a while yet. But, Harpur," she added with a warning, "please don't wake them up!"

"I wouldn't dream of it," Harpur said, slipping into the nursery and closing the door.

Alone with Hart and Meg, Harpur looked down at the twins sleeping side by side in their cradle. Swaddled in blankets as they were, he couldn't tell which one was which. But it didn't matter. His task did not involve knowing one from the other. He removed the amethyst brooch from his ascot and pricked his finger with pin. A purple-red drop of blood oozed out.

"Your mother would likely not approve of this," he whispered as he reached down and drew a runic symbol on one of the babies' foreheads, "but if she knew what was at stake, I'm sure she would forgive me."

He squeezed another drop of blood from his finger and repeated the action on the other baby. "I know my blood already flows in your veins, but this symbol will give it greater strength. In case I don't make it back, I want you both to have my protection."

For a few seconds, the symbols Harpur had drawn on the babies' foreheads glowed electric purple. Then they faded and were absorbed into their soft skin. "Be safe," he whispered and turned to leave.

Alex was behind a privacy screen when Harpur came out of the nursery. A maid was assisting her with her corset and Harpur could hear her grunting as the ties were tugged and pulled to tighten the garment.

"Good bye, Alex," Harpur called as he made his way to the outer door.

"Oh, Harpur?" Alex said, breathlessly.

"Yes?"

"You will be back for the presentation of the twins, won't you?" She grunted loudly.

"I will do everything in my power to be here for it," Harpur said. Not wishing to prolong this discussion, he left Alex's chambers and pulled the door closed behind him.

"I swear," Alex said when she heard the door close, "that tough, old dragon-wizard is turning into a big pile of mush!"

"Indeed, your majesty," the maid agreed.

Spring cleaning, my magical backside! How stupid does Harpur think we are? As much as Anayah had appreciated him defending her newly regained magic, his announcement that he was going to his lair for a few days had produced a fresh wave of annoyance with him. They hadn't seen each other for over a year and he was leaving to go clean up his cave. *Not without me, you're not, dragon!*

She excused herself from the council chambers, telling Sok, Hiro and Bon that she was going to her rooms to practice her magic. "I will be busy all day," she said as she walked out of the council chambers, "so please don't disturb me."

Sok watched her go with narrowed eyes and pursed lips. He no more believed that Anayah was going to hole up in her rooms all day than he believed that Harpur was going to his lair to do spring cleaning. "Well, I'm going to go and meet with Alex to talk about plans for the presentation of the twins." He stood up and walked toward the door leading to the stairs to the upper floors.

"I thought you were going to show me where the shoemaker's shop is so I might get a look at his stitching machine," Bon said.

Sok had forgotten all about that. He stopped at the door and turned around. "Hiro knows the way. I'm sure he won't mind taking you."

Hiro giggled. "I wouldn't mind seeing it myself," he said. "But first I need to go to my laboratory. I need to get something."

Satisfied that the Krist and the android were occupied for the day, Sok continued on. But instead of going up the stairs to Alex's chambers, he went out into the hallway that led around the council chambers and left the castle through the main entrance. He made his way to the city gates and across the Colwygshire Road to the edge of Braydon Wood and hid in the branches of a large oak tree to wait for Harpur to pass. There was a small chance he would leave by the northern gate, but if he did, he would still have to cross the Colwygshire Road and Sok had a clear view of the road past that end of the city wall.

He had just gotten comfortable when he saw Anayah exit the main gate. She stopped and looked up and down the road before turning northward and walking along the forest side of it for a short distance. Then she stopped again, looked around and ducked behind a large bush next to the road.

"Why you sneaky little witch," Sok said to himself. "It looks like Harpur is going to have way more help with his *spring cleaning* than he anticipated."

He half expected Hiro and Bon to be next through the gate, but neither of them showed up. It appeared that the Krist and the android were the only honest members of their little group. While he waited for Harpur, Sok watched people coming and going through the gates. Most were going to or coming from the market, which was beginning to bustle with activity deeper inside the city. A few guards were heading out on patrols. A handful of others were making their way into the forest to look for early mushrooms. There were even some elves delivering firewood to the communal stacks that were stationed around Colwygshire.

Sok was beginning to think that Harpur wasn't coming when the big dragon-wizard himself finally appeared and, as the elf had predicted, turned north and angled across the road to enter Braydon Wood. He scrambled out of the oak tree and cut through the forest in the direction Harpur was heading. He considered looking for Anayah, but decided that if the witch wanted to follow Harpur, she could do it on her own. She would probably give herself away soon enough and he would rather Harpur didn't find the two of them together.

It was easy to track Harpur as he made his way deeper into Braydon Wood. He wasn't trying to be stealthy and he set a fairly steady, though unhurried pace in a roughly north-west direction. Sok had expected him to follow the trails made by the elves and animals that lived in the forest, but Harpur seemed content to avoid them, which made it easier for Sok to remain concealed, but slightly harder to keep Harpur in sight. Now and then, Sok heard Anayah stumbling and bumbling her way through the bush. He couldn't imagine that Harpur hadn't heard her as well and he wondered why the dragon was allowing her to continue to follow him.

The dragon-wizard kept going, though, leading Sok and Anayah deeper and deeper into the forest. After an hour, Sok was amazed that Anayah hadn't given up. After two hours, he began to be impressed by her determination. She was keeping up rather well, if noisily, and then he realized that she was practicing her magic after all. Anayah wasn't following Harpur; she was following a bird she had enchanted to follow Harpur. A yellow-crested tinker was flying back and forth between Harpur and Anayah, leading her forward, then flying ahead, then returning to lead her forward again.

Smart, Sok thought. Yellow-crested tinkers were common enough that Harpur wouldn't pay much mind if he happened to notice one flitting back and forth, nor were they so common that Anayah would get her enchanted tinker mixed up with another one and be led astray.

Thus, it was that the trio made their way through Braydon Wood that morning, travelling together separately. But soon Sok lost sight of Harpur again. One minute the dragon-wizard was about forty feet ahead of Sok and the next minute he wasn't.

The elf wasn't overly concerned about this. He continued to creep forward in the general direction of where he'd last seen Harpur, believing that he would find him again soon enough. When he reached the spot where he had last seen Harpur, Sok looked for signs of his passing and was chagrined to find none at all. To his right, about fifteen yards, the tinker that Anayah had been using to track Harpur began to twitter and chirp loudly. Sok, alarmed, abandoned his search for Harpur's trail and moved quickly toward the bird's call. His first thought was that Anayah had been hurt, though he couldn't imagine how.

As he drew closer to where the witch was, he could see her looking up at the bird that was flitting from branch to branch in confusion. He was just about to step out from behind a bush, when Harpur suddenly appeared behind Anayah, looking none too pleased to see her.

"What are you doing out here?" Harpur boomed, causing a startled yelp to escape Anayah's lips.

The witch spun around to face Harpur. "Harpur! You scared me. How did you know I was following you?"

"I'd have to be stone deaf not to have heard you crashing through the bush." Harpur spat. "Now, I ask you again, what are you doing here?"

Sok crouched down behind the bush to watch and listen.

Anayah crossed her arms and adopted a defiant stance. "I'm following you. What do you think I'm doing here?"

From the look on Harpur's face, Sok could tell he hadn't been expecting such a frank admission. "I don't know... Picking wild flowers?" Harpur suggested sarcastically. "I thought I made it clear that I wanted to be alone."

Anayah flipped her long, red hair over her shoulder and raised her pretty chin. "You did. But I believe you are in some kind of trouble and I want to help."

Harpur rubbed his own chin and sighed. "Anayah, I know it's been a long time since we've seen each other. And I will do everything in my power to make it up to you. But I need you to trust me. There's a trail about ten yards that way," he pointed to his right, "that will lead you right back to Colwygshire. Take it. Now."

"I'm not leaving you, Harpur." Anayah stared at the dragon-wizard.

"You are," Harpur said quietly, "and you will take the elf with you." Without taking his eyes off Anayah, Harpur summoned the elf from his hiding place. "Sok, get your ass out from under that bush and escort Anayah back to the city."

Sok rolled his eyes. *Orhowyn's horned head! How did he know?* He crawled out and joined Harpur and Anayah. "Hey, guys! Nice day for a walk in the woods, isn't it?"

Anayah and Harpur both scowled at Sok, who smiled sheepishly back at them.

"Just once," Harpur said, looking at the two of them, "it would be great if I could get what I ask for. Just once. I'd just like to know how it feels to ask people to do something and actually have them do it. Is that really so much to ask for? Is it?"

Sok and Anayah exchanged glances. "We're worried about you, Harpur. We just want to help," Anayah said.

"Did it ever occur to either one of you that I don't need your help?" Harpur was growing more agitated by the second.

"We're your friends! Why wouldn't you want our help?" Anayah shot back.

Harpur rubbed his hand across his face and sighed again. "There are some things that a dragon has to do alone, Anayah. I am very sorry that one of those things had to coincide with your arrival, but I had no control over that. You are just going to have to accept that I have things I need to do and that they don't involve you. Do you understand?"

"No, I don't understand, Harpur!" Anayah hissed angrily. "And I am not going to accept being shut out of whatever is going on just because you are too proud to..."

Harpur's eyes flared orange-purple and dragon fire cast an orange-red glow through his coat. Sok grabbed Anayah's arm and pulled her away from the furious dragon-wizard. "Come on, Anayah. Let's do as Harpur asks. He will find a way to send word if he needs us."

Anayah was too shocked by Harpur's display of aggression to protest any further and she allowed herself to be dragged away. They didn't run, but neither did they doddle as Sok led them into the protection of the trees toward the trail Harpur had told them to follow back to Colwygshire. He looked back once to see Harpur glaring at them with eyes still burning in fury and he picked up the pace.

When they reached the trail, Sok turned right toward Colwygshire and, still holding Anayah's arm, kept moving. He wanted to put as much distance as possible between them and Harpur.

"What just happened?" Anayah said about one hundred yards into their hasty retreat.

"Thankfully, nothing bad!" Sok said, slowing his pace. "But you better release the tinker. It's going nuts trying to get you to follow Harpur."

Anayah looked up at the squawking bird in the branches above her head and waved her hand at it. The yellow-crested tinker instantly fell quiet and stared down at her with angry, beady eyes. It blasted one last reproachful cry in her direction and then flew off.

"Thanks," she said to Sok. "I forgot about the poor little thing."

"So, how's your magic doing?" Sok asked. "It must feel good to have it back."

Anayah glanced at the elf. There was something in his tone that seemed a little suspicious. "It does. Why do you ask?"

"I was just wondering how your zapping skills are." Sok smiled conspiratorially at the witch.

"You want me to zap us to Harpur's lair?" Anayah asked both alarmed and impressed. She'd have zapped them both back to the castle when Harpur caught them following him, but she was still a little nervous about using her magic. And after Harpur's outburst, she had to question the wisdom of going anywhere near the lair. By any means.

"Not right now," Sok said. "It will take Harpur a few days to reach the lair on foot and there's no point in the two of us sitting up there with nothing to do until he gets there. But, yeah, I want you to zap us to the lair."

Anayah looked back the way they had come. Then she looked at Sok. "I think I can manage that."

"Good!" Sok said with a smile. "For now, why don't you practice by zapping us back to the council chambers? I haven't eaten anything since breakfast and all this tramping through the forest has given me an appetite."

Anayah laughed and shook her head. "It's a wonder you aren't two hundred pounds!" She snapped her fingers and they disappeared in a red plume of smoke.

Chapter Seven

The next two days passed rather uneventfully for all concerned.

Hiro and Bon discussed ways to make a telepathically controlled hover gilly work for the guards, not one of whom had even a modicum of telepathic ability. The only solution they came up with was a remote-control device that the guards would carry with them, but Hiro worried that the devices would get lost or be destroyed frequently. At one point, Bon suggested microchip implants, and while Hiro was intrigued, he doubted very much that Arthur and Davynn would sanction such a procedure. So, they continued to brainstorm.

Sok and Anayah, meanwhile, spent much of their time at Skull's Keep, plotting and planning. The fact that they didn't know what they were plotting and planning for didn't escape them. So, they planned for everything.

"You don't suppose that another dragon has challenged Harpur, do you?" Anayah asked as Sok composed lists of things they might possibly need.

"Nah," Sok said dismissively. "Harpur would have told us that. There's no way that he would face a challenge without preparing us for it."

"Yeah," Anayah said. "Maybe he met someone."

Sok stopped writing and looked up at Anayah. "Harpur? You've got to be joking."

"Well, it makes the most sense."

"How so?"

"Why else would he be sneaking off to his lair alone?"

"He didn't sneak off to his lair. He announced his departure to all of us. Besides, who would have him?" Sok returned his attention to his lists and continued writing.

"Well, I would have at one time!" Anayah sounded a little defensive.

"True," Sok shrugged. "You really dodged an arrow there, didn't you?"

Anayah frowned. Her bizarre infatuation with Harpur had been a disaster. She had come so close to putting Sok and Arthur in serious danger over it. It was a wonder that Harpur had wanted anything to do with her at all after her embarrassing declaration of love for him when they were on Mysturna. They had shared his lair on Earth for several years and her affection for him was genuine. But had she really loved Harpur? That was a question she had asked herself many times. The answer was always the same: It's complicated.

"Personally," Sok went on when she didn't reply right away, "I think you and Davynn are a far better match. The only issue I can see there is the difference in your ages."

"How old do you think I am?" Anayah was shocked.

Sok looked up from his list. "You must be at least fifty. And Davynn is what? Thirty-five? Thirty-six? In forty years, you'll just be reaching the prime of your life and he'll be..." The elf shrugged, "Dead?"

"I don't know whether to admire your candor or turn you into a toad," Anayah said.

"Well, if you decide to turn me into a toad, make it a tree toad. I'd like to keep my connection to the forest." Sok wasn't the least bit concerned about an interspecies transformation taking place. "Now, I think I've covered every eventuality that we've discussed." He pushed the list across the table. "Look this over and let me know if I've left anything out."

Anayah, happy to be distracted from the current topic, picked up the list. "Extra stockings?" she asked, seeing the item about halfway down the third column on the second page lodged between crossbow bolts and bandages.

"We talked about that," Sok said. "It gets cold at night in the mountains still."

"I'm sure it does." Anayah flipped through another four pages of seemingly random items and then handed the list back to Sok. "You've got everything but the kitchen sink. I think we're good."

Sok turned to the last page and prepared to write down kitchen sink. "Do you really think we might need one?"

"I really think we should head back to the castle and get some sleep. Who knows what we are going to face when we get to the lair tomorrow?" Anayah stood up and waited for Sok to follow.

"Let's hope it's just an angry dragon," Sok said, gathering his papers and telling the barmaid to put their meals on the castle account.

While Hiro and Bon brainstormed new ways to make hover gillies work, and Sok and Anayah plotted and planned, Arthur and Davynn rode on toward the Fae Lands. The closer they got, the more nervous Arthur became. He had finally cottoned on to Davynn's trick to shut him up whenever he started complaining and so, to avoid being bounced to death when the horses started trotting, he resolved to try to keep his emotions in better check. He knew he was failing when Davynn leaned forward in his saddle, which was the knight's tell when he was growing annoyed with his king. As soon as he noticed Davynn adjust his seat this way, Arthur changed the subject. Or, if he really needed to vent, he at least changed his tone.

"There's something I don't understand," Arthur said on the morning of their third day on the road. They had just started out and were expecting to arrive at the Fae Lands by mid-afternoon.

"What's that?" Davynn asked.

"If Epoh has been at peace for so long, why do we need an army?"

Davynn looked appalled. "What if Epoh was invaded?"

"By who?"

"By anybody!" Davynn exclaimed. "Harpur is in no condition to defend Epoh and we have been fortunate that none of the neighbouring kingdoms have realized just how vulnerable Epoh has become these past months."

Arthur gulped. "Has Epoh ever been invaded before?"

"Only once. Harpur assisted the first king of Epoh when invaders from beyond the Crysteel Sea attempted to take the kingdom."

Arthur recalled the story of King Ylemnir, a wizard and, as it had turned out, Arthur's ancestor. Harpur had assisted Ylemnir in conquering the invaders, and had granted the wizard the status of king of Epoh as a reward for leading his people as bravely as he had. Much later, Harpur had discovered that Ylemnir had Bounded to Earth and had fathered a child. That was how he had found Arthur, a direct descendent of Ylemnir and, as far as Harpur knew, the only living person on Earth to possess magic, unreliable as it was.

"Right," Arthur said, "I'd forgotten about that. That's the only time there has been a war in Epoh since Harpur inherited?"

"The elves and the Fae have skirmished many times. Harpur has always been quick to intervene, though, and their disputes have not amounted to much. That is another thing we should be thankful for," the knight said with warning in his voice.

"What do you mean?" Arthur asked.

"The Fae are very likely well aware of Harpur's condition. There is little standing between them and an assault on the elves at this point. It would take little provocation for the Fae Queen to order an attack," Davynn explained.

"They hate each other that much?" Arthur could hardly believe what he was hearing.

"The elves hate the Fae more than the Fae hate the elves, as I understand it. But as I told you before, they are anarchists and their queen takes special delight in inciting her people into riotous behavior. Orhowyn only knows why she hasn't crossed the Fae Waters and attacked the elves already." Davynn leaned forward in his saddle.

Arthur didn't know what he had done to annoy the knight. He thought he had been perfectly reasonable throughout this exchange. He decided to risk having to trot anyway. "Why don't I know any of this?"

Davynn sighed and relaxed again. He wasn't really annoyed with Arthur; he had only wanted to avoid what was coming next. "Because Harpur told us not to tell you."

"What? Why?" Arthur couldn't keep the anger and fear he suddenly felt out of his voice.

"Because he wants you to be happy, Arthur." Davynn looked sad. "When Harpur's condition left him unable to use his magic at all, he was going to tell you everything. Then you and Queen Alex announced that you were expecting a baby and Harpur decided not to ruin that for you. He believed he was doing the right thing."

Arthur was shocked. Too shocked to speak.

They rode on in silence for a while before Davynn turned to Arthur again. "I'm sorry, Arthur. We did not want to keep all this from you, but Harpur insisted."

"On pain of death, no doubt," Arthur said, hoping Davynn understood that his scorn was directed at the dragon-wizard and not at him.

"None of us actually believe he would kill us, but that was the general idea." Davynn smirked.

"Your men will be able to protect us if anything should happen between the Fae and the elves, right?" Arthur asked.

Davynn chose his words carefully. "We would do our best, sire."

"You know you only call me sire when it's bad news?"

"I know, sire."

For his part, Harpur relished the peace and quiet of Braydon Wood while he made his steady way toward his lair. He didn't for a minute think that Sok and Anayah were going to simply go back to Colwygshire and stay there and he began to wonder if he shouldn't have let them come with him just so he could keep an eye on them. But he pushed that thought out of his mind in favour of enjoying the glorious solitude his trek to the lair was providing.

Braydon Wood was his favourite part of Epoh. The elves managed it expertly, protecting the old growth and fostering the new growth with loving care. They managed the wildlife within the forest as well and it was a testament to their skill that the animals thrived the way they did. When he was able to live in his natural form as a dragon, he never lacked for fresh meat, such was the abundance of deer and wild boar that roamed the forest.

When things did, upon occasion, get out of balance, Harpur would dine on bear or wolf to bring their numbers back into harmony. Indeed, Harpur had chosen well when he had challenged Orhowyn and won this amazing kingdom and now that his time there was growing short, he took a measure of pride in his stewardship over the centuries. He had no regrets.

He reached the path leading to an alpine meadow that spread out in front of the lair in the mid-afternoon of the third day. *Arthur and Davynn should be at the Fae Lands by now*, the thought as he started to climb above the trees to the meadow. From there it would take them another six days to reach the lair and, if all went well, deliver the Amber Chalice. Though Arthur didn't know it yet, the future of Epoh was in his hands. Or it would be once he got his hands on the chalice. It all came down to timing now. Timing and Arthur's ability to wield his magic like never before. That is to say with accuracy. *There's nothing like a crisis to make a wizard focus*, Harpur thought. *He just has to believe in himself as much as I believe in him.*

And Harpur did believe in Arthur. He knew that Arthur's magic was strong and that the only reason it went so badly so often was because Arthur was afraid of it. Which wasn't entirely a bad thing. A little healthy fear around such great power would keep Arthur humble. Not that there was much chance of him becoming an evil genius. But too much confidence could lead to bad decisions. What Arthur needed was something to tip the balance and force him to find the confidence he needed to use his magic effectively. *Well, my friend*, Harpur thought, *it's time to fly or fall.*

Harpur stepped onto the meadow and paused to take in the spectacular view that spread out before him. The lush, green forests of Braydon Wood spread out as far as the eye could see to the south and east. Beyond the forest, Colwygshire and the fertile planes lay hidden even from Harpur's keen dragon sight. To the west the mountains rose in great jagged spires, forming the border between Epoh and the kingdoms of Ecaep and Rednow. Farther to the east lay the Crysteel Sea and beyond the mountains in the south were the Sands of Sancheera, the vast desert where Harpur, and all dragons on Thraeh, had been born.

There was a time when Harpur had returned often to the Sands of Sancheera. He'd had a mate, a stunning dragon named Karryl Evergreen whose emerald eyes and scales fairly outshone the sun. Against his advice,

Karryl had challenged Khol the Black, the ruling dragon of Rednow, and had lost. Her death had affected Harpur deeply and, save once, when he and Sok and Hiro had Bounded there from Mysturna, he had never returned to the desert. Their only progeny, twin male dragons, were still there, neither of them having yet challenged for a kingdom. But they were still young, barely nine hundred years old, and would find their place in the world in their own time. Harpur was glad that it was neither of his sons who were challenging him now. He didn't think he would be able to enact his plan on his own flesh and blood.

He moved to the edge of the meadow where the mountain dropped steeply down into the valley below and stood beside the skull of the only dragon that had ever challenged him before then. The foolish young red, whose name Harpur could no longer recall, had been far too vain to heed the warnings of other dragons against challenging Harpur and had come in the dead of winter to issue his challenge. Unused to the cold, the young dragon fell fast under Harpur's talons and had died not far from where his skull now lay, weathered and bleached by many years of exposure to the sun. But not before inflicting a few very serious injuries that had left Harpur weak and vulnerable and unable to heal himself completely. If it hadn't been for a travelling healer, from whom Harpur had taken his name, Harpur might have succumbed to his wounds, which would have left Epoh unprotected. In spite of his frustration with the cocky young dragon, Harpur had honoured the challenger by ritually burning his body. But he had kept the skull as a warning to any other dragon bold or stupid enough to challenge him in his prime as this one had done.

In some ways, now that Harpur was facing a new challenge and had many more years of experience behind him, the young red seemed more honourable than his current challenger. The red had not waited for a weak dragon to conquer. Had he been a little older, a little wiser and a little stronger, he might have bested Harpur and taken Epoh for himself.

In his own time, when Harpur had challenged Orhowyn, there was a good chance that he could have lost. Orhowyn was old, but he was still formidable and had much more experience than Harpur. The only reason that Harpur had won against Orhowyn was because he had seen the older dragon fight and knew his tells. Orhowyn always feinted left before striking with his powerful right hand. And he always brought the fight to the ground by tearing at his opponents' wings so they couldn't fly. Harpur had managed to keep his wings intact and the fight in the air, always climbing higher and staying above Orhowyn. Thus, Orhowyn quickly tired and Harpur had delivered the final blow that caused the great silver-blue to fall from the sky to his death. It had been a clean and fair fight where the superior strategy prevailed.

"I am sorry, old friend," Harpur said to the decaying dragon skull. "If the fates are on my side, I will burn what remains of you so you may be whole again and fly free in Arachovor."

Having sworn this oath, Harpur turned and walked to his lair. Leaf litter had blown inside, but otherwise the cave was undisturbed. He could smell his challenger near the entrance, but he knew that no dragon would enter another dragon's lair without an invitation. The scent wasn't fresh; it had been several days since the challenger had been there and Harpur relaxed, knowing that it wasn't near now.

He looked at his hoard, amassed over centuries, and smiled. Nothing gave him as much pleasure as the pile of gold and jewels that filled the cave. Some of it had been Orhowyn's before Harpur had inherited it all, treasures taken in battles fought in a time when dragons were much less civilized than they were now. Some of it Harpur had acquired himself. In his younger days, he hadn't been above pillaging the occasional castle in some far-off kingdom. Some he had bargained for, trading his services, which, truth be told, he would have provided anyway, for chests of gold or other precious gems. And some had been gifted to him. The dwarves were fond of bringing him gilded swords and jeweled crowns that they presented with their entertaining, albeit wholly fictional, tales of heroic defeats over unscrupulous foes. No dwarf in Epoh had seen battle for ages. But Harpur appreciated the embroidery.

He picked up one such crown from the pile and smiled at the memory of his last visit with King Röggenar of the dwarves. Crippled after a boulder crushed his leg in the mines nearly five decades earlier, the cantankerous old monarch had insisted that he had knocked it off an invading king's head himself.

"You're getting sloppy, dragon," King Röggenar had said. "If it wasn't for us dwarves, Epoh would be swarming with foreign dogs bent on taking it for themselves."

Harpur had smiled and nodded. "Thank you, Röggenar. I don't know how I would manage without you."

He had attempted to hand the crown back to the handicapped king.

"Keep it," King Röggenar grunted, waving the crown away. "I don't need it and I'm sure your hoard could use another trinket."

Harpur tossed the crown back onto the pile and took a deep breath. He loved the smell of gold.

He passed the evening lying on top of his hoard. Water dripping from the stalactites throughout the cave and the occasional bird call from outside were the only sounds he heard. As the sun began to set, Harpur began to drift off to sleep, he eyes growing heavy in the fading light. Just as sleep was about to carry him away, he heard another sound. A sound he had been expecting, but one he hoped he wouldn't hear.

"Do you think he's in there?" a whispered voice asked.

"He has to be," another whispered voice answered.

"Should we go in?" a third voice asked.

"Doesn't look like he's done much cleaning," the second voice said.

Harpur sat up and growled. The acoustics in the cave amplified the sound and he hoped the unwelcome interlopers would be fooled into thinking that he had somehow managed to transform into a dragon.

"I told you he wouldn't be happy about us showing up," a fourth voice said, followed by a giggle.

"That was a snore," the second voice said. "He's sleeping."

Harpur slid down off the pile of treasure and walked to the entrance. He stood there, silently, with arms crossed and eyes blazing.

Sok, Anayah, Hiro and Bon all took a large step back.

"I can explain," Sok said, stepping forward again.

Harpur continued to glare.

"You are needed back at the castle," Sod said.

"Why?" Harpur growled.

"There's an emergency. And with Arthur and Davynn away, we thought you had better come and deal with it." Sok gulped.

Harpur's left eyebrow rose a half an inch. "And it took all four of you to come and tell me this?"

"Well, Hiro and Bon have never seen your lair and so we figured, you know, we'd all come and..." Sok said in a nervous rush.

"What is this emergency?" Harpur interrupted. He wasn't buying it, but he figured he had to listen, just in case.

"Several of the guards are running amok," Sod said. "They've taken hostages and have blockaded themselves into the council chambers. They are demanding higher wages. Harpur you really must come quickly."

Harpur looked at the earnest faces of the elf, the witch, the Krist and at the passive face of the android. "Bon is this true?"

Orhowyn's balls! Sok thought. *We're done for now.*

"Not precisely," Bon said. Having been programmed to be truthful, this was the closest he could get to answering Harpur and not outrightly betraying his companions.

"That's what I thought," Harpur said quietly. "Now, here's what you are going to do. You are all going to return to the castle and leave me in peace." Anayah and Sok started to protest, but Harpur put up a hand to stop them. "Just for a few days," he added.

They had not expected that at all.

"A few days?" Anayah repeated.

"Well, six days, to be precise," Harpur said sardonically.

"You want us to come back in six days?" Sok asked for confirmation.

"I don't want you to come back at all," Harpur said. "But seeing as you refuse to mind your own business and now that you've dragged Hiro and Bon into it, I will permit you to return in six days. That is how long I need to..."

"Do your spring cleaning?" Anayah prompted with a measure of sarcasm.

"Precisely." Harpur stared at the witch with a smirk.

In his head, Sok did the math. Six days from then was when Arthur should be arriving with the Amber Chalice. And the Amber Chalice was at the center of whatever Harpur was up to. If they stayed, it would mean six days of living in a damp dragon's lair with nothing to do but wait. Whereas, if they left, they could be in more comfortable surroundings until they were allowed to come back. "Very well," he announced. "Come along, everyone. Let's return to the castle for the time being and leave Harpur to his spring cleaning." Without waiting for an answer, the elf strode away into the growing darkness.

Anayah, not so willing to give up that easily, opened her mouth to object, but Harpur flared his eyes at her once again and thrust his chin in Sok's general direction. "Go."

Harpur watched from the entrance of his lair as Anayah, Hiro and Bon reluctantly caught up to Sok and disappeared down the trail leading away from the lair. *That was too easy*, he thought as he continued to watch and wonder what they would try next. He shook his head at the idea of guards taking hostages for better wages. That had to have been Sok's fabrication. *Orhowyn's fetid breath! How gullible does he think I am?*

Alone once again, Harpur retreated back to the top of his hoard and laid down. *Soon this will all be over*, he thought. *Tomorrow, Elder Dhonna will arrive and we'll prepare for the challenge. I pray Orhowyn, let Arthur get back here in time.*

Not long after Harpur had reached his lair, Arthur and Davynn reached the end of the Colwygshire Road. They had crossed a bridge over the Fae Waters, the only river to run through Epoh, earlier that morning and since then Arthur had been scanning the trees for any sign of the elementals. He had no idea what he was looking for, but he looked all the same.

"What are you looking for?" Davynn had asked when he noticed Arthur's attention was focused on the trees to their right.

"The Fae," Arthur answered.

"You won't see any Fae folk this close to the road," Davynn said. "Their territory begins about a mile to the west."

Arthur nodded, but he kept searching anyway.

Two trailheads led off the end of the Colwygshire Road. One continued south and up into the mountains. The other veered west into Braydon Wood.

Nailed to a tree at the start of the westward trail were three weathered planks with words painted on them.

'Keep out!'

'Turn back before it's too late.'

'Proceed at your own risk!'

Arthur read the signs and his eyes widened in alarm. "Uh, Davynn?" He pointed at the warnings.

Davynn laughed. "Just a bit of dwarven humour," he said, dismounting from his horse.

"So, the dwarves don't like the Fae either?"

"No one *likes* the Fae, Arthur," Davynn said with great patience. "The dwarves and the Fae generally get along reasonably well, though."

Arthur gingerly lifted his right leg and swung it over the back of his horse, trying not to groan as he did. When his feet both touched the ground, he gave his legs a minute to decide whether or not they were going to support him. He was not looking forward to six more days on horseback.

He walked off some of the stiffness as best he could while Davynn tethered the horses to a tree where they had access to grass. He patted their necks and informed them that he and Arthur would be back as soon as possible.

"We're walking?" Arthur asked, unsure if he was up to a hike through the forest.

"It's not far to the Fae Lands," Davynn said. "I thought you'd be glad not to have to ride for a while."

I'd be glad not to ever have to ride again, Arthur thought to himself. "Lead on, good sir knight," Arthur said, forcing a smile and willing his legs to carry him forward.

The trail meandered through the trees in a lazy serpentine path that was wide enough for the two of them to walk side by side. The ground was well packed and mostly dry, with only a few places where melting snow collected to form shallow puddles in dips and depressions. They had been walking for about twenty minutes and Arthur was just about to comment that his legs were feeling much less stiff and sore when they came to a standing stone in the middle of the path. It stood about eight feet tall and was about two feet in diameter. Intricate runes had been carved into it on all sides.

"I take it we've reached the Fae Lands?" Arthur asked, stopping to examine the monolith.

"That we have," Davynn confirmed. "Beyond this stone, you have no power."

"I have no power on this side of the stone," Arthur scoffed.

They stepped around the stone and continued along the path. Arthur noticed that Davynn's gait had changed. He had positioned himself a few steps in front of Arthur and appeared to be taking each step with deliberate care.

"What are you doing?" Arthur asked.

"Looking for tripwires and pits." Davynn was not only walking cautiously, he was constantly scanning the trees for threats from overhead.

"Great!" Arthur said, staying close to the knight and wondering once again why Harpur had wanted him to do this alone.

Creeping along at a snail's pace, Arthur and Davynn made their way up the trail deeper into the Fae Lands. Every sound in the forest made Arthur jump. "Is that the Fae?" he would ask.

"Possibly," Davynn would answer.

After a dozen possible first-contact opportunities had not resulted in a first contact with the Fae, Arthur stopped walking. "This is ridiculous!" he said.

Davynn stopped as well. "It's not as ridiculous as..." Behind him, Arthur screamed and the knight turned around to see his king hanging by one ankle from a tree. "...that!" Davynn finished as he watched Arthur spinning slowly around at the end of a thick rope.

"Get me down!" Arthur yelled.

Davynn ignored the panicking monarch. "We mean no harm," he called out to the forest in general. "I am Sir Davynn Willhart of Colwygshire and my companion is King Arthur. We are here on an errand for Harpur Diggins."

"Davynn, for the love of Orhowyn, get me down from here!"

"Be quiet!" Davynn snapped. "Once the Fae are certain you aren't a threat, they will cut you down."

Arthur was speechless. "The blood is rushing to my head!"

"You'll be fine for a few minutes. Just stop thrashing about." Davynn looked around, peering into the bush. "Hello! Is anybody here?" he called out.

"We are," a voice said from behind a bush on the other side of where Arthur dangled from the tree.

Davynn turned in the direction the voice had come from and was surprised to see a man and a woman step out of the forest and onto the trail. "Who are you?" he asked.

"Who is who?" Arthur asked. He was facing away from the voice and had to wait until the rope spun him around again. When it finally did, he gasped. "Ralph and Holly! What are you doing here?"

"You know these people?" Davynn asked.

"We prefer Jack and Diane now," Jack said.

Arthur spun around to face Davynn. "They are my guardians." He spun away again.

"Huh!" Davynn didn't know what to make of the strangely dressed couple. He'd heard about Arthur's guardians, but he had imagined them... differently. In all the stories he'd heard about them, they were described as nearly naked. The couple standing before him now were fully dressed. As pirates.

"I don't suppose you could get me down from here?" Arthur asked as he spun back toward Jack and Diane.

"We could," Diane said.

"But we think it's best if you wait for the Fae," Jack said.

Arthur brought a hand to his face and covered his eyes. *Here we go again!*

When he took his hand away again, a movement in the tree above him caught his eye. He looked up to see a strange creature with a body carved out of a log and a face made out of leaves kneeling on the branch holding what looked like a very sharp knife. The creature smiled menacingly down at him and then began sawing through the rope.

"Davynn!" Arthur shouted "A little help, please!"

Davynn looked at Arthur, and then followed the terrified king's gaze upward. He leapt forward just as the knife severed the rope and caught Arthur before he landed on his head. He laid Arthur down on the ground and reached to untie the knot holding the rope around Arthur's ankle. "Don't get up too quickly," he warned the king.

"Why not?" Arthur asked, sitting up, then swooning back down as the blood rushed back out of his head.

"That's why not!" Davynn pulled the rope free and shook his head at the dizzy king groaning on the ground. When he looked up at the tree branch again, the creature that had freed Arthur was gone.

Jack and Diane, formerly known as Ralph and Holly, stood by watching passively as Davynn helped Arthur get up slowly.

"I think your friends are spooking the Fae," Davynn said. "Can you get them to leave, at least until we've finished our business here?"

Arthur looked at his guardians. "I doubt it, but I can try." He smiled at Jack and Diane. "Hey, guys! Good to see you again."

"It's good to see you, too, Arthur," Diane said.

"I love your outfits, by the way." Arthur felt steady enough to let go of Davynn and walked closer to them.

"Thank you! We love them too." Ralph did a pirouette so Arthur could get the full effect.

"Right," Arthur said, scratching his head. "Do you think you guys could do me a big favour?"

"Anything at all," Diane said. "That's what we're here for."

"Great!" Arthur rubbed his hands together. "Um... Davynn and I are on an important mission here and we think that it would be best if you two waited for us by the standing stone back there until we are done." He pointed back in the direction of the boundary marker on the trail.

"Except that," Jack said.

Arthur sighed and dropped his chin to his chest.

"You asked for our help," Diane explained. "We can't leave until you release us."

Arthur looked helplessly back at Davynn, who closed his eyes and shook his head in disgust.

"Remind me again," Arthur said, "how exactly I do that."

Diane laughed. "Silly Arthur," she scolded, "when you no longer need our help we will be released."

"That's just it," Arthur said, "I have Davynn here to help me. I don't really need you."

"Not even to make sure you don't get caught in any more of the Fae's traps?" Jack asked.

Arthur had to admit that did sound helpful. "Well, that would be awesome, but..."

"Look," Davynn said impatiently, "I think the Fae are afraid of you. If they are afraid of you and they decide you are a threat, they could harm Arthur."

Arthur shot an alarmed look at the knight. "Just me?"

Davynn rolled his eyes. "And they might not give us what we came here for. And if they don't give it to us, Harpur will be very angry with Arthur."

"Just me?" Arthur repeated, even more horrified.

Davynn covered Arthur's mouth with his hand to shut him up. "All we need right now is for you two to wait by the standing stone until we have met with the Fae and Arthur gets what he came here for."

"We will not let any harm come to Arthur," Jack said, drawing the sword that hung at his waist from its scabbard.

"Put that away!" Davynn shouted. "Are you trying to get us killed?"

"Killed?" Arthur also shouted as he pushed Davynn's hand away. "You said the Fae didn't kill people."

Davynn took Arthur by the arm and led him a short distance away from Jack and Diane. "They don't know that," he whispered through clenched teeth.

"Actually, we do!" Diane said, walking up to Davynn and Arthur. "We also know that the Fae are eager to give the Amber Chalice over to Arthur and be rid of it."

"Did you tell them what we came for?" Davynn asked.

Arthur shook his head. "I think that they are part of me and so they know what I know."

Davynn pulled his hand through his hair. He turned to Diane. "How do you know that the Fae are eager to give Arthur the chalice?"

"It's what we do," Jack said, sword still in hand. "We help Arthur when he needs us."

"And we know things," Diane added.

Davynn stared at the pirates. "How do you explain what just happened here, then?"

Jack and Diane looked back at the rope that had snared Arthur and then up at the tree branch above. "It's not us," Jack said.

"It's you," Diane said.

"Me?" Davynn was incensed.

"You did say that the Fae might not be too happy to have an armed knight in their territory," Arthur contributed.

"You are not helping, sire!" Davynn snapped.

"There really is no reasoning with them, *Sir* Davynn," Arthur said, making a point of using the knight's title against him.

"This is getting us nowhere!" Davynn threw his arms up in the air. "Harpur sent me here to protect you." He pointed at Arthur. "And now I have to look out for a couple of pirates as well."

"You don't have to look out for us," Diane said.

"We don't need looking out for," Jack added.

Arthur shrugged.

Davynn groaned.

"In fact," Jack began, "why don't you follow us?"

"We will take you right to where the chalice is." Diane smiled.

Arthur shrugged again.

Davynn sighed. "Lead on," he said, sweeping his hand out in the direction they needed to go. "And for Orhowyn's sake, put that damned sword away."

Jack slid the blade back into its scabbard. Then he took Diane's hand and the two guardians started walking back toward the standing stone.

"Where are you going?" Davynn called after them.

"The chalice is this way," Diane called back over her shoulder.

Arthur shrugged for a third time and followed the guardians.

Davynn stood with his hands on his hips and counted to ten. Then he followed Arthur.

Soon, they were back at the standing stone. Davynn looked questioningly at Arthur who looked questioningly at Jack and Diane.

"It's under the stone," Jack said.

Davynn sized up the three tons of solid granite that stood before him. "And how do you propose we get it out from under the stone?"

"You dig for it," a gravelly voice behind him said.

Arthur yelped in surprise and turned around to see the creature that had cut him down from the tree standing next to him. He yelped again and jumped back bumping into the standing stone.

The elemental stood about four feet tall. Its eyes were yellow-green with horizontal pupils like a goat and its arms and legs were made from thick, twisted vines. The log from which its body was formed was partially charred by fire and the leaves that made up its face were a mixture of holly and oak. Arthur was as fascinated as he was repulsed by the thing. *No wonder Sok doesn't like the Fae.* But he kept that thought to himself.

"Thank you," Davynn said to the elemental, keeping his voice calm. "I don't suppose you have a shovel we could use?"

"I do not!" snarled the Fae. "But I'm certain your king can conjure one up for you."

"Me?" Arthur replied. "I have no idea how to conjure a shovel."

"I can smell the dragon blood in you from here," the elemental said. "With that much power you should be able to draw the chalice out without having to dig at all. But whatever you do, do it quick and be gone. The *queen* does not care much for having a human knight in our midst." The creature glared at Davynn.

Davynn leaned closer to Arthur, but kept his eyes on the Fae creature. "Try, sire," he whispered forcefully.

"You saw what happened with the pastry the other day. What do you think will happen with this rock?" Arthur couldn't believe that anyone expected him to conjure a shovel, let alone draw the chalice out with his magic.

"Nevertheless, you must try." Davynn coaxed.

"You're insane. I'll end up killing someone if I do that," Arthur cried in protest.

"Arthur," Diane stepped forward and put a hand on Arthur's arm, "there is nothing you need to fear. Your magic is a good force, a gift for you to use to help yourself and others. As you will it, so it is."

Arthur felt a calm settle over him and he knew that Diane had done something to him. He wanted to be angry with her, but instead he felt something stir in his chest, a feeling of strength and confidence he'd never felt before.

"I'm waiting," the elemental said.

Arthur looked at Davynn, who nodded encouragement at him. He wiped his hands on his pants and stepped closer to the standing stone. Though he didn't know why, he placed his hands on the stone and closed his eyes. *As I will it, so it is. As I will it, so it is. As I will it, so it is.*

For several long seconds nothing happened. But then the stone began to tremble and the earth around its base began to loosen. Davynn took three long steps backward and away from the stone and prepared to dive into the bushes if things went the way they usually did when Arthur attempted to use his magic. If Arthur pulled this off, it would be nothing short of a minor miracle. And one, Davynn knew, that would change everything in Epoh for as long as Arthur lived. Not having magic, the knight didn't fully trust it. He'd seen the good it could do. He'd also seen the evil. Edlyngton Bloomregaard had been a good example of that evil. A vain and pitiful man, he had been one of the few humans that had disavowed Harpur's sovereignty over Epoh. Why Harpur had allowed the odious little man to keep three wraiths and use them to terrorize the people of Colwygshire, was something the knight never understood. He believed that it had something to do with the fact that Harpur was totally focused on Arthur for a long time. When Bloomregaard had murdered King Gnik, Harpur did step in. But was it because he wanted to protect Colwygshire? Or was it because the entire incident had helped to open the door to get Arthur from Earth to Thraeh and take his place as king? Davynn never had the nerve to question Harpur about it, but just then, as he watched Arthur straining to control his magic and draw the Amber Chalice from beneath the standing stone, he promised himself that he would sit the dragon down and get some answers.

The ground at the base of the stone looked as if it was boiling and Davynn was tempted to call Arthur off. If it wasn't for Jack and Diane's cool resolve as they calmly watched Arthur's excruciatingly slow progress, the knight would have intervened. But he waited. And he watched. And suddenly, a small hole opened up at Arthur's feet and a rusty old cup popped out of the ground and rolled toward Davynn.

Arthur removed his hands from the stone and wiped a sheen of sweat from his brow. "I did it!" he said with a huge grin. "Did you see that, Davynn? I did it!"

"You sure did," Davynn agreed. He came out of the bushes and bent down to pick up the chalice.

"No!" shouted the elemental, who had moved farther up the trail to get away from the poisonous iron in the cup. "Only the one with the dragon blood can touch it."

Davynn snatched his hand away just in time. He stood up and looked at the Fae creature, who was looking at the cup from a safe distance with unabashed fear in its eyes. "Arthur, I think he means you." Davynn stepped away from the chalice and allowed Arthur to retrieve it himself.

In awe of what he'd just done, Arthur picked up the chalice with a shaking hand. It really was an ugly old thing. He turned it to see the amber stone that was embedded in the side. "Look at this, Davynn," he said holding the cup up for the knight to see.

Davynn glanced over at the Fae creature who was still standing on the path. It looked ready to run away any second. Now that the Amber Chalice was free from the stone, the Fae being had lost all of its bravado. "What is it?" He stepped closer to Arthur and looked at the amber stone. "Wow!"

The amber was a perfect oval about two inches long and an inch wide. Unlike the rusted iron cup it was embedded into, the amber possessed a clear, polished sheen. Its smooth surface shone like glass, reflecting the afternoon sun. But what caused Davynn's amazement were the streaks of green and purple and orange that swirled in a vortex in the center of the stone and the flashes of blue and white light that sparked like lightning around the edge of it.

"That must be Willow's essence," Arthur said in even greater awe.

"Be careful with it," the Fae creature said.

Arthur tore his gaze away from the amber. "How has Willow's magic survived all this time in the iron?" He directed his question at the elemental.

"The amber protects it."

"Okay, well, thank you..." Arthur paused. "I'm afraid I don't know your name."

"My name is of little consequence," the elemental replied. "Now, take that wretched thing away from here."

Arthur wasn't at all sure if the Fae creature was referring to the chalice or to Davynn. "We're leaving right away."

Together, he and Davynn stepped past the standing stone, still and in solid ground once again.

"Oh, and dragon-man," the elemental called out. Arthur and Davynn stopped and turned back to face it. "Tell Harpur Diggins that the queen awaits her gold."

Arthur frowned. He was about to ask the creature what it meant, but it disappeared into the trees and was gone. So, he asked Davynn instead. "What gold?"

"You will have to ask Harpur when we see him," the knight said.

The foursome walked back to the horses and Arthur carefully wrapped the chalice in a spare shirt from his saddle bag. "I hope Finch knows how to get rust stains out of cloth," he said, tucking the bundle back into the saddle bag.

"Who cares?" Davynn said as he mounted his horse. Then he looked at Jack and Diane. "I assume you are coming with us. Which one of you wants to ride with me?"

"We do not need to ride," Diane said. Then she and Jack transformed into dazzling balls of blue-white light and hovered a few feet above the ground.

Arthur, wincing as he swung himself up onto his own horse, smiled at the knight. "They can be annoying, but they are low maintenance."

Davynn kicked his horse into a trot, signaling Arthur that there was to be no conversation for the first leg of their journey to Harpur's lair.

Chapter Eight

Sok had led the others away from Harpur's lair down the path from the meadow and back into Braydon Wood. Unphased by the darkness, he walked on with purpose until they came to a fork in the trail. Instead of taking the path to the left that led back to Colwygshire, he turned to the right and headed south.

"Where are you taking us?" Anayah said. She had assumed that Sok would want her to zap them all back to the castle.

"There is a ravine not far from here," Sok said. "It has a clear view of the lair. We are going to camp there and keep watch on Harpur. Hiro, do you still have those spy glasses you showed me a few moons back?"

The Krist giggled. "I do! They are in my satchel."

They walked through the dark forest for an hour until they came to a small canyon that ran roughly perpendicular to the meadow in front of Harpur's lair. Sok guided them along the edge of the canyon and then down into it along a narrow ledge that was cut into the steep rock walls. When they reached the bottom, Sok stopped and threw his hands out to his sides.

"Welcome to your home for the next six days!" he said with a flourish. "Anayah, do you have the list?"

"No," said the witch. "I thought you had it."

In the darkness, Anayah, Hiro and Bon heard Sok blow a frustrated puff of air through his lips. "I specifically told you to bring it with you."

"And I specifically told you to bring it yourself." Anayah snapped her fingers and a bright ball of light appeared in her hand, illuminating their surroundings. The look on her face made it clear that she wasn't about to zap the list to the elf.

Sok and Hiro blinked multiple times as their eyes adjusted to the sudden brightness.

"All that work for nothing," Sok complained to Hiro and Bon. "I spent hours putting that list together and *she* doesn't even bother to bring it!"

Anayah walked a short distance away, took a deep breath to steady her nerves and waved her hand. Two tents appeared. "You three can sleep in that one," she pointed to one of the tents. "This one is mine." She lifted the flap on the tent she had claimed for herself and disappeared inside. With the ball of light. Her confidence in her magic was growing.

"Well, that hardly seems fair," Sok said. "She gets a tent to herself and we have to share one."

"I do not require sleep," Bon said. "I will keep watch."

"And I will sleep on my hover gilly under the stars," Hiro said. "You are welcome to have the tent to yourself."

Sok sighed. "I'd rather have a hammock in the trees." The tent meant for the men disappeared and in its place a rope hammock appeared on the ground. "Thank you," Sok called out, but Anayah did not answer.

"Anyone want a bedtime snack before we turn in?" Hiro asked with his signature giggle.

"I do," Sok said.

While Hiro prepared the snack, Bon left the ravine to gather wood for a fire and Sok picked up the hammock and went to the top of the ridge to look for a place to hang it. At the north end of the canyon, a narrow clearing opened up, which, in the light of day, would give them a clear view of the meadow and the entrance to Harpur's lair. Sok chose two trees next to the ridge where the canyon and the clearing met and fastened the hammock to the trunks so it hung between them. When he was done, he looked to the north. The mountain into which the lair was burrowed was a black silhouette against the blue-black night sky. No light came from the lair and Sok wondered how Harpur was managing without any magic. *What is he doing for food? Did he bring blankets with him?*

"We're only a finger snap away if you need us," he said out loud before returning to the ravine.

Bon was laying the fire when Sok approached. Within minutes, crackling flames threw dancing shadows on the canyon walls. Sok, having no other option, sat cross-legged on the ground next to Hiro's hover gilly and accepted a large mug of ale from the Krist.

"I thought I'd keep it simple," Hiro said, handing Sok a large bowl of warm peach cobbler smothered in clotted cream and sprinkled with cinnamon and sugar.

Sok put his ale down beside him and spooned the decadent dessert into his mouth. "Oh, Hiro!" he said. "This is delicious!"

"I got the recipe from Bon," the Krist said, sounding quite proud of himself. "Apparently, it is an old Earth favourite."

"How is it you know about Earth recipes?" Sok asked the android.

"Anayah and I discussed Earth customs many times when we were together in the Sphere," the android answered.

"Have you ever been to Earth?" Sok prodded.

In the past, Bon had been reluctant to discuss his past or his origins. He perpetuated this habit now. "I have been to many worlds," he said.

Sok let it go. He was much more interested in eating the cobbler than he was in knowing how Bon knew the recipe for it.

The light went out in Anayah's tent. Sok and Hiro took that as a sign that they, too, should retire for the night. They finished their snack and Sok bid his companions a good night. Before he left, he asked Hiro for a blanket, which the Krist produced from his satchel. As he climbed out of the ravine, a thought struck him. *Does today count as day one of the six days? Or is tomorrow day one?* But that was a debate for another time. He made his way to his hammock and settled in under the warm woolen cover where he was gently rocked to sleep by a cool spring breeze.

Harpur woke early the next day, refreshed and energized for having slept on his bed of gold. He slid down the from the pile in an avalanche of coins and jewels and all but laughed out loud at the joy he felt being back in his lair. It was as much the solitude as it was the gold that had lifted his spirits. As much as he cared about his little band of misfits, not having to listen to their constant chatter and solve their endless problems was a salve for his soul. He stretched the kinks out of his shoulders. This not so pleasant aspect of his human existence was something he'd grown to accept, but he did enjoy the release as his muscles loosened and his bones thunked into place.

Dawn was just beginning to break when he exited the lair and made his way out into the meadow. The pale light was not yet strong enough to bring out the full colour of the valley below, but it was just strong enough to draw his attention to a rising plume of smoke from a campfire in the ravine a mile or so to the south. His keen vision picked up movement at the edge of the ridge above the ravine. He'd know that long silvery hair anywhere. "So, that's where you went," Harpur said as he watched Sok make his way from the hammock along the ridge back to the ledge leading down into the ravine. In an odd way, Harpur took comfort knowing that Sok, Anayah, Hiro and Bon were close. "At least you're giving me some space," he said. "Just stay out of the way for the next six days."

To his left, he heard a rustle coming from the bush near the path from the valley and he turned to see Elder Dhonna emerge onto the meadow. The guild master's bright red hair was disheveled and her face and purple kaftan were smudged with ash. She stumbled forward and Harpur rushed toward her to catch her before she fell. As usual, she was barefoot.

"Elder Dhonna! What happened to you?" Harpur was surprised to see her there that early, but her ash-smudged appearance was what alarmed him.

It took a moment for the typically elegant elf to catch her breath and steady herself. "I used the dragonfoil ash to zap myself here. It's a wee bit more powerful than I anticipated." She leaned on Harpur as he guided her toward the lair and seated her on a boulder just outside the entrance.

Elven magic was not like dragon or witch magic. Elves did not have the natural ability to zap themselves from place to place. Some elves, particularly those with Elder Dhonna's skill level and power, could enhance their magic with dragonfoil ash. Though it was not strictly forbidden, such practices were deeply frowned upon by the Council of Elders. For Elder Dhonna to breech the protocols of magic like this was somewhat unexpected.

"Why would you do such a thing?" Harpur asked as he wiped a smudge of ash from the slightly dazed elf's face.

"I had intended to walk," Elder Dhonna said a little hoarsely. "But there was a problem with some of the herbs in the garden and I had to assist in

132

getting that sorted out. If I was to get here in time, I had to take drastic measures."

Harpur was touched. "Using dragonfoil ash wasn't just drastic, Elder Dhonna," Harpur said with concern. "It was dangerous. You could have burned to death."

Elder Dhonna waved away Harpur's distress. "I was careful," she assured him. "I just didn't expect it to pack such a punch!"

Harpur had to stifle a smile. "Well, let's get you inside so you can clean up a bit. Did you bring everything we need?"

Elder Dhonna patted the satchel that hung from her shoulder. A tiny puff of smoke burst out from under the flap with the impact. "I hope so," she said and gingerly lifted the flap so she could look inside.

They both breathed a sigh of relief when they saw that the contents of the satchel were unharmed.

"Do you really need all those potions and powders?" Harpur asked when he saw the incalculable array of bottles and pouches the guild master had packed in the bag.

Elder Dhonna flipped the flap back into place. "I'm a healer. I come prepared for any eventuality."

Elder Dhonna went into the lair to freshen up and then joined Harpur outside again on the boulder next to the entrance. "I see you have company," she said, indicating the smoke from the campfire in the ravine.

"They mean well." Harpur sighed. "I just hope they stay where they are until..."

"There isn't much they can do to interfere at this point is there?" Elder Dhonna asked.

"Have you not met Sok and Anayah?" Harpur countered.

"Our young Sok is a tenacious little devil," Elder Dhonna conceded. "And from what I saw of the witch, she seems to be..."

"Stubborn? Pigheaded? Obstinate?" Harpur suggested with a good-natured grunt of laughter.

Elder Dhonna patted the dragon-wizard's leg. "As you said, they mean well. Now, why don't you and I go for a walk? I think there is a patch of rueflower not too far from here and I would like to gather some while I'm in the area." She stood up and waited for Harpur.

"Rueflower, hey?" Harpur said, offering the guild master his arm. "Are you expecting a wart epidemic?"

"Aren't you a clever dragon?" Elder Dhonna teased.

"One doesn't spend time with the best healer in the land and not pick up a thing or two," Harpur said, smiling sideways at her.

"If I didn't know better, I'd think you were flirting with me," Elder Dhonna said with a laugh.

Harpur didn't reply. *If I were ever to flirt with anyone, it would be you,* he thought to himself.

They crossed the meadow to the west and Harpur scanned the distant clearing by the ravine. He could see Sok and Anayah standing near the trees. They were holding what looked like metal tubes up to their eyes and he realized that Hiro had provided them with spy glasses. He was tempted to wave, just to let them know that they weren't getting away with anything, but he resisted.

"We are being watched," Harpur told Elder Dhonna.

"Oh?" she said with worry in her voice. "Is it time?"

"No," Harpur assured her. "It's just our friends in the ravine keeping tabs."

Elder Dhonna leaned forward and looked around Harpur toward the canyon. She had excellent vision, as all elves do, but from that distance she was unable to make out any people. "I'll take your word for it," she said, thinking that if she couldn't see Sok and Anayah, they were unlikely to be able to see her and Harpur.

They followed a narrow path leading out of the meadow and down the slope of the mountain into the valley in search of the rueflower patch that Elder Dhonna was looking for. They found it about a half mile to the west of the lair and Elder Dhonna recited a blessing of gratitude before they began harvesting the delicate orange flowers and long, thin leaves from a few of the plants. When they were done and the medicinal foliage was safely stowed in Elder Dhonna's satchel, they continued meandering through Braydon Wood for the better part of the morning. The path they took circled back near the clearing where Anayah and Sok were taking turns scanning the meadow through their spy glasses waiting for the dragon-wizard and the elf to return. Harpur steered them away from the clearing to avoid being seen and they made their way eastward to the trail that led to the meadow from that direction.

"There they are!" Anayah exclaimed.

"Where?" Sok asked. He lifted the spy glass to his eye and directed it westward, expecting Harpur and Elder Dhonna to be returning from the same direction they had gone in originally.

"The other side," Anayah said, pointing to the eastern path. "How did they get over there?"

Sok swung his own spy glass to the right. Sure enough, Harpur and Elder Dhonna were crossing the meadow toward the lair from the eastern side. "They probably came back around on a trail leading right past us."

"I wonder why Elder Dhonna is there," Anayah thought out loud.

"Clearly the six-day rule does not apply to her," Sok complained.

"I told you Harpur had something going on with someone," Anayah said, elbowing the elf in the ribs.

"Don't be daft!" Sok scolded. "Elder Dhonna is a revered Guild Master. She would never consort with a dragon in that way."

"I don't know," Anayah insisted. "They look pretty friendly to me."

Sok snorted. "It would never happen."

"Why else would they be up there alone together?"

Before Sok could answer, Hiro and Bon arrived with brunch.

"Any action?" Hiro asked as he spread out a blanket on the ground and began pulling steaming quiches out of his satchel.

"Elder Dhonna is with him," Sok said, lowering his spy glass and following the appetizing aroma of the egg pies to the blanket.

"Really?" Hiro said with a giggle. "Doesn't the six-day rule apply to her?"

"I think she and Harpur are romantically involved," Anayah said.

"That makes sense," Hiro said with a nod. He joined Sok on the blanket and helped himself to a large helping of cheesy, meaty quiche.

"It does not make sense," Sok insisted. "I'm telling you, Elder Dhonna would never—ever—do that! She's there for another reason. And it has something to do with the Amber Chalice."

Anayah had to admit that the mysterious cup Arthur had been sent to get did not factor smoothly into her theory. Unless it was just a diversion.

But then why wouldn't Harpur have sent all of us to get it? "You're right, Sok," she conceded. "Something else is going on."

"I know I'm right," Sok said, then washed a mouthful of quiche down with a large drink of jamba. "It's absurd even to think such a thing. Are you going to eat?"

Anayah lowered her spy glass and turned to look at the late-morning feast that Hiro had brought. "I don't know where you two put all that food. I'm still stuffed from breakfast. But I wouldn't mind a cup of tea."

Hiro reached into his satchel and pulled out a carafe of tea and a fine porcelain cup. "It's mint. I hope that's alright." He handed the hot beverage to Anayah.

"It's perfect," she said. "Thank you."

The remainder of the day consisted of Sok, Anayah, Hiro and Bon taking turns spying on Harpur and Elder Dhonna, who spent most of their time sitting on the boulder next to the entrance to the lair chatting and laughing. By the time Hiro served supper, Anayah was quite bored.

"Is this really all we're going to do for the next five days?" She speared a thick slice of roast pork onto her plate and drenched it in gravy.

"Technically," Sok said, "we only have to do this for three more days." He'd decided that the previous day was day one.

"Harpur said we couldn't go back for six days." Anayah was confused. "You've only accounted for four."

Sok put his plate down on the blanket and held up a thumb. "Yesterday was day one." He held up an index finger. "Today is day two." Middle finger. "Tomorrow is day three." Ring finger. "The day after that is day four." Pinky finger. "The day after that is day five." Other thumb. "And the day after that we go back to the lair." He held up his hands to show the six raised fingers. "That's six days total."

"I don't think that's what Harpur meant," Anayah argued. "I think that today is day one."

And the debate was on.

A lengthy and heated discussion about when they could safely return to the lair ensued. Bon and Anayah took the position that the current day was day one, while Sok and Hiro agreed that this was day two. Both sides remained immovable and, in the end, Anayah had stormed off to her tent, leaving the other three to come to the very quick conclusion that they should wait and see if anything significant happened before making a final decision.

By then the sun was setting. The elf, the Krist and the android also concluded that nothing significant was likely to happen after dark, so they packed up the remnants of their latest repast and returned to the ravine to sit by the campfire where Hiro introduced Sok to the fine art of marshmallow roasting. This latest delicacy from Earth was another of Hiro's growing repertoire of culinary delights and Sok nearly made himself sick on them.

"Tomorrow, I shall give Hiro the ingredients for S'mores," Bon announced when they finally agreed it was time to retire.

"Sounds amazing," Sok mumbled sarcastically as he left to take his protesting stomach to his hammock. He couldn't remember the last time the thought of food had been so unappealing.

Much farther to the south, Arthur and Davynn were making their way through Braydon Wood, followed closely by two glowing orbs of bright light. Davynn had found the guardians to be somewhat disturbing in their human forms, and was no less disturbed by the bobbing, weaving balls of energy that dogged them through the forest. Arthur didn't seem to have any control over Jack and Diane and he couldn't help but wonder what sort of help Arthur could possibly need from them.

"I'm bored," Arthur announced in the late afternoon on the day following their experience with the Fae creature.

They had taken the Colwygshire Road back to the bridge and had made camp there for the night. Early that morning, Davynn had taken them into the forest following a trail that led into Braydon Wood just a short distance north of the bridge. While the forest was beautiful in the spring, even Davynn found the closeness of the trees had quickly grown tedious. He could totally relate to Arthur's sense of ennui.

For Arthur, it wasn't the trees that were creating the monotony; it was the constant, rhythmic motion of the horse underneath him. His body was protesting considerably less to being stuck in a saddle for hours on end, but now he was finding himself hard pressed to stay awake as he swayed back and forth in time to the horse's steady footsteps.

"Not much I can do about that," Davynn said. "We can take a short break if you like. Stretch our legs a bit. But I would like to ride until dusk if we can. The longer we ride each day, the sooner we'll get to the lair."

Arthur didn't need to be asked twice. He reined in his horse and dismounted. "How long until dusk?" he asked as Davynn followed suit and hopped down off his own horse.

"A couple of hours."

Arthur groaned. Two more hours of this was going to be hard. Five more days of it was going to be impossibly difficult. "My kingdom for a hover gilly!" he said, patting his horse's rump, and then pulling his water skin from the saddle bag. As he did every time they stopped, he checked to see that the Amber Chalice was okay. It was. Arthur took a long drink of water and poured some over his head to wake himself up.

The moment Arthur's feet touched the ground, Jack and Diane became human again and stood next to the path near Arthur's horse.

"We could sing you a song of our people," Jack offered as a means to relieve Arthur and Davynn's boredom.

Arthur and Davynn looked at each other. When Davynn shrugged to let Arthur know it was his choice, Arthur scratched his head to buy himself a bit of time to come up with a diplomatic refusal. "Maybe we could save the entertainment for another time." Arthur recalled when he first met Jack and Diane and they had told him their real names. His ears had rung for hours afterward.

"I think you will like this song, Arthur," Diane said with a smile.

"Go on, Arthur," Davynn said, taking a seat on a fallen log. "Let them sing us a song."

Arthur shook his head furiously at the knight. "I really don't think this is a good idea."

"We will just sing the first verse," Jack compromised.

"And if you don't like it, we will stop." Diane finished the bargain.

Arthur sighed. "Very well. But let me get something to eat first." He took some of the jerked meat out of his saddle bag and sat down next to Davynn on the log. "Plug your ears."

The knight's face adopted a worried expression and Arthur braced himself for the worst with a twisted wince while Jack and Diane moved to the center of the path facing them. The guardians smiled at their audience and then Diane began to sing.

Instead of the screeching that Arthur had expected, Diane's voice was pure and crisp, soft yet powerful. Arthur could only describe it as angelic. He couldn't understand the words for she sang in a language he'd never heard before, but the melody was like that of a spirited lullaby, both uplifting and soothing at the same time. When Jack added his perfectly pitched tenor, the knight and the king were completely mesmerized and failed to notice the group of elves that had heard the song and had gathered behind them to listen. It wasn't until the song ended and the elves joined their applause with Arthur and Davynn's that they realized they weren't alone.

The knight leapt to his feet and spun around, drawing his sword in a single reflexive motion and stood ready to defend Arthur to the death if need be. When he saw the six elves, whose clapping had ended abruptly, staring back at him in confusion, he relaxed his stance.

"My apologies," Davynn said to them. "I didn't hear you approach." But his sword remained unsheathed.

"It is us who should apologize," said one of the elves. "I am Stellah. I and my companions were working not far from here when we heard the singing and stopped to come and listen. We did not mean to frighten you."

Davynn, deciding that the elves were no threat, slid his sword back into its scabbard. "I cannot blame you for being drawn to the music," he said. "Jack and Diane are truly gifted minstrels."

Stellah turned his attention to Arthur. "Ah, King Arthur! What brings you into the Wood on this fine spring day?"

"We are on our way to Harpur's lair," Arthur said truthfully.

Stellah frowned slightly. "You are taking a roundabout route, aren't you? Or has Harpur moved his lair to the south?" They were quite a distance south of Colwygshire and the elf was confused as to why they would come this way and not travel directly to the lair from the city.

"Actually," Arthur began, "we have just come from the Fae Lands..." Two of the elves spat on the ground in contempt. "...and we are now heading north again."

"What business could you possibly have in the Fae Lands?" Stellah asked scornfully.

Davynn opened his mouth to intervene, but before he could say anything, Arthur took a menacing step forward. "What business is it of yours what business I have with the Fae?"

Davynn cleared his throat and stepped forward, rather less menacingly, and placed a hand on Arthur's arm. "We are simply taking advantage of the delightful spring weather to tour the kingdom. King Arthur had never been to the Fae Lands before and he just wanted to see it for himself. But I think we are forgetting what brought us together on this fine evening." Davynn turned and waved an arm in the direction of Jack and Diane. "Let's not allow our disdain for the Fae to ruin the moment. Another song, perhaps?"

Stellah's eyes shifted from the knight to the guardians and then back to Arthur. "Again, I must apologize, your majesty. It's difficult to hear the name of those vile creatures spoken without my temper rising. Another song would be a lovely way to end our day in the Wood."

All eyes turned to Jack and Diane.

"We are losing daylight," Jack said.

"It is time for Arthur and Davynn to continue on their journey," Diane said.

"Of course," Stellah replied. "We will not keep you any longer. Thank you for the song. I hope we might hear more of your talents someday."

To show that there were no hard feelings, Arthur and Davynn shook hands with all of the elves and mounted their horses. The six elves looked on in utter astonishment as Jack and Diane transformed into brilliant balls of light and followed them down the path.

"What was that?" one of the other elves asked.

"I have no idea," Stellah answered, "but I would bet my treehouse that the human king did not visit the Fae Lands out of mere curiosity."

Two of the elves spat on the ground again.

Chapter Nine

The next day started out much the same as the previous day had. Arthur and Davynn awoke early, climbed on their horses and rode through the forest. Harpur and Elder Dhonna awoke early and sat on the boulder outside the lair and reminisced. Sok, Anayah, Hiro and Bon awoke early, ate copious amounts of food and took turns staring through the spy glasses at Harpur and Elder Dhonna. And whether they counted it as the second or the third day, it would, in time, be remembered as the first of several unforgettable days.

Just as the sun reached its zenith, Arthur and Davynn reached a small clearing and decided it was a good place to stop for lunch. The horses were left to graze freely while their riders settled on the ground and tried to drum up some interest in the jerked meat, hard cheese and flat bread. After five days of eating nothing else, they had reached the point where strong hunger pangs were required before they stopped to eat.

Arthur bit into a piece of flat bread and chewed it unenthusiastically. "What do you think about the idea of me zapping us to the lair?"

Davynn ripped a piece of jerky off the strip he was holding and worked it thoroughly with his teeth before answering. "In principle, I think it's a wonderful idea. But I'm not sure that I am willing to allow you to test your ability to do it successfully on me. Besides, horses do not take well to being relocated by magic and I'm not going to abandon them."

Arthur wasn't surprised. He wasn't sure he was willing to test his zapping abilities on himself either. He turned to Jack and Diane, standing in human form again, at the edge of the clearing. "Do you two think I can do it?"

"We know you can," Jack said.

"But we think it would be best if you followed Harpur's instructions and arrived when he asked you to." Diane smiled at him from across the clearing.

"Why is it so important that I arrive in four days?"

"That is when Harpur will be ready for you." Jack said.

"So, what you're saying is," Arthur theorized, "that if I get there sooner with the chalice that something could go wrong?"

"What we are saying is the chalice will not change the outcome by arriving sooner," Diane said.

"I see," Arthur, now distracted from his boredom by a mystery of sorts, took a bite of jerky and washed it down with water from his waterskin. "You know what's going to happen, don't you?"

"We know that Harpur trusts you to fulfill your destiny," Jack said.

Davynn listened to this exchange between Arthur and his guardians with great interest, if also great confusion. He remained silent, hoping that something the guardians said would make sense.

"I thought I already did that by walking into the dragonfoil fire and becoming the king of Epoh," Arthur said.

"Before that, you had to become Entangled with Sok. You had to become king so that you can do what needs to be done now. Your destiny is not confined to a single event," Diane said.

"Is there any chance at all that Harpur can defeat his challenger?" Arthur asked, dreading the answer.

"He can only defeat his challenger if he is defeated first," Jack said.

"What does that mean?" Arthur asked.

But before Jack or Diane could provide another enigmatic answer, Davynn jumped to his feet. "Look!" he shouted, pointing at the sky.

Arthur did as he was told and looked up. In a flash, he too was on his feet. A large, teal dragon flew over them heading north west. Right toward Harpur's lair.

Arthur started jumping around, waving his hands and snapping his fingers. Davynn stared at the bundle of insanity that was leaping around the clearing.

"Arthur, what are you doing?" the knight, also under the influence of an adrenaline rush, asked.

"I'm trying to zap us to the lair!" Arthur shouted. "We have to warn Harpur! We have to save him!"

Davynn turned to the guardians who were standing calmly on the sidelines. "I think this is the part where you help him." It was half order, half plea.

"We are helping him," Jack said.

"We are preventing him from zapping you both to the lair," Diane said.

Davynn didn't know how to interpret that, but it seemed obvious that neither Jack nor Diane was going to prevent Arthur from spooking the horses. The last thing they needed was for their mounts to run off, so he dealt with them first. Once he had caught their reins and tethered them to a tree away from Arthur, he attempted to get the wild mage to settle down.

"Arthur!" Davynn yelled. "Arthur, stop!" But Arthur's frenzied antics only grew more frenzied. "Orhowyn's blazing backside! Arthur, stop!" the knight shouted again.

When Arthur failed to stop, Davynn did the only thing he could think of. He rushed toward his king and tackled him to the ground.

"Oof!" Arthur's lungs emptied of air as Davynn smashed into him and he landed on his back on the ground with the knight on top of him. "I can't breathe," he wheezed.

Davynn rolled off of Arthur and came up onto on knee. He was ready to take Arthur down again if he had to. "I'm sorry, sire," he said quietly, "but you were out of control."

It was times like this when Davynn realized how difficult it was to be friends with Arthur. Tackling Arthur was one thing; tackling the king was quite another. And Davynn wished he knew how to separate the two. Next to him, Arthur rolled onto his side and then slowly pushed himself up to a sitting position and stared forlornly down at the ground.

"There's nothing we can do to save him, is there?" Arthur asked quietly.

"No, there is not," Davynn answered honestly. "But he has tasked us with bringing the chalice to the lair, so we must do that."

"What's the point?" Arthur dropped his head into his hands and tried to keep from sobbing.

"I don't know. But I do know that Harpur would not ask you to get it without a good reason." The knight placed a comforting hand on Arthur's shoulder.

"A few days ago, you thought this was nothing but a wild dragon chase," Arthur sniveled. "Now you want us to finish this."

"A few days ago, there wasn't a big, blue-green dragon making its way to Harpur's lair."

A short while after Davynn had tackled a panic-stricken Arthur to the ground, Sok watched Harpur suddenly stop talking to Elder Dhonna and stand up. The dragon-wizard pointed to the south-east and as Elder Dhonna looked in the direction he was pointing, her eyes widened. *In fear?*

Sok swung the spy glass in the same direction and scanned the sky, but whatever they were looking at was hidden by the trees behind him. He lowered the spy glass and walked out into the middle of the clearing to see if could get a better view. Raising the spy glass to his eye again, he moved it slowly back and forth just above the treetops. With each fruitless pass, he lifted the spy glass slightly and repeated the back-and-forth motion scanning from the east to the south. The only things he saw were a few birds soaring high above the forest.

He focused on Harpur and Elder Dhonna again to check if they were still looking at whatever had caught Harpur's attention. Harpur had moved out into the middle of the meadow and was still looking south-eastward at the sky. Elder Dhonna had remained by the entrance to the lair and was holding one hand flat above her eyes. She, too, was looking to the south-east.

"What are you two seeing up there?" Sok asked aloud as he turned the spy glass back to the area that Harpur and Elder Dhonna were looking toward. All he could see were birds and he couldn't imagine why Harpur would be remotely interested in a bird.

"What are you doing way out here?" Anayah asked, coming across the clearing toward Sok.

"Harpur saw something in the sky and I'm trying to see what he's looking at." Sok continued scanning with the spy glass.

Anayah, lifted her own spy glass to her eye and pointed it south-eastward. "Oh, no!" she exclaimed.

"What? What is it? What do you see?" Sok matched the angle of his spy glass to that of Anayah's.

"It's a raven! Whatever shall we do?" she mocked.

"A what?" Sok lowered his spy glass.

"All I see is a raven," she said.

"What's a raven?" Sok asked, realizing that she was taunting him.

"Those big, black birds that are all over the forest. Don't you call them ravens?" She kept scanning the sky.

"You mean worcs," Sok corrected her.

"Whatever," Anayah said. Then she gasped.

"Stop mocking me," Sok said. He wasn't going to fall for it again.

"No, look!" Anayah pointed farther to the east. "It's a dragon!"

Sok repositioned his spy glass to match Anayah's again. A few seconds later, he gasped too.

"Harpur *is* being challenged!" they both said at the same time. They lowered their spy glasses. "We've got to tell the others!" Then they ran back to the ravine.

Harpur had been aware of the dragon even before Davynn had seen it. But he said nothing to Elder Dhonna until it was close enough for her to make it out for herself. He was more interested in watching Sok watching him and wondered what the elf would do. When he saw Sok move out into the middle of the clearing, he knew it was only a matter of time before the elf figured out what was going on. And when he saw Sok and Anayah run back to the ravine, he knew that time had come.

Remember your history lessons, elf, Harpur thought, *and keep the others in check for a few more days.*

"What should we do?" Elder Dhonna asked. She was not as mentally prepared for this as she thought she would be.

"Stay calm," Harpur said. "She won't hurt you."

"She?" Elder Dhonna cried. "Your challenger is female? Won't that make things...?"

"Weird?" Harpur finished the thought for the elf. "Yeah, well, unfortunately, dragons don't get to choose their challengers."

"But Harpur, if this works, you'll..." Elder Dhonna was desperately trying to figure out how Harpur's plan was going to work.

"I know, Bella Dhonna," Harpur interrupted. He used his pet name for her, hoping it would calm her. He could only imagine what was running through her mind at that point. "It will all be okay."

"Are you sure you still want to do this?" Elder Dhonna couldn't keep the shock and disbelief from her voice.

"I don't think I have any other choice."

As the blue-green dragon approached the meadow, Harpur positioned himself squarely in front of the entrance to his lair and stood with his feet apart and his arms crossed. He cut a striking figure with his signature top hat and his expertly tied ascot. For the first time in many months, he wished he still had his amethyst-topped walking stick. But that had been lost nearly two years before in a fight with the three wraiths and he had chosen not to replace it. Well, maybe he had one small regret.

The blue-green dragon flew over the meadow and then rose up into the air. She began circling above Harpur, watching him closely.

"What is she doing?" Elder Dhonna asked from just inside the lair. "Why doesn't she land?"

"She's waiting for me to transform," Harpur said over his shoulder. He, too, was keeping a close eye on his challenger.

"But..."

"I know," Harpur said. "This is unconventional, but she will land soon enough and issue her challenge to me regardless."

Elder Dhonna wondered if Harpur really knew what he was doing. *What is to stop her from burning Harpur to a crisp where he stands?*

The unspoken answer to Elder Dhonna's unspoken question was a simple one. That was not the way of dragons. There were protocols, traditions that dragons followed when a challenge for a kingdom was made. The challenge first had to be stated and accepted verbally. Then a time and place would be agreed upon. It was the prerogative of the dragon being challenged to choose where and when the fight would take place, and as long as it was within a reasonable amount of time, the challenger would accept it. This gave the dragon whose kingdom was at stake time to get his affairs in order, which, for the most part, Harpur had already done.

Once arrangements for the fight were made, the challenger would ask if the dragon being challenged had any final requests. The challenger was not required to comply with these requests, but it was a matter of honour to do so, again, as long as it was within reason. It also showed respect for the incumbent ruler of the kingdom whose very life was likely to be forfeited in the process.

In turn, the challenger would be asked if he—or she—had any final requests. It was equally possible that the challenger would not survive the fight and so it was customary to express any final wishes, particularly in regard to the disposal of the body. Almost all dragons asked for their bodies to be burned where they fell. While in life, dragons were impervious to fire, in death they were not and it was believed that this ritual released their spirit so it could travel to Arachovor, the spirit world of dragons.

The final step in the issuing of the challenge was for the two dragons to agree upon a witness. The witness was, without exception, another ruler of a kingdom. It was this dragon's job to attend the fight and to make sure that all aspects of the challenge had been agreed upon and were being honoured. Again, it was the dragon being challenged who got to name the witness, but the challenger was honour bound to ensure that the witness was notified. In the rare case where a witness could not attend the fight, the challenge became void and the challenger would have to wait for a year and a day before issuing the challenge again.

Harpur had no fear of this possibility playing itself out then. Months earlier, before he had lost control of his magic entirely, he had made arrangements with his chosen witness, who had assured him that it would be his honour to fulfill the role. It was not his habit to leave anything to chance if he could possibly help it, and he had been preparing for this eventuality ever since his condition had started to decline. The only variable that he had absolutely no control over was who his challenger would be. And as his challenger finally alighted in the meadow, he felt the first pangs of doubt about his plan creep into his bones.

Why did it have to be you?

Sok and Anayah ran along the ridge above the ravine until they were even with the camp. Below them Bon was giving Hiro instructions on how to make a dish he called lasagna and the Krist's mouth was watering in anticipation of their evening repast.

"Get up here, you two!" Anayah shouted down at them.

"Harpur is being challenged!" Sok added.

The witch and the elf didn't wait for the Krist and the android. They dashed back to the clearing and aimed their spy glasses toward the lair just in time to see the blue-green dragon land in the meadow.

"I thought you said Harpur would have told us if this was going to happen," Anayah said accusingly to Sok.

"It never occurred to me that he wouldn't," Sok said without apology. "Harpur would never leave us without preparing us."

"Maybe this isn't a challenge," Anayah said hopefully. "What other reason would a dragon come to Epoh for?"

"The only other thing I can think of is to ask Harpur to be a witness at some other dragon's challenge," Sok said, "but he's in no condition to do that."

"Hop on," Hiro said, gliding up beside Sok and Anayah in his hover gilly. "I can get us there in a few seconds."

Anayah, jumped onto the back of the hover gilly next to Bon. "Come on, Sok. What are you waiting for?"

"No," Sok said. "We can't go barging up there right now."

"Why not?" Anayah asked.

"Because if this is a challenge, Harpur would not be happy if we intruded on this part of it." Sok continued to watch the dragon and the dragon-wizard through the spy glass. "That's probably why Harpur hasn't told us yet. He hadn't actually been challenged."

"I don't understand," Anayah said. She lifted her spy glass to her eye, but stayed on the hover gilly.

Sok gave his companions a brief outline of how a dragon challenged worked. "Right now, if this is a challenge, they are setting the terms. Once that is done, the other dragon will leave and Harpur will probably send for us."

"But he doesn't know where we are." Anayah pointed out the flaw in Sok's logic.

But Harpur did, of course, know where they were. And Sok knew he knew where they were because he was signaling them. "Not to worry, Anayah," Sok said with a smile. "Harpur wants us to stay here until Arthur and Davynn come with the Amber Chalice."

"How do you know that?" Anayah was mystified. "Don't tell me you can read lips!"

"Read lips?" Sok had never heard of such a thing.

"Interpret what people are saying by watching their mouths as they talk," Anayah explained.

"That's a thing?" Sok asked in wonderment.

"That's a thing," Anayah confirmed.

"That's a thing I have got to learn!" Sok immediately saw the potential in such a skill.

"So, we are not going to the lair?" Hiro asked with a giggle. He had pulled a third spy glass out of his satchel and was watching the tableau unfolding on the meadow with the others.

"Not today," Sok said.

Bon, who had no need for a spy glass simply zoomed in with his android vision and stepped down from the hover gilly. "It appears the challenger is about to leave," he said.

They all watched as the blue-green dragon launched into the air and flew away to the west.

"Where is it going?" Hiro asked.

"I believe she is going to Rednow," Bon said. "Likely she's going to seek the help of a witness for the challenge as Sok described."

"She?" Sok, Anayah and Hiro said in unison.

"If I'm not mistaken, that is a female of the species," Bon said.

"Poor Harpur," Sok said.

"Why poor Harpur?" Hiro asked.

"Such a great dragon and he's going to be killed by a girl."

Anayah, too, stepped down from the hover gilly and punched Sok in the arm. "You're an idiot!" she hissed and then stomped away back to her tent.

"Ow!" Sok rubbed his arm.

Hiro and Bon both just shook their heads and then followed Anayah to the camp.

"What?" Sok asked their retreating backs. But neither of them stopped to explain it to him.

The blue-green dragon landed in the middle of the meadow and looked at Harpur, who stood his ground near the entrance to his lair.

"Will you not meet me in your true form, Xzynthyrius Dreamfinder?" she asked.

"If you have come to challenge me, challenge me as you see me. I will not transform for your satisfaction." Harpur chose not to rise to the bait and ignored the use of his original name.

"Very well," the dragon said. "Xzynthyrius Dreamfinder, I challenge you to a fight to the death for possession of the Kingdom of Epoh."

"I accept your challenge." Harpur could have asked why the blue-green was issuing the challenge, but he didn't care. And he didn't want to drag this out any longer than necessary.

The blue-green was taken aback by his terse response. She had expected more bravado from the great Xzynthyrius Dreamfinder. "Name the time and place for..."

"Right here at midday three days from now," Harpur interrupted.

The teal dragon shifted nervously on her feet and looked away from Harpur to the skull at the edge of the meadow. There had been rumors, but to see his last challenger's bones bleached and cracked like this was disconcerting. She swung her great head back around to face Harpur again. The dragon-wizard was stroking his beard with one hand while holding his other hand over his heart. She had no idea what to make of it, but sensed there was a greater meaning in it.

"Do you have any last requests?" she asked, suddenly wanting this to end as much as Harpur did.

"I do," Harpur said. He stopped stroking his beard, removed his top hat and placed it top down on the ground in front of himself. "I ask that you allow the citizens of Epoh now under my charge safe passage out of the kingdom and sufficient time to make arrangement to relocate should you choose not to permit them to stay."

The blue-green's gaze moved from Harpur to Elder Dhonna. "I understand that the elves manage the forest. What services do the other races provide?"

"The humans work the land, the dwarves mine the mountains and the Fae protect the river," Harpur said. "Do you agree to my terms?"

"I agree to your terms," the blue-green said. "But know that I have not yet decided which races, if any, will be permitted to stay if I inherit. Is there anything else?"

Harpur noticed the use of the word if and had to suppress a smile. This dragon still feared him. "There is." Harpur then had to clear his throat. This request was not easy for him. "I wish that you do not burn my body or enter the lair for eight days if I should lose."

The teal dragon was rendered speechless. She stared at the dragon-wizard in disbelief.

"I simply want my friends to have the chance to mourn my death according to their customs. I know there are some among the humans and elves who will wish to perform their own rituals." Harpur qualified this request and was relieved to see that it seemed to satisfy his challenger.

Harpur's challenger nodded her head and wondered how it was that a dragon became friends with members of the lesser races. "I will do as you ask," she agreed.

"And what requests do you make of me?" Harpur asked formally, reminding his challenger that she may not be the one granting the final wishes.

"I simply ask that my body be burned immediately." She looked back at the skull. "All of it. I do not wish any part of me to become a monument."

Harpur picked up his top hat and placed it back on his head. "I will see it done."

"Do you know which of our kind you wish to act as witness?"

"I choose Khol the Black of Rednow as witness."

Another surprise! "You want the dragon who defeated your mate to be your witness?" She was unable to keep the astonishment from her voice.

"Do you oppose my choice?" Harpur countered.

The teal dragon felt like she should oppose Khol as the witness, but she had no good reason to do so. Nothing Harpur had said was in breach of the protocols of a challenge. Except for his rude interruption, he had conducted himself appropriately, if strangely. Then again, this legendary dragon had changed his name to Harpur Diggins and had lived as a human on Earth for several years. She supposed that, for him, such eccentric behavior was normal.

"I see no reason to oppose Khol the Black of Rednow as witness."

"Good," said Harpur. "Now, if you don't mind, my friend and I have plans to gather thistle shoots for her apothecary. I will see you here again in three days."

Harpur tipped his top hat at his challenger. Then he turned to Elder Dhonna, who was as perplexed as the teal dragon was, and held an arm out for her to take.

Somewhat shaken by the whole experience, the blue-green watched Harpur and Elder Dhonna walk past her across the meadow and down a path leading into the valley. For an awkward minute or so, she stood in the meadow, wondering what had just happened. Finally, she launched herself into the air and flew westward toward the kingdom of Rednow to entreat Khol the Black to act as witness for the challenge.

Chapter Ten

She waited until the teal dragon was just a spec in the distance, and then Elder Dhonna stopped walking and turned to face Harpur. "I have a few questions," she said.

"I thought you might," Harpur said and waited for the guild master to gather her thoughts.

"First, what was the beard stroking and holding your hand over your heart and putting your hat on the ground all about?"

Harpur chuckled. "That was me telling Sok that all was well and to stay calm and stay put for three more days. Putting my hat on the ground reinforced that I was serious and that no matter what, he is to keep away for the agreed amount of time."

"You know that they will come early in the day," Elder Dhonna said. "They will be here when your challenger returns. They could interfere."

"I am aware that Sok and Anayah will not wait a minute longer than they have to," Harpur said. "And because of that, I'm afraid I'm going to have to ask you to use the dragonfoil ash again. Are you up to it?"

Elder Dhonna frowned. "What do you want me to do with it?"

"Nothing drastic," Harpur assured her. "Just ward the entrance to the lair and trap them inside when the time comes."

"That will require some preparation ahead of time," Elder Dhonna said. She was relieved that was all he wanted her to do. "They will know what I'm doing."

"We can get things ready the night before. Then when I go out to meet my challenger, all you will need to do is enact the spell. Simple!" Harpur smiled at the elf.

"You are remarkably astute for a dragon who is about to face his death," Elder Dhonna said.

Harpur took that as confirmation that she was on board with the plan. They continued walking along the path through Braydon Wood.

"I don't know why you don't just let them come now," she said after a few minutes had passed.

"Honestly," Harpur said with a smirk, "I'm rather enjoying the peace and quiet. Especially now that they know about the challenge. I would rather spend my last days with you than have to deal with their emotional trauma."

"Oh, but my emotional trauma is okay," Elder Dhonna teased.

Harpur stopped walking again and turned the guild master to face him. He placed his hands on her arms and looked her directly in the eye. "Your emotional trauma is not okay," he said. "But there is no one I trust more to help me get through this than you. Your being here means everything to me and I know I cannot thank you enough for what you are doing. I wish you didn't have to be here to see this."

"Again with the flirting," Elder Dhonna joked as she tried to choke back a sob.

Harpur pulled her close and held her while she cried. He was beginning to understand this hugging thing. It really did help.

As soon as she was able, Elder Dhonna composed herself enough to pull away from Harpur. She wiped the tears from her eyes and smiled up at him. "Thank you," she whispered and resumed walking. "I just remembered something," she said as they rounded a bend in the path.

"Oh, right! We were going to look for thistles." Harpur assumed that was what she was referring to.

"I don't know what thistles are." Elder Dhonna had forgotten about the thistles. "I thought you had made that up."

"Ah, yes. You know them as barbed Faeleaf. Thistle is the Earth name for them," Harpur explained.

Elder Dhonna smiled. "I think I like thistle better," she said. "But that wasn't what I wanted to ask."

Harpur didn't reply. He wasn't sure he wanted to field any more questions, so he waited silently for her to continue.

"What ever happened with that Morgaine Fayle woman? You mentioned that you had some business with her before you came to the lair. Were you able to deal with that?"

Harpur stiffened beside her. He didn't want to hesitate too long, but he hadn't expected Morgaine Fayle to come up. *How do I answer?* "That is all being dealt with even as we speak."

"Who is she?" Elder Dhonna persisted. "What did she want?"

It's like being with Sok and Anayah! Harpur thought as he took a deep breath and searched again for an answer that would satisfy the elf. "She is from Andonsheer. She just brought me a message from the Sands of Sancheera. Nothing you need worry yourself about. Oh, look. Thistles!"

Elder Dhonna decided to let it go. She assumed that the black-haired beauty had come to Colwygshire to warn Harpur that he was going to be challenged soon. They gathered some barbed Faeleaf and headed back to the lair.

Now that the challenge was common knowledge, at least among those closest to Harpur, the dragon-wizard fell into a mild state of melancholy.

First, I start hugging people. Then I get all mopey about dying. What's next? Kissing the red-headed guild master?

Indeed, that very thought had crossed Harpur's mind a few times of late. He had always admired Elder Dhonna, but this odd attraction he was feeling toward her was something he was having great difficulty reconciling. His dragon-self rejected the possibility entirely. It was, after all, entirely inappropriate for dragons to mingle in that way with other races. To his human self, however, the idea felt completely natural. She was an attractive, mature woman to Harpur, the man, and the man saw nothing wrong with the urges he was feeling.

I only have to control myself for three more days. Once I'm dead, this won't be a problem.

Elder Dhonna found the situation somewhat more amusing than Harpur did. In a slightly heartbreaking way. Seeing him struggle with his feelings wasn't easy for her, but she thought it would be good for him to experience some real human emotions. The timing could have been better, but she was confident that she would be able to let him down easy if she had to. In the meantime, she didn't discourage him from going for walks by himself once in a while and she refrained from teasing him about his increasingly shameless flirting, choosing instead to act oblivious to his awkward attempts at seduction. Not that she wasn't curious. She was simply more determined to stick to the vows she had taken and remain true to her calling as a healer.

Since the challenge had been issued and accepted, time began to pass both agonizingly slowly and astonishingly quickly for the residents of the lair. They weren't bored, exactly, just irritated by being slaves to the waiting. Harpur was even tempted to go and visit the campers in the ravine. But then he would see them watching him and he was reminded all over again that their company would entail preventing them from trying to save him. Which, if he was honest with himself, was a notion he was growing more and more fond of. If not for the fact that the proverbial gauntlet had been thrown down and he had picked it up and any interference at this point would most likely result in them being burned alive, he might have given in to the temptation. Had he known the waiting was going to be so excruciating, he might have given his plan more thought and found a way to speed up the process. As it was, Arthur was the one with all the control. And all Harpur could do was prepare to face his challenger and pray to Orhowyn that Arthur would find the strength to play his part.

On the eve of the day the challenge was scheduled to take place, Arthur and Davynn stopped to make camp next to a small pond. They had pushed the horses as hard as they dared since seeing the blue-green dragon and though it was not quite dusk yet, they stopped for the day to give the animals the rest they needed for the final leg of their journey the next day.

"How much farther?" Arthur asked for the hundredth time.

"With an early start, we should be there by mid-afternoon tomorrow." Davynn understood Arthur's anxiety, but he wished the king would stop asking how much farther they had to go. "You can see the mountain from here," he added, pointing through a gap in the trees to the north west.

"What if we are too late?" Arthur asked.

If we are too late, we are too late, Davynn thought, but did not say out loud. "I am not familiar with all the subtleties of dragon challenges, sire, but I do know that there is some time between the challenge being issued and the actual fight. Perhaps the dragon we saw was here to issue the challenge."

"But we didn't see it fly back again," Arthur persisted. "Why wouldn't it come back again if it was only here to issue the challenge? And what if the time between the challenge being made and the actual challenge has already passed?"

They had had this conversation several times over the past two days. Davynn's answer was the same then as it had been every other time Arthur had asked the question. "I have no answer for you."

"Maybe we should keep going," Arthur said. "Get as close as we can tonight."

"The horses need rest." Davynn pulled the saddle off of his mount and ended the conversation. He was not going to harm the beasts that had served them so well for the past eight days. No matter what they found when they reached the lair, sacrificing the well-being of the animals was not going to change it.

After they had eaten, Arthur reached into his saddle bag for the Amber Chalice. He unwrapped it and held it up to the fire light so he could see it better now that the sun had set. "It's just an old piece of junk," he said.

"I dare say it's more than that," Davynn said. "There must be a reason you are the only one who can touch it. I think that means there is something very special about it."

Arthur turned the cup around in his hands, examining it closely. In places, rust had eaten through the cup, leaving several holes in it. "It can't be the chalice itself that matters," Arthur theorized. "It has to be the amber stone with Willow's essence that Harpur needs."

That seemed obvious to Davynn and he wondered why someone as supposedly powerful as Arthur would question that. "I don't know much about magic," he said, "but don't you... sense anything from it? As I understand it, and I'm just guessing here, magic is in the feeling of things."

Arthur looked across the fire at the knight. "That's what Harpur always says. 'Feel the magic, Arthur.' I don't know what that means. I don't know what it is supposed to feel like."

Jack and Diane, who had been standing a little apart from Arthur and Davynn, now moved closer and sat down next to Arthur in the grass.

"What did it feel like when you drew the cup from beneath the standing stone?" Diane asked.

Arthur thought back to the day in the Fae Lands when he'd used his magic to retrieve the chalice. "It felt... tingly," he said, "like an electric shock going down my arms into the stone and searching for the chalice. But it didn't hurt or anything. It just felt... tingly."

"That was your intention being transmuted into energy," Jack said. "But what did you feel? How did you know where to direct your intention?"

Arthur looked at the ugly cup in his hands and tried to remember exactly what happened. "First, I pictured the cup in my mind and then... It wasn't so much a feeling as it was a sound. A kind of hum. And somehow I knew that was the cup." Arthur looked up from the chalice at Davynn, his face aglow with excitement. "Oh, wow! I get it now! I heard the hum, but I felt the connection."

Davynn didn't like the way Arthur was looking at the piece of jerky he held in his hands. "Not my..."

But it was too late. The jerky was yanked out of his hand by an unseen force and floated over the fire right into Arthur's outstretched palm. He stared at it in wonder.

Next to Arthur, Diane started clapping. "Well, done!

"Indeed!" Jack chimed in.

"Can I have my dinner back now?" Davynn said. He was impressed, but that was the last of the jerked meat.

Arthur tore a large chunk of the piece of jerky with his teeth and then pointed what remained at the knight. "Wouldn't you rather have an apple?" Arthur laughed. "Wait! How about some ale?"

He stood up and closed his eyes. Davynn wasn't sure what to expect, but experience told him to get ready to duck. Several long seconds passed before Arthur snapped his fingers and a large mug of ale appeared in the air in front of Davynn, then promptly fell and spilled all over the knight's lap.

Davynn yelped. He jumped to his feet and glared at Arthur. "What is it with you sorcerers and dumping drinks on me?"

"You were supposed to catch it!" Arthur exclaimed, turning his palms up in a what-the-hell gesture. "Here, let me fix that for you."

"No!" Davynn shouted. "I will change my pants myself. You practice on someone else." He walked over to his saddle bag to get his spare pair of pants. "But not the horses! Do not do anything to the horses."

"Geez," Arthur said, sitting down again. "A little gratitude for the effort would be nice." He closed his eyes again and conjured two more mugs of ale. This time he had them appear safely on the ground near the fire.

While Davynn, bastion of modesty that he was, was in the bushes changing his pants, Arthur conjured two apples and two bowls of pudding for himself and the knight. Davynn rinsed the ale-soaked trousers out in the pond and then laid them down to dry next to the fire. He looked at the treats Arthur had conjured suspiciously.

"They're perfectly safe," Arthur assured him and spooned a large scoop of pudding into his mouth.

Davynn waited until Arthur had eaten more of his pudding before he allowed himself to take a tentative test taste of his own dessert. "Not bad," he conceded. "Thank you."

Soon the two road-weary adventurers' appetites were fully sated and they felt more relaxed than they had in days. The food had helped to take the edge off, but neither of them had forgotten what they were there for and where they were going. When they were ready to bed down for the night, Arthur offered to conjure them each a pillow.

"Remember, Arthur, everything you conjure comes from somewhere. You do not create it," Jack said with a note of caution in his voice.

Suddenly, Arthur felt guilty about the apples, ale and puddings. "Is there a way to know where things come from?"

"Not always," Diane said. "Magic is a privilege, not a right. Use it wisely."

"I'm fine without a pillow," Davynn said. But Arthur heard the disappointment behind the words.

"Thank you for helping me with my magic," Arthur said to Jack and Diane. "You told me the same thing Harpur did, but in a way that makes sense."

"We can only tell you what you already know," Diane said.

And we're back to the crazy, woo-woo stuff! Arthur leaned back on his saddle and closed his eyes. The trepidation he felt mixed with elation over his new understanding of his magic. It all made sense. Well, it made more sense than it ever had before. His mind was churning with fears and fantasies vying for dominance and he knew sleep would not come easily. The harder he tried to clear his mind, the more insistent his thoughts became. He was just about to give up and go for a walk when Davynn spoke from the other side of the dying fire.

"Did you put the chalice away?"

Crap! Arthur sat up and felt around for the precious relic. "I can't find it!"

Davynn sat up, too, and looked past the fire at the ground where Arthur had been sitting with it. "It's right there." He pointed at a spot next to the ring of rocks that contained the fire.

"Where?"

The knight sighed and crawled closer to the flames. "Right here!" He pointed again.

"Oh! I thought it was a rock."

The chalice had rolled, or been knocked, against the fire ring and was laying with the amber stone down. In the shadow of the rocks, it looked very much like another rock. Arthur picked it up and wrapped it in the shirt again for protection. He tucked it safely back into his saddle bag and laid back down.

"Harpur wouldn't be too pleased with you if you lost it," Davynn said, laying back down also.

Arthur shrugged. "I'd just find it again with my magic," he boasted.

In the darkness, the knight rolled his eyes. *There will be no living with him now!*

Sok was pacing back and forth behind the campfire in the ravine. "I'm missing something," he said. Repeatedly.

"Yes," Hiro said. "You're missing out on this delicious apple crumble." He walked around the fire and handed Sok a bowl filled with the scrumptious dessert he had conjured out of his satchel.

Sok took it and kept pacing. He scooped a spoonful out of the bowl and ate it. "Mm! Is that cardamom?"

"It is," Hiro replied and giggled. "I'm thinking of showing this recipe to Finch to serve at the feast for the twins."

"Good idea," Sok said, spooning another bite into his mouth. His pacing continued.

"Have we decided if tomorrow is day five or six yet?" Anayah asked. She was sipping tea instead of consuming more calories.

"I believe that we have established that tomorrow is the third day after the challenger's visit to Harpur," Bon said. "Which makes it the sixth day after Harpur told us not to come back for six days."

"Yes, but is tomorrow the day of the challenge?" Sok wondered.

"What difference does that make?" Anayah asked.

Sok stopped pacing. "These things are usually set for dawn."

"Why do men always want to kill each other at dawn?" Anayah scowled. "Why not after breakfast? Or after lunch?" The aroma of apple crumble was beginning to have an enticing effect on her.

"Because everybody knows exactly when dawn is," Sok said as he resumed his pacing.

"Do they?" Anayah countered. "I mean is it first light or when the sun actually rises? Seems to me dawn is a period of time, not a specific moment."

"Everyone knows that when something is scheduled for dawn, the participants start to gather at first light and then wait until the sun is up to commence the event," Sok said. "And technically, Harpur is a dragon, not a man, so you really shouldn't stereotype like that."

"You know what I mean," Anayah said. She gave in to her craving for the apple crisp and turned to Hiro. "I think I will try some of that, please."

Hiro giggled and handed her a bowl of the latest Earth cuisine. "I suppose we should turn in soon if we intend to be at the lair for dawn."

Anayah nibbled at her dessert. "I don't know if I want to go," she said quietly.

Sok stopped pacing again. "You have to go," he said. "Your magic is the only thing that might save him."

Anayah pushed a chunk of apple back and forth in the bowl. "I don't think he wants to be saved."

"What are you talking about?" Sok said, also accepting another bowl of apple crisp from Hiro. "You don't think he wants to die, do you?"

"Why do you think he's kept us away?" Anayah asked. She put her bowl down next to the fire. "He doesn't want us to interfere."

"I think Anayah's right," Hiro said. "Harpur has taken great pains to keep us away."

"That's because he has a plan," Sok said. "There's no way Harpur's going to lose to that other dragon."

"I think we should stay here until after it's over," Anayah said.

"Well, you can stay here if you want to," Sok said, "but I'm going to go and do everything I can to help Harpur."

Anayah sighed. She stood up and walked toward her tent. "Do what you think is best."

Sok watched Anayah disappear into her tent. "You two are coming with me, right?"

Hiro and Bon exchanged looks.

"Let's sleep on it," Hiro suggested, "and see how we all feel in the morning. We don't even know for sure if the challenge is going to take place tomorrow."

"Just a thought," Bon said, noting Sok's distress. "Perhaps we might consider going to meet Arthur and Davynn in the morning. By my calculations, they won't arrive until mid-afternoon. Harpur must know that as well. But no matter what transpires tomorrow, it may be a good idea if we all arrive at the lair together."

Sok hadn't thought about when Arthur and Davynn would arrive, or how that might factor into whatever Harpur's plans were. "But they could be anywhere. Braydon Wood is enormous. How would we find them?"

"It seems to me," Bon posited, "that Davynn will take the most direct route from the Fae Lands. I have examined the maps of the forest and the most direct route is a trail that leads from just north of the bridge across the Fae Waters and joins the trail from Colwygshire three miles east of where we are now."

Sok was impressed with the android's knowledge of the forest. "I don't know." He began pacing again. "I can definitely see Davynn taking that route. It makes sense. But what if we miss them? What if Harpur needs our help sooner?"

"Harpur sent Arthur for the Amber Chalice for a reason," Bon continued. "And that reason must have something to do with the challenge. Harpur needs the chalice, Sok. The chalice is the key to everything. You said so yourself. Perhaps Arthur and Davynn have information we do not. I believe that the best course of action would be to find them and go to the lair together as a group."

"Why didn't you say this earlier?" Sok said. He was beginning to see the logic in what Bon was saying. But he still felt like he needed to get to the lair as early as possible.

"It only just occurred to me," Bon admitted. "When Anayah and I were in the Sphere together for all that time, she talked about Harpur. A lot. She talked about you and Arthur as well. And when she said that she thought he might not want to be saved, I realized that she meant by us. Arthur, on the other hand, has some role to play in all of this yet. I believe that he is going to need our help more than Harpur will."

Sok took a moment to process the android's words. "I think Hiro is right. We should sleep on it and see how we feel in the morning."

Hiro began clearing away the dishes from the apple crisp. He reached for the bowl Anayah had abandoned next to the fire, but Sok got to it first.

"Waste not, want not," the elf said and carried the dessert, now warm from the fire, to his hammock next to the clearing.

As the elf climbed out of the ravine and Hiro got comfortable in his hover gilly, Bon scanned the ridge along the east side of the ravine until his eyes came to rest on a particular tree he'd been keeping watch on for the past hour. "Good night, Harpur Diggins," he mouthed silently in the tree's direction. "Rest well."

Harpur approached the lair from the east side of the meadow. He could see Elder Dhonna sitting on the boulder outside the cave entrance. She was looking toward the west with a worried expression on her face. He cleared his throat to let her know he was there and smiled when she jumped at his arrival from an unexpected direction.

"Where have you been?" she said, shifting her bottom over to make room for the dragon-wizard on the boulder.

"Oh, just wandering around the Wood." Harpur looked out past the meadow toward the ravine.

"You went to the ravine, didn't you?" Elder Dhonna accused.

"Just to take a peek," he admitted. "I'm growing to like the android more and more."

"You spoke to them?" Elder Dhonna was a little shocked.

"No, I did not," Harpur assured her. "But Bon was aware that I was there. He really is a remarkable... man?"

Elder Dhonna did not have enough experience with androids to comment on their gender assignments. "So, did you gather any useful intelligence while you were spying on them?"

"I did," Harpur said. "It's very likely that they will go meet Arthur and Davynn in the morning."

"We don't have to ward the lair, then?" Dhonna asked hopefully. She wasn't feeling terribly enthusiastic about working with the dragonfoil ash again.

"It wouldn't hurt to be prepared." Harpur dashed her hopes. "Sok is reluctant to go. But Anayah said she didn't want to be here for the... big event. I'm not sure if she just doesn't want to watch me die, or if she's still mad at me and hopes that I do."

Elder Dhonna cuffed Harpur on the arm with the back of her hand. "Of course, she doesn't want to watch you die! How could you think otherwise?"

Harpur was silent for a moment. "You don't have to stay either," he said quietly.

"I'm not leaving," Elder Dhonna asserted. "Whatever happens tomorrow, I promised you that I would be here for you. And I will."

Harpur took her hand and kissed it. He slipped his arm around her and pulled her close to him. "You are the greatest treasure I have ever known." The dragon part of him winced as he spoke. But Harpur, the man, wished this moment could last forever.

They stayed together on the boulder as the evening wore on. A waxing crescent moon floated among the stars that twinkled against the velvety black sky and they took turns pointing out different constellations until thick, dark clouds rolled in from the east to obscure the spectacular view of the firmament above them. A chilly spring wind and the first, heavy drops of rain finally drove them inside shortly after midnight.

They still had work to do.

Sok climbed into his hammock and pulled the blanket over himself. As he devoured Anayah's apple crisp, he, too, gazed up at the stars. His eyes settled on Draconis Major, hovering protectively over the mountain where

Harpur's lair was. The nine stars that made up the constellation shone brighter than the other stars in the sky. It was said that Draconis Major took on the colour of the ruling dragon from whichever kingdom it was being viewed from. He took great comfort in the deep violet glow shining down on him from the Great Dragon of the Sky.

He wondered what it looked like from a kingdom that was ruled by a black dragon. Would it even be visible? Perhaps someday he would travel to Rednow and find out.

It struck him how little he knew about other kingdoms. His whole life, he had focused on learning the history of Epoh, but he'd never given much thought to what life was like in other places on Thraeh. He knew that humans, elves and dwarves lived in Rednow and that elves and dwarves lived in Ecaep. The Fae were not permitted in either of Epoh's neighbouring kingdoms and of that Sok approved wholeheartedly. *Such awful creatures! I wonder what Arthur will have to say about them.*

The wind began to pick up and Sok's hammock began to sway. He didn't mind the chill it brought with it. He didn't even mind the rain as it started to fall over Braydon Wood and drip through the canopy onto him. Elves were simply not affected by the weather like other races were. But he grew sad when the clouds blocked his view of Draconis Major. *I wonder what colour you will be tomorrow...*

Chapter Eleven

Harpur woke up early on the day of the challenge. He was vibrating with nervous energy and rather than disturb Elder Dhonna who was sleeping a few feet away from him on top of his hoard, he carefully rolled away from her, slid down to the ground and went outside onto the meadow. He could see Sok still asleep in his hammock near the edge of the ravine. But if the elf and his companions were going to go meet Arthur and Davynn, Sok likely wouldn't remain there for long. He returned to the boulder by the entrance to the lair, sat down, leaned back and closed his eyes. The rain had stopped, but the thick clouds that blocked the rising sun drifted lazily over Epoh, undecided as to whether or not to release more precipitation.

When the rain had chased them inside the lair the night before, Harpur and Elder Dhonna had prepared the spell to ward the entrance. Just in case. After that they had one last task to complete before they could turn in.

Elder Dhonna pulled a small blue bottle out of her satchel and set it carefully down on a flattened stalagmite in the centre of the lair. It contained a potion she had mixed up at the Guild House before she came. "There is more than enough to last through the challenge," she said. "I'm just not sure how much dragonfoil ash it's going to take to activate it or how quickly it will work."

Harpur noted the doubt on his dear friend's face. "The good news is that the dragonfoil ash isn't going to harm me no matter how much you use. The bad news is that the more you use, the worse it could be for you."

Elder Dhonna shuddered as she recalled the explosive effect the small pinch of dragonfoil ash she used to zap herself to the lair had. She looked from the small, blue bottle to Harpur. "We didn't think this through very well, did we?"

"The worse news is that I'm going to need as much as I can get. The more the better." He felt terrible. "But I think I will absorb most of its power. You'll be directing the magic at me, not you."

"And here I was thinking Arthur had the hard part," Elder Dhonna said. "You know Anayah..."

"...would be better at this?" Harpur finished for her. "That may be, but she can't know what we're doing. No one can, Bella Dhonna."

"Are you going to still call me that if this all works out?" Elder Dhonna asked.

The question threw Harpur for a bit of a loop. "I don't know." Harpur winked at the elf.

"Arthur is going to figure it out," Elder Dhonna deflected back to the topic at hand.

"That can't be helped," Harpur said. "But we aren't going to worry about that right now."

"No," Elder Dhonna said. "First we have to worry about not blowing me up with dragonfoil ash."

The contents of the small, blue bottle were little more than some herbs suspended in water. On its own, the potion might give whoever drank it a temporary boost of energy. But with magic added, it would allow Harpur to transform into his dragon form so he could fight his challenger. Since Harpur was unable to use his magic, Elder Dhonna had to activate the magic using a spell. And the only way she could do that was to use dragonfoil ash to enhance her own magic, which was not of the sort that could achieve the desired results by itself. For the spell to work, Elder Dhonna had to first enchant herself with the dragonfoil ash. This alone held an element of danger as too much could kill her and too little would mean that she might not have enough power to cast the spell and make it powerful enough to do what Harpur needed it to do, namely transform him into a dragon. Worst case scenario: Elder Dhonna died and Harpur faced his challenger as a man. Even Harpur didn't know what the protocols were for that! But there was also a chance that he could transform into something else. A baby dragon, for instance. Or he might only partially transform. As it was, even if everything went according to plan and Harpur transformed into his true dragon form, his wounds would not be healed. He would still have a broken wing. The scales on his left leg would still be missing. And the scale he had torn from his chest to save Arthur from a murderous forest on Mysturna would still be gone and his heart would still be exposed. Best case scenario: Elder Dhonna wasn't killed, Harpur transformed into his injured self and the fight didn't last too long.

They finally devised a plan to use just enough of the dragonfoil ash to make an invisible shield from behind which Elder Dhonna could cast the spell. They did a test run to see if it would work and the results were promising. But they didn't want to waste the precious dragonfoil ash that they had, and so decided that they were as ready as they were ever going to be.

Elder Dhonna put the small, blue bottle back into her satchel and headed toward the back of the lair that she had made to sleep on when she first arrived.

"Bella Dhonna?" Harpur had called out softly to her from the top of his hoard that first night.

"Yes, Harpur?"

"Why don't you come sleep up here?"

Only the dripping of water from the roof of the cave could be heard for a long, long minute while the implications of Harpur's invitation played themselves out in the guild master's head. Then finally, she rose from her bed of leaves, walked over to the base of the mountain of treasure and looked up at the dragon-wizard. "Are you flirting with me again, dragon?"

"Who knows if I'll ever get another chance?"

Sitting on the boulder, Harpur now smiled as he recalled Elder Dhonna scrambling to the top of his hoard and nestling into a layer of gold coins. "This is much more comfortable than I imagined," she had said. "I might have to collect a hoard of my own to sleep on."

"Take as much as you want with you," Harpur told her.

"You're giving me your gold?"

"It's still mine to do with as I wish," Harpur replied. "I wish you to have as much as you want."

Elder Dhonna had not responded. She simply reached out for Harpur's hand and held it as she fell asleep.

Harpur sensed a dragon approaching and he opened his eyes. It was a bit early for his challenger to be arriving and he was relieved to see that it was Khol the Black of Rednow approaching from the west. He sat up straight and watched the black dragon glide toward the lair and land next to the skull at the edge of the meadow. It was a bit early for the witness to be arriving too.

Khol was not overly large as dragons go. But he was deceptively strong for his size and had a reputation for being quite ruthless when he needed to be. When he had bested Harpur's mate, Karryl in her challenge for his kingdom, many had been surprised that Harpur hadn't retaliated. If dragons were gamblers, which they were not, most would have safely betted on Harpur to win. But Harpur had accepted Karryl's loss with his usual stoicism and maintained a civil relationship with Khol, who had done nothing wrong. Harpur had warned Karryl not to challenge Khol. She had chosen not to heed his advice. If Harpur had felt any anger toward any dragon, it was Karryl for not listening to him.

But that was long ago and now, as the black dragon touched down on the meadow, Harpur was glad that Khol was to be his witness. He was also intrigued by Khol's appearance so far ahead of the actual challenge. Harpur stood and walked out to meet his neighbour.

"You're a bit early," Harpur said by way of a greeting.

Before he answered, Khol transformed into his own human form, a stocky, dark-skinned man. His crimson robes were embroidered with silver dragons and his pointed hat sat at a jaunty angle on his bald head. Every inch the wizard. "I thought we should talk," he said, hoping for an invitation into the lair.

Harpur had never seen Khol in his human form. He didn't know whether to laugh or to appreciate the effort Khol was making at being respectful. Khol was the only dragon who knew the full extent of Harpur's condition and so Harpur chose appreciation over the risk of alienating his witness.

"What should we talk about?" Harpur asked, ignoring the glance Khol had made toward the entrance to the lair.

"You do not have to do this," Khol said. He accepted that Harpur chose not to invite him inside. He wouldn't have either.

"Oh?" Harpur raised one eyebrow in curiosity.

"You have sons," Khol continued. "You have the right to declare them heirs to Epoh. You don't have to be killed today."

Harpur had already thought of this. And he'd rejected it. "I've already accepted the challenge."

"Yes, yes," Khol said dismissively, "but you can still invoke the Right of Survivorship and give Epoh to them as a living bequest. As your witness, I am bound to ask if you have had a change of heart. You won't be dishonoured if you exercise your right to name your sons as your heirs."

"But I would have to leave Epoh now. Where would I go?" Harpur had no intention of naming his sons as heirs to Epoh, but he was curious about how Khol thought this would work. And what hidden agenda Khol might be attempting to forward.

"You can go to Andonsheer," Khol suggested, "and live out your days there as a..." Khol had no idea what Harpur could live out his days as in Andonsheer. Without his magic, he would have to take up a trade of some kind. *A blacksmith, perhaps?* "Well, you could ask your sons to allow you to stay here as a liaison between them and the people. At least you would still be alive."

"I just love how everyone assumes I'm going to lose today." Harpur looked down at the shorter dragon-wizard and was amused at the confusion that contorted Khol's face.

"You can't even transform!" Khol exclaimed. "How do you expect to survive in combat with a full-sized dragon?"

"I believe that I can transform," Harpur said, "and, in spite of my physical short-comings, my challenger will not find me easy to defeat."

Khol frowned. "Do not underestimate your opponent, Harpur Diggins. She is as ruthless as they come."

Just then, Elder Dhonna came out of the lair. She had woken up and heard the two dragon-wizard's voices. When she saw Harpur and Khol standing in the middle of the meadow, she stopped, unsure of what she was looking at.

Khol looked at the elf in surprise and Harpur turned, not surprised at all.

"You cannot use magic to win the challenge!" Khol was incensed.

"I cannot use magic against my challenger, you are correct." Harpur said. "Khol, meet my friend Elder Dhonna, Guild Master of Healing in Braydon Wood." He extended a hand as invitation for Elder Dhonna to join them. "Elder Dhonna, this is Khol the Black of Rednow. He will act as witness during the challenge today."

"Pleased to meet you," Elder Dhonna said as she took her place next to Harpur. "Are all the dragons going to be in human form today? Should Harpur be sharpening a sword and polishing his armor?"

Harpur smiled at the guild master's wit. "I'm afraid that won't be necessary," he said. "I will be meeting my challenger as planned; in my dragon form."

You hope! "I'm not sure which is better." She paused. "Or worse." She turned to Khol. "May I ask why you've come so early?"

"Khol just wanted to apprise me of a possible way around the challenge," Harpur said truthfully.

"Do you think it's wise to say anything in front of..." Khol tilted his head toward Elder Dhonna.

"I have no secrets from Elder Dhonna," Harpur said.

"What possible way around the challenge?" Elder Dhonna asked, hardly able to keep the excitement from her voice.

"Khol thinks that I should invoke the Right of Survivorship and bequeath Epoh to my sons," Harpur explained.

Elder Dhonna blinked at Harpur. "No. No secrets at all," she said sarcastically. "Right of Survivorship? Sons? Why don't I know any of this?"

"Technically, I have the right to name my sons as my heirs and give Epoh to them. Before the challenge begins, Khol will ask me if I wish to do this. It's part of the protocols. If I were to agree, the challenge would be deferred until my sons were installed as the rulers of Epoh. One of them would then have to accept the challenge. If he lost, then the other one would have to accept the challenge. If he lost, then my challenger would get the kingdom. I, of course, would be banished from Epoh and would have to leave immediately," Harpur summarized.

As Harpur spoke, a variety of emotions flashed across Elder Dhonna's face. When he stopped speaking, she took a few minutes to process what she had learned. Finally, she punched Harpur in the arm. "I should kill you myself!" She stormed back to the lair.

Khol, open-mouthed in abject shock, watched her stomp away. He, too, needed a minute to process what he had just witnessed. "An elf just punched you!"

"Yes, she does that once in a while," Harpur confirmed.

"And she's still alive!"

"Yeah, well, she probably has a right to be upset with me. She'll get over it." Harpur wasn't concerned.

"You, my friend," Khol said, pointing an accusatory finger at Harpur, "have been in human form too long!"

Harpur simply nodded. He watched Elder Dhonna disappear into the lair and knew that he had to go and make things right. He turned back to Khol. "We go ahead with the challenge as planned."

Khol transformed back into his dragon form. "You are a fool, Harpur Diggins." And with that he launched into the air and flew back toward Rednow.

Arthur opened his eyes. Jack and Diane were standing just outside the lean-to that Davynn had built in the middle of the night after it had started raining. The pirate guardians were bent over, hands on their knees, smiling down at him. It was still raining, but instead of the torrential deluge that had forced the hasty construction of the lean-to, what was falling from the sky was a mere drizzle in comparison. Beyond Jack and Diane, Arthur could see the tattered remnants of the tent he had attempted to conjure for them lying on the muddy ground. He couldn't say exactly what had gone wrong, but had blamed being tired for the misfire. He noted, also, that Davynn was not in the lean-to with him.

"Where's Davynn?" he croaked.

"He is saddling the horses," Jack said.

"He wanted us to come and wake you up." Diane beamed.

"So, why didn't you?" Arthur said. He sat up and crawled out from under the makeshift shelter.

"We didn't want to disturb you," Jack said.

Bewildered by that response, Arthur chose not to pursue it. He stood up, stretched and headed over to Davynn and the horses. "Good morning!"

Davynn looked at him over the back of his horse, but did not reply.

"Oh, come on," Arthur wheedled. "You aren't still mad at me about the tent, are you?"

"No, sire," Davynn said, yanking on the cinch.

"I said I was sorry," Arthur pleaded.

And he was. When he'd first conjured the tent, all seemed in perfect order. Then Davynn had entered it through the flap and it had promptly collapsed around him. He'd had to cut his way out with his dagger. Which is why it was in tatters. Arthur had tried to repair it, but the supports kept collapsing and by the time he had given up, Davynn already had the lean-to half built.

Davynn tossed the reins to Arthur and mounted his own horse without further discussion.

"Don't you want to have breakfast before we start out?" Arthur asked the back end of Davynn's horse as it walked past him.

"I already ate," Davynn said over his shoulder.

Arthur turned back to Jack and Diane. "He's in a mood!"

The guardians said nothing.

Arthur decided to conjure two cups of jamba before he mounted up himself. He was a little nervous after the tent debacle, so it took a couple of tries. To be safe, he had them appear on the ground a few feet away from where he was standing. Then he realized that he still had to get up onto his horse and he couldn't do that while holding onto two cups of hot jamba.

Diane picked up the jamba and handed one cup to Jack. When Arthur was safely seated in his saddle, she handed the cup she was holding to him. "Jack will catch up to Davynn with the other one," she said.

After nine straight days of riding, Arthur finally felt confident enough to ride without holding onto the saddle horn. At least at a walking gait. But Davynn was far enough ahead of him now that he either had to trot to catch up, or hope that Davynn took pity on him and stopped at some point to wait. He opted for the latter, deciding that if Davynn got too far ahead, he would make the attempt at a faster pace and switch his hope to not ending up wearing his jamba in the process. Besides, Davynn was clearly still cranky about the tent and the lack of sleep Arthur's magic had contributed to. *Best to let him have some space for a while.*

This gave Arthur a chance to think. At first, his thoughts were on Harpur and what they might find when they got to the lair. But that just led to all sorts of speculation, none of which was at all comforting. *What if Harpur is dead? What if that blue-green dragon we saw is now the ruler of Epoh? What if it banishes the people from its kingdom? What will happen to us? What will happen to Alex, Hart and Meg? How will I look after them if I'm not the king anymore?*

As the morning wore on and these frightening thoughts continued to plague Arthur, a longing to see Alex and the twins again swept over him. Hart and Meg were ten days old now. And he'd missed all but the first of those ten days. He wondered how much they had changed. *Babies change fast, don't they? I'll never get this time back. I'll bet Sok hasn't missed a moment with them.*

Suddenly, Arthur felt a pang of jealousy sweep the longing for his family away and take firm hold of his psyche. The elf was spending time with his children! The elf was getting to see them grow and change in their first days of life. The elf was probably singing them lullabies and telling them stories. This was unacceptable.

"Davynn!" Arthur shouted as he kicked his horse into a trot. He'd lost all concern for either his jamba or staying seated on his horse.

Davynn heard the cry from behind and pulled his horse to a stop. He looked over his shoulder, expecting Arthur to be quite a bit farther back on the trail than he was, and watched, helplessly confused, as Arthur bounced past him slopping jamba all over himself and his horse.

"We've got to get moving," Arthur huffed as he passed. "Sok is not going to bond with my kids before I do!"

Davynn looked back down the trail. His first thought had been that some threat was coming from behind, but he couldn't reconcile that with the odd statement Arthur had uttered. Nor could he grasp what Arthur meant by it. *Bond with his kids? Is that like Entanglement?*

Jack and Diane swished by with Arthur as glowing balls of energy. Davynn wasn't certain, but he swore he heard them laughing rather gleefully. He took one more look behind to be certain that there was nothing coming after them, then kicked his own horse into a canter to catch up to Arthur.

As he drew next to the bobbing king, he slowed his horse and reached out for Arthur's reins. Bringing both horses to a stop, he stared in bewilderment at his Jamba-soaked companion. "What is happening?" he asked.

"What are you doing?" Arthur shot back. "We need to get to the lair. We don't have time for idle chit-chat." He tried to get his horse to move again, but Davynn held onto his reins and wouldn't let him go.

"I get that we need to get to the lair," Davynn said, "but what's this about Sok bonding with Hart and Meg? What does that mean? And how do you know it's happening?"

Arthur slumped in his saddle. "We've been gone from the castle so long," he wailed. "And I know that Sok is spending too much time with the twins. We need to get to the lair and get this business... Whatever it is! ...over with as soon as possible."

Davynn had no idea how Arthur had come to this conclusion, but he suspected that the time they'd spent apart on the trail had provided Arthur's imagination with too much freedom to roam. "So bonding is spending time with someone?" Davynn persisted.

"Yes!" Arthur cried. "You saw how Sok was with them the day they were born, trying to take them out of the nursery. He's had nine days to himself with them! Can you imagine what he's filling their heads with while I'm out here in the middle of nowhere?"

"They're babies," Davynn said. "What could Sok possibly fill their heads with at this stage? All they do is eat and sleep."

"It doesn't matter!" Arthur shouted. "He's there with them. And I'm not!"

"Okay," Davynn said as soothingly as he could. "I understand that you are missing your children. This all couldn't have happened at a worse time. But do you think that Alex will allow Sok to interfere in any way?"

"She let him name them!" Arthur was truly horrified. It was as if the reality of those first few hours after Hart and Meg were born were just then sinking in.

Davynn got the horses to start walking again, but he continued to hold onto the reins of Arthur's horse. Hopefully, progress, even slow progress, toward their destination would help appease his frantic king. "Well, yes, she did do that," Davynn agreed. "But only sort of. She picked Hart's real names. And Meg's names didn't change from what you had chosen. He only created nicknames for them from their initials."

"That's not the point," Arthur insisted.

"What is the point?" Davynn asked.

"The point is, I want to go home!"

Just ahead of them, two bright balls of energy hovered in the middle of the trail. Davynn looked at them sternly as if to say, "A little help here, please?"

The guardians seemed to sense Davynn's dilemma and transformed into their human pirate guises. They fell into step alongside Arthur's horse. "Sok is not bonding with Hart and Meg at the castle," Jack said.

"How do you know that?" Arthur asked.

"Because he's with Anayah, Hiro and Bon on the hover gilly coming toward us," Diane said.

"What?" Arthur and Davynn asked in unison. They both looked up the trail, searching for a sign of the hover gilly and its multi-racial cargo.

"You should meet them before the sun reaches its zenith," Jack said.

"Why didn't you tell us this?" Arthur demanded. He neither expected, nor received an answer.

Davynn looked up at the sky. The clouds were thin enough by then that he could tell it was getting close to midday. "Good. The Krist will be able to conjure us some food without putting our lives at risk." He let go of Arthur's reins and kicked his horse back into a leisurely cantor.

Arthur scowled at the guardians and followed suit. He felt bad, but he tossed his empty jamba cup into the bush so he could hold on with both hands.

Sok woke up and flipped gracefully out of his hammock. It had become his habit upon waking to check on the lair, but he had left his spy glass in the ravine the night before and so all he could make out was a small, dark hole in the side of the mountain. If anything was happening up there, he could not tell.

He stretched and headed back to the ravine where Anayah, Hiro and Bon were already breaking camp. Hiro tossed Sok a biscuit.

"That's it?" Sok asked. "This is breakfast?" He took a bite of the warm rusk and savoured the flaky layers as they melted in his mouth.

Hiro handed him two slices of crispy bacon. "You're welcome." The Krist giggled.

Bon had extinguished the fire and Anayah had disappeared her tent. All that was left was to leave the ravine and begin their trek eastward; hopefully to meet Arthur and Davynn somewhere on the trail. Sok sat down on a log and devoured the bacon.

"Shouldn't we discuss this?" he asked.

"No," Anayah said. "I think that Bon's idea to go and find Arthur and Davynn is the best thing to do." She started walking toward the narrow path that led out of the ravine.

"Well, I think we should go straight to the lair," Sok said.

"Do whatever you want," Anayah called back over her shoulder. "We are going to find Arthur and Davynn."

Sok looked at the Krist and the android. "Is that what you want to do?"

Hiro stepped into his hover gilly. "It is," he said with his usual giggle. "I do hope you will come with us."

Bon's answer was to step onto the hover gilly and stand next to the Krist.

Sok sighed. "Is that really all I get to eat?" he asked as he stood up and joined the others aboard the floating chariot.

Hiro giggled again. "I saved something special for you. Just reach into my satchel and..."

The elf was already bent over and lifting the flap on the magic shoulder bag. "Hiro, you are my hero!" he exclaimed as he pulled an enormous, fruit-filled pastry out and took a big bite.

They caught up to Anayah at the trees where the hammock had been tied. She had already zapped it away. She handed the bowl and spoon from the apple crisp to Hiro to discard in his satchel and then became the last passenger on the hover gilly. As they drifted across the clearing to the path that would lead them to the path that would lead them to the trail that Arthur and Davynn should be on, Anayah lifted her spy glass to her eye and pointed it at the lair.

"Anything happening up there?" Sok asked, fruit filling from his pastry dripping down his chin. His spy glass must have been put back in the satchel. But his hands were both occupied with the pastry.

"Harpur is sitting on the boulder. Alone." She lowered the spy glass.

They entered the forest and their view of the lair was obscured by the trees. Only Bon had noticed the black spec in the sky flying toward the lair from the west. He said nothing to the others.

Harpur stood in the meadow for a few minutes after Khol had flown away. He had some explaining to do to Elder Dhonna and he didn't know if he was up to it. Part of him knew that she would understand. But another part of him felt like this was too big to put into words. *Then again,* he thought, *I was the one who opened my big mouth. Best go take my lumps.*

Elder Dhonna was filling her satchel with gold and jewels from his hoard when Harpur entered the lair. For a second, he forgot that he had told her she could take what she wanted. Still, the sight of her stuffing bits and pieces of the cache into her bag while she muttered elven expletives under her breath was an affront to his dragon nature. He had to take a moment to calm himself.

"You said I could take what I wanted," Elder Dhonna said without looking at him. She crammed a jeweled dagger into the satchel.

"I did," Harpur said. "And I meant it." *Did I really, though?*

"Are you going to tell me about these sons of yours?"

A golden goblet disappeared into the satchel and Harpur had to wonder if it was like Hiro's magical satchel and just how much of his treasure it would hold. "If you want me to." He walked over to the flattened stalagmite where they had discussed the magic potion the night before and sat down. *No! Not that one!* He cringed as Elder Dhonna packed away a particularly valuable coronet that once belonged to a princess from... *Where was that spoiled brat from?*

"It's all in the book, isn't it?" the elf paused. She was holding an enormous ruby in her hand.

"It is," Harpur confirmed.

"So, there's no reason for you to think that I didn't already know," Elder Dhonna said. "It's not like I haven't spent many, many hours poring over the story of your life."

"When you were young and first started coming to the lair, you once asked me about them," Harpur said. "You saw their pictures and you asked me if they were my children. Do you remember that?"

The guild master turned her back on the hoard and stared at the dragon-wizard. "I do not."

"It was late summer," Harpur continued, "and you had just gotten in trouble for picking the wrong flowers for Aurrow, the guild master at the time."

Elder Dhonna was instantly transported back to her youth. She remembered how Aurrow had banished her from the guild house and gardens for the remainder of the season. "He was a strict mentor," she said. "I remember that. But I don't remember coming here when it happened."

"Well, you did," Harpur said. "You were inconsolable. You were certain that you would never be allowed to enter the Healing Guild and you insisted that I let you live here with me forever."

Elder Dhonna's memory began to clear. She couldn't help but smile at her long-forgotten bout with youthful angst. "And to cheer me up you told me about your sons?"

"I gave you the book to look at. Personally, I wanted you to just leave. Distraught adolescent elven girls were not my forte." Harpur chuckled. He was never more afraid of another being than he was of Elder Dhonna that day. He'd flown off and killed three cows in the planes south of Colwygshire, hoping she would be gone when he returned to the lair. But she wasn't.

Elder Dhonna put her satchel down and joined Harpur on the stalagmite. "I don't suppose that's changed since then?"

"It has not," Harpur said. He shifted a little to his right to make room for his friend. "Anyway, you were looking at the pictures. You couldn't read the writing in the book yet, but you loved looking at the pictures and asking me about them."

"What did you tell me about your sons? I really don't remember ever hearing about them."

"Not a lot. I told you that I had once had a mate named Karryl Evergreen and that before she challenged Khol the Black and lost, we had produced a rare set of twin boys named Framanjesk and Phiercesten. You laughed at their names."

Suddenly it all came back to Elder Dhonna. "I do remember," she whispered. "I was worried about what would happen to them without their mama to look after them."

"By then, they were old enough to look after themselves," Harpur said, "but I did have to convince you that they had been well cared for after their mother had died."

Elder Dhonna blew a lungful of air out through puffed cheeks and leaned against Harpur. "I am sorry," she said.

"For what?"

"For forgetting. I had no right to get angry with you."

"Were you really angry that you didn't know I had a couple of sons? Or was it learning about the Right of Survivorship that upset you?" Harpur reached across himself and put a hand on top of Elder Dhonna's.

"They kind of go hand in hand, don't they?"

"Relative to the current situation, I suppose they do." Harpur shifted to put an arm around Elder Dhonna and pulled her in close to himself. "You do understand that I can't do that, don't you?"

"I understand that you don't want to do it," she replied, "but I don't understand why you can't."

"Because I don't want to live out my days unable to transform and without magic," Harpur explained. Again.

"Would you really be banished from Epoh forever, if your sons inherited the kingdom?" she asked.

"Definitely," Harpur confirmed. "I could petition Framanjesk and Phiercesten to allow me to stay, but no dragon is going to permit another dragon – in any form – to live in their kingdom. Even without my magic, they would see me as a potential threat. What if I was somehow healed someday and decided to try to take the kingdom back?"

"How would that be any different from any other challenge?" Elder Dhonna asked.

"It would be different because it would be my right. As long as I am alive and living here, Epoh remains mine to rule. If I give it to my sons, they would be regents only. Until I die."

"What if you were banished and were healed? Wouldn't you still have the right to take it back?"

"Technically," Harpur said, "but it wouldn't be that easy. Once I left the kingdom, it would be dishonourable for me to return."

"Dragon politics are complicated," Elder Dhonna said with resignation.

Harpur snorted a laugh. "You should go to Earth someday. You think dragon politics are convoluted? You should see what goes on in some countries there."

"What are countries?"

"They are like kingdoms. More or less."

"I see." Elder Dhonna really didn't.

They sat in silence for a while, each one lost in their own thoughts.

"Is this really the only way?" Elder Dhonna finally broke the silence.

"It's the only way I can think of that doesn't overtly break any rules," Harpur answered.

"It just bends them," Elder Dhonna said.

"Just a little," Harpur said.

"Has the sun reached its zenith yet?"

Davynn dropped his chin to his chest and groaned. "No, sire. But I'm sure we will meet them soon." *Orhowyn's withered wings, I swear if he asks me that one more time...*

"There they are!" Arthur spurred his horse into a cantor and bolted ahead of the king-weary knight.

Davynn's head snapped back up. He was tempted to keep his horse at a walk so he could enjoy a few minutes by himself. But he couldn't see a hover gilly anywhere, so he urged his own horse to match Arthur's horse's gait and followed, hoping Arthur wasn't leading them into some kind of danger.

Not that the threat of danger was all that likely in Braydon Wood. But one never knows...

When Davynn caught up to Arthur, the king was stopped in the middle of the trail looking up at the forest canopy. "Where are they?"

"Up there." Arthur pointed through a small gap in the leaves overhead.

Davynn followed Arthur's finger. At first, he didn't see anything but the thin clouds. "Where?"

"There!" Arthur pointed again. He cupped his hands around his mouth and shouted toward the tree tops. "Hiro! Anayah! Sok! Bon! We're down here."

Davynn still couldn't see them. "What would they be doing up there?" *Arthur, you're daft.*

"I don't know." Arthur swung his horse around and started heading back the way they had come. "Sok! Anayah! Hey! We're down here!"

Davynn turned his own mount around and followed Arthur. He kept his eyes on the sky whenever the leaves above permitted, but all he saw were the occasional bird. And more clouds. "Arthur!" he called after the excited king. "Arthur, I don't think they are up there. Let's keep going. I'm sure we will meet them on the trail."

Arthur did stop. But not so they could continue westward. He dismounted and started climbing a tree.

"I don't think that's a very good idea," Davynn said as he approached and stopped next to Arthur's horse. "You are not an elf."

"I've seen Sok do this a thousand times," Arthur grunted, pulling himself awkwardly onto the first branch. "How hard can it be?"

"This is going to end badly," Davynn said.

"What did you say?" Arthur called down from the second branch.

"Nothing. Carry on," Davynn said with a sigh. He stayed on his horse, considering his options. "Sire?" Davynn called up as Arthur reached the third branch.

"What?"

"This may not be the best time to remind you..."

"Remind me of what?"

"Your aversion to heights."

Arthur didn't reply.

Davynn moved closer to the tree trunk and looked up to see Arthur clinging to the trunk with his eyes squeezed tightly shut. "You looked down, didn't you?" Davynn asked.

"I guess I didn't think this through very well," Arthur replied. "What do I do now?"

"Well, *that* is a very good question," Davynn murmured.

He climbed down off his horse and tethered it to a bush next to Arthur's mount. Then he went back to the tree. "Do you want me to come up there and help you get down?" *Please, say no.*

"No. That's probably not a good idea either."

Thank Orhowyn. "I don't have any rope. And short of chopping the tree down, which will take..." Davynn eye-balled the thick trunk. "...about a day with my little hatchet, I don't know what else to do. You're just going to have to come down on your own."

"Maybe you could keep going and see if you can find Sok and the others. Bring them back and get Anayah to zap me down. They are not too far east of us."

Davynn was impressed. "That sounds like a good idea. Except that I don't think we passed them. I'm going to keep heading west and when I find them, we'll double back for you."

"We did pass them!" Arthur insisted. "They are above the trees. I saw them fly over in the hover gilly."

Davynn sighed. He hadn't seen anything and while he wanted to believe Arthur, he couldn't justify going back the way they came and losing more time. Then again, according to Jack and Diane, they should have met by now. He turned to the glowing balls of energy that were hovering, ever so unhelpfully, on the path near the tree. "I don't suppose you two could get him down?"

Jack and Diane transformed into pirate people.

"We cannot," Jack said.

"But Hiro or Anayah can," Diane said.

"Great," Davynn said. "I will carry on then and bring them back. You two stay here and keep him calm." He untethered his horse, climbed back onto it and turned it westward.

"The hover gilly is the other way," Jack said as Davynn trotted past them.

Davynn reined in his horse, turned back around and looked at the guardians. "Are you sure?"

Jack and Diane nodded in unison.

"Very well, then." Davynn spurred his horse forward. Then he stopped again. "I don't suppose that one of you can go and find them?"

Jack and Diane exchanged glances.

"That is not possible," Diane said.

"We are Arthur's guardians. We must stay here with him." Jack explained.

"Figures," Davynn mumbled. He started back down the trail again.

"Hurry!" Arthur shouted after him.

Davynn left at a cantor, determined to find the hover gilly and its passengers as quickly as possible. He hadn't gone far when he came across Stellah and his crew coming toward him along the trail. They were out looking for trees in need of healing and did not appear to be looking too hard or too closely. Davynn stopped and hailed them. "Greetings, friends," he said. "Have you seen Sok anywhere? He'd be with three others in a sort of floating chariot."

"I told you that was Sok in the hover gilly," one of the elves in Stellah's group said.

"So you did!" Stellah replied. "I shouldn't be surprised. That young elf grows less elf-like every passing day. Imagine flying around in one of those silly things!"

"Where did you see him?" Davynn interrupted. He had no time for a debate on the merits of hover gillies.

"About two or three hundred yards back that way." Stellah pointed with his thumb over his shoulder. "Heading east toward Colwygshire, I suspect."

"You didn't talk to him?" Davynn asked.

"No chance!" Stellah said. "They flew over us in the clearing back there. Looked like they were in a hurry."

Orhowyn's fiery breath! "Thanks. I better get a moving then." Davynn walked his horse past the group of elves and then kicked it back into a cantor.

As his horse covered more ground, Davynn realized how futile it was to keep going. Particularly above the trees, the hover gilly was way more maneuverable than he was and had the advantage of far greater speeds than he did. *What are they doing up there anyway?* he wondered. *It makes no sense for them to be flying above the trees when we are on the ground. Maybe they aren't looking for us.*

With that thought now rattling around in his head, Davynn decided to abandon his quest for the hover gilly and return to Arthur, about whom he was growing more anxious by the second. *Maybe the elves will get him down before I get back there.* He turned his increasingly confused horse around again and headed back to the tree to find it completely vacant of acrophobic kings.

Chapter Twelve

As midday drew nearer at Harpur's lair, he began to wonder if he'd gotten the day wrong. He was perched on the hillside above the lair, watching the sky to the west and to the south-east, which remained empty of dragons. Beside him, barefoot and slightly soot-stained from dragonfoil ash, Elder Dhonna sat cross-legged on the ground, unable to keep her eyes off the magnificent, if somewhat damaged dragon next to her.

They had activated the potion about an hour before midday with only a minor backfire from the dragonfoil ash that had left black smudges in Elder Dhonna's hair and on her face and caftan. The shield she had created to protect her had done its job. Mostly, and much to both her and Harpur's great relief.

When Harpur had transformed for the first time in many moons, he did so with a roar of pain that, had they been inside the lair, would have deafened the unprepared elf. As it was, Harpur had elected to transform on the hillside in a spot that left no room for either his challenger or Khol to land nearby. They would have to land in the meadow. This was Harpur's higher ground, so to speak, a place from which he intended to start the fight with at least some advantage.

So far, things had gone well. *Too well?* Harpur wondered. He was all too familiar with plans not going according to expectation and an absent challenger was wholly unexpected. He couldn't even begin to imagine why Khol would not show up.

"Is this some kind of dragon tactic?" Elder Dhonna finally asked. "Is she playing mind games with you; trying to undermine your confidence?"

"If it is," Harpur growled, "it's bloody brilliant. I think I'm becoming what Arthur calls a wreck."

Elder Dhonna looked up at the enormous dragon. If he was nervous, it didn't show. But if he was feeling half as anxious as she was, he would, indeed, be a wreck. She wanted to say something to comfort him, but words failed her. Silent companionship seemed most fitting for the occasion. And less likely to cause her to burst into tears. This waiting, though, was pure torture.

The sun reached its zenith and still there were no dragons anywhere to be seen. Then a glint of sunlight reflecting off a shiny surface to the east caught his eye and he zoomed in on it. "What in Orhowyn's name are those fools doing?"

"What fools?" Elder Dhonna asked. She turned in the direction that Harpur was looking, but she could not see what he was seeing.

"Sok and the others. They are flying the hover gilly over the tree tops," he said.

"Where?" Elder Dhonna craned her neck, but all she saw was a sea of trees spread out below them in the valley.

"Not far," Harpur said. "They should have met up with Arthur and Davynn long before this."

"What do you mean by not far?" Elder Dhonna asked, alarmed. They weren't expecting Arthur and Davynn to make it before mid-afternoon.

"They still have a couple of hours before they reach the lair," Harpur assured her. "It will all be over by the time they get here."

"That's if your challenger even shows up!"

Reminded of his challenger's tardiness, Harpur swung his big head back toward the west, scanning the sky for any sign of either dragon. "There!" he said.

"Where?" Again, Elder Dhonna's keen elf vision paled in comparison to Harpur's even keener dragon vision.

"Khol is about a quarter of an hour out," Harpur said.

Elder Dhonna squinted in the direction Harpur was looking. A tiny black spec could be seen against the clouds. "What happens if she doesn't show up?" she asked.

"She forfeits and she can never challenge me again," Harpur answered.

"I hope she forfeits," Elder Dhonna said.

"If it's not this one, Bella Dhonna, it will be another. The entire dragon nation will be aware that the challenge has been made. If she doesn't come today, you can be certain that another one will come soon."

Elder Dhonna swore in elven. "I hate this!" she cried. "I hate this so much!"

Harpur did not respond to the outburst. "Perhaps Khol knows something," he said.

A few minutes later, Khol alit on the meadow. "I'm not going to ask how you managed that trick," he said, referring to Harpur's transformation, "but I am pleased to see you in your true form, Harpur Diggins."

"Welcome back," Harpur said. "First you come early; now you arrive late. Not as late as my opponent, however."

"She will be along shortly," Khol said.

"You met with Harpur's challenger?" Elder Dhonna asked. This didn't feel right to her.

"It's alright, Bella Dhonna," Harpur soothed. "It's Khol's prerogative as the witness to meet with both sides prior to the challenge."

"Hmph!" Elder Dhonna exclaimed. "So, what's her excuse for keeping Harpur waiting?"

"Not that I have any obligation to explain things to you, elf," Khol said with a snort of smoke, "but I asked her to delay her arrival."

"Why is that?" Harpur asked.

"So that I could appeal to you one more time to give up this suicide mission," Khol said.

"How is accepting a challenge a suicide mission?" Harpur countered.

"Harpur, you know that I have nothing but respect for you," Khol continued, "but this is not a fair fight. You are in no shape to defend your kingdom. I beg you, bequeath Epoh to Framanjesk and Phiercesten. There's no need for you to die at the talons of..."

"What is your challenger's name, by the way?" Elder Dhonna asked, interrupting Khol's plea. "You haven't told me."

Harpur looked down at Elder Dhonna. "You never asked. But you will find out soon enough," he said. "She is coming."

All three of them looked southward to see the blue-green dragon gliding toward the meadow.

"Impatient *seetah*," Khol swore in draconian. Then he turned back to the great purple dragon. "It's not too late, Harpur."

Harpur's eyes stayed on his challenger. "Thank you for your concern, Khol, but I will meet my challenger in battle as agreed."

Davynn was certain he was at the right tree. There were no hoof prints leading up the trail past where he stood. The ground was still soft enough after the rain that he could see his and Arthur's horse's prints quite clearly. There were no prints from any passing elves, so he couldn't be sure that Stellah and his crew had made it this far. But Davynn was not surprised. Elves tended not to leave prints behind. It was kind of spooky to him. He'd had to carry Sok before, and, for such a slim fellow, there had been a fair bit of heft involved. But his immediate concern was for his king.

"Arthur!" he called out as he searched the bush around him. "Sire? Where are you?"

"Right here!" Arthur said, stumbling out of the forest a few yards behind Davynn. "Where are Sok and the others? Did you find them?"

Davynn turned his horse around to face Arthur, who was pulling leaves and twigs from his hair and brushing dirt off his clothes. "I'm afraid I did not. How did you get out of the tree?"

"Funny story," Arthur said. "I had to pee, so I figured I would try to climb down. I kind of lost my balance and... Well, thank Orhowyn for that bush over there; it broke my fall. Anyway, I must have spooked my horse when I yelled. It took off into the bush." He pointed vaguely in the direction he'd come out of the forest from.

"Are you hurt?" Davynn asked with grave concern. "Where is your horse now?"

"I'm fine." Arthur threw his hand out to his sides to show he was okay. "I haven't found the horse."

Davynn, from his higher vantage point atop his horse, scanned the forest, looking for the missing horse. It was nowhere to be seen. "Well, climb up behind me. We need to get moving."

"No," Arthur said. "We need to find my horse! The Amber Chalice is in the saddle bag."

Davynn shook his head. "Um, sire?"

"Yes, Davynn?"

"I can't believe I'm about to say this, but we really don't have time to go searching for a horse that could be anywhere by now. Why don't you just zap the chalice here?" he winced when he said the word zap.

"Oh, yeah!" Arthur laughed. "Why didn't I think of that? But aren't you worried about the horse?"

"I am," Davynn agreed, "but right now I'm more worried about getting you safely to the lair." *The sooner the better.*

Arthur closed his eyes so he could concentrate on his magic. He was feeling for the chalice when Davynn interrupted him. "Sire, do you mind going a little farther back that way before you..." He waved his hand in the air in a vaguely magical gesture.

Arthur opened his eyes. Mainly so Davynn could see him roll them. He didn't really blame the knight for being cautious, but a little support would have been welcome. Then again, if Davynn got beaned on the head by a rusty old cup, he would feel bad. So, he walked a few yards away and closed his eyes again.

"Did anyone lose a horse?" a voice called out from behind Arthur.

Davynn looked up and Arthur spun around to see Sok riding Arthur's horse up the trail. The knight was never happier to see the elf than he was at that moment.

"Sok!" Arthur cried out when he saw his friend and his horse approaching. "You found it!"

Sok assumed Arthur meant the horse, but he was referring to the chalice. "She was grazing by the side of the trail a way back. I thought it was yours."

"Why did you think it was mine?" Arthur asked as he flipped open the saddle bag and pulled out the bundle containing the chalice. Just then Hiro, Anayah and Bon came around a bend on the hover gilly. "Oh, hey! You're all here! We've been looking for you."

"What's that?" Sok asked, dismounting. He decided it was safer to ask about the bundle than it was to answer Arthur's question.

Davynn's relief was replaced by ardour when he saw Anayah. Their eyes locked. Davynn beamed at her and Anayah returned his smile with one of her own. He jumped down from his horse and tethered it securely to a tree branch before he ran to meet her.

A noisy reunion ensued as the six friends all greeted each other by exchanging bits and pieces about the last nine days and naturally slipping into a lively discussion about what it all meant. Eventually, they circled back to the bundle in Arthur's hand.

"It's really an ugly thing, isn't?" Sok said when Arthur finally unwrapped the Amber Chalice and held it up for them all to see.

Anayah stared at it through a frown on her face. "Wow! I expected it to be shiny and with fewer holes," she said.

"It's been buried under a huge standing stone in the Fae Lands for a long time. All things considered, I think it's in remarkable shape."

"Hmm..." Anayah reached out to touch it, but Arthur pulled it away.

"You can't touch it!" he snapped. "Only I can touch it."

"Sorry!" Anayah exaggerated the apology to the point of parody.

Arthur wrapped the chalice up in the shirt and tucked it back into the saddle bag. "We really should get going. It's past midday and..."

"I'm hungry."

Everyone looked at Sok.

"I'm going to start calling you Jughead Jones," Arthur said as he mounted his horse. Then his own stomach growled. "Hiro, you got anything we can munch on while we ride?"

The Krist giggled and then obliged by handing out sandwiches from his satchel to everyone.

"Who's Jughead Jones?" Sok asked. He took a bite of his chicken sandwich.

"He's a tall, skinny guy from Riverdale who never stops eating," Arthur said. He waited for the others to mount and board their respective modes of transportation.

"Riverdale. That's in Ecaep, isn't it? How do you know someone from Ecaep?" Sok was genuinely curious.

"Never mind, Juggie," Arthur said with a giggle of his own. "Let's get moving."

As the reunited group moved along the trail toward the lair, they continued to chat. Davynn wanted to know why they had taken the hover gilly above the trees the way they had.

"That was Sok's idea," Anayah said. "He wanted to keep an eye out for the teal dragon as well as look for you two. And he thought he could do both from up there."

"Did you see it?" Arthur asked.

"No," Sok said.

"You didn't see us either," Davynn added.

"It was Anayah's turn to watch the trail." Sok defended himself. "She's the one that didn't see you."

"How was it my turn?" Anayah asked. "I didn't even know I was supposed to be watching the trail."

"Well, *someone* was supposed to be watching the trail!" Sok snapped.

"Sorry I asked," Davynn said. "When is the challenge supposed to take place anyway?"

"Mid-afternoon today, I think," Sok said.

"How do you know that?" Arthur asked.

"Harpur signaled me from the lair," Sok explained.

"He signaled you? How?"

"We have a secret code," Sok said.

"You're about as helpful as Jack and Diane!" Arthur rolled his eyes.

"Who are Jack and Diane?" Anayah asked.

Arthur stopped his horse and looked around. "Where are Jack and Diane?"

Davynn did the same. "I have no idea. They were with us at the tree, weren't they?"

"Who are Jack and Diane?" Sok repeated Anayah's question.

"My guardians," Arthur said. "They are back."

"I thought your guardians' names were Ralph and Holly," Anayah said, confused.

"They were on Mysturna," Arthur said with a shrug, "but here they prefer to be called Jack and Diane."

"And they are dressed like pirates," Davynn contributed.

"Pirates?" Sok and Anayah said at the same time.

"More or less," Arthur said. "They don't have eye patches, peg legs or parrots, but other than that, they look the part."

Sok and Anayah tried to imagine the nearly naked couple they met on Mysturna in pirate garb.

"Why pirates?" Sok wondered aloud.

"Why nearly naked?" Arthur shot back. "Who knows? I'm just glad they were fully dressed."

"So, when did they show up?" Anayah asked.

"Just before we got to the Fae lands," Arthur said. He looked around again for his swashbuckling guardians, unsure how he felt about their disappearance.

"You look worried," Anayah said.

"It's just odd not having them around," Arthur replied.

"I for one am glad we don't have to watch them... you know... every time we turn around," Sok said. He was not concerned in the least.

"They aren't like that here," Arthur said. "They've actually been kind of helpful."

"Seriously?" Sok was staring at the half-eaten sandwich in Arthur's hand. "Are you going to finish that?"

Arthur looked down at his food. "Yes," he said, taking a bite, "I am!"

"Hiro, are there more sandwiches in your bag?" Sok asked.

Hiro giggled and told the elf to help himself. "Thanks!" Sok pulled two thick slices of dark bread filled with shredded pork drenched in a spicy sauce. "Whoa! This is fantastic!"

"Do you think we should look for Jack and Diane?" Arthur asked Davynn.

"I think Jack and Diane are quite able to take care of themselves," Davynn answered. "They said they would stay as long as you needed their help; maybe you don't need their help anymore."

"Yeah," Sok said. His lips were covered in the spicy sauce. "You got us now! We're obviously all the help you need."

Davynn glowered at the elf. "He was doing just fine with me."

"No offense, Davynn," Sok mumbled around another mouthful of what Bon informed him was called barbequed pulled pork, "but it can't be a coincidence that Arthur's guardians appeared when it was just the two of you and then vanished when we showed up. You guys have got to try one of these sandwiches!"

As they progressed closer to the lair, the banter faded away. No one on that trail through Braydon Wood knew what they would find when they reached their destination and not even barbequed pulled pork was enough to distract them from their fear for long. The idea of losing Harpur was more than any of them could begin to fathom, in spite of the fact that he had told them all that at some point he would be challenged. And he might lose.

Whenever there was a gap in the canopy or they passed through a clearing, they all scanned the sky, looking for the teal dragon to make an appearance. As time wore on, and there was no sign of the dragon, they began to dare to hope that Sok had been mistaken about the challenge. Or at least the time it was supposed to take place. Subconsciously, they picked up their speed until they were galloping through Braydon Wood as fast as the horses could go, for as long as the horses could sustain the gait.

All too soon, Davynn reined in his beast and slowed back down to a walk. He expected Arthur to protest, but the king acquiesced without complaint, possibly more relieved by the sedate pace than anxious to get to the lair. Either way, Davynn was grateful that he didn't have to justify his actions.

"We're not far from the lair," the knight said. "The trail is going to start to climb the mountain shortly. Harpur keeps a paddock below the lair just a short way off the main path to the meadow. We'll settle the horses there and then walk up the rest of the way."

Davynn led the way up the mountain path. The trees were thinner and shorter, giving them more opportunity to watch the sky. The closer they got, the more hopeful they felt.

"Sok, are you sure Harpur's signals meant mid-afternoon today?" Anayah asked.

"I'm positive. He was very precise." The elf said.

"You didn't count the days wrong again, did you?"

"I didn't count the days wrong the first time." Sok felt compelled to defend himself.

Anayah chose not to take the bait. "How much longer, Davynn?" she asked.

"The path to the paddock is just ahead," he replied. "From there, it's only a short walk to the meadow."

"I hope we're not too late," Sok said.

"Why would we be too late?" Anayah asked. "It's just mid-afternoon now."

"Alas, whatever business Harpur had today with the teal dragon, it is finished," Bon piped up.

"What do you mean?" Arthur twisted around as far as he could in his saddle to address the android.

"The teal dragon has come and gone," Bon said flatly.

"Bon?" Anayah said, "What are you saying?"

"She flew over us toward the lair just before we met in the woods," Bon explained, "right about the time Sok found Arthur's horse. She and a black dragon returned just after we passed the last clearing."

"Why didn't you tell us?" Anayah shouted.

"It did not seem prudent, Anayah," Bon said calmly. "Knowing would not have gotten us here any faster. It would, however, have contributed significantly to the level of stress each of you is experiencing. I believe that Harpur planned for you to arrive after the challenge was complete. I wanted this last leg of our journey to be as pleasant for you as possible."

For a while no one spoke. Arthur and Anayah were dumbstruck. The idea that the challenge could be over, was overwhelming. Davynn and Hiro saw the sense in Bon's actions and accepted it. Sok, on the other hand, surprised them all even more.

"Thank you, Bon," the elf said, laying a hand on the android's shoulder. "That was very kind of you."

They reached the path to the paddock and Davynn and Arthur veered off with the horses, leaving the occupants of the hover gilly to wait on the main trail. They unsaddled their mounts and left the saddles on a rock sheltered by an overhanging outcropping next to the small enclosure. Arthur used a bucket that he found tucked in next to the fence to fetch some water for the animals from a nearby waterfall that trickled down the mountain into a small creek. He filled the trough while Davynn wiped the horses down and when the animals were settled, they picked up their saddle bags and returned to the hover gilly.

Sok, Anayah and Bon all shuffled forward to make room on the floating chariot for Arthur and Davynn, but Arthur declined the silent invitation. "I think I prefer to walk," he said quietly.

Davynn nodded and joined his king at the front of the hover gilly and together they started up the trail. A moment later Sok fell into step beside them, followed by Anayah, who slipped her hand into Davynn's as they ascended the mountain.

Bon also stepped down from the hover gilly. But he walked behind it. As the newcomer to the group, his place was still uncertain and so he deferred to their solidarity as Harpur's long-time friends and companions.

Thus, the little parade made its way to the meadow.

Chapter Thirteen

The blue-green dragon drew near the meadow and Khol moved to the western end of the grassy field to make room for her to land. To Elder Dhonna, the expanse of grassland suddenly seemed small, filled as it was with the great bodies of the black and teal dragons. She gave Harpur one last pat on his huge foot.

"Orhowyn's blessings, my friend." She scrambled down from their perch above the lair and retreated, reluctantly, into its safety.

Harpur, the largest of the three dragons on the mountain, watched the elf until she entered the lair. Then he turned his attention to his challenger. "Welcome," he said.

The teal dragon nodded her head at the magnificent purple dragon. She sensed Harpur's weakness, but his size alone gave her pause. She took in the misshapen wing and the missing scales on his leg. It would be a ground fight, where his size could be to his disadvantage. "Greetings, Xzynthyrius Dreamfinder, Khol the Black. I apologize for being late. Khol asked me to give him some time with you before..."

"Khol has already explained," Harpur boomed. "Let's get this done."

Khol stepped forward to begin the proceedings. "Xzynthyrius Dreamfinder, also known as Harpur Diggins, you have been challenged for the ruling ownership of the kingdom of Epoh. Have you accepted this challenge willingly and without coercion?"

"I have," Harpur said.

"By whom have you been challenged and is your so named challenger present?"

"She is indeed present," Harpur said, "and her name is..."

"Wait!" A voice called out from the sky to the west.

Harpur, Khol and the challenger all turned to see two more dragons gliding toward the meadow. One purple and one green, each with the iridescent shades of the other running through their scales.

Harpur glared at Khol. "What have you done?"

The black dragon, nonplussed, shuffled to the eastern side of the meadow next to Harpur's equally astonished challenger. "This is not my doing, Harpur," he assured his host.

As the two new dragons alit on the meadow, crowding Khol and the challenger closer together, Elder Dhonna stepped out of the lair and stared at the spectacle before her. The sight of the four huge beasts, sparkling in the midday sun like giant gems, left her in awe. She wanted to climb back up to Harpur's side and talk to him, but she knew that he would not want her to. And then she realized who these two new dragons were.

"Framanjesk and Phiercesten, I presume," she said before she could stop herself.

Five sets of dragon eyes all swung in her direction. "Why is there an elf on the field?" the challenger hissed menacingly.

"Harm her," Harpur bellowed, "and not one, but four dragons will die in this meadow today."

Each of the dragons below him took the threat quite seriously and diverted their attention back to their host. In spite of his weaknesses, Harpur still presented an imposing figure and commanded their respect.

"What are you two doing here?" Harpur addressed his sons.

"We have come to petition for joint regency of Epoh," Phiercesten, the purple one announced.

Orhowyn's dusty bones! This can't be happening! Harpur was frantically trying to figure out how to get rid of his offspring. Their interference could put an end to his plan. And he couldn't have that.

"You have recognized us as your sons and have granted us the name Dreamfinder," Framanjesk, the green one said. "We demand..."

"You demand?" Harpur roared. "You demand what? To strip me of my right to defend *my* kingdom? The kingdom that I fought and killed for. What honour is there in obtaining rulership without earning it? If you wish to rule a kingdom, challenge a dragon and fight for it. Do not come to me begging for something you have not earned. Neither of you are fit to bear the Dreamfinder name."

Framanjesk and Phiercesten both lowered their heads.

"We meant no disrespect, Father," Framanjesk said.

"But know," Phiercesten continued, "if you lose to your challenger today, we will return to challenge her. She will not rule long in your stead. If you will not grant us joint regency, one of us will rule Epoh absolutely."

Harpur's sons shuffled awkwardly on the crowded meadow to turn around so they could leave. They'd made their point.

"Framanjesk and Phiercesten?" Harpur said before his purple son launched into the sky. "Scalla ap Averborn."

The young dragons exchanged looks, but did not reply. First Phiercesten, then Framanjesk sprang to the sky and flew northward over the mountain.

"Are you having second thoughts?" Khol whispered to the challenger before he returned to the spot Phiercesten had just abandoned.

The blue-green dragon was indeed having second thoughts. Harpur, even as weak as she sensed he was, was going to be difficult to defeat. His sons, however, would be impossible. But if she withdrew her challenge now, she would do so in shame, and she was not going to return to the Sands of Sancheera in anything but victory.

Elder Dhonna watched Phiercesten and Framanjesk fly away, but her thoughts were on Harpur's last words to them. Scalla ap Averborn. *Is that a name? Is it a place? What does it mean?* She retreated back into the entrance of the lair. The proceedings were about to resume.

Khol, also wondering about Harpur's enigmatic dismissal of his children, decided to get things moving along. Before anything else disrupted them. He knew that Harpur was planning something; he just didn't know what it was. And he didn't want to know. The faster this challenge was done, the faster he could return to Rednow and resume his life.

"You were about to name your challenger," Khol said to Harpur.

Harpur looked directly at the blue-green dragon standing below him in the meadow. "My challenger is present. Her name is Karrys Evergreen, sister to Karryl Evergreen."

A loud gasp was heard from the entrance to the lair and, once again, Elder Dhonna stepped out onto the meadow. "You're Harpur's mate's sister?" she demanded confirmation straight from the dragon's mouth.

"Bella Dhonna," Harpur said, "go back inside. Now is not the time for this."

The guild master walked further out into the meadow so she could glare up at Harpur. With her hands on her hips, she turned toward Khol. "Can I have a moment with Harpur, please?" She had so many questions.

"No!" Khol and Harpur shouted at the same time.

Elder Dhonna sensed Karrys shifting behind her and she turned to face Harpur's challenger. There were tendrils of smoke drifting out of the teal dragon's nostrils. Harpur was right; now was not the time for this. She retreated, muttering and cursing in Elven, back inside the lair.

Khol took a deep breath and pressed on. "And what are the terms of the challenge?"

"Karrys and I will fight until one of us is dead. Whichever one of us survives will rule Epoh. If I lose, Karrys agrees to give the people of Epoh safe passage and sufficient time to leave if she does not wish to allow them to stay within the kingdom. She also agrees not to burn my body or enter the lair for eight full days – starting tomorrow – to give my friends time to perform their death rituals in my honour," Harpur said.

"And if I lose, Harpur promises to burn my entire body where I fall immediately." Karrys looked at the skull on the edge of the meadow.

Khol followed her gaze and nodded. *That was not a very honourable thing to do to a challenger.* "Very well," he said, "and you both are in full agreement to these terms?"

"Yes."

"Yes."

"As your witness, it is my duty to ask if either of you wish to withdraw from this challenge. Harpur, you may invoke the Right of Survivorship, having two recognized heirs to which you may grant regency over Epoh if you wish." This last was delivered without hope.

"I do not wish to withdraw, nor do I wish to invoke the Right of Survivorship and bestow Epoh upon my sons," Harpur announced formally.

"And I do not wish to withdraw my challenge and lose my honour among dragonkind," Karrys said.

"Finally," Khol said, "Xzynthyrius Dreamfinder, also known as Harpur Diggins, do you vow to honour the final requests of Karryl Evergreen if you win?"

"I do."

"And do you, Karrys Evergreen vow to honour the final requests – no matter how peculiar they might be – of Xzynthyrius Dreamfinder, also known as Harpur Diggins, if you win?"

"I do."

"Then, as your witness, I declare this challenge valid. May the victor rule with honour; may the conquered find peace in Arachovor."

Khol had barely finished speaking when Harpur launched himself off of the mountainside with every ounce of power he could muster, straight down on top of Karrys. Not for a second had he given any thought to making this easy for her. He would fight for his life, fight to win, though he harboured no illusions about his chances for success. All that he had put in motion, his great contingency plan, was just that; a contingency plan.

He didn't believe that Karrys was doing this out of any desire for revenge for her sister. That would have been directed at Khol, had it existed. And it would have happened long before now. Like Harpur, she had warned Karryl against challenging Khol and had accepted the outcome. No, Karrys might have been ruthless, but she would not seek to destroy Harpur for the sake of destroying him. Her motivation to issue the challenge was one of opportunity. Harpur was weak enough to beat. It was that simple.

A deafening screech rose from Karrys as Harpur's weight and momentum drove her to the ground. She felt one of her talons snap off as it hit a buried rock when her left arm was driven straight into the earth beneath her. The jar to her shoulder sent a second wave of pain through her body and she collapsed, unable to rally from the unexpected blow in time to keep herself from being flattened.

Harpur clamped his mouth around Karrys' good arm and lifted it back and up, enabling him to reach the fleshy spot where her arm met her body and dug his talons into it, searching for an artery. If he could get to it, she would weaken fast and bleed out quickly. He felt the flesh give and was rewarded by a warm gush of blood.

Karrys screeched again. The realization of what he was trying to do to her gave her the impetus she needed to extract herself from her potentially fatal position. She worked her back legs under herself and with all her might, pushed herself up and forward, sending Harpur rolling away to her right. As soon as his weight was off her, she pulled herself up to her full height and leapt toward Harpur, mouth open, ready to clamp her strong jaws around his neck. But Harpur ducked and Karrys flew past him. He twisted and reached up, aiming for her groin and hoping to tear it open the same way he had her underarm. Karrys, sensing what he was about to do, kicked her leg forward into Harpur's own jaw and sent him reeling backward toward the drop off at the edge of the meadow. She fanned her wings out to slow her momentum and stop herself from sliding over the edge as well.

Harpur tucked his own wings in close to his body and twisted around so that he was facing his opponent. Karrys' maneuver gave Harpur time to right himself again and prepare for the next attack. He was behind her now, so he backed away to give himself room to launch himself at her again. She didn't notice his tactical retreat and swung her tail past the spot he had so recently occupied with the intention of knocking his legs out from under him. Her tail failed to meet with any resistance and the force of the swing was enough to throw her off balance so that when Harpur's body came at her again, the talon he'd intended to stab into her underarm met with her left eye instead.

Karrys reared up, screaming in pain. She blindly threw her neck and head at Harpur's unguarded shoulder, sending him flying off to the side. Too late, as Harpur tried to regain his balance, he saw the skull of the dragon that had challenged him so long ago. Time slowed as Harpur watched the single remaining upturned horn growing closer to his body. His full weight came down on the skull, crushing it to dust. But not before that weathered horn found the spot on his chest with the missing scale and pierced his heart.

"You have beaten me at last, my old friend." Harpur's last words drifted across the valley unheard.

The great purple dragon was dead.

Chapter Fourteen

Silence filled the meadow after Harpur Diggins fell.

Elder Dhonna, paralyzed by horror and grief, stood in the entrance to the lair with her hand over her mouth to stop herself from screaming. She wanted to run to him, but she dared not do it. There was no telling what Khol or Karrys might do to her. Without Harpur's protection, she had no idea if they would allow her near her friend's body. So, she stood where she was, tears pouring from her eyes. Afraid to move; afraid not to.

The world around her, blurred by her tears, was suddenly different. Empty. Lonely. Andy terrifying. *What if his plan doesn't work? What if Arthur can't do what he needs to do?*

The elf's mind reeled with dark thoughts, fueled by her grief. If ever she needed Sok to show up, it was then. But the senior advisor to the king of Epoh was still miles away.

On the other side of the meadow, Khol the Black approached Harpur's body and looked for signs of life. It was his duty as witness to ensure that death was final before declaring either opponent the winner and this he did with great sorrow. He had admired Harpur Diggins. As unconventional as he was, Harpur had always been an honourable dragon. Well, most of the time. The irony of Harpur meeting his demise the way he had was not lost on Rednow's ruler. *You should have burned all of him.*

"I hereby declare Karrys Evergreen the new ruler of the kingdom of Epoh," Khol said after he had made certain that Harpur was dead. He then turned to the victor. "How bad are your wounds?"

Karrys came forward, slowly. "I will heal," she said. "My eye, though…"

"Will be a reminder of this day for as long as you live," Khol said. "Why did you do this? Why Harpur? Why Epoh?"

"I grew tired of the Sands of Sancheera," she said. "And Harpur was…"

"Easy prey?" Khol finished for her, angrily.

"I didn't kill him, Khol," she said after a moment had passed. "He did not die from any wound inflicted by me."

"A mere technicality," Khol said. "You challenged him, the two of you fought and he died. That is the outcome you wanted, wasn't it?"

"I wanted to inherit Epoh honourably," Karrys hissed. "This isn't honour. This is Harpur Diggins' hubris come full circle. I cannot claim Epoh as mine, not like this."

Elder Dhonna, upon hearing this, gasped. The teal and the black dragons' heads turned slowly in her direction. Khol started toward her.

"No, Khol!" Karrys shouted. "You will not harm her."

"She's a witness. She knows what really happened." Khol continued toward the entrance to the lair.

Karrys leapt painfully in front of Khol to stop him. "I will not let you do this. We will seek the Council's advice. We will tell the truth. And we will accept whatever decision is made."

"So Harpur can have died for nothing? No, Karrys. If the Council rules against you, Framanjesk and Phiercesten will get the kingdom." Khol moved to step around Karrys.

"So be it," Karrys answered, shifting again to block his way.

"What happened to you, Karrys?" Khol asked. "You used to be so..."

"Pitiless? Brutal?" Karrys offered. When Khol did not respond, she continued, "I have learned that honour is all we have as dragons. Why are you so determined to cover this up? You were the one who didn't want me to challenge Harpur. You wanted him to invoke the Right of Survivorship and give Epoh to his sons. What happened to *you*, Khol?"

Khol puffed out a thick plume of black smoke. "You're right, I didn't want you to challenge Harpur. I admired Harpur. I suggested the Right of Survivorship because I didn't want to see him... come to his end like this. He was so very weak, Karrys. He didn't stand a chance against you. I thought you challenging him was dishonourable."

It was Karrys' turn to release a puff of smoke. "There was no weakness in the dragon I fought today. His injuries may have kept him on the ground, but Harpur was not feeble in any way."

An expression of realization passed over Khol's face. He looked around Karrys at Elder Dhonna, still standing in the entrance to the lair. "Elf, tell me what you did to make Harpur so strong? How did he manage to transform from his human guise?"

Elder Dhonna froze. *I'm going to die.*

"What are you talking about?" Karrys asked, confused.

"Harpur lost his magic months ago," Khol said. "I knew he was up to something, but..." He looked at Elder Dhonna again. "Tell us, elf. How did Harpur transform?"

"I... I gave him an herbal remedy to boost his strength," Elder Dhonna stammered. A half-truth was better than an outright lie. Not that she had the wherewithal just then to come up with a plausible lie.

"And what exactly was in this herbal remedy?" Karrys asked, turning to face Elder Dhonna head on.

"Just some bitterroot, some barbed Faeleaf, a bit of oak sap," she said. All true. She left out the dragonfoil ash and the incantation to activate it."

"You didn't use your magic to give Harpur his power?" Khol asked.

"I most certainly did not!" Elder Dhonna thought it was time to defend herself with a bit of good offence. "How dare you suggest such a thing! I am a healer. And an elf. I do not possess such magic. I couldn't have performed such a feat if I wanted to. And I sorely wanted to! If I could have helped Harpur win today using magic, you can bet your slimy scales I would have!" She crossed her arms and glared as menacingly as she could at the two huge beasts before her.

Khol and Karrys looked at each other.

"We are going to the Council of Dragons," Karrys reaffirmed. "And you, elf, are coming with us."

Elder Dhonna had not expected this. She couldn't leave the lair. Not now. Not until Arthur arrived with the chalice and she told him what he needed to do with it. "I can't go to the Sands of Sancheera! I wouldn't last five minutes there."

"We will take you to Andonsheer. There's a compound there for dragons. You will be kept safe," Karrys said.

"No!" Elder Dhonna shouted. "I will not go with you. You two can go and sort out your problems on your own." She backed into the lair and rushed over to her satchel. Reaching inside it, she retrieved a stylus and some parchment and scribbled a quick note to Sok. "You can't come in here. You can't make me go with you."

Khol and Karrys both grimaced impatiently.

"Do you want to do it? Or should I?" Khol asked.

"I'll do it," Karrys said. "I don't want her crushed or dropped before we get to Andonsheer."

With that, the one-eyed teal dragon waved her talons and magically pulled Elder Dhonna out of the lair and into her grip.

While the terrified and angry guild master struggled and cursed in Karrys' hand, the two dragons moved to the edge of the meadow and got ready to fly to Andonsheer.

"Are you okay to fly?" Khol asked.

"I'm fine. My wounds were all fairly superficial. But stay on my right so I can see where you are." Karrys waited until Khol was airborne before launching herself skyward.

Arthur was the first to see Harpur's body lying in the grass at the edge of the meadow. He dropped the bundle containing the Amber Chalice on the ground and ran across the lea.

"No, no, no, no, no," he repeated as he dropped to his knees next to Harpur's head. "Please don't be dead," he begged. "Please don't be dead."

He barely noticed Sok and Anayah join him and lay their hands on Harpur's head. A soft blue light flowed from their palms into the dragon's body and when, only a few minutes later they withdrew it, Arthur grabbed their wrists and pushed their hands back onto Harpur's scales. "Don't stop! Why are you stopping?"

"He's gone," Anayah said softly. She pulled her hand away from Arthur's and stood up.

"Sok?" Arthur looked pleadingly at the elf.

Sok just shook his head. "Come," he said. "Let's go find Elder Dhonna and find out what happened here."

Together, Sok and Anayah helped Arthur to his feet. Tears betrayed their calm repose as they guided their distraught king away from Harpur's corpse. As they passed Davynn, who had remained standing a short distance away from them, Anayah let go of Arthur and let the knight fold her into his arms. They stood there, holding each other, while the others continued on to the lair to look for Elder Dhonna.

The lair, of course, was empty when the four companions entered it. Sok called out to Elder Dhonna, hoping she was just hiding somewhere among the treasures that filled the vast space. When she didn't answer, he felt panic seize him. "Elder Dhonna! Where are you?" he shouted. But only his own echo replied.

"Her satchel is here," Hiro said. "She can't have gone far." He floated on his hover gilly to the flattened stalagmite on which it sat. Reaching over the side of the chariot, he lifted the satchel and found the scribbled note that the guild master had left for Sok. Wanting to believe it was an assurance of her safety, a missive to inform them she had just gone into the woods for some reason and would return soon, he picked it up. "She's left us a note, but it's written in Elven."

Sok left Arthur sobbing where he stood and walked over to Hiro. Wiping the tears from his eyes, he took the note from Hiro and read it. His pale features grew even paler as the words on the parchment sunk in. He read it again, hoping it would say something different this time.

"What does it say?" Bon asked.

"Elder Dhonna has been taken," Sok whispered, his voice hoarse with fear.

Arthur's head snapped up. "What?" He sniffled. "Taken where?"

Sok, gripping the parchment with both hands, read it again. This time out loud. "'Sok. Need help. In Andonsheer. Dragons are questioning outcome of challenge. Arthur must fill chalice with Harpur's blood. Now. ED'"

"What does that mean?" Arthur asked. "What questions? How do I fill a holey cup with blood? Why would I even try?"

The signs of a classic Arthurian meltdown were evident in the high pitch of his voice and Sok didn't have time to indulge one. "Where is the chalice, Arthur?"

Arthur looked at his empty hands. "I don't know! I don't know!"

"Orhowyn's blood and bones!" Sok shouted.

He wanted to grieve for his dead friend. Instead, he had been thrown into full crisis mode. Elder Dhonna was in Andonsheer, probably taken there by Harpur's challenger. Arthur was having one of his fits and was in no shape to follow the vague instructions Elder Dhonna had left for him. And there were questions about the outcome of the challenge. Clearly, Harpur had lost. There was no question about that. The proof was laying lifeless in the meadow. *What happened here?*

He looked at Arthur, ranting in abject misery next to the hoard. *Nothing to do but let that run its course.* Then he turned to Hiro and Bon. "Let's go look for the chalice while he..." Sok flapped a hand in Arthur's general direction. "We need to find that chalice."

Sok marched out of the lair and nearly ran into Davynn and Anayah who were on their way in. The teary-eyed witch and the stoic knight side-stepped out of the charging elf's way and stopped to let him pass.

"Where are you going?" Davynn asked.

Sok did not reply.

Hiro and Bon floated past them in the angry elf's wake. "Arthur lost the chalice. We are going to look for it." Hiro supplied the answer to Davynn's question.

Davynn and Anayah looked at Arthur. He was pacing and babbling incoherently about dead dragons and holey chalices and kidnapped guild masters and missing his wife and babies. By mutual consent they opted to go back out and help search for the chalice.

Sok went back to Harpur's body. It seemed the most likely place for Arthur to have dropped the chalice. Hiro and Bon floated in the opposite direction to the trail they had come up on. Anayah and Davynn stood in between, unsure which way to go.

"Found it!" Hiro called.

They all ran over to where the hover gilly hovered next to the bundle containing the Amber Chalice and stood there looking at it. No one dared pick it up. Even though it was wrapped in Arthur's shirt, they weren't sure if don't touch it meant don't actually touch the cup or don't handle it at all.

"Someone needs to stay here and guard it," Sok announced. He was relieved to know where it was.

"Where's it going to go?" Anayah asked.

"I don't know, Anayah!" Sok barked. "But we can't let it out of our sight again!"

"I will stay and keep watch over the chalice," Bon volunteered.

The others looked back at the entrance to the lair. They could still hear Arthur's voice coming from inside. None of them wanted to go back in there. They turned toward Harpur's body. No one wanted to go there either. Sok did the only thing he could in the moment. He dropped to the ground, buried his face in his hands and cried.

Eventually, Davynn and Anayah did move back over to Harpur to pay their respects and say their good-byes. When they were done, Hiro and Bon did the same, leaving Sok where he was next to the chalice.

Arthur finally emerged from the lair, shaken and pale, but relatively more composed than he was when his friends had left him to his stress-induced paroxysm. "Guys?" he called out tenuously. He cleared his throat and tried again. "Guys?"

Three sets of puffy eyes turned in his direction along with two sets of clear, but sad, ones. No one moved.

"Guys, did you find the chalice?" Arthur asked humbly.

"It's over here," Sok said. He wiped away the tears and stood up. "We haven't touched it."

Arthur strode over to Sok. Before he bent to retrieve the precious bundle, he embraced the elf. "I'm sorry, Sok. We'll figure this out."

"That we will, sire," Sok said. "For Harpur."

"For Harpur." Arthur released his friend and picked up the chalice.

They convened by the entrance to the lair. Arthur sat on the boulder that Harpur and Elder Dhonna had occupied so often in the days leading up to the challenge while the others formed a semi-circle in front of him. He didn't feel much like a king, much less a leader capable of sorting out whatever had happened and finding a solution. That, it seemed to Arthur, had always been Harpur's job. *Now who will guide us?* he wondered.

Sok recognized the uncertainty in his king. Now that he had worked through the first bout of grief, he was ready to step up and do his best for their motley little band. But first he would give Arthur the means to allow him to do so. "What do you want to do next, sire?" he asked.

Arthur stared at the ground and shook his head. "I guess we need to make a plan," he said.

"Agreed," Sok said, testing the mantle of authority. "May I suggest that we start with what we know."

"What do we know?" Anayah asked.

"Well," Sok said, holding up a finger to enumerate the short list of facts at his disposal, "we know that Harpur did not survive the challenge. We know that there is some question about the outcome of the challenge, but we don't know what that is. We know that Elder Dhonna has been taken to Andonsheer, but we don't know why. And we know that Arthur has to fill the Amber Chalice with Harpur's blood, but we don't know how seeing as it's full of holes."

"How do we know all these things?" Davynn asked.

"Elder Dhonna left a note," Hiro said, pulling said note out of his satchel where he had stowed it after Sok left the lair to look for the chalice. He handed it to Anayah.

"It's in Elven," she said, handing it to Sok.

"Basically, it says that Elder Dhonna needs our help and that she's been taken to Andonsheer. She mentions that something happened during the challenge that brings the outcome into question and that Arthur needs to fill the chalice with Harpur's blood. Now!" Sok summarized.

"Hadn't Arthur better do that then?" Davynn suggested. "Harpur has been dead for several hours now; the longer he waits the harder it's going to be."

Arthur raised his head and unwrapped the chalice. "How?" he asked, holding it up so they could all see the holes. "It's a sieve."

"Trust the process," Sok said, standing and clapping Arthur on the shoulder. "If Harpur says you have to fill the chalice, then it's got to be fillable. Somehow."

"Why do I have to fill it with his blood, though?" Arthur shuddered at the thought.

"That we don't know," Sok said, beckoning Arthur to follow him to Harpur's body. "Yet!"

Once again, they all made their way across the meadow to Harpur's body.

"I don't see any wounds," Arthur observed with a glimmer of hope in his voice.

Davynn and Bon both began walking around the enormous corpse, searching for an open wound from which Arthur could draw blood. Harpur lay prone at the edge of the meadow, his legs and arms splayed outward under the wide expanse of his wings. There was little room between his body and the steep drop off to the valley. Davynn inched along the length of Harpur's neck on the valley side until he reached Harpur's leg. Beneath the canopy of the wing, he could see where the blood from Harpur's fatal wound had spread out and trickled over the edge.

"However he died, the wound is on his chest," Davynn reported from his precarious perch. He reached down to feel the sticky purple-red fluid that had pooled on the ground. "It's not quite dry. If we can roll him over, maybe we can get to the wound and get what we need."

"Roll him over?" Arthur said. "How in Orhowyn's name are we going to do that?"

"Oh, I don't know," Davynn said sarcastically. "If only we had a powerful witch or a burgeoning wizard to help us."

Arthur blushed. He'd quite forgotten his new-found ability to wield magic with some measure of success.

"I don't know if I can do it alone," Anayah said as she considered how to use her magic to move the enormous cadaver.

"I can help," Arthur said.

"I've heard about your adventures with magic," Anayah quipped. "Apparently, they leave a lot to be desired. I will try it myself."

"No!" Arthur said forcefully. "I can do this. Jack and Diane helped me figure it out. I wonder what happened to them anyway."

"I told you, Arthur," Sok chimed in, "you have us now; you don't need their help anymore."

Arthur frowned at the elf.

"Arthur really is getting better with his magic," Davynn said supportively. "He pulled the chalice out from under a standing stone and he conjured jamba and food for us on the trail." Kindly, he didn't mention the mishaps with the ale and the tent.

"Alright, then," Anayah said. "Let's give it a try. But we have to work together. We'll need to lift him straight up and then roll him over so we don't break his legs."

"Got it!" Arthur exclaimed.

Prudently, in spite of his glowing endorsement of Arthur and his magic, Davynn moved to the far side of the meadow near the mountain and motioned for Sok, Hiro and Bon to join him. Arthur scowled at their retreating backs, but when Anayah moved back and toward the end of Harpur's tail, he realized that Davynn's pragmatic move was more than a mere gesture. He too stepped back and toward Harpur's head.

"Okay, Arthur," Anayah called from her end of the body. "We're going to lift until his legs are clear of the ground and then roll him toward the mountain."

Arthur gave her the thumbs up and closed his eyes to concentrate.

Anayah glanced over at Davynn, who gave her a double thumbs-up accompanied by an encouraging smile and a nod. She took a deep breath and then turned her full attention to the task at hand. She could sense Arthur's magic building from across the meadow and she was impressed by its strength and stability. As she added her own magic to the mix, Harpur began to shift. They focused their efforts on the mass of his body, letting his head, neck, limbs and tail follow the huge bulk as it rose. *Steady, Arthur. Keep it steady.*

Arthur's eyes remained closed as Harpur's body slowly levitated farther from the ground. Anayah wasn't sure if she should say anything; the risk of distracting him was too great. In spite of his self-imposed blindness, as soon as Harpur's feet cleared the ground, Arthur's magic shifted subtly and the body started to rotate. She could see the strain on Arthur's face, but his magic remained smooth, steady and strong. When Harpur was turned so that he was laying on his side, Arthur's magic shifted again and the enormous purple dragon started moving parallel to the ground toward the mountain. Anayah wasn't expecting this. She looked at Arthur, ready to shout at him to stop, but the strain she had noted a moment before was gone, replaced by a blissful calm, and she instinctively let him take over and finish the job. Moments later, Harpur lay on his side in the middle of the meadow and Anayah ran to Arthur and threw her arms around him.

"That was amazing!" she cried. "You did it!"

A volley of cheers rose from the small audience on the other side of the meadow and the others jogged or floated back to them.

Arthur returned the embrace. "I felt you working with me, and then you were gone."

"You seemed to have everything under control. I didn't want to mess anything up for you." Anayah laughed. "I'm not sure I could have done it by myself. Well done, wizard-king!"

Arthur liked the sound of that. But before he could celebrate his achievement, he needed to complete the chore he'd been assigned by the deceased Harpur Diggins. Fill a hole-ridden cup with the dragon's blood.

He had set the chalice down in the grass before performing the magical relocation and he picked it up again. Unwrapping it, he walked around Harpur to look for a wound from which he could gather the required gore. When he reached the belly side of the body, he nearly dropped the chalice again. There, sticking out of the middle of Harpur's chest, was what looked like a large shard of bone.

"Whoa! Where did that come from?" Arthur asked in repulsed awe.

"Where *did* what come from?" Sok asked as he came up to Arthur from the other end. "Orhowyn's horns and... Wait!" Sok spun around and examined the edge of the meadow. "I think I know what happened."

One by one, the others made their way to where Arthur was standing, staring at the fatal wound in Harpur's chest. Blood still trickled out between the bone shard and the flesh it had torn through, enough, it appeared to fill the chalice. If only the chalice could be filled. Arthur was baffled.

Sok was squatting next to a large pile of blood-soaked bone fragments at the edge of the meadow. "Look at this," he said.

Everyone turned to look.

"What is it?" Arthur asked.

"Notice anything missing?" Sok countered.

"The dragon skull," Davynn deduced. "Harpur fell on the dragon skull and the horn pierced his heart."

The significance of it was lost on Arthur, Anayah, Hiro and Bon.

"Exactly!" Sok exclaimed, standing up again. "The wrong challenger killed Harpur."

"What are you talking about?" Arthur asked.

"Dragons cannot use weapons of any kind against each other in a challenge. They typically don't use weapons ever, but never in a challenge. Technically, the challenger that Harpur defeated here hundreds of years ago killed him, not the challenger he fought today," Sok explained. "Thus, the questions about the outcome."

"And because Elder Dhonna saw what happened, they took her to Andonsheer to... What?" Davynn asked.

"That I don't know," Sok said. "But I do know that Arthur had better fill that chalice before Harpur's blood is completely drained."

They all turned and faced the wound again. "This isn't going to work," Arthur said.

Sok moved to stand next to his king. "Like I said before, Arthur. Trust the process."

Arthur shrugged his shoulders and forced himself to approach Harpur's body. He stepped carefully to avoid the blood that was pooling on the ground beneath the wound. Bracing himself with one hand on Harpur, he reached over and pressed the Amber Chalice against the scales just below the protruding horn.

"It really is an ugly thing!" Davynn reiterated the sentiments of everyone who had seen the chalice and was rewarded with nods of agreement.

The rim of the chalice diverted some of Harpur's blood over its edge and down the inside of the cup. At first, as Arthur had expected, the purple-red fluid simply drained back out of the holes. Then something strange began to happen. The chalice started to feel warm in Arthur's hand. The more blood that ran into it, the hotter it got until it was glowing like an ember in a fire. Being impervious to fire due to the dragon's blood that flowed in Arthur's own veins, the heat was not an issue. All he felt was a pleasant warmth.

"Orhowyn's ashes!" Arthur cried.

"What?" five voices behind him asked.

"The chalice! It's... It's healing itself!" He didn't know how else to describe what he was seeing.

The others moved in closer to see for themselves, but the heat from the chalice kept them from getting close enough to see anything through the blinding glow surrounding it and Arthur's hand.

"This is incredible!" Arthur said excitedly.

Arthur kept the chalice in place for several more minutes while a spectacular transformation unfolded before his eyes. First, the holes sealed. Then the surface of the cup smoothed out and a stem and pedestal formed at the bottom. A bright gold veneer appeared, covering the entire surface. And, finally, a pattern of embossed runes appeared around the top of the cup just above the amber stone. It began to cool and when it was full, Arthur pulled it away from Harpur's body and held it up for the others to see.

"It's beautiful!" Anayah said in a tone hushed by awe.

"Trust the process, indeed!" Arthur said. Then he noticed the amber stone. "Does this mean that Willow isn't pleased with what I've done to the chalice?"

He turned the cup around so the others could see the vortex in the center of the stone. Purple-red swirls were now mixed with the green, purple and orange ones that were there when Arthur first recovered the chalice. And the blue and white sparks around the edge were infused with purple-red ones as well.

"No," Sok said. "I think that means that Harpur's essence is now in there with Willow's"

"Cool," Arthur said, slightly relieved and hoping that Sok was right. "Now, what do I do with it?"

That was another question that no one knew the answer to.

The sun was beginning to set in the west and as the light faded, so did their collective energy. A wave of grief swept over them again and more tears began to flow. They were tired. They were sad. And they were hungry.

"Might I suggest a wake for Harpur," Hiro said, his signature giggle replaced by a gentle sniffle.

"I think that is a wonderful idea," Arthur said. "There's not much we can do for Elder Dhonna until we can form a plan and we're all too tired to do that now. Let's celebrate our lost friend. Then we can decide what to do next after a good rest."

Sok was torn. He was worried about Elder Dhonna and wanted to help her as quickly as possible. But he knew that Arthur was right. "Yes, let's celebrate that cranky old dragon's incredible life."

"I'm going to go check on the horses," Davynn announced, "and make sure they are okay for the night."

"I'll go with you," Anayah said between fresh sobs.

While the witch and the knight walked arm-in-arm across the meadow, Hiro began setting things up for a picnic near the entrance to the lair. Arthur placed the transformed Amber Chalice on the boulder next to the entrance and then managed to create some magical glowing orbs that floated above them, providing light. Bon gathered wood and laid a small fire and Sok sat on the boulder next to the chalice, thinking.

By the time Davynn and Anayah returned from tending the horses, the feast was ready and they all sat down on the ground, except for Sok, to begin eating some of Harpur's favourite foods and toasting his memory with large flagons of ale. Soon they were sharing stories of their adventures with the larger-than-life dragon-wizard. There were more tears. There was some laughter. But all too soon it was time to call it a night. Arthur and Anayah conjured mats, blankets and pillows for everyone who needed them. Hiro, of course, pulled his own from his satchel.

"Do you want me to conjure a hammock for you, Sok?" Anayah asked, knowing that the elf would prefer to sleep outdoors.

"No, thank you," Sok replied from his place on the boulder. "I'll be fine."

Anayah simply nodded. She patted Sok on the shoulder and bid him good night.

Bon, not needing to sleep, informed the group that he was going to spend the night exploring the forest and that he would return in the morning.

When everyone had settled into their beds, Sok returned to Harpur's body. "I know this isn't the end of our story, old friend," he said as he curled up in the crook of Harpur's jaw and went to sleep.

Elder Dhonna sat in her cell in the dragon compound on the outskirts of Andonsheer. She may not have been in the desert proper, but it was still hot in this part of the world and her soot-stained dress was clinging to her in ways she felt were somewhat less than dignified.

She had been escorted to the cell by Karrys Evergreen and warned not to try to escape. They would come for her when the Council was ready, which, to Elder Dhonna, was beyond farcical. The cell itself would have felt cramped and confining to any dragon, but to her it was on a palatial scale, some sixty wide, forty feet deep and at least fifty feet high. And the bars, clearly designed to imprison much larger beings than elves, were set a good three feet apart. All she had to do was walk through them. Which she did. Several times.

There were no guards to be seen anywhere. But the cell was situated in an enormous building right in the middle of the northern wall of the compound and the only dragons present, namely Karrys and Khol, were in dragon form. She doubted she would get very far if she tried to escape. An elf running around a dragon fortress would be noticed. And probably burned to a crisp on the spot. So, she stayed put and hoped that Sok found her note and figured out a way to rescue her.

In spite of its size, the cell offered little worth exploring. In one corner there was a pile of junk, broken forges and pieces of wagons, presumably there as a mocking parody of a dragon hoard on which the usual type of prisoner was meant to sleep. In the opposite corner was a large trough big enough that Elder Dhonna could have swum in it. But she wasn't sure if it was there to provide hydration or serve as a commode. Either way, she wasn't touching the fetid water it was filled with. All she could do was sit and wait. And hope she didn't die of thirst before she could get out of there.

She was hot, thirsty and tired. More than this, though, she was terrified. Harpur was the only dragon she had ever known and she had always felt safe with him. Whether he was in dragon form or his human guise, she never once feared for her life or her safety. The thought of him brought on another wave of tears, precious fluid she could not afford to lose. It took all of her willpower to fight against the grief and not allow herself to cry. So, she sat and waited.

As evening descended, so did the temperature. Elder Dhonna found herself shivering violently. She didn't know which was worse, the heat or the cold. She forced herself to run around the cell to warm up, but that just made her thirst worse. Then she noticed some wood, broken pieces of planking, among the junk in the corner. She wrestled it out into the middle of the cell and then went back to look for something she could use to cut it down into smaller chunks and found a broken tip from a plough and heavy iron bar. She used these to split the dried-out old planks and laid the thinner pieces out crisscrossing each other in a pile. She gathered the larger splinters that had fallen off of the planks to use as kindling.

In Elder Dhonna's long career as a healer, she often had to use heat to soothe sore muscles. She sometimes did this by applying her hands to the affected area and generating heat through her healing magic into the patient's body. She had no idea if she could generate enough heat to ignite the wood, but she had to try. She could have applied this same warm healing to herself, but only in small patches and not for long. A fire would keep her warm all over and last throughout the night.

She wedged a thin splinter of wood between two larger pieces and cupped her hands around its end. A soft blue energy flowed from her palms, growing darker and more intense as she focused on making it heat up. But she had to stop after only a few seconds; the heat was too much for her to bear. She needed something to make a tinder bed with, something that would ignite faster than the wood. The only thing in the cell that might work was her own dress. So, she tore a strip off the hem and shredded it as best she could in the hope that the natural fiber would burn.

Once again, she applied her healing magic to it, heating it up as much as she could stand. Several long and painful seconds passed, but finally a thin tendril of smoke started to rise from the shredded cloth. She kept her magic flowing hot for a few more seconds until she saw a tiny flame, and then quickly withdrew her hands and applied cooling magic to them. The tiny flame grew and spread across the fabric tinder bed. It lasted long enough for the kindling to catch it and soon she was sitting next to a blessedly warm fire.

"Thank Harpur," she muttered.

Just as the heat from the fire had chased the worst of her shivering away, Karrys Evergreen appeared at the cell door. "What are you doing?"

Elder Dhonna stood up and glared at her captor. "I'm trying not to freeze to death! You leave me here in this Orhowyn-forsaken cell with no food or water, not even a mat to sleep on. I sweltered in the heat and froze when the sun went down. Do you have a problem with me trying to stay alive long enough to do whatever you brought me here to do?"

"My apologies," Karrys said, taken aback by Elder Dhonna's outburst. "That was an oversight. I will bring you food and water and something to sleep on." She turned to leave.

Elder Dhonna ran over to the door and leaned out between the bars. "Why don't you just conjure it up now?"

"I beg your pardon?" Karrys said. "What makes you think that I am capable of such a feat?"

Elder Dhonna was starting to shiver again. "I know all about the scope of dragons' magic. I know you have the ability to conjure. So, conjure already. I'm cold and I'm hungry!"

It was true that dragons tended not to use their magic openly in the presence of other races. Even Harpur had maintained the ruse and only presented himself in his natural dragon form to the people of Epoh. Until he discovered Arthur on Earth and realized that he possessed magic of his own. Harpur had then chosen to stay on Earth to keep an eye on Arthur, living in his human form most of the time and, thus, sacrificed his own magic and healing ability. He had revealed his magic to Edlyngton Bloomregaard and, unknown to him at the time, had been seen by Sok. After that, there was not much point in pretending that his only skills were breathing fire and terrorizing villages.

"Harpur really did do things unconventionally, didn't he?" Karry noted. "How many others are aware of our abilities?"

Too late, Elder Dhonna realized that she had gone too far. She had no idea how bad it was that Harpur's magic had more or less become common knowledge in Colwygshire. *Do dragons kill people to keep the secret?* "Only myself, as far as I know," she lied, not wanting to put any of Harpur's friends or subjects in danger. "Harpur and I were very close."

"I see," Karrys said. "I hope that is true." She lowered her head to Elder Dhonna's level and turned it to stare at the elf with her one good eye. "I also hope you are good at keeping secrets."

The teal dragon turned and left Elder Dhonna in her cell.

"Don't forget my food and water!" the elf called out. "And a blanket and a mat!"

Karrys did not respond. But she did return only moments later with a mat and a blanket, a waterskin and a whole cooked goose.

"I trust that these will suffice," the dragon said as she passed the welcome comforts through the bars of the cell.

"Thank you, yes," Elder Dhonna said. "I will also need a commode of some sort."

"Of course," Karrys said with restrained politeness. "I should have realized. I will be right back."

Again, the dragon left the cell and again she returned a few minutes later, this time with a large bucket. "Will this do?"

"It will." Elder Dhonna accepted the improvised latrine. "Thank you. How long do I have to stay here?"

"Not long," Karrys said. "The Council will convene in two days. Khol and I will present our versions of the challenge and then they will deliberate. That could take a day or so. They may or may not decide that they want to hear your account of things. Either way, they will want to know that you are aware of our magic."

Elder Dhonna blanched. "What will they do to me when they find out?"

"It's hard to say," Karrys answered. "There are a few dragons on the Council who look favorably upon the elven race. If you can convince them that you will not share what you know about us with anyone, they may set you free."

"And if I can't?" Elder Dhonna asked.

"I promise you, your death will be quick."

With tears of desperation in her eyes, Elder Dhonna returned to her little fire and ate the most ironic meal of her life.

The occupants of Harpur's lair awoke to a dull day. The sky, stippled in a dense cloud-cover, threatened more rain. They elected to break their fast inside and Hiro quickly set to work preparing an elegant repast of something Bon called Eggs Benedict with hash-browns.

"Mmm..." Anayah cooed. "It's been ages since I've had this." She recalled eating the rich breakfast at a little restaurant she and Harpur frequented when they lived on Whyte Avenue in Edmonton.

Arthur, too, was savoring his meal, a favourite of his from home on Earth. Unaware of the various Earth food that Bon had taught Hiro to conjure, he was curious how Hiro came to create it. "Where did you learn to make Eggs Benedict?" he asked.

"Bon has been teaching me how to prepare food from your world," the Krist replied. "I'm learning all sorts of interesting new recipes. When we get back to Colwygshire, Bon is going to show me how to make something called turducken!"

"Turducken?" Arthur was impressed. "That ought to be interesting. Bon, how do you know how to cook Earth food? I thought you were from Mysturna."

"I know many things from many places." As usual, Bon's answer was vague and enigmatic.

"Where is Sok?" Anayah asked. She knew that even if pressed, Bon would not relent and reveal where he came from. Orhowyn only knew how hard she'd tried to learn of his origins when they were alone in the Sphere on Mysturna.

The elf had yet to join them.

"He's probably still sleeping in a tree somewhere," Arthur theorized. "He'll be along soon. His stomach will lead him back to us, I'm sure."

Everyone laughed.

"What did you call him yesterday?" Davynn asked.

Arthur laughed again. "Jughead Jones. He's a character from a comic book who eats a lot of hamburgers."

"What's a comic book?" Hiro asked, hooked by the word book.

"Um,... They're books with drawings that help tell the story," Arthur explained in the simplest of terms. "I'll bet Bon knows what they are."

Everyone looked at the android who recognized the bait he'd been thrown. "I am familiar with the concept of graphic novels," he said. But he offered no more.

"When we get back to the castle," Anayah said to Hiro, "I will show you what they look like. I think you will enjoy them."

"Speaking of getting back to the castle," Arthur said, patting his full and sated stomach, "we need to round up Sok and figure out what we are going to do about Elder Dhonna."

"I will go and look for him," Bon offered. He left the lair without waiting for a response.

"Why won't Bon tell us where he's from?" Davynn asked.

"He's just a private android, I guess," Anayah said, shrugging. "I tried to get him to open up when we were in the Sphere, but he masterfully deflected every attempt I made to get him to tell me. Eventually, I gave up. I'd like to believe he will tell us when he's ready."

"Well, that was delicious, Hiro," Arthur said. "Thank you. I can't wait to try the turducken."

"What exactly is turducken?" Davynn asked.

"It's a deboned chicken inside a deboned duck inside a turkey. I don't know if the turkey is deboned or not," Arthur said.

"The turkey is deboned as well," Anayah contributed. "Harpur and I had it once on Whyte Avenue. It was very good."

"Why would anyone stuff a chicken and a duck into a turkey?" Davynn asked.

"Mostly because they can," Arthur said. He stood up and stretched and patted his stomach again. "Hiro, I don't suppose you have a toothpick in your satchel. There's a piece of ham stuck in my teeth."

"What's a toothpick?" Hiro and Davynn both asked.

Anayah conjured a toothpick for Arthur and the knight and the Krist watched in fascination as he used it to release the offending piece of meat from between his molars.

Just then Bon returned with Sok following behind him.

"Good morning," Arthur greeted the elf.

"What's for breakfast?" Sok asked, then hastily added, "Good morning."

"Eggs Benedict," Hiro announced, handing Sok a plate.

"Smells divine!" Sok said, lowering himself to sit cross-legged on the ground and taking his first bite. "Wow!" As he chewed and swallowed, he gave Hiro a thumbs up.

"While Sok catches up on breakfast," Arthur said, "we might as well figure out what we are going to do."

"We are going to Andonsheer to rescue Elder Dhonna," Sok said.

"Obviously," Arthur retorted. "But what's the plan?"

"We go to Andonsheer, find out where the dragons are keeping her and we rescue her." Sok took another bite of egg smothered in Hollandaise sauce.

Arthur sighed. "How?"

"How what?" Sok asked.

"How do we get to Andonsheer? How do we find out where Elder Dhonna is? How do we rescue her?"

"One step at a time, Arthur," Sok said. "First, we get to Andonsheer. I vote Anayah zaps us there."

Everyone looked at Anayah. "I can do that," she said.

"We can't leave the horses here unattended indefinitely. We have to take them back to Colwygshire first," Davynn said with finality.

"That will take three days," Sok said. "We can't waste that much time. We don't know why the dragons took her there or how long they intend to keep her."

"Sok's right," Arthur said. "And in all honesty, I don't think we all need to go. Davynn, why don't you take the horses back to the castle? Hiro and Bon can stay here and make sure nothing happens to... Does anyone remember where I put the chalice?" He scratched his head and looked contrite.

"Seriously, Arthur?" Sok shook his head.

"The chalice is still on the boulder outside the lair." Bon quickly resolved that potential argument.

"Right!" Arthur said, trying to sound like he'd intended to leave it there.

"So, I just take the horses back to the castle and then what? I don't get to be part of this anymore?" Davynn sounded insulted.

"You're the one who's more concerned about a couple of horses than you are about Elder Dhonna," Sok shot back.

"Stop it, you two," Anayah snapped. "How about this? Davynn will take the horses to Colwygshire and when we return with Elder Dhonna, I will zap myself to the castle and zap us both back here to the lair. Nobody gets left out."

"So, just you, me and Arthur are going to Andonsheer," Sok clarified.

"I think it will be easier for three of us to get in and get out without drawing too much attention to ourselves, don't you?" Anayah reasoned.

"That makes sense," Arthur said, "but can I suggest one little change to that plan?"

"What's that?" Davynn asked.

"It's not that I don't want to help rescue Elder Dhonna," the king and new father said, "but I want to go with Davynn and see Alex and the twins. It's been nearly a fortnight since I left them and, well, two is even more discreet than three." He looked at Sok, pleading for understanding.

Sok heaved a great sigh and stood up. He wanted to be angry, but he understood. He looked at Anayah. "Do you think we can handle this on our own without killing each other?"

"We managed not to kill each other while we were holed up in the ravine," Anayah said. "Besides, I think we're far more likely to be killed by the dragons than we are by each other. If Bon and Hiro are okay with waiting here with the chalice, I think we have a plan."

Bon merely nodded.

"That sound good to me," the Krist said with a gleeful giggle. "I know it's not entirely above-board, but under the circumstances, I don't think Harpur would mind if I poked around a bit in here..." Hiro's eyes shifted toward the hoard.

"Just don't take anything," Arthur warned him.

"Oh, no! I wouldn't dream of it," Hiro said innocently.

And with that, the six companions prepared for their respective new missions.

Chapter Fifteen

Elder Dhonna had spent a fitful night alone in the vast cell. The fire she had lit the night before had gone out and the cell was as cold as it was before she had lit it. As she would soon discover, it would remain that way until mid-morning when the hot Andonsheer sun would force the cold out of the stone walls that surrounded her. She sipped from the water skin Karrys had brought her, rationing the life-saving liquid it contained. She didn't know if Karrys would even return, much less check on her to see if she needed anything. Then she chewed on some more irony, knowing that the heat would spoil the goose carcass in short order.

She had not slept well, waking at every little noise in hope that it was Sok come to rescue her. Not knowing if he had even found her note, she couldn't help but worry that she might just be left to the mercy of the dragons. As the morning dragged slowly on and the temperature began to soar, Elder Dhonna decided that she needed to find a way to keep busy. It was the only way she was going to keep dark thoughts from taking over.

She rummaged around in the junk pile for a while, discovering a few more boards, which she pulled out to make more firewood with, and more scrap metal, none of which she could think of a use for. In one corner, she did find parts of an old suit of armor. She pulled the helmet out and lifted the flap. Inside, the desiccated head of the knight who once owned the armor smiled horribly up at her. She quickly closed it again and put the helmet back in the pile.

Wiping her hands on her dress, Elder Dhonna abandoned her exploration of the junk heap and wandered over to the cell gate. She poked her head out between the bars and, as usual, saw no one in the wide corridor. So, she stepped through the bars and started walking. If Karrys returned, she would tell her she was bored and was just getting a little exercise.

She passed two more cells, just like the one she was *imprisoned* in before she came to a T-junction in the corridor. To her right was another wide, long hallway that sloped downward eventually vanishing into pitch blackness. There were no doors or openings that she could see and she quickly discarded any notion of going that way. Descending deeper into the compound did not seem like a very good idea. To her left was the way she had entered with Karrys, a hallway the length of the cells that opened onto a courtyard as equally vast as the cells. Karrys had landed in the middle of it when they had arrived at the compound and had brought her directly to her cell. She remembered seeing an opening in the far wall of the courtyard opposite to the cells. Even at a run, it would take her a good minute to cross the expanse. And then what? She had been too frightened to absorb any details of the compound from the air. If she made it to the opening, she had no clue as to what lay beyond. With a heavy sigh, she returned to her cell, curled up on the mat and waited for whatever fate had in store for her.

Davynn and Arthur set out for their three-day trek back to Colwygshire with the horses after Arthur moved the Amber Chalice inside, placing it on a safe ledge at the back of the lair. Arthur was excited to be going home to Alex, Hart and Meg, even if it was only going to be a brief visit. Sok had informed him that he had left Berryl, the most reliable member of the council, in charge in their absence. Court had been cancelled until Arthur and Sok returned, but Berryl was to collect any petitions and privately resolve the minor ones to prevent a huge backlog on the docket when court reconvened. It was likely that Arthur would not have more than a day at the castle before Anayah came for him and Davynn again and he intended to spend every second of it with his family. The petty petitions of the people could wait.

Hiro and Bon bid the others a quick good-bye and good-luck and immediately delved into their intended pastime of digging through Harpur's hoard. Both the Krist and the android were eager to look for historical artifacts that might be buried within the huge, glittering mound of gold and, as was his wont, Hiro planned to catalogue them for his own interest. It would keep them both occupied while they waited for the others to return with Elder Dhonna. Since she was the only one who knew what Harpur wanted Arthur to do with the chalice, anything else they could do was contingent upon her safe return.

"How are you finding it here on Thraeh?" Hiro asked Bon as they began picking through the treasure.

"I was looking forward to spending time with Harpur and learning about dragon culture," Bon replied. "It is a subject that I am sadly lacking data on."

"Weren't we all?" the Krist replied sorrowfully. "Weren't we all?"

But it was Sok and Anayah that faced the biggest challenge. They were going to a place neither of them was familiar with, with no clue as to where Elder Dhonna might be. Or if she was even still alive.

Anayah zapped them to the outskirts of Andonsheer. If it came to it, she wanted them to be able to blend in as much as possible, but first she would need to observe the people, see what their attire was like and hear their speech. There was a good chance they would have to interact with the locals if they wanted to get any information and she was not sure how well strangers would be received.

They arrived in a small clearing, surrounded by stunted, scrabbly trees, barely surviving in the parched earth they grew from. Sok was shocked at the pitiful condition of the trees, but he was even more shocked to see a Boundary right in the middle of the clearing. "I wonder where it goes," he said. A feeling of nostalgia swept over him as he recalled his adventures with Harpur, Arthur and Anayah and the Bounds they had made to Earth and Mysturna.

"Wherever it goes, it's good to know that it is here," Anayah said. "If we have time once we are in the city, we can try to find out."

Sok shifted his attention back to the trees. "Obviously, there are no elves about. They would never allow this to happen!"

"We don't have time to worry about the trees, Sok," Anayah said.

"I know, I know," Sok replied. "But Harpur's heart and soul, this is heartbreaking to see."

Anayah's eyebrows shot up. *Harpur's heart and soul? What happened to Orhowyn?*

"What?" Sok asked, seeing the witch's astonished expression.

"Nothing," Anayah said, deciding not to pursue it right then. "I'm going to make us invisible so we can move about and observe without being seen. Maybe we can pick up the information we need without having to draw any attention to ourselves. Are you okay with that?"

Sok nodded. "That sounds like fun."

"We are observing and listening only," Anayah warned. "No playing tricks on the Andonsheerians."

"Are they Andonsheerians? Or Andonsheerites?" Sok was genuinely curious.

"What difference does it make?" Anayah snapped.

"Andonsheerites sounds more appropriate for the climate."

"What?" Anayah said before she could stop herself. "Never mind. I don't want to know how you accomplished that mental leap. Are you ready?"

"Let's do this," Sok said.

Anayah told Sok to hold on to her shirt. They would have to stay connected in order for them both to be invisible. When he'd gotten a good grip, Anayah snapped her fingers and they both vanished. And not a moment too soon.

"Who is there?" a deep and booming voice demanded.

Sok and Anayah stood stock-still and watched as a large man dressed in shimmering green pants that were gathered at the waist and knees, and a short, grey vest with green embroidery to match the pants, stepped into the clearing. He was tall, heavily muscled and bald. A thin, black beard traced his jawline and rose to two sharp points at the corners of his full lips. His eyes were nearly as black as his beard and two gold hoops looped through his ears. He was carrying an empty sack in one hand and a curved and vicious-looking sword in the other.

"Who's there?" he demanded once again as he scanned the clearing looking for the source of the voices he'd heard on his approach. "Show yourselves!"

Sok and Anayah remained perfectly still and quiet.

When no one gave in to his demands, the hulk of a man walked up to the Boundary and leaped through it.

Sok and Anayah released the breaths they had been holding.

"I wonder where he's going," Sok whispered.

"I'm not sure I want to know," Anayah said. "Let's go."

Invisibly, they left the clearing and started up a path leading through the scrubby forest to Andonsheer.

"It's hot," Sok complained a few minutes later.

"We're in the desert," Anayah said.

"I know that!" Sok said. "I'm just saying it's hot. Maybe we should change into something more suitable to the weather. Those pants that guy was wearing looked comfortable."

"Really?" Anayah snorted out a laugh. Then she snapped her fingers.

Sok felt loose folds of soft cloth replace the snug leather he'd been wearing. "Ooh!" he exclaimed. "That's interesting. I wish I could see what they look like."

Anayah stifled a laugh. "Me too," she said.

They continued walking for another ten minutes until they came to a wide stretch of sandy land separating the forest and the city of Andonsheer. It was dotted with clumps of yellow grass, but was otherwise a barren and forlorn expanse of drab, beige nothingness. To their right, about one hundred feet away, a semi-circle of nine round tents made of dirty yellow and red-striped material was set up. A group of half a dozen men, similar in both build and attire to the man they had seen in the clearing, were gathered around an unlit firepit, drinking and laughing and generally being crass. At one end of the semi-circle stood a rack made of rough-hewn logs against which several long spears leaned.

"Let's go this way," Sok whispered, pushing Anayah to their left, away from the camp and its formidable inhabitants.

"Good idea." Anayah had no desire to mix and mingle with that bunch. Even invisibly.

They made their way across the sand to their left along the edge of the scrubby forest to the city wall. There they stopped to peak around the corner.

"Why are we peeking around the corner?" Sok asked. "We're invisible."

"Habit," Anayah said, thankful he couldn't see her face redden.

Sok was disappointed she couldn't see his eyes rolling.

From where they stood, they could see that the sand surrounding the city led out into the great desert known as the Sands of Sancheera. As far as their eyes could see, there was nothing but a monotonous carpet of sand stretching out to the east and south. A few wispy palm trees grew in clusters in the verge between the wall and desert proper along with more clumps of the yellow grass, but otherwise there was no vegetation. A road, of sorts, wound in from the north-east bringing a steady flow of people to the city, presumably from villages that dotted the edge of the desert. They all wore brightly coloured, long, loose robes and head coverings to protect them from the sun.

"I'm not sure your baggy pants were the right choice," Anayah observed.

"Again, I'm invisible, so it doesn't matter." Sok shifted his hips to renew the sense of freedom his baggy pants provided. "What's the plan?"

Anayah's shrug went unseen. "I suppose we just blend in with the crowd and go into Andonsheer. I'm guessing these people are heading to a market. Let's follow them."

Sok gave her shirt a gentle tug to let her know he was ready to proceed and together they joined the influx of villagers on the packed dirt road. Walking next to the road so they wouldn't bump into anyone, they were close enough to hear the conversations being had by the locals.

"They aren't speaking the common language," Anayah whispered. "I can't understand a word of what they are saying."

"It's probably just a local dialect," Sok whispered back. "I'm pretty sure that the common language is spoken in Andonsheer. When we get to the market, I'll bet they will convert to it."

"I hope so. Otherwise, we are not going to learn anything."

Upon entering the city gates, they quickly realized that not bumping into anyone was going to be a challenge. The streets were teaming with people going in various directions without any organizational flow. The good news was that their voices blended in with the cacophony of noise all around them and they no longer had to whisper. Shouting was, in fact, the only way the Andonsheerians seemed to be able to communicate.

"Which way do we go?" Anayah hollered.

"There!" Sok shouted back, pointing uselessly at a man carrying a large basket filled with long, narrow loaves of bread.

"Where?"

"Straight ahead," Sok said, keeping his eye on the man. "I'll guide you by pulling on your shirt. Which you're going to have to change first chance you get. You're a little sweaty."

Anayah elbowed the elf in the stomach. "Yeah, well, you're not so sweet-smelling either."

They started moving slowly forward as Sok raised his arm and sniffed his pit. "Touché!" He borrowed the phrase from Arthur.

Luck was with them. The man with the bread led them right to the market square situated next to the south wall of the city. Strangely, it was not as crowded as they had expected it to be. People seemed to be making their way in an orderly clockwise direction around the market area. If they wished to purchase something, they joined a cue leading to a stall. This left the center of the market open as all of the stalls were set up on the outer edge of the large rectangular space. Sok and Anayah made their way to the uncrowded center where they could get a better look at the place and decide what to do next.

"You're right," Anayah said, "they are speaking the common language to the vendors. I think we need to get closer again and just listen to what people are talking about."

"That's not going to work. They are only speaking common to the vendors. We won't be able to hear them over the conversations in the lineups. Besides, they are not likely to be chatting with the vendors about current events. I've got a better idea." Once again Sok pointed ineffectually toward a second gate in the south side of the city wall. "There's a group of guards over by the gate. If anyone is going to be talking about anything that might be useful to us, it will be them. Let's go over to there. At least we will be able to stand in the shade of the wall."

Anayah nodded as uselessly as Sok had pointed. "Good call," she added.

There were four guards at the gate, all of them in livery reminiscent of the ruffians in the camp on the opposite side of the city. Their loose pants were made of a royal blue material and they each wore a short, black vest with an insignia depicting a dragon wing embroidered on the left breast.

Their feet were clad in sandals with laces that crisscrossed their legs to mid-calf. They were not as big or as muscled as the men from the camp were, but they looked like they could hold their own in a fight. Each of them wore their long, black hair in a top knot and two were bearded, while the other two were clean-shaven. At their sides hung unsheathed and shorter versions of the curved sword Sok and Anayah had seen the man in the clearing carrying. Sok and Anayah inched as close as they dared, hugging the wall and settled in to listen to their banter.

"I'll be on desert duty come the next moon," said one of the clean-shaven guards, a young man Anayah placed in his early twenties.

"Desert duty is such a waste of time," complained the other beardless guard.

"Actually, I'll be accompanying the general," said the first guard. "He's going to negotiate with the dragons to see if he can get them to stop burning crops up near Andon."

"Better take a couple of virgins with you then," one of the bearded guards suggested. "That will keep the scaly bastards in check. At least for the season."

The other bearded guard, the largest of the four men and the oldest, was leaning with his arms crossed against the archway of the gate. He snorted derisively. "Such a waste."

If Sok and Anayah could have seen each other, they would have exchanged looks of contempt.

"Yeah, well, I prefer my women to have a little experience," said the second beardless guard.

"What women?" the first bearded guard scoffed. "You couldn't get a woman if you paid her."

The others laughed.

"That's the only way Hamyd could get a woman," the first beardless guard said, "and even then, he'd have to pay double."

They laughed again.

"Mock me all you want," Hamyd said defensively. "I've had my share of women!"

"It's a good thing his share leaves plenty for the rest of us," the first beardless guard said.

More laughter. Anayah balled her invisible fists and gritted her teeth.

"Like you can talk?' Hamyd sneered. It was time to change the subject. "Did you hear about the dragons that came into the compound yesterday?"

"No," said the first bearded guard. "Did you say *dragons*? As in more than one?"

"Yes," Hamyd confirmed. "Two of them. A black and a blue-green. They came in from the north and they had a passenger."

Sok and Anayah both perked up and inched a little closer.

"A passenger?" the oldest guard asked. It was strange enough that two dragons arrived together, but with a passenger? "What kind of passenger?"

"A woman with bright red hair. She was screaming like a Fae on fire. Half of Andonsheer saw them." Hamyd reported.

"Must be a virgin sacrifice from one of the northern kingdoms," said the first bearded guard. "But why would they bring her here? Don't they just roast them on the spot?"

"I doubt she's a virgin sacrifice if they brought her to the compound," the oldest guard said. "I suspect that she is somehow involved in a dispute between the black and the blue-green. Better prepare for the Dragon Council to convene."

"The Dragon Council?" The first beardless guard was alarmed.

"That's my guess," the oldest bearded guard said, obviously speaking from experience. "It's going to be a hot time in Andonsheer when they get here."

Sok and Anayah did not wait around to find out what that meant. They slipped past the guards out of the city and ran down a packed roadway that led to another patch of scrubby forest to the south.

When they were safely among the trees, they stopped to catch their breath.

"Can I let go of your shirt now?" Sok huffed. "My fingers are starting to cramp up."

"No!" Anayah said. "It's best that we stay invisible. There's no telling who, or what, we might run into out here."

"Well, let me change hands then." He reached out with his free hand until he found Anayah's back and took hold of her shirt. Then he let go with his other hand and shook the stiffness out of it. "I don't suppose you have any idea where this compound is?"

"The guard said that the dragons flew in from the north over the city. That means they were heading south. I say we follow this road and see where it goes." Anayah started to walk, pulling the elf behind her.

"It could be miles away," Sok whined.

"Or it could be just around the next bend," Anayah countered. "Either way, we have to find Elder Dhonna and this seems like our best bet."

"Can't you just conjure or zap her from wherever she is?" Sok asked.

"Not without knowing where she is," Anayah said. "Conjuring things is not the same as zapping people. If I wanted a cup of tea, I would envision it and then send the magic to find one and bring it to me. But with living beings, the magic doesn't work the same way. It has to be precise and while I could send my magic to find Elder Dhonna, it could just as easily find an elf that looks like her and bring that one to me. You should know this already."

"I was just hoping you knew a loophole so we could get out of here faster. These trees are depressing." Sok was struggling in the bleak environment.

"I get it," Anayah commiserated. "This is no Braydon Wood. Hopefully, the compound isn't too far."

They walked on, staying on the road. At one point, a snake slithered out of the bush and paused for a moment, unable to see them, but sensing their presence. As they walked around it, it hissed and then continued on its way.

"Are there poisonous snakes here?" Sok wondered aloud.

"Let's try not to find out," Anayah said.

They finally came to a bend in the road. From there it curved steeply down into a vast and, to Sok's delight, lushly forested valley. It was as if they had stepped into a whole other world. If only the heat had abated with the stark barrenness, but it only grew hotter and more humid the farther they descended into the valley.

"On the upside," Anayah said, fanning her face with her hands, "I think we've found the compound."

In the middle of the valley was an enormous, walled enclosure. From their vantage point on the road above it, they could see that it was just a huge fenced-in open expanse with what appeared to be a covered area running the length of the north wall and four smaller fenced spaces on the outside of the south wall. On the east side, there appeared to be a raised platform. A gate on the west wall opened on the jungle-like forest and the road Sok and Anayah were on led straight to that gate. At the north-west corner, a sloped stone roof extended out from the wall. They could see two dragons sitting on the platform and estimated that the compound could easily accommodate a hundred more. They seemed to be alone.

"What do we do about our scent?" Sok asked and they resumed their journey toward the compound.

After six long days in the ravine and the morning in the sweltering heat, they were both feeling pretty ripe.

"I can conjure us up some perfume if you like," Anayah offered, missing the point entirely.

"What I mean is, invisible or not, the dragons will smell us before we get into the compound. They will know we are there." Sok explained.

Anayah blew out a deep breath of frustration. "What do you suggest?"

"I suggest we create a distraction," Sok said, "something to draw them away from the compound long enough for us to get inside and look for Elder Dhonna."

"Like what?"

"How about a series of explosions starting at the top of that hill on the other side of the valley and leading to the far side of it? The first one will get their attention, then a few more will draw them away."

"What if only one of them goes to investigate?"

"They're dragons," Sok said. "They will both want to be the one to vanquish any threat."

"That makes sense," Anayah conceded. "But we'll need to get close enough so we can get into the compound as soon as possible when they leave."

"Right," Sok agreed. "There's a clearing down there that should be far enough away from them that they won't pick up our scent, but close enough that we can run in after they leave."

"You know, Sok," Anayah said, smiling invisibly, "when we put our minds to it, we make a pretty good team."

"Let's not count our dragons before they hatch," Sok said, nudging the witch forward.

They reached the clearing and Anayah prepared to create the illusion of a series of successive explosions going up and over the hill on the south side of the valley. The first explosion was loud enough and close enough to rock the foundations of the compound. Sok was watching through the trees for the dragons, but when several seconds passed and neither of them appeared, he urged Anayah to do two or three in quick succession. Anayah was happy to oblige and supplied three rumbling blasts accompanied by dramatic plumes of thick, black smoke.

That did the trick. "There they go!" Sok said.

"And here we go," Anayah replied.

As they ran toward the compound, Anayah set off more explosions, hoping to keep the dragons busy until they found Elder Dhonna. When they reached the gate, they did a quick recon of the huge courtyard. Finding it empty, they crept inside.

"Well, at least she's not chained to a stake," Sok said.

"This way," Anayah urged. "She's probably in that tunnel somewhere."

Sok followed the witch into the opening leading to the covered area. Every few steps, he looked over his shoulder to see if the dragons were coming back. "Can you give them a couple more explosions?"

A few seconds later, Sok heard, and felt, three more blasts. "Which way?" he asked when they came to the T-junction.

"Hello? Is someone there? What is going on?" A frightened voice came from their right.

"It's her!" Sok exclaimed. "She's alive."

They ran the length of the corridor, looking into each of the other cells as they passed. When they reached the last one, they found a very bedraggled guild master standing at the gate.

"Elder Dhonna, it's me, Sok!" he said.

"Where?" the confused elf asked.

"Elder Dhonna, this is Anayah. Sok and I are invisible. We've come to get you out of here. Can you step through the bars, or is the gate warded?" Anayah explained.

Elder Dhonna didn't know if she trusted her senses. The blasts had woken her up, but she had no idea what to make of them. "Is it really you?"

"It really is us," Sok assured her. "Can you leave the cell?"

Elder Dhonna stepped through the bars, but didn't know where to look.

"Elder Dhonna, I'm going to put my hand on your arm, so don't be alarmed, okay?" Anayah said.

"Okay," the elf replied, looking off to the side of her rescuers.

Anayah took Elder Dhonna by the arm. "I'm going to zap us back to the lair now."

"Did Arthur get the chalice? Did he fill it with Harpur's blood?" Anayah's touch assured her that she wasn't dreaming.

"Yes," Sok said. "We'll tell you all about it when we get back to the lair."

He had barely gotten the words out when they all found themselves standing in the meadow not ten feet from the entrance to Harpur's lair.

Elder Dhonna wept with relief to be back in Epoh. She stumbled over to the boulder and sat down. "Thank you. I wasn't sure you would find the note I left, but I'm so very glad that you did," she said through her tears.

"You're welcome, Elder Dhonna," Anayah said. "Sok, you can let go of me now."

Sok released Anayah's shirt and they both became visible again.

"What in Harpur's good name are you wearing?" Elder Dhonna gaped at Sok in astonishment.

Sok remembered that he hadn't seen the clothes that Anayah had given to him in Andonsheer. He looked down and released a startled yelp. "Very funny, Anayah! Now change them back into proper elf attire."

Anayah was too busy laughing to do as Sok asked. After all the stress of the past two days, she was almost as hysterical as Harpur had been in the great hall the day she had arrived. She needed this!

Hiro and Bon heard their voices and came out of the lair to see what the fuss was about. When he saw Sok, Hiro started to giggle. Then belly laugh. Soon, Elder Dhonna was laughing along with them. Even Bon couldn't suppress an amused smile. And, as much as Sok wanted to be angry, the absurdity of his hot pink pants with purple and orange dragons and the neon-orange vest with green and yellow polka dots made him start to laugh as well.

Then Elder Dhonna noticed Harpur's body, laying in the grass and her laughter was replaced by wonder. She stood up and walked across the meadow. The others, believing that she had been drawn to Harpur by grief, composed themselves and watched her make her way over to the corpse. Then they, too, noticed what Elder Dhonna had. Harpur's body was surrounded by flowers.

"What are they?" Anayah asked as she and the others joined Elder Dhonna next to Harpur.

"They are Harpur's legacy to the land," she said, bending down to pick one. "Like the dragonfoil trees that Orhowyn left, these are Harpur's gift to us. He told me to look for them if he didn't survive."

"They are beautiful," Sok said, picking one for himself. "I wonder what power they hold?"

"Healing," Elder Dhonna said, studying the blossom in her hand.

The star-shaped flowers were about two inches in diameter with velvety, deep purple petals and shiny blue-green streaks running through them. In the center of each were a cluster of five, short, golden stamens. Their fragrance was divinely spicy and woodsy, with an instant calming effect.

"Harpur had no regrets," Elder Dhonna continued, "but he understood the value of natural healing ability, perhaps better than anyone. He wanted to leave his own healing powers to Epoh."

"But he lost his healing ability," Sok said. "He lost all of his magic."

"He only lost the ability to wield it," Elder Dhonna corrected the elf. "Where is Arthur, by the way?"

"We didn't know how long it would take us to find and rescue you," Anayah explained, "so he and Davynn took the horses back to Colwygshire. I'm going to go and get them the day after tomorrow."

"I trust he took the chalice with him?" Elder Dhonna asked.

"No," Sok said. "The chalice is here in the lair."

"Why?" Elder Dhonna seemed confused.

"He didn't know how to carry it on horseback without spilling Harpur's blood," Sok explained the rationale.

Elder Dhonna sighed. "Show me the chalice."

They all returned to the lair. Elder Dhonna leaned in close to look at the transformed Amber Chalice. She clasped her hands behind her back to prevent herself from being tempted to touch it. It was stunningly beautiful.

"There was no need to keep the blood once the chalice was complete," Elder Dhonna said. "But, of course none of you would know that. I wish Arthur hadn't left, though. You could have all gone back to Colwygshire."

"What is Arthur supposed to do with the chalice?" Anayah asked.

"That I cannot tell you," Elder Dhonna said, turning to face the disappointed group behind her. "Only Arthur can know Harpur's plans from here on in. And even he isn't supposed to know everything. Right now, however, we have bigger problems."

Sok puffed out his cheeks and threw his hands up in the air. "Of course, we do! And what might they be?"

"Karrys Evergreen and Khol the Black are going to come looking for me," Elder Dhonna said with a shudder."

"Karrys Evergreen is the name of Harpur's challenger?" Sok asked. "And Khol the Black was their witness?" He knew who Khol the Black was, but he'd never heard of Karrys Evergreen.

Elder Dhonna went on to explain what had happened during the challenge and who Karrys Evergreen really was. "So Karrys refused to accept the inheritance and they took me to Andonsheer in case the Dragon Council wanted to hear my side of the story. I also let it slip that I was aware of the scope of dragons' true magic and, apparently, Karrys thinks I need to answer for that."

Stunned silence followed the guild master's speech as synapses and circuitry put these previously missing pieces into order, which only led to about a thousand more questions. But before they could bombard Elder Dhonna with them, she held up her hands to stop them.

"We need to get Arthur back here to get the chalice. Davynn can take the horses back to Colwygshire on his own. Then Arthur needs to get back to the castle and hide the chalice until it's time for him to use it. Karrys and Khol are likely to come to the lair first to look for me and it will take them a couple of hours to fly here from Andonsheer. I need to not be here when they arrive, but someone needs to stay here and convince them that

I didn't come back." Elder Dhonna spoke with such authority that none of the others dared to argue.

"I will go and get Arthur, obviously," Anayah said. "Who is going to stay here and face the dragons?"

"I will stay," Bon said. "I am the least emotionally involved in all of this. I am also the most diplomatic. But what will the dragons do when they do not find you here, Elder Dhonna?"

"They will be angry," the elf replied honestly. "I don't doubt that for a second."

"If the question of rulership over Epoh is in question, they won't dare cause harm to anyone," Sok interjected. "Until the Dragon Council makes a decision, Epoh technically still belongs to Harpur."

"What happens if they decide against Karrys?" Anayah asked.

"Then Epoh will most likely be given to Phiercesten and Framanjesk. And that can't happen! Karrys must inherit." Elder Dhonna was adamant.

"Why?" Sok asked, perplexed. "And who are Phiercesten and Framanjesk?"

"She just does," Elder Dhonna said. She ignored Sok's other inquiry.

"And how do we make sure of that?" Hiro asked.

Elder Dhonna had been so looking forward to returning to her own treehouse, but she suddenly realized that that was not going to happen. "As much as I hate to say it, I'm going to have to go back to the compound and convince them." Elder Dhonna looked stricken, but determined.

"No!" Sok said. "That's not an option." He forgot about Phiercesten and Framanjesk.

"It's the only option," Elder Dhonna said. "I thought I could hide from them, but with the future of Epoh at stake, I realize I have to return and see this through. Now, Anayah, I want you to zap me back to the compound and then go get Arthur. Once he has the chalice, get him back to the castle and make sure he puts it in the vault with Harpur's book. Tell him to stay in the castle until I come for him. Understood?"

"Not really," Anayah said, "but I guess we have to trust that you know what you are doing."

"No!" Sok said again. "You can't go back there. Even if you do manage to convince the dragons to grant rulership of Epoh to Karrys Evergreen, they will kill you for knowing about their magic."

"Once Karrys is ruler and finds out that half of Epoh knows about dragon magic, she will kill all of us." Hiro said.

"I highly doubt that," Elder Dhonna said.

"What aren't you telling us?" Sok demanded.

"A lot!" Elder Dhonna replied. "Anayah, zap me back to my cell."

"I will," Anayah agreed. "But after I get Arthur, Sok and Hiro back to the castle, I'm coming to Andonsheer to protect you. If the dragons decide to kill you for what you know, I will zap you out of there."

"I'm staying here with Bon," Hiro said. "There's a lot more treasure to catalogue here."

Elder Dhonna looked askance at the Krist. "Just don't take anything!"

"Just cataloguing," Hiro assured her.

"One more thing before I go," Elder Dhonna said. "Please take my satchel back to the castle and keep it safe for me?"

"Of course," Anayah said. Then in a puff of red smoke, she and the elf disappeared.

When the smoke cleared, Sok remembered the names Elder Dhonna had mentioned. "Who are Phiercesten and Framanjesk?"

The Krist and the android had no answer.

Elder Dhonna was back in the late afternoon heat of her cell. She could hear Karrys and Khol talking out in the hallway. They did not sound happy.

"I can't find her anywhere," Karrys snapped.

"She can't have gone far," Khol said. "I'll go and look for her in the forest."

"When you find her, singe her hair," Karrys snarled.

Elder Dhonna's hands went protectively to her crimson mop of curls. It was time to reveal herself. "Did you lose someone?" she called out in a shaky sing-song voice from between the bars.

Karrys was standing in the corridor in front of the farthest cell from Elder Dhonna's. Faster than Elder Dhonna thought possible, the huge dragon spun around and rushed toward her. Instinctively, she backed up and away from the outraged dragon.

"Where were you?" Karrys demanded. Her one-eyed glare was more frightening than her two-eyed glare had been.

"I'm sorry," Elder Dhonna said as contritely as possible. "I was behind the junk in the corner using the commode."

Karrys' eyes narrowed and she turned her head to look at the pile of old iron, measuring the plausibility of the elf's claim. She growled. "Where are the others?"

"What others?" Elder Dhonna didn't have to feign surprise. *How does she know?*

"Don't lie to me, elf," Karrys hissed. "I can smell two others. Both in much need of a bath, I might add. Now, where are they?"

Elder Dhonna shook her head and shrugged her shoulders. "I have no idea what you're talking about. I haven't seen—or smelled—anyone else here." *Please believe me. Please believe me.*

From down the corridor, Khol was losing patience with the interrogation. "Leave it, Karrys," he ordered. "She's where she's supposed to be. That's all that matters."

Karrys looked at the black dragon and then back at Elder Dhonna. "You better not be up to anything."

"What could I possibly be up to in here?" Dhonna shot back. "But since you're here, I could use some fresh food and water. The meat you brought me last night has already gone off in this infernal heat."

Karrys growled again. "Bring me the carcass."

Elder Dhonna complied. Happily. She handed the quickly putrefying goose to Karrys, who sniffed it and then dropped it, whole, into her mouth. "It's fine," she sneered. "But I will bring you some fresh meat and some water.

Elder Dhonna breathed a sigh of relief as the teal dragon retreated down the corridor. She really wanted something stronger than water, but she didn't dare ask for it. While she waited for Karrys to return, she sat on her mat and thought about the flowers that had sprung up around Harpur's body. The blossoms were quite striking, beautiful but not delicate. They were purple and teal, the same colours as Harpur and Karrys. That meant something. But in her current state of stress and fear, she couldn't recall what it was.

Karrys' return distracted Elder Dhonna from her thoughts. "Your food and water, elf," the dragon said from outside the cell.

Elder Dhonna got up and went to retrieve the full waterskin and what appeared to be a leg of mutton from her warden. "Thank you," she said.

The dragon snorted a column of smoke in her direction and turned again to leave. Then it struck Elder Dhonna. She wasn't sure if she was right, but she thought it was worth a try.

"Karrys?" she called to the dragon's back.

"What it is now?" Karrys stopped but did not face the guild master.

"When a ruling dragon is challenged and loses, it leaves behind something of itself to the land, right?"

"Yes. And?" Karrys was curious to know where the elf was going with this.

"And it's always the colour of the conquered dragon, isn't it?"

"It is a blend of the colours of both dragons involved in the challenge. Why do you ask?"

Elder Dhonna could barely conceal her excitement. "Then if you are not the rightful heir to Epoh, whatever Harpur is leaving will not have your colour in it."

"What are you saying?" Karrys demanded, turning now to look at Elder Dhonna.

"I'm saying go to the lair and see if anything is growing near Harpur's body. If it has already appeared, it will be definitive proof of whether or not you should rule Epoh." Elder Dhonna watched the dragon as she processed this information.

"That is an excellent idea, elf," Karrys said, already scheming her next move. "But why would you help me in this way?"

"Because I believe you are the rightful heir. It was your blow that caused Harpur to fall on the skull." She did not add that she had already seen Harpur's legacy to the land.

"I still do not understand why you would help me." Karrys' suspicious nature could not let this go.

"Because if I am right, I expect a favour from you in return." Elder Dhonna swallowed her fear.

"And what might that be?" Karrys asked, her curiosity piqued.

"I want you to let me go and keep what I know about dragon magic to yourself."

Karrys was impressed. She couldn't blame Elder Dhonna for bargaining for her life. "You forget that Khol also knows what you know. I cannot prevent him from speaking up to the Council."

Elder Dhonna knew she was grasping at straws. "Then defend me as a subject of Epoh under your rule and protection. Tell them you will deal with me, make an example of me in Epoh so that all of your subjects will know that your rule is absolute."

"You are clever. For an elf," Karrys said. "Tell me, though, what is to prevent me from betraying you? You have already played your hand with the information about Harpur's legacy to the land. You have nothing to hold over me."

"I may not," Elder Dhonna said, "but you do."

"I have something to hold over myself?" Karrys asked. The elf was becoming more interesting by the minute.

"That's right," Elder Dhonna replied. "You have your honour. Any dragon that would not accept victory in a challenge due to a technicality would not break a promise. Even to an elf."

Karrys laughed. She understood why Harpur had liked this elf so much. "Very well. I will fly to Epoh and look for Harpur's legacy tonight. If I find it, and it proves I am the rightful heir, then you have my word. I will not mention your knowledge of our magic to the Council when it convenes tomorrow. And if Khol does, I will defend you as my subject. But know this, elf, I cannot guarantee the outcome. Dragons do not take this lightly and I may not be able to save you."

"I understand," Elder Dhonna said solemnly.

Karrys turned to leave again, then stopped and sniffed the air. "There's that smell again!" She whipped around, threw open the gate and entered the cell. "Who is here with you, elf?"

Elder Dhonna backed up to the wall opposite the gate, pressing herself against the stone. "No one! I swear!" *Not now, Anayah!*

Karrys tore through the pile of junk, sniffing angrily. The helmet with the desiccated head flew across the room and rolled to Elder Dhonna's feet, giving her an idea.

"It's probably some dead animal somewhere," she said with desperation.

Karrys turned and glared at the terrified elf. "If I find out you are hiding something from me, our bargain is off!"

"I... I swear I am not hiding anything from you," Elder Dhonna stammered. She pressed herself harder against the wall, squeezed her eyes shut and waited to be roasted alive.

Karrys shot one more glance at the corner where the pile of junk used to be and growled loudly. Then she left, slamming the heavy gate behind her.

Elder Dhonna slid down the wall and sat vibrating with fear, her head on her knees. A few moments later, she felt a hand on her arm.

"Anayah?" she whispered into the growing darkness. "Is that you?"

"Yes," Anayah's disembodied voice said next to her. "I'm sorry about that. I just wanted you to know that I am close by. I heard what you and the dragon were talking about. You are the most courageous woman I've ever met."

"You can't stay here," Elder Dhonna said, tears welling up in her eyes at the compliment. She didn't feel very courageous.

"I know. I will hide in the forest tonight. But I will check on you again in the morning. Can I get you anything?"

"No, thank you, I will be fine," Elder Dhonna said. "It gets cold at night. You'll need to find a way to keep warm."

Anayah's rueful smile went unseen. "I will be fine too. Don't worry about me. Just stay safe and I will see you tomorrow."

"Will I see *you*?" Elder Dhonna's tears were flowing freely now.

"Absolutely. The moment it is safe." Anayah patted the guild master's arm and then zapped herself out of the cell.

Elder Dhonna forced herself to her feet and wiped her tears away with the back of her hand. She was glad to know that Anayah was close by, but now she had to worry that the dragons could, literally, sniff the witch out. She set about laying the fire for the night and wished she had asked Anayah to do this for her as she ripped another strip of the bottom of her dress. *One way or another, this will all be over the tomorrow. Hopefully.* Her dress would not last much longer.

When the fire was glowing merrily in the gloom, she sat down on her mat and tore a piece of mutton off the leg Karrys had brought her. The meat was dry and tasteless, but she needed to keep herself occupied, and eating was her only option as she faced another long night alone in the cell.

With her belly as full as she could stand, Elder Dhonna drew her blanket around her shoulders and laid down on the mat. As she waited for the respite sleep would bring, she remembered something else. *Scalla ap Averborn.* The words Harpur had said to Phiercesten and Framanjesk before they left the lair. *What did he mean?* It seemed to have eased the young dragons' minds in some way. And they had flown away to the north. *Why did they fly north? Where did they go? What else has Harpur done?*

These thoughts carried the elf off to sleep. Soon she found herself dreaming that she was flying over the mountains above Harpur's lair. On the other side, a vast tundra opened up and stretched as far as she could see to the north. The ground was covered in a light dusting of snow through which dazzling gold rocks protruded. At first, the rocks were randomly strewn across the plane, but as she flew farther, they began to form a huge labyrinth. In the center of the labyrinth were seven gold standing stones, forming a circle around a crystal-clear pool of water. Elder Dhonna was entranced by the vista, feeling the sacredness of the white and golden landscape.

She wanted to land and walk the labyrinth, but no matter what she did, she was unable to do so. Something was keeping her in the air. She circled the standing stones and then stopped to float above the pool in their center. She expected to see her reflection in the glassy water. Instead, she saw nothing. Not even the sky was reflected. The sensation this invoked was disturbing, so she tried to fly away again back to the mountains. But she couldn't move. She was suspended in the air above the pool, held there by some invisible power that forced her to keep looking into the water below. Rather than struggle against it, Elder Dhonna made herself remain calm. She sensed that there was something she needed to see, something she needed to know, so she watched and waited.

Below her, the surface of the water began to ripple and then roil like a cauldron on a hearth. Fascinated, she stared at the tempest bubbling and frothing on the surface of the pool as if it was trying to expel something from its depths. Then, just as suddenly as it began, the churning waters calmed and the face of a teal dragon appeared on the surface. *Karrys?*

Scalla ap Averborn. Scalla ap Averborn. Scalla ap Averborn.

Elder Dhonna heard the words Harpur had spoken to his sons repeated by the dragon in the pool.

"What does it mean?" she called down to the teal dragon.

But as soon as she spoke, the dragon disappeared and, without warning she started to fall. Just as she was about to hit the water, Elder Dhonna sat up, wide awake, on her mat in the chilly cell once again.

The fire was dwindling, so she added a couple more boards and laid back down. She could make no sense of the dream, but she wondered if Averborn was the name of the labyrinth and whether it was to play some part in Harpur's plan.

"Bloody dragon," she mumbled, cursing her dead friend. "Drag me into this Fae-brained scheme of yours and look where it's got us all. I'm stuck in Andonsheer at the mercy of all dragonkind. Anayah is out there alone in the jungle, one sniff away from being discovered and probably roasted alive. Arthur has no idea what he's supposed to do with the chalice. A Krist and an android are rummaging around in your hoard. And Sok! Did you see the fool's garb he ended up in? On your broken wing and charred scales, I swear if I die here and can't get back to help Arthur finish the job, I'm going to find my way to Arachovor and kill you again!"

She spent the rest of the night tossing and turning on her mat. Grief and hope and terror all vied for control over her heart and mind. She wished she had told Sok and Anayah what Arthur needed to do. In case she didn't make it back, someone had to be able to guide him. No matter what Harpur's wishes were. She had to hope that if things didn't go well for her with the Council, one of them would find the spell Harpur had torn out of the book in the archives at Colwygshire and figure out what to do with it.

After Anayah and Elder Dhonna had zapped out of the lair, Sok realized that he was still wearing the colourful baggy pants and vest that the witch had provided for him in Andonsheer. While they were comfortable, they were far more suited to the desert heat than the cooler northern climate of spring in Epoh.

"Harpur's horns!" he exclaimed. "Anayah forgot to give me my clothes back."

"I think I can help you with that," Hiro said, reaching for his satchel while he eyed up the elf for size and fit. He pulled out a pair of rich brown breaches, a cream-coloured tunic and a warm beige vest along with a pair of leather boots to match and handed the neatly folded pile of clothes to Sok.

"Very nice," the elf said as he shamelessly stripped down and redressed. "You have good taste, Hiro. These are perfect."

"What was Anayah thinking when she conjured these up for you?" Hiro asked, stuffing the baggy pants and vest into his satchel to get rid of them.

"I'm guessing there's a theatre company in Andonsheer that is short a costume," Sok said. "Anayah probably requested the wildest set of clothes her magic could find, just to be funny. And those were the result."

The Krist nodded. "Here," he said, passing Sok one of two large pastries he pulled from his satchel, "eat this. It should tide you over until Anayah returns and you can go back to the castle."

Sok accepted the fruit-filled pastry with thanks and sat down on the broken stalagmite to eat it. "Harpur would have your hides if he knew you were snooping around in his hoard like that," he observed.

"We aren't taking anything," Hiro assured the elf. "I just want to see if there is anything of historical significance among the treasure."

"And is there?" Sok asked.

Hiro drew a broken sword with a bejeweled hilt out of the pile. "I suspect there is a good story behind this beauty," he said, holding it up for Sok to see. Even broken, he needed two hands to hold it.

"I believe that is Withersong," Sok said casually. "Some prince in one of the southern kingdoms wielded it once upon a time."

"How do you know this?" Hiro asked, curious.

"It's in a book in the archives," Sok shrugged. "I think it's called Famous Weapons of Thraeh or something unimaginative like that. Anyway, Withersong was gifted to the prince by a wizard who assured him that he could use it to kill dragons."

"And did this prince kill dragons with it?" Bon's own thirst for knowledge was aroused.

"He tried," Sok said, "but it broke when he stabbed his first dragon in the foot with it."

"What happened to the prince?" Hiro asked, frustrated at having to coax the story out of the elf piecemeal like this.

"The dragon burned him, of course." Sok said. "What do think happened to him?"

"So, the wizard lied?" Bon posited.

"No," Sok said, taking another bite of his pastry. "The prince was just a lousy fighter; had no idea how to kill a dragon. But that thing is still loaded with magic. Even in its current condition, it could kill a full-grown dragon. If it was wielded by a skilled fighter."

Hiro handed the broken Withersong to Bon, who scanned it to store its image for future reference.

"I wonder how it ended up here," Hiro ruminated aloud.

"The same way everything else in Harpur's hoard ended up here. Harpur took it." Sok popped the last bite of his pastry into his mouth. Then he spied the second pastry Hiro had pulled from his satchel, uneaten in Hiro's hand. "Are you going to eat that?"

"Eventually," Hiro replied, putting it back in his satchel. "Why do dragons hoard treasure? These things should be in a museum."

"Because that's what dragons do," Sok said as if it should be obvious. "They like shiny things. It makes them happy to be surrounded by shiny things. And a happy dragon is a dragon that is not burning crops and villages and eating livestock."

Hiro asked Bon if he'd recorded all the information about Withersong and, upon confirmation from the android that it was all indeed safely stored in his data banks, resumed rummaging through the pile of treasure.

"How did dragons come to dominate Thraeh?" Bon asked.

"In a dragon egg shell," Sok began, "they only evolved on worlds where magic could evolve. Essentially, they are the original wielders of magic. Dragons have existed on Thraeh since long before any of the other races appeared. Back then they shared this world with other creatures, who, for reasons unknown—except maybe by dragons, and they aren't telling anyone—went extinct. Some say the Fae were the first race to develop, but again, who really knows? When elves, humans and dwarves came along, they were mostly contained in the lands in the east across the Crysteel Sea and the dragons mostly left them to their own devices, believing that they would eventually wipe each other out.

"As time passed, technology advanced and all but choked magic out among the races. There were great wars of mass destruction fought between the races that almost accomplished what the dragons had hoped for, but you can thank the elves for setting things right."

"How so?" Hiro asked.

"Technology evolved into magic, as first discovered by the elves who used it to destroy the humans' and dwarves' technology. The humans and dwarves called it the apocalypse, but the elves saw it as the advancement that it was. While the dwarves retreated underground and excelled at mining and manipulating ore, the humans tried to get in good with the elves. It is believed that any magic among humans stemmed from cross-breeding with elves and while the elves turned their magic toward nature and healing, the humans that assumed magic formed strong cliques, or classes of magicians, that took different paths. Wizards are generally conjurers and spellcasters. Sorcerers tend to control their environments. Witches are basically herbalists with darker proclivities than us elves. Now, magical humans are quite rare, the classes having all but died out. Only the elves and the Fae continue to possess magic across their populations.

"When things settled down, the dragons created the kingdoms and offered the races their protection. That's about it." Sok finished his history lesson for the day.

"As I understand it, some dragons do not allow all of the races to live within their kingdoms, though," Bon said.

"That is true," Sok confirmed. "Each ruler of a kingdom has the right to decide whether or not to allow any or all of the races to live within its borders. There are some regions on Thraeh where the races live without the protection of dragons. But the dragons monitor them closely and will not tolerate any... What's Arthur's word for it? ...shenanigans."

Just then Anayah and Arthur appeared at the entrance to the lair.

"Hi, honey, I'm home," Arthur sang out as he entered the lair and retrieved the Amber Chalice from the ledge where he'd put it that morning.

"It seems our history lesson has come to an end," Bon said. "Thank you, Sok, for being such a good teacher. But how do you know this?"

"You're welcome," Sok replied. "Harpur told me. I think he might have been a little drunk, though."

"I see you found some new clothes," Anayah said to the elf.

"Hiro kindly helped me out," Sok said. "And I see you found our king okay."

"Arthur and Davynn were on the main trail back to Colwygshire. Davynn is camping out with a group of elves led by a fellow called Stellah. Do you know him?" Anayah explained.

"Stellah? Yes, I know him. He's a good elf." Sok saw the concern on Anayah's face. "You don't have to worry about Stellah. He and his crew will make good company for Davynn."

"Shall we?" Arthur asked as he joined them.

"First, I have to get Elder Dhonna's satchel. She asked me to keep it safe for her." Anayah looked around and then spotted the precious case next to the broken stalagmite. She grabbed the strap to lift it off the ground. "Oof! What has she got in here?"

"Maybe she stole some of Harpur's treasure," Sok said with a laugh as he helped the witch settle the heavy bag on her shoulder.

"Like that would ever happen!" Anayah rolled her eyes. "Ready, boys?"

"Ready."

"Ready."

"No sign of the dragons?" Anayah asked as Arthur and Sok took their places next to her.

"Not yet," Hiro said.

"Okay. That's good. I'll come back for you as soon as I can. Stay safe." She didn't wait for a reply; she snapped her fingers and once again vanished with the elf and the king in a puff of red smoke.

All this zapping back and forth was wearing Anayah out. After dropping Arthur and Sok back off at the castle and giving Sok the satchel for safe keeping, she had zapped herself back to Andonsheer to check on Elder Dhonna. That near disaster had left her quite shaken. The timing of her appearance in Elder Dhonna's cell had put the elf in danger. *Or had it?* Anayah didn't think that the dragons would harm Elder Dhonna. At least not before the Council met and made its decision. Some good had come of it, though. She had overheard Elder Dhonna bargaining with Karrys. She knew that Karrys was going to look for the flowers, which would prove that she had rightfully inherited Epoh. *If only I knew why Elder Dhonna is so determined to make sure the Dragon Council decides in Karrys' favour.*

"I guess I will just have to wait to find out," she said aloud as she set up her minimalist camp in the same clearing she and Sok had stopped at earlier.

"Wait to find out what?" A gruff and thickly accented voice asked from behind her.

Anayah spun around to see the large man from the Boundary, sans sack, but still carrying the vicious-looking blade. He was accompanied by two other men, similarly attired and equally armed, who stared at her with cold eyes.

"What are you doing out here alone in jungle?" the large man demanded.

Knowing that she could zap herself away at the first sign of any trouble from these three, Anayah decided that the truth was the best tactic she could employ. They might provide her with some useful information.

"My friend is being held prisoner in the dragon compound," Anayah said with as much confidence as she could muster. "I'm hoping to find a way to help her."

The three men laughed.

"How is tiny woman going to help friend against hundred dragons?" the large man asked.

"I haven't figured that out just yet," Anayah said. "I don't suppose you three big, strong men would care to help me?" Anayah batted her eyes and smiled.

Again, the three men laughed.

"Not even Drengrokil crazy enough to take on Dragon Council," the large man said, gesturing to include his comrades. "You should go home. Forget friend. Friend is dead."

"Elder Dhonna is not dead!" Anayah stated emphatically. "At least not yet. And I will not go home without her."

"Your friend is elf?" the large man asked, obviously surprised. "How is witch friend with elf?"

How does he know I'm a witch and Elder Dhonna is an elf? "I'm friends with lots of different people. What does it matter?"

"Does not matter," the large man said. "Is just not common. Where do you come from?"

"Epoh." Anayah took a deep breath to steady her nerves. "How did you know I am a witch?"

"Drengrokil kill many witches across Crysteel Sea," the large man said. "We remember how witch's magic smell, no? But no witches live in Epoh. I believe this is lie."

Clearly, the Drengrokil were not to be trifled with and Anayah realized that she would be far better off making friends with them than enemies.

Still confident that she could zap herself to safety if she had to, she steeled her courage and pressed on. She explained that she was from Mysturna and that she was now living in Epoh at the invitation of the ruling dragon, Harpur Diggins. She thought it was prudent to leave out the fact that the ruling dragon was dead and rulership over Epoh was in question.

"You are Bounder?" Again, the large man sounded surprised. "Drengrokil Bounders also. Have not Bounded to Mysturna, though." He said something to his comrades in a language Anayah did not understand and they nodded in reply. "Perhaps we go there someday. Kill more witches."

"The witches of Mysturna are peaceful," Anayah said desperately, wishing she hadn't revealed so much about herself. "We are not like the witches here on Thraeh."

One of the large man's companions made a comment and the others snickered.

"My friend says is true you are not like witches on Thraeh. Much prettier."

Anayah swallowed her flattered disgust. "Thank you. Now, if you won't help me, please leave me alone. I'm tired and I need to rest before the Council meets tomorrow."

The large man in the baggy green pants stepped toward Anayah and she prepared to disappear if he tried to grab her. But he walked past her, bent down and picked a handful of fern-like fronds from a plant at the edge of the clearing. "Drengrokil help with this," he said, handing it to her.

"What is it?"

"Is called deer fern. Crush leaves and rub juice on hair and body. Will cover your scent so dragons cannot smell you. You can make yourself invisible, yes?

"Yes," Anayah said, both relieved and surprised. "Thank you."

"Is pleasure of all Drengrokil to assist such beautiful witch," the large man said as his friends started to leave the clearing. Before he joined them, he turned back to Anayah. "I am Frode of Ordyr, leader of Drengrokil clan. Much luck saving friend, witch."

"Well, that was interesting," Anayah said to herself with a good measure of relief after Frode and his friends left the clearing. "And thank you, Harpur, for watching over me. This deer fern is a real blessing." *If it works...*

Anayah fell asleep thinking about Frode and the Drengrokil. They were obviously not from this part of the world. *Are they mercenaries?* she wondered. *I will have to see what I can learn about them once all this – whatever this is – is over.*

Anayah had zapped Sok and Arthur into the council chambers in the castle at Colwygshire and reminded Arthur to hide the chalice with Harpur's book until Elder Dhonna could return and tell him what he needed to do next.

"I know. I will," Arthur said, like a teenage boy addressing his nagging mother. *Eventually.*

Once she was gone again, Sok turned to Arthur. "Will you attend supper in the great hall?"

"Not if I can help it," Arthur said. "I want one night with my family before I have to be the king again."

Sok nodded and watched Arthur dash to the back door of the council chamber. *I wonder if he even knows where his crown is.* Sok thought. He made a mental note to find it and put it on Arthur's head in the morning. First, though, a hot bath and some of Finch's fine cooking.

While Sok was making his way toward a long, relaxing soak in a tub, Arthur was running up the stairs to the queen's chambers. As always, he was slightly out of breath when he reached the top and had to take a minute to get his heartrate back down to normal. He did this behind a pillar out of sight. He did not want anyone to know he was back. He also didn't want to enter Alex's room huffing and puffing like he'd just run up three long flights of stairs. When his breathing normalized, he peeked around the pillar, then, seeing that the corridor was clear, made another quick dash to the unguarded door to his wife's rooms.

He was about to knock when the realization that there were no guards posted where they should have been hit him.

"Where are the guards?" he asked the empty hall way.

He reached for the knob, found it unlocked, and pushed the door open. The room was dark, but he could feel the abandonment.

Arthur retrieved a torch from a sconce in the hall and returned to Alex's rooms. The fireplace was cold. The bed was stripped down to the mattress. There were no toiletries on the vanity. Not a single dress hung in the large wardrobe. The less he found, the more he panicked.

He ran to the connecting nursery door and pushed it open to find that room as unoccupied as the other. Not only were there no twins, there was no crib and no Alma. Though he had been hoping for the last nine days that the mid-wife would have moved on before he returned, her absence made his blood run cold.

By the light of the torch, Arthur searched the main room again, looking for anything that would indicate where his wife and children might be. There was nothing, not even a note. Dizzy with fear, he left the room and ran on shaky legs in the opposite direction from which he'd originally come to the secondary stairs and followed them down to the floor below. Not caring anymore if anyone saw him, he ran to the second door on the left and flung it open.

"Sok!" he shouted into the spacious room, softly lit with candles. Dozens and dozens of candles. Elder Dhonna's satchel hung from a hook on the wall next to a large screen that sectioned off one corner of the room in front of a double set of doors leading out onto a small balcony. Still holding the torch, he approached the screen and there he found the elf, naked and about to step into a round tub overflowing with woodsy-scented bubbles.

"Sok!" Arthur repeated. "Get dressed. Alex and the twins are missing!"

Sok stood with one foot hovering inches above the bubbles, which he looked at ruefully. "What do you mean they are missing?"

"I mean missing, as in they aren't in their rooms." Arthur looked around for a robe or something he could give to Sok to cover himself.

"They are probably at the great hall for supper." Sok lowered his foot an inch.

"You don't understand!" Arthur shouted, still searching for a robe. "Alex's rooms are empty. All of her things are gone. There's nothing there!"

Sok sighed. *So close.* "Okay, don't panic. I'm sure they are around here somewhere." He retracted his foot and walked out from behind the screen to get dressed.

He had just stepped into his pants again when Finch, the head housekeeper appeared at the door with a tray of sandwiches, fruit and pastries, and a large mug of ale. "Like I don't have enough to do getting supper ready for the mob in the great hall, I have to bring a feast all the way up here for the likes of you." Failing to curtsy before her king, she waddled across the room and plunked the tray down on a table by the window. Then she turned and waddled back toward the door, her lopsided, grey bun bobbing with each step. "First the queen insists on changing rooms. Needs to be near the gardens, she does. It's better for the twins, she says. And that mid-wife! Orhowyn's silvery scales, but that's a crusty one, that is! Took all day with her snapping orders at me. At me, can you imagine? Then the elf shows up after being Orhowyn knows where for days on end and demands food be brought to his room!"

"Thank you, Finch!" Sok called out to the long-suffering housekeeper's back.

"Uh... Finch?" Arthur said, following her out into the hall. "Did you say that the queen moved to rooms near the garden?"

Finch did not stop walking. "That I did. Had the whole castle in an uproar over it too. No time to plan things out properly, just get it done. Like I don't have other things to tend to. Orhowyn only knows how I'm ever going to get caught up on the laundry now. Probably have to stay up all night to get it done."

And then she turned the corner to take the stairs back down to the kitchens.

Arthur returned to Sok's room to find him removing his pants again. A pastry was sticking out of his mouth.

"What are you doing?" Arthur asked.

"I'm going to have my bath," Sok answered, removing the pastry, "before the water gets cold."

"What about Alex?"

"You heard Finch, she's in new rooms by the gardens. You do know where the gardens are, don't you?"

Arthur heard splashing as Sok sank into his bath and he made a face at the screen. "I think I can figure it out." He turned to leave.

"Oh, Arthur?" Sok called from his woodsy-scented tub. "Before you leave, can you bring the food and ale in here? I forgot to grab it."

Arthur pretended not to hear, but he tip-toed over to the tray and helped himself to a sandwich, an apple and a pastry.

"Arthur? Are you there? Arthur?"

Arthur closed the door and headed down to look for his wife and children.

Chapter Sixteen

Karrys Evergreen had left Elder Dhonna's cell filled with intrigue and suspicion. The elf was clearly up to something. What that was, exactly, the teal dragon couldn't begin to fathom. But it did seem as if the elf genuinely wanted her to inherit Epoh. *She is a clever little thing,* Karrys thought to herself as she approached the platform where Khol the Black was sitting and staring southward.

"Expecting more explosions?" Karrys said to the stout black dragon.

"They were obviously a distraction to lure us away from the compound," Khol huffed.

"Obviously," Karrys agreed, "but just as obviously, the ruse failed. The elf is still where she's supposed to be." She didn't mention that she had smelled in interloper. "I have warded the cell to make sure no one can get in."

Khol studied the teal dragon. "I wish you had just accepted the inheritance upon my witness and let me kill her. All this fuss over an elf is preposterous."

"You are right," Karrys said.

Khol's large eyes widened in surprise. "I am?"

"I think I may have a way to settle the dispute. We may not need the Council after all."

"Oh?" Karrys had the black dragon's full attention.

"Harpur's legacy to the land," Karrys said simply.

"What of it?"

"If I am the rightful heir to Epoh, his legacy will be purple and teal. I'm going to fly back to Epoh and see if it has shown up yet. Legacy plants often do appear within hours of death." She made it sound like it was her idea.

"And what of the elf, then? If you do find the legacy and it does prove you are the rightful heir, there's still the matter of her knowing about our magic," Khol said.

"As ruler of Epoh, I will take care of it." Karrys replied.

"How?"

"When I announce my rulership, I will make an example of her before all of Colwygshire."

"I would like to be there when you do." Khol sensed something was off.

"I thought you might," Karrys said. "But if Epoh is truly mine to rule, I will do it my way and without your interference."

"How will I know it is done if I'm not there to see it?"

"Don't you trust me, Khol?" Karrys feigned shock.

"Not particularly," Khol admitted.

"Regardless, I am giving you my word and that's all I'm giving you. You will just have to hope that I don't find the legacy." Karrys left the platform and moved out into the center of the compound enclosure to prepare to take off. "You may come with me if you like. That way, if Harpur's legacy does prove that Epoh is mine, you can just go back to Rednow and be done with all this."

Khol's big head swung toward the cells. He could see the faint glow of Elder Dhonna's fire through the high window. "You're just going to leave her here unattended?"

"As I said, I have warded the cell. She will be safe enough until I return."

Khol really did not want to stay in Andonsheer any longer than necessary. *If only Harpur had listened to me,* he thought as he joined Karrys in the air. *If only Karrys had listened to me!*

Two hours later, the teal and the black dragons landed in the meadow in front of the lair. Hiro and Bon, sitting on the boulder, watched them land.

"What are they doing here?" Hiro whispered. "Did Anayah not take Elder Dhonna back to Andonsheer?"

"They seem to be looking at Harpur's body," Bon replied.

The Krist and the android watched the two dragons approach Harpur's corpse. Then Karrys scooped up some of the flowers that had sprung up around it and held them out for Khol to look at.

"So, I was right," Khol said. "Congratulation, Karrys. You *are* the new ruler of Epoh."

"Looks like we'll be neighbours, Khol," Karrys said. "Let's try to be peaceful ones."

"You will have no trouble from me," Khol said, happy to have his part in the challenge over with. Then he added, "As long as you take care of that other business as you promised."

"You have my word," Karrys said.

Then Khol the Black flew away to the west and Karrys Evergreen flew away to the south. Neither of them having given Hiro and Bon a modicum of attention.

"What was that all about?" Hiro asked.

"It appears that the flowers have somehow settled the question of Karrys Evergreen's inheritance," Bon said.

They both walked over to Harpur and picked up a few of the flowers Karrys had ripped out of the ground. But the flowers did not reveal any answers to their questions.

Arthur slipped down the secondary stairs to the main floor of the castle. He passed Hiro's laboratory and the kitchens, then took a right turn toward the kitchen garden on the eastern side of the castle and followed the sound of a crying baby to the conservatory that flanked the north end of the garden.

The baby with the lungs was Meg. When Arthur entered the room, he saw Alex bouncing the fussing infant in her arms and his heart melted. He paused at the door to relish the sight of his cute hippie girl wife and his beautiful daughter. Already having missed too much of these precious first days of his children's lives, he wanted to burn this sight into his memory.

Alex appeared to be alone with Meg in the conservatory. She was wearing, of all things, a teal gown with a train that fell from the scooped neckline at the back of her dress and her unruly curls were pinned back with sparkling silver combs. *Ready for supper in the great hall*, Arthur thought as he gazed at the love of his life. *Time for a change of plans.*

Arthur cleared his throat to get Alex's attention. She turned to see who had come in and Arthur nearly cried with joy when her face lit up with recognition.

"Arthur!" Alex cried as she deftly kicked the train of her gown behind her and moved toward her husband. "Look, Meg, Daddy's home."

Arthur threw his arms around his wife and daughter and kissed Alex deeply while Meg renewed her vocal protest between them.

"Oh, Arthur," Alex said, "it's so very good to have you home, but you need a bath." She waved a hand in front of her nose.

"Yes, sorry about that," Arthur said. "I'm sure I am a little punky. I just needed to see you. I have so much to tell you."

Alex saw the sadness in his eyes. "Arthur, what is it? What happened?"

A footman came into the conservatory and announced that supper was ready to be served.

Alex thanked him and informed him that she and the king would be eating in the conservatory instead and asked him to send Rupert, Arthur's valet, to fetch some clean clothes for the king.

"Finch will have kittens when she finds out she has to prepare plates for us," Arthur said, deflecting Alex's concern.

"Finch could send a maid if she wanted to," Alex replied, "but I think she prefers to have something to complain about."

Arthur laughed. "I missed you so much," he said, moving in for another kiss.

"I missed you too," Alex said, pulling away. "But no more kisses until you get cleaned up. You can bath in my room. It's just through there." She pointed to a door to the right of the entrance to the conservatory.

"Right!" Arthur backed away from his wife. "Make sure Rupert doesn't bring one of those frilly outfits he wishes I would wear."

Arthur retreated into the room Alex had sent him to. Clearly this new arrangement was a work in progress. The bed was barely more than a cot and all of Alex's gowns were laying on top of tapestries on the floor. A cracked mirror hung above an old table that held her hair brushes and a few toiletries. As in Sok's room, the tub was tucked in a corner behind a screen. There was one small window on the east wall over which a blanket had been tacked up to serve as a curtain. An open door on the north wall led to a smaller room where Arthur found his son, Hart, sleeping soundly.

"There you are, little man," Arthur cooed softly. "It's so good to be back and see you and your sister again. I hope that Alma hasn't been giving you a hard time."

"Alma has been giving him exactly what he needs to thrive," a stern voice said from behind Arthur.

He spun around to see the mid-wife standing in the doorway with her arms crossed. The typical look of disapproval was cemented in place on her face.

Speak of the devil. "Alma," Arthur said, "I didn't see you there."

"Obviously." The mid-wife approached the crib and craned her neck to check on her charge. "What are you doing here? I thought you were off on some errand for that dragon."

"That dragon has protected Epoh and all of the people who live here for centuries. Just because he's dead, it doesn't mean you can be anything less than respectful toward him." Arthur's nostrils flared in ire.

"Harpur Diggins is dead?"

Arthur and Alma turned to see Alex standing in the doorway holding Meg, her eyes wide with shock and disbelief. The baby was sleeping. Finally.

Arthur glared at the mid-wife. "If you don't mind, the queen and I need some privacy." As Alma walked toward the door, he continued. "If you tell anyone about Harpur, I will personally throw you in the dungeons and leave you there to rot. Do you understand?"

Alma stopped, but did not turn around. "I understand," she said quietly.

Arthur went to his stricken wife and wrapped his arms around her. "I'm so sorry, honey," he said. "That's not how I wanted you to find out."

"How did it happen?" Alex sniffled into Arthur's chest. Meg stirred and fussed, but did not wake up.

Arthur took the princess from Alex and laid her down in the crib next to her brother. Then he led his wife back out into the bedroom and settled her on the edge the straw-filled cot. *I will have to get Sok to get a proper bed in here if Alex intends to stay.*

He told her everything he knew about the challenge and how Harpur had died.

"Then why did he send you to the Fae Lands to get the..."

"The chalice!" Arthur jumped up.

Just then Sok walked in holding a leg of roast turkey. "You left it in my room. Don't worry, I didn't touch it. And I put two guards outside my door and told them not to let anyone but you or me in." He looked at the sobbing queen. "You told her?"

"Not now, Sok," Arthur snapped.

"Harpur's top hat, Arthur, calm down!" Sok said defensively. "I just wanted to see Hart and Meg. Are they in there?" He pointed to the door on the north wall.

"Seriously, Sok," Arthur said, "read the room. This is not the time."

Sok took a bite of the turkey leg while he considered his dismissal. Then he took a good look at the shabby room. "What..."

"Sok. Get. Out!" Arthur said through gritted teeth.

"Fine," the elf conceded. "I'll wait in the conservatory."

Arthur pushed the door firmly closed behind Sok and returned to Alex. He knelt down on the floor in front of her and took her hands. "I have to go and put the chalice in a safer place. But I'll be right back, okay?"

Alex nodded and Arthur stood back up. He kissed the top of her head and left the room.

Sok and Alma were staring menacingly at each other from opposite sides of a table bearing two large plates of food that Finch had delivered for the king and queen. Arthur didn't stop to say anything to either of them. *Maybe they will kill each other before I get back.*

But upon his return from stowing the chalice in the vault with Harpur's book, however, not much had changed in the conservatory. The elf and the mid-wife were still glaring at each other. One of the plates was noticeably emptier, though. Arthur shook his head and went into Alex's room.

It broke his heart to see her red-rimmed eyes filled with such grief. But he was relieved that she seemed to have gotten her sobbing under control. She was holding a baby again; this time it was Hart.

"I'm so glad we named him Harpur," Alex said as she rocked the serious infant in her arms.

"Me too," Arthur said. "I'm also glad that Harpur got to meet this little guy before..." He let the thought go.

"What does this mean for Epoh? What's going to happen now?" Alex asked.

"Harpur has a plan." Arthur reached out to take his son from Alex.

"How can Harpur have a plan? He's..." She couldn't say it either.

Arthur shrugged. "It's something he put in motion before the challenge. Until Elder Dhonna gets back from Andonsheer—if she gets back from Andonsheer—we're all as much in the dark about it as you are."

"You seem to be taking this all rather well," Alex observed. She handed her son to his father.

Arthur kissed his son's forehead and then looked off into the distance. "When I first saw him lying in the meadow, I thought I was going to die. I couldn't believe that he was really gone. But then I got this feeling that it isn't over yet. I don't think we've seen the last of Harpur."

Alex studied her husband's face. It was filled with conviction and hope. "Did you say Elder Dhonna is in Andonsheer?"

Arthur nodded. Then he filled her in on that part of the story.

"I'm glad Anayah is there," Alex said, "but what if something goes wrong? Shouldn't you and Sok be there too?"

"Anayah said she could handle it." Hart started to fuss and Arthur responded by bouncing him in his arms. "If they aren't back soon, we'll figure out the next step. Right now, though, I think this little guy is as hungry as his daddy is."

As if on cue, Alma entered the room and scooped the baby out of Arthur's arms. "Is the elf still alive?" he asked the mid-wife's back as she swept away to change Hart's nappy.

"For reasons I cannot explain, he is," she answered as she kicked the door shut behind herself.

Alex and Arthur exchanged looks, then returned to the conservatory where Sok was drinking from a flagon of ale that was meant for Arthur.

"I've ordered more," the elf said. Then he looked at the almost empty plate on the table. "I've ordered more food too. When can I see the twins?"

Arthur shook his head. "They are being changed and fed. I'm sure you will get to see them later."

Arthur held a chair for Alex and then seated himself across from her at the small table. There were only two chairs, so Sok dragged another one from across the room and joined them. "Alex, what's with the monk's cell? You have beautiful rooms upstairs. Why are you living down here in virtual squalor?"

"Yeah," Arthur said. "I was scared out of my mind when I went to your chambers upstairs and found it abandoned."

Alex smiled. She wasn't quite ready to laugh yet. "I just wanted a change of scenery and I love the conservatory. I don't think that I will stay down here forever. But with spring finally here, I wanted to be closer to nature. I'm sorry you were frightened, my love."

"It's alright," Arthur said, patting her hand. "If it makes you happy to be on the other side of the castle from me..." He winked to let her know that he was teasing.

Alex gave him an exasperated look. "It's the other side of the castle, not the other side of the kingdom."

"Still..." Arthur took a bun from a basket on the table and bit into it.

Sok watched this exchange between lovers and sighed. He thought of Yna and wished that he could share moments like this with her, then he made a mental note to go to Braydon Wood and check on the progress on the house he was having built.

He'd chosen a copse of oak overlooking the training grounds and the Wood Guild was working with the trees to turn it into an elegant treehouse. If Yna approved, maybe she would give him serious consideration as a suitor. Then again, now that Harpur was no longer the ruling dragon of Epoh, the whole undertaking could end up being moot.

"That reminds me," Arthur said. "Sok, can you arrange for a proper bed to be installed down here for Alex. That cot isn't fit for a dungeon."

"Why don't you just conjure one?" Sok suggested.

"Don't be silly, Sok," Alex scoffed. "Arthur can't do anything that complicated with his magic."

Arthur and Sok looked at each other knowingly.

"Watch this," Arthur said, standing up and walking back into the bedroom.

Alex put her fork down and got up to follow her husband. "What are you going to do?"

Arthur didn't answer. Instead, he closed his eyes and took a deep breath as he imagined a big, soft, luxurious bed in place of the grungy cot. Slowly, he started to raise his hands out in front of himself. When they were chest height, he drew them toward himself and then pushed them outward again. The room filled with a puff of amber smoke and when it cleared, the cot had been replaced by a big, soft, luxurious bed.

Alex squealed with delight. "Arthur, that was fabulous! How did you do it?"

Arthur buffed his finger nails on his shirt in a gesture of pride. "Jack and Diane helped me figure out how to use my magic properly."

"Jack and Diane?"

Another explanation was in order and Arthur brought her up to speed on his wayward guardians on the way back to the table.

"Pirates?" Alex said and Arthur nodded. "And you have no idea where they went or why."

"None whatsoever," he said. "They just showed up when Davynn and I got to the Fae Lands and then vanished when we met up with Sok and the others in Braydon Wood."

"Huh!" Alex didn't know what to make of these guardians. She'd heard about the nearly naked couple on Mysturna and had always hoped that they would never show up again. She shook them out of her head. "So, what happened to Hiro and Bon? Where did those two get to?"

"They are at Harpur's lair, cataloguing his hoard." Sok finished the ale and stood up to go and find out what was keeping the refill and the food.

"Is that wise?" Alex asked.

"Probably not." Arthur shrugged. "But it's keeping them busy. And it makes me feel better to have someone there with Harpur."

Tears filled Alex's eyes again at the mention of Harpur. She dabbed them with the corner of her linen napkin. "I'm really going to miss him."

Arthur went to her, knelt down beside her and held her close. "It's going to be okay," he whispered.

Sok returned with the tardy plate and ale, having saved Finch the complaint-generating trip. "I wish my room was this close to the kitchen. When you decide to move back upstairs, I think I'm going to move in here."

Arthur gave him a dirty look over Alex's shoulder, which went largely unacknowledged, as Alex disengaged and wiped the tears away with the napkin. "I want to see him."

"See who?" Arthur already knew the answer, but he had to ask, if only to buy himself time to come up with an answer.

"Harpur. I want to see Harpur." Alex looked pleadingly at Arthur, who looked helplessly at Sok, who looked innocently up at the ceiling. "You both got to see him and say good-bye. I want to, as well."

Arthur reached up and gently brushed a tendril of curly blond hair from Alex's brow with his fingertips. "I know you do, honey," he said, "but it's a three-day ride to the lair. What about the twins?"

"What about them?" Alex said. "Alma is here and there are two wet nurses to feed them. They will be fine."

"I don't think that's a very good idea, Alex," Arthur said. "What if Karrys comes back while we're there? I think we should stay here and wait for Anayah and Elder Dhonna to return. Once they are back and we have a better idea of what we need to do, then maybe..."

"I want to see him, Arthur!" Alex demanded.

Arthur stood up and sighed. "Okay. I'll figure something out. Let's finish our dinner and get a good night's sleep first. We'll talk about it again in the morning."

"Good idea," Sok said. "That will give Arthur time to take a bath."

Karrys Evergreen took her time flying back to the compound. With her rulership over Epoh now confirmed, she needed to alert the Council that there was no need for them to convene. But first she had to deal with the elf.

The bargain they had made was that Karrys would let Elder Dhonna go if Harpur's legacy to the land proved that she was the rightful heir to the kingdom. Beyond that there were no agreed upon specifics as to what letting the elf go entailed, so she considered doing just that; letting Elder Dhonna go. *Maybe the Drengrokil will take care of her for me,* Karrys thought, knowing that the mercenaries would be out patrolling the jungle around the compound.

Then again, the elf had been helpful and could prove useful when she took over the kingdom. *What would Harpur Diggins do?* She wondered. If Harpur's reputation was anything to go on, he would have seen the elf safely back to Epoh. But Karrys still had the feeling that the elf was up to something. With six more days until she could burn Harpur's body and enter the lair, Karrys needed to stall the elf as much possible and on her own, it would take much longer than six days for Elder Dhonna to get back to Colwygshire. *But what of that other person I smelled in the cell?* Obviously, whoever that was possessed magic and could help the elf. *This whole honour-among-dragons thing can be tricky.*

Still, Karrys would not begin her reign with a shadow over her wings. She had challenged Harpur fairly and she had won. She would honour her agreement with the elf and let her go. She could always deal with Elder Dhonna later. As for her promise to Khol, Karrys hadn't been specific as to how she would make an example of the elf. With a bit of luck, the Drengrokil would dispatch Elder Dhonna before whoever had been lurking in the cell could help her. It wasn't a great plan, but it was the only plan Karrys had that didn't compromise her honour.

The great teal dragon landed in the compound shortly after midnight and went immediately to Elder Dhonna's cell to find the elf sleeping on the mat next to the dying fire. "Wake up, elf," Karrys said, raking her talons across the cell bars. "You are free to go."

Elder Dhonna sat up slowly. Consciousness was reluctant to engage. "What?" she asked, blinking the sleep out of her eyes.

"I said you are free to go," Karrys repeated. "Harpur's legacy is as you predicted, confirmation of my victory over him."

Elder Dhonna pulled the blanket tighter around her shoulders. "Free to go where?"

"Anywhere you want." Karrys stepped back from the bars to grant her prisoner passage out of the cell.

"It's the middle of the night," Elder Dhonna said. "You're just going to turn me out. I don't even know where I am."

"Just follow the road from the compound. It will lead you to Andonsheer. Off you go!"

Elder Dhonna stared at the teal dragon. "You need to take me back to Epoh."

"I do not need to do that," Karrys said. "Our bargain was that I would let you go if Harpur's legacy proved my right to rule Epoh. It did. Now I'm letting you go. And I strongly suggest that you go quickly. I have things to do."

Elder Dhonna stood up. She adjusted the blanket again and then picked up the water skin. "Fine. But I'm keeping the blanket and waterskin." She walked to the gate. "How far is it to Andonsheer?"

"Not far," Karrys said as she estimated the distance. "You should be there well before dawn." *If the Drengrokil don't find you first.*

Elder Dhonna stepped through the bars and looked up at the dragon. "How am I supposed to get back to Epoh?"

"That's not my concern," Karrys said. "But if you're lucky you'll come across *someone* who will help you." *Like whoever was in your cell earlier.*

Something in Karrys' tone made Elder Dhonna think that she was referring to Anayah. "Is there anything I need to be wary of? Beasts? Snakes? Should I have a weapon?"

"I'm sure you will be fine if you stick to the road," Karry said. "Now, get moving before I am forced to give you a reason to." A blue-green puff of smoke rose from the dragon's nostrils.

Elder Dhonna wanted to say something snide, but decided to hold her tongue. She started walking as quickly as she could without appearing to be as terrified as she felt. It was decidedly uncomfortable having a fire-breathing dragon behind her, but she was determined not to let her fear show. When she reached the corridor that led into the open compound, though, she ran as fast as she could until she was through the arched gate and out onto the road to Andonsheer. Behind her, she heard Karrys' wings flapping as they lifted her skyward, but she didn't look back. *Anayah, if you're out here, now would be a good time to appear.*

But Anayah did not appear. So, Elder Dhonna kept walking. The cold night air, made to feel colder by a gusty breeze, bit through the blanket and set her teeth to chattering. Her elven physiology helped some, but she was not used to the dampness given off by the dense jungle that surrounded her. Even her feet, bare as usual, started to feel numb as the road began to curve and climb out of the valley. The strange animal noises coming from the bush did nothing to ease her tense nerves. All she could do was walk on and hope that Anayah showed up before she got to the city.

She was about halfway up the hill when three very large men stepped out onto the road in front of her and effectively barricaded her way forward. Elder Dhonna stopped and took in the impressive physiques of the swarthy-skinned, bald giants dressed in loose, baggy pants and short, sleeveless vests. They stood with their feet apart, their hands resting on the hilts of their long, curved swords.

"You are friend of witch, yes?" the largest of the three very large men asked.

Elder Dhonna had never heard an accent like his. She had never seen men like them. She was altogether too tired, too cold and too frightened to respond. She nodded slightly and wondered if her numb feet would allow her to outrun them.

"We are Drengrokil. We are also friends of witch," the big man said with a smile. "Why did dragons let you go?"

Drengrokil? Friends of a witch? Anayah? Elder Dhonna forced her tongue to work. "You know Anayah?" she asked, ignoring his last question.

"If Anayah is beautiful witch with red hair, then, yes, we are friends of Anayah," he confirmed.

"If you are her friend, why don't you know her name?" Elder Dhonna was as curious as she was suspicious, but she had to find out if they knew where she was.

The big man cocked his head to the side. "Our friendship is very new," he explained. "Witch did not tell us name yet."

"Do you know where she is? Can you take me to her?" Dhonna asked hopefully.

"First tell us why dragons let you go," the Drengrokil leader said. "Is not like dragons to set prisoners free."

Elder Dhonna considered her answer carefully. "I made a bargain with them," she said. "If I helped them solve a problem, they agreed to let me go." *Bloody dragons, have to take everything so literally.*

"What is this problem you helped them with?"

He's a tenacious one, this Drengrokil. "There was a question about an inheritance of a kingdom. I helped them find the answer to the question."

"This kingdom is Epoh, yes?"

How much did Anayah tell them? "It is," Elder Dhonna answered simply.

"This means great purple dragon, Harpur Diggins, is dead," the big man said. "Which dragon is new ruler of Epoh?"

Elder Dhonna took a deep breath. She sensed no real threat from these Drengrokil men, but she didn't fully trust them either. Nor did she want to stand out in the cold night air any longer than she had to. "Why don't I tell you all about it while you take me to Anayah?"

"Apologies, Elder Dhonna, I see you are cold and..." he began.

"Wait! You know my name?" Elder Dhonna interrupted.

"Witch tells us your name; you tell us witch's name," he said with a laugh. "Everything works out."

"And who is going to tell me your name?" Elder Dhonna asked.

Again, the big man laughed. "I am Frode of Ordyr, leader of the Drengrokil. We will show you where witch is now. This way." He pointed back down the hill. "Is not far."

Elder Dhonna was not sure she wanted to be going back toward the compound. She wasn't even sure that she trusted the three giant men. They could be holding Anayah prisoner somewhere and this could be a trap. But she was now certain that she couldn't outrun them and if there was even a small chance that they could lead her to Anayah, she had to take it. Then Frode, seeing her hesitation, transferred his sword to his left hand and offered her his right arm. *The way Harpur used to.* Elder Dhonna forced back the tears that threatened to spill from her eyes and linked her own arm through Frode's.

They hadn't walked far when Elder Dhonna stumbled on a rock in the road. Frode immediately handed his sword to one of his comrades and then scooped the startled elf up into his big arms and cradled her like a small child. Her first impulse was to protest, but the warmth of his body seeped through her blanket and she decided that her dignity could be put on hold for a while.

"Tell us who is new ruler of Epoh," Frode reminded the elf.

"Her name is Karrys Evergreen," Elder Dhonna said.

Frode stopped in his tracks. "Karrys the Ruthless? Drengrokil will go to Epoh and kill this scourge for elf and witch."

Behind him the other two Drengrokil raised their swords and roared in support.

"No!" Elder Dhonna said in alarm. "You can't do that."

"Why not?" Frode asked. "Karrys the Ruthless kill four good Drengrokil men. We will avenge our comrades and free Epoh from her tyranny." He started walking again.

"Really, I beg you, Frode," Elder Dhonna said, "if you are my friend, you cannot kill Karrys Evergreen. You just can't!"

"You want vicious worm to rule your land? Why?" Frode demanded.

"I understand that you want to get revenge for your friends, but Karrys has to live." Elder Dhonna felt the desperate panic rising up in her.

"You must tell me why," Frode said.

"I can't," Elder Dhonna said. She couldn't hold back her tears any longer. "I can only ask you to trust me. Please."

"Frode of Ordyr swore to kill Karrys Evergreen," he said. "I must know why you want me to break oath."

Elder Dhonna felt the throes of desperation tighten around her heart. "If I tell you, will you promise not to tell anyone else?"

"Frode of Ordyr gives his word," Frode agreed.

Elder Dhonna pulled herself up closer to Frode's ear and whispered into it. *Forgive me, Harpur.*

When she was finished, Frode looked into her eyes and nodded. "Is good plan," he said. "Is weird plan. But Drengrokil will go to Epoh. If plan fails, then we kill rotten dragon."

Elder Dhonna slumped against Frode's chest. *What have I done?*

They continued walking down the hill until they were even with the clearing where Anayah had made her camp. Frode made his way through the trees and when they saw the lovely witch curled up and sleeping under a thick fur rug, he set Elder Dhonna down on the ground. She ran to Anayah and gently shook her shoulder.

"Anayah, wake up," Elder Dhonna whispered loudly.

Anayah opened her eyes. When she saw Elder Dhonna leaning over her, she sat up and hugged the elf. "What happened? How did you get away from the compound?" Before Elder Dhonna could answer, she noticed the three Drengrokil standing in the middle of the clearing. "Frode? What are you doing here? Did you rescue Elder Dhonna?"

"Karrys set me free," Elder Dhonna explained. "I ran into our new friends on the road to Andonsheer and they brought me to you."

"She set you free?" Anayah asked. "Why?"

"It's a long story. Let's get back to Colwygshire so I only have to tell it once," Elder Dhonna said.

"Okay. I'm good with that." Anayah got up and zapped away the fur she had been sleeping under. "Thank you, Frode, for bringing Elder Dhonna to me. I hope we'll meet again someday."

"About that," Elder Dhonna said. "I believe that Frode and his friends will be coming with us."

"What? Why?" Anayah stared at her disheveled friend in disbelief.

"Another long story," Elder Dhonna said. "Let's just go. I'm tired and I'm cold and I just want to get out of here."

"First we get Drengrokil brothers from camp on north side of Andonsheer," Frode said when Anayah lifted her hands to zap the five of them back to Epoh.

"Drengrokil brothers?" Elder Dhonna asked. "How many?"

"Six," Frode said. "Is that problem?"

You have no idea. "Is it a problem, Anayah?"

Anayah shrugged her shoulders and shook her head. "I... guess... not?"

"Very well," Elder Dhonna sighed. "Where is this camp?"

"I know where it is," Anayah said as she picked up the deer fern fronds from the ground.

"Ah!" Frode said. "You were at Boundary yesterday. Is all making sense now." He tapped his temple with his fingers as he made the connection between the voices he'd heard by the Boundary and Anayah.

"Shall we?" Anayah said and a moment later they were all in the Drengrokil camp.

While Frode roused his clan from their tents, Anayah and Elder Dhonna sat on stumps next to the fire pit.

"What are those?" Elder Dhonna asked, pointing to the leaves in Anayah's hand.

"Deer fern," Anayah answered. "The juice is supposed to mask your scent so dragons can't smell you. I thought Hiro and Bon would like to analyze them."

"I wish you'd had some of that when you came to the cell." Elder Dhonna shuddered. "I thought Karrys was going to roast me alive when she smelled you there."

"I'm so sorry about that, Elder Dhonna," Anayah said. "I didn't think she would be there."

Elder Dhonna patted Anayah's leg. "It's alright. Don't give it a second thought."

The guild master and the witch watched in awe as the Drengrokil efficiently broke down the camp in a matter of minutes. Before they knew it, nine very large men were gathered around them with their gear packed cleverly inside their tents, which they had strapped to their backs. Their swords were tethered to their sides and each one held a spear half again as tall as they were.

Frode smiled at the two relatively small women. "Drengrokil ready. Do not worry, Frode told Drengrokil brothers you are good witch."

"Good to know," Anayah said, standing up and taking Elder Dhonna's hand. She leaned over and whispered to Elder Dhonna, "Are you sure about this? I could just zap the two of us back to Epoh."

"We have enough problems without making enemies of this bunch. Best to just take them with us."

Anayah snapped her fingers and moments later they were all standing in the council chambers in the castle in Colwygshire.

"Now, what are we going to do with nine Drengrokil?" Anayah asked as she watched the large men check out the room they found themselves in.

"Drengrokil will make camp outside city," Frode said. "You will show us where is best place, yes?"

"Follow me," Elder Dhonna said, then turned to Anayah. "I'll set them up on the north-west side, outside the walls. It's on my way back to Braydon Wood."

"It's late. Wouldn't you rather stay here for the night? I can find someone to show you to a room near me." Anayah offered.

"Thank you, but I just want to sleep in my own bed," Elder Dhonna said. "I'll come back in the morning."

Anayah was concerned for the elf. "Let's show these guys where to make camp together and then I'll zap you to the Wood."

Elder Dhonna smiled. "That's not necessary. It's not that far and I could use some time in the forest."

Anayah frowned, but acquiesced. "You're sure you'll be okay?"

"I will be just fine. Now that I'm close to home again, I feel better already." She hugged Anayah and then went to the council chamber door. "Come on, boys! Let's find you a home."

Anayah followed them out into the wide castle foyer. A handful of guards on night duty were mingling near the outer door and she had to stifle a laugh as their bulging eyes watched the bedraggled elf lead the parade of enormous Drengrokil out of the castle into the night. *Thank Orhowyn... or is it Harpur now?* The guards were too shocked to draw their swords.

Arthur had slept like a rock. After supper with Alex and the invading Sok, he had cleared Alma, the wet nurses and the twins out of Alex's rooms so he could take a bath and put on clean clothes. Of course, Rupert, the fashionista valet, had delivered an outfit that was a little more flamboyant than Arthur preferred. So, he had taken the opportunity to practice his magic and conjured up a more sedate pair of black pants that he paired with a dusty-green poet's shirt. While he soaked the miles of traveling he'd done over the previous days out of his pores, Sok got to play with the twins under the watchful supervision of a disapproving Alma and Alex busied herself by working on a macramé project she intended to give to Anayah.

The evening ended with a nightcap with Sok after Alma had settled the babies into their crib and had retired to her own new room across the hall from the conservatory, an arrangement that was not popular with the mid-wife at all.

"I will not be able to hear the twins if they wake up," she had protested.

"But I will," Alex replied.

"Hmph!" Alma snorted as she swept out of the conservatory.

"It's so good to be home," Arthur said when the affronted mid-wife was finally gone.

"I suspect that this will encourage her to find a new situation for herself," Alex said casually, thus, revealing her true motives for the move from her former chambers.

"She's finally gotten to you, then?" Arthur asked and tipped his cup of ale to his lips.

"She has too many rules," Alex said with a sigh. "I just want to enjoy my babies."

"Me too," Sok said. He looked at Arthur's shirt suspiciously, but didn't comment.

"They are not your babies," Arthur reminded him.

"You know what I mean," Sok replied. "They really are amazing. I would love to show them around Braydon Wood."

"Perhaps when they are older," Arthur said.

"If we had a stroller, we could take them out to the forest for an afternoon. The weather is getting much warmer during the day and some fresh air would be good for them," Alex suggested.

"What's a stroller?" Sok asked.

"it's kind of like a cradle on wheels that you can push the babies around in." Arthur always found it strange to have to describe common things from his world.

"On Earth, the cradle part converts to seats for when the children are old enough to sit up," Alex added.

"That's a fantastic idea!" Sok said. "Leave it to me." He drained his glass, said good night and left the king and queen to themselves.

"Alone at last!" Arthur said. He took a seat on a sofa and patted the space next to him.

Alex abandoned the tangle of ropes from her macramé project and joined her husband. As soon as she sat down, she yawned.

Arthur gathered her into his arms and kissed the top of her head. "Maybe we should call it a night."

Arthur conjured some sheets and pillows and a thick down quilt, hoping he wasn't taking someone else's bedding in the process. They had arrived folded, so he told himself they must have come from a storage closet to appease his guilt. That reminded him that he didn't know where the bed had come from either and he resolved to be more discerning about his conjuring in the future. If anyone complained, he'd make it right, but for now, all he wanted to do was crawl under the covers and fall asleep with his cute hippie girl wife in his arms.

When he woke in the morning, he slipped quietly out of the bed and got dressed in the clothes he'd conjured for himself the night before, leaving Alex sleeping peacefully. There hadn't been a peep from the twins all night, so he crept into their room to check on them. Both were sleeping as peacefully as their mother. *And I thought babies were bad for sleep.* He blew them a kiss and tip-toed out to the conservatory.

Alma was standing in front of the door to Alex's room with her arms crossed, waiting for Arthur to get up and leave.

"They're all still sleeping," Arthur told her, but she pushed past him and went inside to see for herself. "Good morning to you too!" he said sarcastically and then made his way to the council chambers.

Sok and Anayah were sitting at the round table drinking jamba and eating toast and eggs when he arrived.

"Anayah!" Arthur said with relief and joy. "You're back. Where's Elder Dhonna?"

"She went back to her treehouse last night," Anayah answered. "She's a bit rattled, but she'll recover. She said she would come to the castle later this morning."

Arthur sat down and Sok got up to go and order more food and jamba.

"How did it go? What happened in Andonsheer?" Arthur asked the witch while he waited for his morning repast.

"We agreed to wait until we are all together so we only have to tell the story once," Anayah said. "I zapped over to the lair to let Bon and Hiro know that they can come back here. They decided to take the hover gilly and catch up to Davynn. The three of them should be here this afternoon."

"You're really going to make me wait until then?" Arthur complained. He was dying to know what he was supposed to do with the Amber Chalice, but it made sense to wait for everyone to be together before making any further plans.

"We have to wait for Elder Dhonna," Sok said, sitting down again. "Besides, we have another problem to deal with."

"No!" Arthur wailed. "I just got home. I don't want to deal with any more problems."

"This one might actually be interesting," Sok said. "Berryl brought it to my attention this morning. Something to do with a group of strange men camped just north of the city. Folks are concerned."

Anayah's toast hovered a few inches from her open mouth. She had hoped to break the news of the Drengrokil to everyone later. "Yeah, about that..." she began.

Sok and Arthur both turned to look at the witch.

"You know about this?" Sok asked.

"They're kind of my new friends from Andonsheer." Now that she actually had to explain them, she was at quite a loss. "They're harmless. I think. They just have a teeny little problem with our new dragon."

"Your new friends from Andonsheer?" Arthur asked.

"A teeny little problem with Karrys Evergreen?" Sok asked.

Anayah sighed. "I was waiting until we were all together to tell you about the Drengrokil..."

"There are Drengrokil in Colwygshire?"

Arthur, Sok and Anayah all looked toward the door leading to the kitchens where a footman stood holding Arthur's breakfast tray. Sok got up and took the tray from the alarmed servant. "It's nothing for you to worry about. Do not say a word of what you heard here to anyone. Understand?"

The footman nodded and backed out of the council chambers.

"He's going to tell everyone he sees," Sok said, placing the tray on the table in front of Arthur. "Should I have him locked up in the dungeon?"

"No!" Arthur said. Then he looked at Anayah. "Should he?"

"No! There is no need to lock anyone up anywhere." Anayah shook her head and rolled her eyes. "It's not like Frode and his men haven't already been seen."

"So, why did the footman look like he needed to change his drawers when he heard their name?" Sok demanded. "Are we going to have a mass panic on our hands?"

"I told you, the Drengrokil are harmless," Anayah insisted. "I think."

"Well, I think we better go meet these Drengrokil of yours," Arthur said, looking regretfully down at the plate of steaming eggs and toast he wasn't going to get to eat.

Sok stood up. "Take your jamba with you and conjure up a pastry to eat on the way," he suggested. As he passed Arthur's chair, he clapped the king on the back. "Nice shirt, by the way. I used to have one just like it."

"I'll make sure you get it back." Arthur grabbed his jamba and followed the elf and the witch out of the council chambers.

They left through the main gate and followed the wall to the north side of the city. It was faster than navigating the maze-like streets. Easier, too, as it turned out. When they turned the corner at the end of the wall, they could see a throng of people blocking the north gate. Guards with drawn swords had formed a line to keep the mob safely separated from the nine gigantic men who were sitting around an open firepit ignoring them completely.

Just as they had been in Andonsheer, nine red and yellow-striped tents were set up in a semi-circle around the firepit and nine long spears leaned against a rack made of rough-hewn logs. The only difference Anayah could see between the camp here and the one in Andonsheer was the clothes the Drengrokil were wearing. Instead of the loose, cool, baggy pants and short vests, they were all wearing leather pants and boots. But even in the chilly, spring-morning air, they remained shirtless. Then she spotted another difference. Among the big men, a relatively petite elf with a shock of bright red hair sat on a log, also ignoring the guarded mob at the gate some fifty yards away.

Arthur and Sok took in the tableau with justified alarm. The Drengrokil made Harpur in his human form seem small. And he had been the biggest man either of them had ever seen.

"Harpur's amethyst ascot!" Sok said. "Those aren't men; they're small mountains."

"Come on," Anayah said. "I think you'll actually like Frode."

"Frode?" Arthur asked.

"Frode of Ordyr, their leader." She strode forward into the camp.

Sok and Arthur straightened their backs, puffed out their chests and followed Anayah bravely into the midst of the Drengrokil.

"Anayah!" Frode boomed when he saw the witch approach.

"Good morning, Frode. I'm happy to see you got settled in okay." Anayah allowed the small mountain to embrace her.

"The peoples of Colwygshire not so happy to see Drengrokil," Frode said. "Peoples of Colwygshire afraid of Drengrokil."

"Nonsense," Anayah said as reassuringly as she could. Then she turned to Arthur. "Arthur, maybe you can go and put their minds at ease?"

"This is great King Arthur?" Frode reached out a massive hand to shake Arthur's.

"Well, I don't know about great," Arthur said as he watched his own hand disappear into Frode's fleshy paw. When it came back whole and unshattered, he stared at it in awe.

"And this is the great elf, Sok, no?" Frode turned his attention to the elf and repeated the hand-shaking ritual.

"I am," Sok said, with much less humility than Arthur, who thumped him on the arm with the back of his whole and unshattered hand. Sok rubbed his arm and glared at his king.

Frode laughed. "Come, come. Join Drengrokil." He swept his trunk-like arm toward his circle of friends. "Wolf, get more stumps for guests," he ordered one of his comrades.

Arthur watched one of the Drengrokil men get up and go into the forest. "His name is Wolf?"

"Short for Wolfengaard. Is good name for him, no?" Frode said.

"Arthur," Anayah interrupted. "You really should go and say something to those people. They look like they are about to riot."

Arthur looked over his shoulder at the mob by the gate. They really did look—and sound—upset. "What am I supposed to say to them?"

"Just tell them that the Drengrokil are your guests and that they have nothing to fear from them," Anayah suggested.

"You think," Arthur said as he strode toward the gate.

"Harpur's violet eyes! I forgot to look for his crown," Sok said. "I swear I'm going to have to nail it to his head."

A few minutes later, Wolf returned carrying three stumps and Sok gasped in horror. "Um... What have you done?"

Across the firepit, Elder Dhonna was drawing her fingers back and forth in front of her throat and shaking her head emphatically. Sok looked at her, confused and infuriated.

"Is okay, Sok," Frode said when he saw the look on Sok's face. "Drengrokil friends with forest. Just like elves."

"But..."

"Is okay!" Frode repeated. "Drengrokil know about treaty with elves. Elf named Stellah mark trees we can use. Sit, sit!"

I'm going to have a long, long talk with Stellah when I see him, Sok thought to himself. He leaned closer to Anayah and whispered, "What have you gotten us into?"

"Just sit down and be nice," Anayah whispered back.

"I can't wait to see the look on Davynn's face when he sees this," Sok said to the witch. "He's going to have a fit."

Anayah flipped her long red hair over her shoulder and took a seat on a stump Wolf had set down next to Elder Dhonna. The two women smiled at the small mountains. Then Anayah looked at Sok and nodded her head to one of the empty stumps beside her. The elf relented and finally sat down.

Arthur returned and sat down next to Sok. He sipped his jamba.

"What did you say to them" Sok asked, craning his neck to see the crowd at the gate. "It doesn't look like you put their minds at ease."

The group around the firepit all looked toward the north gate. Sok was right, the mob did not look appeased.

"I just said what Anayah told me to say, that the Drengrokil are my guests and that they have nothing to fear. I don't think they believed me." Arthur took another sip of Jamba.

"Maybe if you would wear your crown once in a while, they might listen to you better," Sok snapped.

"Is no need for crown." Frode shook his head. "True king lead with his heart. Crown just decoration."

"Ha!" Arthur said, giving Sok another thump on the arm. "Told you."

"And what do you know about being a king?" Sok asked the Drengrokil leader.

"I am king," Frode replied, thrusting his thumb toward his chest.

"I thought you were a leader," Sok challenged. This time, Anayah thumped him.

"King. Leader. Is all the same," Frode said with a shrug.

"Thank you, Frode," Arthur said. "I appreciate that."

"I will go talk to crowd," Frode said, standing up.

"No!" Sok shouted. "I will do it."

Frode sat back down and Sok stood up. He walked over to the gate, spoke a few words and then returned. Behind him the crowd dispersed and the guards relaxed.

"What did you say to them?" Arthur asked as the elf sat back down.

"I told them the Drengrokil were your guests and that they had nothing to fear," Sok said.

"And you weren't wearing a crown either," Arthur said snidely.

"No, but they listened to me." Sok leaned back to avoid another thump on the arm and laughed when Anayah and Arthur's fists met just inches from his chest.

Anayah, not missing a beat, brought her elbow up and back, knocking Sok off his stump. The Drengrokil burst into laughter.

"Drengrokil think Epoh will be fun place to live," Frode said and motioned for two of his men to help Sok get up. "King Arthur," he continued, "elf is only trying to make you better king. He has great love for you. Frode sees this. You should listen to elf's advice."

Sok, surprised by this glowing endorsement, stared at the Drengrokil leader. "You just told him he doesn't need to wear a crown."

"Is true for Drengrokil," Frode said, nodding his head. "Maybe not so true for king of Epoh. I apologize for mistake."

In spite of himself, Sok was beginning to warm up to the small mountain. "Apology accepted."

Arthur wanted to ask Frode why he and his men had come to Epoh, but Elder Dhonna spoke up before he could ask any questions.

"Frode, this has been wonderful," she began, "but Anayah, Arthur, Sok and myself do have some important business that we need to attend to. Perhaps we can join you again later. We are expecting more friends to arrive today and we'd like you to meet them as well."

"Of course," Frode stood up. "Drengrokil understand. Go, take care of business."

The four Epohians bid the Drengrokil farewell and headed back to the castle.

"I can't believe you knocked me off my stump!" Sok said when they rounded the corner of the city wall.

"I can't believe you would mock your king in front of visitors from another kingdom," Anayah snapped back.

"Is okay, Anayah," Arthur said, mimicking Frode's accent. "Like Frode said, Sok loves me; he's just hard on me because he wants me to succeed." He threw his arm around Sok's shoulders. "Right, Sok?"

"Right," the elf agreed. "So where is your crown anyway?"

"I swear I will look for it the moment we get back inside." Arthur actually crossed his fingers behind his back as he and Sok strode ahead of the women.

"Men!" Anayah snorted.

"Can't live with them and you can't thump them hard enough on the arm to make a difference," Elder Dhonna concurred.

Davynn, Hiro and Bon arrived shortly after noon. They saw the horses settled in the stable and then went directly to the council chambers where Arthur and Sok were engaged in an argument over Arthur's missing crown.

"Did you even try to find it?" Sok said.

"I looked for it." Arthur had, in fact, made cursory scans of the different rooms he'd been in since returning from Harpur's lair, but the illusive coronet had failed to jump into his hands on its own.

"Where?" Sok was exasperated. "Where did you look for it?"

Davynn dropped a saddle bag onto the round table and flipped the flap back. "Are you talking about this?" He reached into the bag and pulled out a silver circlet.

"Oh, yeah," Arthur said. "I forgot I put it in there." He accepted it from Davynn and promptly put it down on the table next to the saddle bag.

"On your head, Arthur," Sok groaned. "It goes on your head."

Arthur scowled. "It gives me hat hair. I hate having hat hair," he complained as he plonked it on his head. Crooked.

Sok pinched the bridge of his nose.

"I see things haven't changed around here," Davynn said.

Anayah started the welcome home proceedings by giving Davynn a hug. "I'm glad you're back"

"I'm glad to be back." Davynn held the witch tightly as, around them, the others exchanged greetings.

They settled into chairs around the round table and Sok, pen in hand, paper at the ready, brought the meeting to order. "Now that we're all together again, I suggest we all share what we know so that we all know what each other knows. I'll start." He paused to gather his thoughts. "Harpur is dead, and we know his challenger, one Karrys Evergreen, may not have legitimately inherited Epoh in the challenge..."

"Actually, we do know that Karrys is the rightful heir to the kingdom," Elder Dhonna interrupted.

"We do?" Arthur asked.

"We do? Sok repeated.

Elder Dhonna stood up and pushed her chair back. She was wearing a teal and purple caftan that looked to Arthur like it had been tie-dyed. It was clearly an homage to Harpur and the new ruling dragon of Epoh and he sensed that the elf had chosen it specifically to represent the fact that she knew more about everything than anyone else gathered around the round table that day. He rested his elbows on the table and leaned in to listen to what she had to say.

The guild master explained how she had realized that the flowers that had grown in the meadow around Harpur's body were proof of Karrys' victory and that she had used that information to bargain for her freedom.

"In five days, Karrys will return to Epoh to claim her inheritance," Elder Dhonna said. "She will burn Harpur's body, according to his wishes, and the lair and all of its contents will be hers."

"So, where does the Amber Chalice come into all this?" Hiro asked.

"I'm getting to that." Elder Dhonna watched as all six of her companions focused intently on her. "First, where is my satchel?"

"It's in my room," Sok said. "I can send someone to fetch it for you."

"Please do," Elder Dhonna said. She waited until Sok had found and dispatched a guard to retrieve the satchel. When he was seated again, she continued. "When my satchel gets here, Arthur and I will repair to his private chambers. I'm afraid that I cannot share anything more with all of you. What comes next is for Arthur's ears only."

"Aw!" Sok groaned. "Come on, Elder Dhonna. You can trust us."

"There is one thing I can tell you," she said, deciding to throw them a bone. "If what Harpur wants Arthur to do fails, the Drengrokil have sworn to kill Karrys Evergreen in retaliation for her having killed four of their men."

Five of the six people at the round table exchanged looks of alarm. Only Bon remained impassive as he searched his internal data bases for any information on the Drengrokil.

"Did you say Drengrokil?" Davynn asked.

"I did," Elder Dhonna confirmed. "A small group of them are camped outside of Colwygshire right now."

Davynn leapt to his feet. Only Bon's quick reaction stopped the knight's chair from crashing to the floor behind him.

"Is Frode with them?" Davynn sounded excited.

"Yes," Elder Dhonna said, confused.

"That's fantastic," the knight said as he stepped around his chair. "I have to go and see him."

"You know Frode?" Anayah asked.

"Well, I don't know him, know him," Davynn said, bobbing his head from side to side. "But I met him once when the Drengrokil landed at the sea port. They'd just crossed the Crysteel Sea and King Gnik wouldn't grant them passage through Epoh. I was with the guards that were sent to keep them from coming ashore. Wow! Frode is here! Where is he?"

Anayah turned to Sok and stuck her tongue out. The elf curled his lip back at her.

"I will show you," Anayah said, standing up without causing her chair any distress. "If Elder Dhonna says we can't know what Arthur has to do, I might as well hang out with the Drengrokil."

The knight held out his arm for the witch and the two of them left the council chambers as Davynn excitedly told her the story of how he had met Frode of Ordyr, leader of the Drengrokil clan.

"Come on, Bon," Hiro said, backing his hover gilly away from the table. "Let's go meet these dragon killers."

Bon stood and boarded the floating chariot behind the Krist and the two of them floated out of the room.

The guard Sok had sent to get Elder Dhonna's satchel arrived and hefted the heavy bag onto the table. He asked if Sok or Arthur needed anything else and when Sok said that would be all for now, he bowed and took his leave.

"Arthur," Elder Dhonna said, "shall we go upstairs?" She reached for the satchel and when Arthur saw her strain to lift it, he quickly stepped in to carry it for her.

"What do you have in here?" He grunted as he pulled the strap over his shoulder.

"Harpur left me a few trinkets," the elf said. She walked to the back door of the council chambers.

"Just a few?" Arthur quipped as he opened the door and held it for the guild master.

Sok, alone in the room, looked around the empty table and sighed. "Meeting adjourned."

Chapter Seventeen

Elder Dhonna entered Arthur's private chambers and felt a sharp tug at her heart. The last time she'd been there, Harpur was with her, and his absence now was keenly felt. The cup he'd abandoned on the table by the sofa was gone, cleaned and put away by a maid just doing her job. But for some reason, this made Elder Dhonna angry. Then sad. *This has to work*, she thought, taking a breath and holding the tears back.

She sat in the chair Harpur had occupied when they told Arthur about the challenge. She had hoped she would feel his presence. But it was just a chair.

"Do we need the book?" Arthur asked. He put the heavy satchel down on the floor next to Elder Dhonna's chair. "Or the chalice? I can get them out of the vault."

Elder Dhonna smiled up at him. "Yes, bring them both. The book might be helpful to us."

Arthur nodded and went into the adjoining bed chamber to get them.

Elder Dhonna opened her satchel and rummaged around until she found the torn page from the spell book. She pulled it out and with it came two of the purple and teal flowers from the meadow. *How did they get in there?* She didn't remember putting them in her bag, but she must have. She picked them up off the floor and lifted them to her nose. Their spicy, woodsy fragrance filled her with calm.

Arthur returned with the book and the chalice and placed them both on the low table by the sofa. He sat down and watched Elder Dhonna looking at the transformed golden relic. The inside was stained with a bit of Harpur's blood that had congealed while it sat on the ledge in the lair. "Sorry, about that," Arthur said. "I should have cleaned it properly."

"Not to worry, Arthur," the elf said with a doleful smile. "It won't affect what you need to do."

"What *do* I need to do?" Arthur asked.

Elder Dhonna handed him the page from the spell book. "Start by reading this."

Arthur looked at the elf and then at the page. He read the first few lines. "It's a spell of some kind."

"Keep reading."

Arthur kept reading. About half way down the page, his eyebrows shot up and his eyes followed them to Elder Dhonna's face. "You can't be serious?"

"Keep reading."

Arthur read on. When he reached the bottom of the page, he put it on the table and slid it back toward Elder Dhonna. "Not happening," he said.

"Not even for Harpur?" Elder Dhonna asked.

"Harpur is dead," Arthur said. "What good could plucking the eye out of a dead snake and slicing my own hand open to drip my blood over it possibly do him?" He shivered convulsively at the thought.

"You won't have to actually pluck the eye out of the snake," Elder Dhonna said. "I can do that for you. And you don't have to slice your hand open. You can prick your finger tip instead. You only need a few drops for the spell to work."

Arthur put his hand between his knees and squeezed them together. Another convulsive tremor shook his spine. "What is this spell supposed to accomplish anyway?"

"I can't tell you that." Elder Dhonna took a deep breath and braced herself for one of Arthur's famous outbursts.

But Arthur just stared at her for a long moment. "Let me see if I understand things so far," he began, resting his elbows on his knees and clasping his fingers together. "First, Harpur somehow intuits that he is going to be challenged and so he sets some sort of plan in motion, not to save his life, but to ensure that Karrys Evergreen wins. Then he sends me off to the Fae Lands to get a chalice that he's been saving for Orhowyn knows how long because it contains the essence of a Fae girl whose magic he does not intend to use for himself, because he's going to die. And now that he is dead, I have to cast a spell with the chalice using snake eyes and my own blood, but you can't tell me why. Did I get that right?"

"Yes," Elder Dhonna said. "I think that sums things up fairly accurately."

"Well, if you can't tell me why, I can't perform the spell." He leaned back on the sofa and crossed his arms.

"I told Harpur you would refuse if you didn't know the whole story." If not for Harpur's flower, she might have had a fit herself.

"Then tell me the whole story. Harpur's never going to know," Arthur said. "And don't tell me you made a promise to him and you can't break it."

"I did make a promise to Harpur not to tell you. But I think I always knew that I might not be able to keep it. Not if I wanted Harpur's plan to work. And I do." Elder Dhonna reached for the book on the table and opened it to the last page. As she expected, Harpur's death was recorded.

Normally, a dragon's death was the last entry in its life book, but after the short article chronicling the last moments of her friend's natural life, there appeared two other short entries. The first was a picture of the purple and teal flower with a description of its healing powers; the second was an account of the Drengrokil arriving in Epoh. Harpur's story wasn't over yet. She looked up at Arthur and smiled. *Maybe I can keep my promise after all.*

"Let me show you something." Elder Dhonna stood up with the book and moved to the sofa to sit beside Arthur.

"What is it?" Arthur asked as the elf spread the huge book open across both their laps.

She pointed first to the entry about Harpur's death. "This talks about how Harpur died. This is about his legacy to the land. And this is about the Drengrokil's arrival in Epoh."

Arthur looked at the writing, but didn't grasp Elder Dhonna's point. "Okay. What does any of this have to do with the spell?"

"Usually, when a dragon dies, the last thing to be written in its life book is its death." She watched Arthur, waiting for him to make the connection. He seemed to be straining rather harder than she thought he should.

Finally, the light came on in Arthur's head. "Oh!" he said. "So, that's what he's up to."

Elder Dhonna breathed a sigh of relief. She gestured like a player in a game of charades with the time about to run out to get him to give the actual answer.

Then the light went out again and Arthur shook his head. "No. That can't be right."

"Oh, for Harpur's sake, Arthur, it isn't alchemy!" Elder Dhonna pushed the book onto the table and stood up again.

"Is that what we're doing now? Saying Harpur instead of Orhowyn?" Arthur looked at up at the nearly apoplectic elf.

"I need ale!" she sighed.

Arthur stood up as well and went to a table by the window where he poured them each a cup of ale. "I'm sorry, Elder Dhonna," he said handing her one of the cups, "I don't mean to be so thick. But this doesn't make any sense to me. It was almost as if Harpur wanted to die."

Elder Dhonna took a drink of ale and sat back down in the chair she had first occupied. "And why would Harpur want to die, Arthur?" She would coach him through this if it killed her.

Arthur remained standing between the chair and the end of the sofa. "He was injured and unable to heal. He couldn't transform into his true dragon form. He couldn't wield his magic. I imagine all that would make him want to give up."

"No, Arthur," Elder Dhonna said, "all that was why he needed to be challenged. There's a difference."

Arthur frowned. "Yeah, so he could die an honourable dragon death."

"And?" the guild master prompted.

"Oh!" Arthur said a few seconds later. "Really? That's weird!"

Finally! Elder Dhonna thought. "Now will you agree to cast the spell?"

"You are going to handle all the icky parts, right?"

"I will handle all the icky parts." She drained her cup.

"Okay, then, I'll do it. For Harpur."

"You don't know how happy I am to hear you say that," Elder Dhonna said, handing Arthur her cup for a refill. "Now, let's go over the details. There are a few modifications we have to make to the spell."

Arthur filled both their cups and then they settled in to make their plans for the final part of Harpur's plan.

The head table in the great hall was almost full for the first time in over a fortnight that night, though the seating arrangement had been slightly altered. Davynn now sat next to Alex. Beside him was Anayah, and beside her was Hiro. Sok and Bon sat on Arthur's right. An empty chair next to Arthur separated the elf and the king. Elder Dhonna had elected to return to Braydon Wood to eat with her own people.

There had been some debate about leaving Harpur's chair empty. They were not ready to announce his defeat just yet, but to Arthur, leaving him out felt wrong and so a place was set for the dragon-wizard and Sok was to announce simply that he was at his lair. It was, after all, the truth. Arthur had also wanted to have Frode sit at the head table, but the Drengrokil leader declined saying that he would sit with his men. And so, a table was reserved at the front of the hall for the nine small mountains.

As the guests filed into the hall, the usual rush to sit as close to the head table as possible didn't happen. When they saw the Drengrokil, the noble folk and even the knights hung back and the tables filled from back to the front. The latecomers who were left with no choice but to sit next to the Drengrokil did so hesitantly. There was no open discrimination, but Arthur leaned over to Sok and instructed him to say something about being respectful and welcoming. "Make sure they understand that I will not tolerate any racist behaviour anywhere in Epoh."

Sok signaled the footman to blow his horn and after three short blasts, the guests fell quiet and turned their attention to the head table.

"Welcome, guests!" Sok began, emphasizing the word guests to let everyone in the hall know that they were there at the king and queen's pleasure. "It is good to be back among you all once again. As you know, King Arthur, myself and our good friends have been away on business for Harpur Diggins. Harpur will remain at his lair for the foreseeable future.

"I would like to thank Berryl for seeing to the day-to-day business of the castle in our absence. Your copious notes are greatly appreciated." The councilman who normally sat at the front of the hall, stood up and waved from the very back of the room, accepting his accolades at a safe distance from the Drengrokil. Sok nodded in his direction and then continued. "The presentation of the twins will be announced soon. Prince Hart and Princess Meg are growing like dragonfoil trees and the king and queen are looking forward to having you all meet them. The event will be by invitation, so watch for those to be delivered in the coming days.

"Finally, I ask you all to welcome our esteemed guests, Frode of Ordyr and his men, to Colwygshire. We are all honoured to have them visiting our kingdom and the king and queen know that you will treat them with the respect they deserve. Epoh is a kingdom of diversity and home to a variety of races who live together in unity and cooperation. Let's show our Drengrokil brothers how great Epoh is and welcome them with open arms to our city." He lifted his cup. "To the Drengrokil! May their stay here be a peaceful one"

"To the Drengrokil!" Arthur said loudly, standing and raising his own cup.

Murmurs in kind drifted throughout the hall as the guests, eyes down, followed suit.

Frode and his men remained seated while the other guests concluded their half-hearted efforts and resettled themselves. They were well-aware of their effect on people and only accepted the invitation to dine in the great hall out of respect for their seven new friends at the head table.

"That was great, Sok," Arthur said as he sat down. "I was expecting upon-pain-of-death threats or at least long terms in the dungeons. Your diplomacy skills are improving."

The elf looked at Arthur. "You don't really expect anyone to challenge them face-to-face, do you?"

"No," Arthur said, "but you saw that mob earlier today."

Sok didn't reply. Instead, he signaled the footman to do his thing with the horn and get supper started.

Alex leaned close to Arthur. She hadn't taken her eyes off the Drengrokil since they had arrived. "They are fascinating," she crooned.

Arthur instinctively inflated his chest. "They aren't that fascinating."

Supper was followed by entertainment. As was customary, Olly, Versifier to the Court, a title the skinny blond bard had adopted for himself, started the evening off with a few songs. Usually, the minstrel's lyrics were humorous, bordering on bawdy, but that night his offerings were more subdued with melodies that were upbeat enough to get the audience swaying to the music without inciting any overt merrymaking. By the end of the night, the only casualty was a plate, dropped by a serving girl who was somewhat distracted by Wolfengaard's charming smile.

Arthur and Alex were the first to excuse themselves and once the monarchs had retired to the conservatory, the crowd began to disperse as well. Only the occupants of the head table and the Drengrokil remained and Sok invited everyone back to the council chambers for a nightcap.

"Arthur was in a chipper mood tonight," Anayah observed while stirring her tea. The others, except for Bon, of course, were having ale.

"Whatever Harpur had planned for him and the chalice must be easy, otherwise he'd be brooding about it." Sok said.

"No one else knows the plan?" Frode asked.

"Only Elder Dhonna," Anaya said. "Not even Arthur is supposed to know everything."

"Frode thinks plan is good," Frode said.

"You know the plan?" Sok cried, jumping out of his chair and nearly knocking over his ale.

Frode looked at each of the Epohians, who were all staring at him with various expressions of disbelief. "I do not know plan," he lied. "I only mean I think plan must be good."

Sok sat back down slowly, eyeing the Drengrokil leader with suspicion. "Why are you here?" he asked.

"Drengrokil in Epoh to see if plan works out," Frode said. "If plan not work, we kill Karrys the Ruthless."

Davynn, who was enthralled by Frode, was as confused as the others. "So, you know there is a plan, but you don't know what the plan is, but if it doesn't work, you're going to kill our new ruler?"

"This is correct," Frode said.

"Why?" Davynn asked.

"Karrys the Ruthless kill four Drengrokil. Frode of Ordyr swore to avenge deaths of good men. Also swore to wait until plan is done. We will see." Frode wasn't sure he could get himself out of the corner he'd backed himself into.

"Frode?" Anayah said. "What did Elder Dhonna tell you exactly?"

"Elf friend only tell me she has plan," Frode said. "Nothing else."

Sok, Anayah, Davynn, Hiro and Bon all looked at each other incredulously.

"Arthur must be going to kill Karrys," Sok said. "But why? How would that help Harpur?"

Everyone looked back at Frode.

"Plan must be different," he said. Then he turned to Bon, hoping to change the subject. "Friend Bon, why you not have drink with us?"

Bon had been running the information he'd just learned through his internal circuitry to determine the most likely missing aspects of Harpur's plan. His head jerked slightly as he switched his attention back to the room. "I have no need for food or drink."

"This ought to be interesting," Davynn said quietly to Anayah.

"Everyone has need for food and drink," Frode countered.

"Bon is an android," Anayah said.

"What is android?" Frode asked.

"An android is a machine that looks and acts like a person," Hiro explained.

"This is impossible," Frode said. "How can machine look and act like person?"

Bon stood up and unfastened his soft gray outer robe. Then he unbuttoned his white tunic and exposed his upper torso. He pushed gently on his chest and thirteen pairs of eyes widened as a panel about eight inches square popped out of his skin. Beneath it was a mass of wires and circuits. Tiny blue and green lights glowed on a plate of brushed metal near the top of the opening.

"What sorcery is this?" Frode asked in a hoarse whisper. The look of fear on his face was as much of a shock to see as Bon's unprecedented revelation was.

"It is not sorcery," Bon said calmly as he replaced the panel and buttoned his shirt. "It is technology."

"Where you come from?" Frode asked, working hard to keep his composure.

Sok, Anayah, Davynn and Hiro all turned to look at Bon with hopeful anticipation.

"Not here," Bon said and sat back down.

Sok, Anayah, Davynn and Hiro all groaned in disappointment.

"Okay, I have to ask," Sok said. "Why won't you just tell us where you're from? What's the big secret?"

Bon had done what he'd done for one simple reason; to distract his friends from any further discussion about Harpur's plan. The analysis he'd run had revealed the only possible goal Harpur could have had in mind and, even with what little he knew about dragon culture, it was obvious that it was in the best interest of everyone not to know what that was. It was also obvious that Frode knew what the plan was and had sworn not to tell anyone. Bon assumed that Elder Dhonna had been the one to share what could only be termed as highly classified information with the Drengrokil leader, probably under duress, perceived or otherwise, and he felt that he now needed to protect her most of all. Though it went against his mandate, he made a decision.

"I am from Earth," he said and he watched Anayah's eyes narrow with skepticism. "I was created there in the year twenty-five eighty-three and am one of several hundred androids scattered throughout time on different worlds. My assignment is to monitor and report on the progress of the cultures in the worlds I am sent to. You could say I'm an experiential archeologist."

"But it's only twenty-twenty on Earth," Anayah said after she processed what she had just heard. "How can you...? Oh, wow! You're from the future!"

Bon nodded. "On Earth I am from the future, but here on Thraeh, in this time, I am actually from the past. My kind are not usually permitted to visit future worlds, but I was able to procure permission to come here for one Thraehian year to study how magic has evolved beyond technology. My creators are particularly interested in dragon culture."

"Fascinating," Hiro mused. "Have you ever been to present-day Earth to see what life on your home world was like in the past?"

"I have not," Bon said. "And I would not want to go there now."

"Why not?" Anayah asked, giddy with the thrill of finally knowing where Bon came from.

"Because Earth is about to experience a global pandemic of epic proportions. Over the next two years some two hundred and twenty million people get sick and over four and a half million people die from a disease called COVID-19. Many of these deaths could be avoided, but too many people will insist that the protocols that the governments put in place to help stop the spread of COVID-19 infringe upon their rights. It is a very sad period in Earth's history," Bon explained.

The conversation continued between Bon, Anayah and Hiro. No one else understood half of what they were talking about. Sok was lost on words like pandemic, vaccine and medical system and something called WHO, which, according to Arthur, was a musical quartet that was famous for playing something called rock and roll. Sok couldn't fathom what *that* meant, let alone how it related to a disease that killed a tenth of the entire population of Thraeh. Davynn tuned out at the first mention of Bon being from the future and poor Frode was reeling from seeing Bon's entirely unnatural innards exposed without any harm to Bon. The rest of the Drengrokil just looked uncomfortable.

"Well, this has been great," Sok said over the unintelligible chatter. He affected a convincing yawn. "But I think I'm going to turn in. Good night."

Sok emptied his cup and left through the back door of the council chambers.

Frode, seeing this as an excellent opportunity to escape as well, stood up and signaled to his men. "Drengrokil return to camp now," he said and led his comrades away.

"I'll come with you," Davynn said. He looked hopefully at Anayah, but she was engrossed in a story Bon was telling about... *Space ships?* He shook his head and ran to catch up with the Drengrokil.

Several hours later, fatigue got the better of Anayah and she finally bid Bon and Hiro a good night. "I wish Harpur was here. I would have loved to see the look on his face when he found out you are from the future. And the past," she added with a weary giggle. "I don't know why I never guessed that you are a time traveler." She raised her hand to snap her fingers and zap herself to her room. Then a thought occurred to her. "Could you take me back into the past so I can see Harpur again?"

"I'm afraid I do not have the capacity to do that for you, Anayah," Bon said apologetically. "But have faith. The day may come when you will find a way to connect with him again."

Taking that to be some form of android spiritual comfort, Anayah smiled. "Good night, boys. And thank you, Bon, for sharing your story with us." She snapped her fingers and was gone.

Hiro giggled. "If you like we can go and work on the hover gilly plans for the rest of the night."

"I would like that very much, but do you not wish to sleep?" Bon asked.

"Don't tell the others, but mostly I just pretend to sleep." The Krist giggled again.

Bon stepped onto the hover gilly and the odd couple floated to the laboratory.

Arthur woke up and rolled over to find Alex's side of the bed empty. His disappointment turned to contentment when he heard her softly singing *Twinkle, Twinkle Little Star* in the adjoining nursery. He threw the covers back, conjured a fresh outfit of dark blue pants and a grey tunic, hoping that Sok's closet would not end up missing anything. He dressed and went into the make-shift nursery.

Alex raised a finger to her lips to shush him so he wouldn't wake Meg. Alex had just gotten her back to sleep after a nearly all-nighter of fussing. Hart was in the crib, wide awake but quiet. His little hands were balled into fists and he seemed to be concentrating on the wooden side wall of his bed.

Arthur gave Alex a kiss and motioned to let her know that he was going let Alma in. She nodded and whispered that she would see him later.

He opened the door to the conservatory and the mid-wife marched in past him, not bothering to exchange salutations, but Arthur didn't let her rude behavior dampen his good mood. On his way out of the conservatory, he ran into Rupert, the valet, carrying an armful of clothes.

"Good morning, your majesty," the valet said as he bowed awkwardly behind the mound of clothing in his arms.

"Good morning, Rupert," Arthur chirped. "Whatever you have there, take it all back to wherever it came from. I seem to have managed to dress myself today." He backed away from the valet.

"But sire, I've just come from the tailor. He assures me these are the latest fashions." Rupert peeked balefully over top of a particularly awful shade of mustard brocade.

Arthur sighed. "Leave them in the conservatory. I'll look at them later." He took a few steps down the hall.

"Your majesty?" Rupert called after him.

"What is it, Rupert?" Arthur stopped and turned around.

"I've arranged an appointment with the barber for you for mid-morning today. I thought you might..."

"I'm not sure I can make it, but thanks for thinking of me." Arthur turned and sprinted down the hall before Rupert could finish whatever he was going to say.

"...like a shave, sire." Rupert sighed. He took the pile of clothes into the conservatory and placed them on the sofa. Then he looked around to make sure he was alone. *This gorgeous mustard brocade jacket is probably too narrow in the shoulders for Arthur. I think I will just take it for myself.* He draped the coat over his arm and strode back out into the hall. If anyone asked, he'd just say he was taking it to be cleaned. Arthur's reluctance to dress like a proper king was good for Rupert's own wardrobe.

Arthur strode into the council chambers to find the room empty. He counted twelve ale mugs and one tea cup, the remnants of the nightcap his friends had imbibed without him the night before. Must have been a late night, he thought as he carried on through to the kitchens where he pilfered a cup of jamba from an urn that had been set out for the kitchen staff. Then he wound his way back through the hallway to Hiro's laboratory.

The Krist and the android were discussing hover gilly magic technology and seemed to once again be facing a brick wall on the path forward. How could they get a telepathically controlled device to work for people without telepathic abilities? It seemed impossible.

"Good morning," Arthur said from the open doorway. "You are up early."

Hiro and Bon looked up from the latest sketches.

"Good morning." Bon removed a pile of books and papers from a stool so Arthur could sit down.

"Good morning," Hiro said. "What brings you to this side of the castle?"

"No one else is up yet, so I thought I'd come and see if you were awake. What are you working on?" Arthur sat on the stool and cocked his head to look at the sketches.

"We're still trying to figure out how to make hover gillies for Davynn's men." Hiro giggled.

"What's the problem?" Arthur asked. He cocked his head the other way. The new perspective didn't help make sense of the drawings.

"Hover gillies rely on magic that humans don't possess. We have been trying to come up with some sort of external magical device to compensate, but everything we have thought of lacks efficiency," Bon said.

"Hmm..." Arthur sipped his Jamba. "Too bad you don't have an anti-gravity propulsion system."

For a few seconds, Bon stared blankly past Arthur. He appeared to be in a trance. Arthur looked at Hiro. "Is he okay?"

"I'm perfectly fine," Bon answered for the Krist. "I was just scanning my data base for viable anti-gravity propulsion system specs that we might modify for our purpose."

"And?" Arthur asked.

"And I think I might have something we can use," Bon said. "Thank you, Arthur. I believe you may have simplified things for us rather nicely."

Arthur nodded. "You're welcome. Nothing will get your hover gilly project off the ground like a simple anti-gravity propulsion system." He laughed at his sarcastic pun.

"Indeed," Bon concurred.

Sok walked into the laboratory, yawning. "What are you working on?"

"Anti-gravity propulsion systems for the new hover gillies," Arthur said as if he knew what he was talking about.

Sok had a flashback to the night before and felt his barely conscious brain threaten to shut back down. He held up a hand to stave off any further explanation. "I haven't had any jamba yet. And that sounds like a post-jamba conversation."

Arthur stood up. "Well, let's go find you some rocket fuel, then," he said, clapping the drowsy elf on the back and heading to the door. "Have fun you two."

Sok followed Arthur. "I've ordered porridge for breakfast," he announced, ignoring the rocket fuel comment.

"Porridge? Yuck. What's wrong with pancakes?"

"If you don't like what I pick, order your own breakfast."

"I will.

"Good."

Hiro and Bon listened to the king and his senior advisor bicker until they disappeared around the corner. "Porridge actually sounds pretty good," Hiro said. He pulled a steaming bowl of hot cereal out of his ever-present satchel and then hunkered down with the android to discuss anti-gravity propulsion and how they could incorporate it into hover gillies.

When Arthur and Sok arrived back in the council chambers, two large bowls of porridge were waiting for them on the round table along with a large jug of jamba. The empty cups from the night before had all been cleared away. Sok poured himself a cup of the energy-boosting fluid and topped up Arthur's own cup. Arthur stared at the porridge in front of him.

"Do you think Finch will be insulted if I switch this for pancakes?"

"I think you should just eat the porridge." The elf shoveled a heaping spoonful into his mouth. "Ooh! Hot!" He waved his hand in front of his mouth and forced himself to swallow.

"Serves you right," Arthur said, scooping up some of his own porridge and blowing on it to cool it down. "Next time order proper food for breakfast."

Anayah popped into the room and plopped down on a chair across from Arthur. She was wearing a dark red vest and matching leggings with a black bustier over a silky, cream-coloured shirt. Her hair was a mess.

"Late night?" Arthur asked the yawning witch.

"Did you lose your hair brush?" Sok asked.

Anayah looked upward through the tangle of red waves that fell across her brow. She snapped her fingers and her hair rearranged itself into a tidy braid, tied with a black ribbon. "It was a very late night," she said. "Bon told us where he's from."

"Did he now?" Arthur said. "What prompted him to do that?"

Anayah shrugged. "Frode asked him and he told us."

"Just like that?" Arthur was surprised.

"Just like that," Anayah confirmed.

"You should have seen it, Arthur," Sok said, awe and wonder creeping into his voice. "Bon pressed on his chest and it opened up. He's full of wires and blinking lights and little bits of metal. It was the creepiest thing I ever saw."

"I suspect that's normal for androids. What did you expect him to be made of?"

"Gears and pullies. I thought he'd look more like a clock on the inside."

Arthur laughed. "Never saw a computer made with gears and pullies,"

"A what?" Sok asked. Then he thought better of it. "Never mind. I don't want to know."

"So, are you going to tell me where Bon is from?" Arthur asked.

"Earth," Anayah said.

"Earth?" Arthur parroted. "That's impossible. Technology on Earth isn't advanced enough to make an android like Bon."

"He's from the year twenty-five eighty-three," Anayah said.

"Oh! Well, that makes sense." Arthur spooned more porridge into his mouth.

"How in Harpur's lair does that make sense?" Sok couldn't help himself.

"So, we *are* doing that now," Arthur said.

"Doing what?" Sok was confused.

"Saying Harpur instead of Orhowyn. Elder Dhonna was doing that too."

"Well, of course, we're saying Harpur instead of Orhowyn. Harpur was our last ruler." Sok looked at Arthur like he was daft.

"I was wondering about that myself," Anayah said. "I sort of get why people use Orhowyn's name. He was more or less revered as a god. But I don't understand the transition to Harpur."

"I think we should stick to Orhowyn," Arthur said.

"That's not how it works," Sok admonished. But he couldn't explain how it did work, so he steered the conversation back to Bon's origins. "You didn't answer my question."

"What question?" Arthur pushed his empty porridge bowl away from himself and reached for the Jamba jug to refill his cup.

Sok pushed his cup closer to Arthur to be refilled as well. "How does it make sense that Bon is from the future?"

"Because that's how it works," Arthur quipped.

Anayah rolled her eyes. "Twenty-five eighty-three is five hundred years in the future. Presumably, Earth's technology will have advanced to the point where time traveling androids are normal by then. Arthur is basing his acceptance on science-fiction."

"I'm basing my acceptance on Bon," Arthur said. "He's living proof that science-fiction will become science-fact."

"You know what?" Sok said, standing up.

"What?" Arthur asked.

"I'm going to Braydon Wood to talk to the trees. *They* make sense."

"Want some company?" Arthur asked sarcastically.

"No!"

Arthur and Anayah snickered as they watched the elf march out of the council chambers.

"And what are you up to today?" Arthur asked.

"I don't have any plans."

"Why don't you come with me to see Hart and Meg?"

"That sounds like a plan!"

Davynn woke up under a tree. He'd spent the night in the Drengrokil camp, drinking ale—too much ale—and listening to Frode's hyperbolic tales of battles won and maidens wooed. His head felt like it had been run over by a wagon and it hurt to listen to the birds chirping merrily all around him. He couldn't remember crawling over to the tree or being covered by the thick fur rug he was under. He sat up, groaned and laid back down. As long as he kept his eyes closed, the world wasn't spinning.

Harpur, if you let me live through this, I swear I will never drink ale again.

Someone kicked his foot and he forced one eye open to see Frode towering over him with a cup in his hand. Just the thought of more ale made the knight's stomach lurch violently. He closed his eye and pulled the fur painfully over his head. Frode kicked him again.

"I bring you this," Frode said. "Will clear head and settle stomach. Drink." He knelt down beside the knight and lifted his head.

Davynn didn't have the energy to argue. "What is it?" he croaked.

"Is good for what *ails* you." Frode laughed. "Drink."

Davynn opened his mouth to allow Frode to pour the contents into it for him. Whatever it was, it tasted like tar and farts and suddenly Davynn had just enough energy to roll over and spit it out. "Harpur's missing scales, are you trying to kill me? What is that?"

"Is called dragon piss," Frode said.

Davynn rolled the rest of the way over, came to his hands and knees and vomited onto the ground. "Dragon piss?"

"Is just called that," Frode said. "Is not real dragon piss. Drink." He thrust the cup toward Davynn.

"I'll pass, thanks." Davynn squeezed his eyes shut again.

"I'll leave here for you." Frode put the cup on the ground. "Hold nose and drink all at once. Will be easier." He got up and left the hungover knight to make his own choice.

Davynn looked at the cup. It was filled with a honey-coloured liquid that appeared benign enough. He wanted to trust Frode, especially if it meant he would feel better. He lifted the cup and sniffed it. It smelled as bad as it tasted, but just one whiff made the pounding in his head recede a little. *Dragon piss, hey? Here goes nothing.* He plugged his nose and brought the cup to his mouth. He hesitated for a moment while he braced himself for the vile taste. Then he chugged the entire contents in one go.

When the cup was empty, Davynn sat still, not sure what to expect. A few minutes later a huge belch escaped his lips and though he had to endure the essence of tar and farts one more time, he felt great. His head was clear. His stomach was settled. It was as if he hadn't consumed eleven flagons of ale. *I've got to get the recipe for this!*

He folded the fur and returned it with the cup to Frode who was waiting for him by the firepit with the other Drengrokil. "Thank you, Frode. I really do feel better."

"Is my pleasure," the Drengrokil leader said, motioning for one of his men to take the cup and the fur. "Stay close to latrine for next while. Dragon piss good for hangover, but also cleans you out..."

Just then, Davynn's lower abdomen emitted a loud rumble. "Oh-oh!"

The Drengrokil all laughed as they watched the knight speed-walk awkwardly toward the north gate.

Arthur, Sok, Anayah, Hiro and Bon all gathered in the council chambers later that afternoon and were having a pre-supper/post-afternoon-snack snack, which consisted of something Hiro pulled out of his satchel that Bon called brownies.

"These aren't *special* brownies, are they?" Arthur asked, biting into a chewy, chocolate morsel.

"What would make them special?" Hiro asked.

Arthur and Anayah exchanged looks.

"I believe Arthur is referring to the addition of cannabis to the recipe," Bon offered.

"What is cannabis?" Hiro asked. "And how does it make brownies special?"

"Cannabis is a plant that contains tetrahydrocannabinol, or THC, a psychoactive compound that when smoked or ingested produces a sensation of feeling high," Bon recited from his internal database.

"Can we not talk about weird Earth things today?" Sok complained.

"So, you put this cannabis into the brownies and then when you eat them you float up into the air?" Hiro paraphrased.

Arthur laughed. "No, Hiro, cannabis doesn't make you float up into the air. Although, that would be pretty special."

"Being high is sort of like being drunk. But... different," Anayah said.

"I see," Hiro said.

"What do you know about being high?" Arthur asked Anayah.

"Harpur and I had our share of special brownies when we lived on Whyte Avenue," she answered.

"Really?" Arthur was surprised. "Harpur never mentioned he used pot." He noticed the confused looks on Sok and Hiro's faces and added, "That's a nickname for cannabis."

"Sok, are there any plants like that in Epoh?" Hiro asked.

"You looking to get stoned, Hiro?" Arthur teased.

"Stoned is another way of saying high," Anayah explained.

"I would like to analyze it." Hiro reached for another brownie.

"Elder Dhonna would be the one to ask about mind-altering plants," Sok said. "Has anyone seen Davynn today?"

"Not since he left with Frode and company last night," Anayah answered.

"Why is it called pot?" Hiro's curiosity would not be quelled by Sok's mere attempt to change the subject.

Everyone looked at Arthur, but it was Bon who provided the answer. "Pot is derived from the Spanish word potaguaya, a wine in which the buds of a cannabis plant have been steeped. It literally means the 'drink of grief.'"

"I did not know that," Arthur said. "Cool."

"You're just a walking library, aren't you?" Sok said to Bon. "Is there anything you don't know?"

"I am certain that there are many things that I don't know," Bon said.

The door to the council chambers opened and Davynn walked in. He looked a little peaked.

"Where have you been all day?" Anayah asked, pushing the chair next to her out so he could sit beside her.

"Don't ask." The knight folded his arms on the table and rested his forehead on them.

"Are you alright?" Anayah was alarmed.

"I'll be fine," Davynn moaned. "But if anyone ever offers you dragon piss, just say no."

"Duly noted," Arthur said, not wanting to know what that was. "Brownie?"

Davynn lifted his head and looked at the dwindling plate of brownies. "No, thanks." He put his head down again.

"Who gave you Carver's tincture?" Sok asked. "That's another name for dragon piss, by the way."

"Frode." Davynn suddenly stood up and ran out of the room.

"Where's he going?" Anayah asked. She stood, wondering if she should follow him and make sure he was okay.

"Probably to the nearest water closet," Sok said. "If he drank a large amount of Carver's tincture, he'll be wanting to stay close to one for a day or two."

Anayah sat back down and grimaced.

"Bon, remind me to look up Carver's tincture when we get back to the laboratory," Hiro said to the android.

The android nodded. "I will also remind you to talk to Elder Dhonna about psychoactive and hallucinogenic plants when you next see her."

"Yes! Thank you, Bon."

"That reminds me," Anayah said. "I brought back some leaves from a plant called deer fern. I thought you might want to study it. Apparently, the juice from the leaves masks your scent so dragons can't smell you."

Hiro giggled with delight. The Krist hadn't had this much new stuff to investigate in months. "That sounds interesting. Thank you, Anayah.

The back door of the council chambers opened and Alex entered. "Is Davynn okay? I just saw him running down the hall like his pants were on fire."

"Well, not his pants exactly," Arthur said with a laugh.

"What?" Alex looked questioningly at her husband as she joined him at the table.

"Never mind. I'll tell you later." Arthur kissed his wife. "What are you doing here?"

"The twins are both sleeping," she said, "so, I thought I'd sneak out and see what you were up to. Ooh! Brownies!" She reached for one of the last three remaining squares. "Are they the special kind?"

Sok planted his face in the palm of his hand.

Chapter Eighteen

The next day was court day. Arthur traded his disliked coronet for his loathed jeweled crown. He donned the fur-trimmed royal robe without complaint and Sok actually tested his forehead for fever.

"Stop that!" Arthur said, batting the elf's hand away from his face.

"Just checking, sire," Sok said. "You'll be pleased to know that there are only eighteen petitions today. Berryl left a few things for you, but it's all pretty minor."

"If Dun and Jacko are on the docket today, tell them to work it out for themselves." Arthur adjusted his crown.

"They are not. I think they finally got the message last time they were here." Sok double-checked the list of petitioners just to be sure he wasn't lying to his king.

"Good. Those two are tedious." Arthur started to head to the great hall and then stopped. Thinking about the butcher and the shoemaker reminded him of something else. "I don't suppose Morgaine Fayle is on the list?"

"Should she be?"

Arthur hadn't thought about the sultry, raven-haired beauty since he and Davynn had been on their way back from the Fae Lands. It suddenly seemed odd to him that there had been no mention of her since his return to the castle. "That was all a bit strange, don't you think?"

Sok shrugged. "My sources tell me that she left the Shire Bend Inn a few days after Harpur went to his lair and hasn't returned. Maybe she changed her mind."

"Hmm... Maybe." Arthur put her out of his mind and went into the great hall to take his seat on the throne.

For the next four hours, Arthur listened to his subjects whine, complain, wheedle and grumble about various petty differences they had with their neighbours, friends and family. One by one, he pronounced judgement, doled out punishments or dismissed the cases as he deemed necessary. By the time they reached the last case, Arthur was slumped down in the throne with his chin resting in his hand, barely able to keep his eyes open.

"One more," Sok said after the second to last petitioner had left the hall.

"Thank Orhowyn," Arthur said, refusing to convert to the new way of doing things. He sat up straight. "What is it?"

Sok scowled, but did not comment. He would grant Arthur a grace period to adjust. "It's not clear, sire," the elf said. "The petition is being brought forward by a man from a village at the base of the mountains near the end of the Colwygshire Road. He refused to tell us what his problem is, saying that it is for your ears only."

"A private audience?"

"He didn't specifically request that, but he did say that he would prefer that there not be any other petitioners allowed in the hall when he spoke to you. He seems quite anxious." Sok didn't sound overly concerned.

"What's his name?"

"Ned Krats, sire."

"Do you really have to call me sire?" Arthur asked.

"This is court, sire," Sok said. He knew the crown and robe thing was too good to be true. "Here, I am not your friend; I am an officer of said court. Your Majesty."

Arthur stifled a sigh and gestured for Sok to continue. "Let get this over with."

Sok signaled the guards at the door to admit the final petitioner of the day. Ned Krats was a stocky man in his mid-forties. His reddish-brown hair was kissed with gray at the temples and fine lines fanned out from the corners of his light green eyes. He was wearing what most villagers who worked in the fields wore, a pair of thick canvas pants and a simple brown coat. He carried a battered hat in his hands and he continually worried at a loose thread on the brim. Anxious was as good a way as any to describe his demeanor.

"Mr. Krats, welcome to Colwygshire. How can I help you today?" Arthur said in his most kingly voice.

Ned Krats bowed nervously. "Thank you, your majesty. I'm here on a matter of some urgency."

"And what is this urgent matter, Mr. Krats?" Arthur prompted.

"It's the Fae, your majesty."

Sok's head snapped up. He was sitting at a small table to the left of Arthur's throne recording the proceedings. "What about the Fae?" he asked before Arthur could respond.

Ned Krats' eyes shot over to the elf and then back to the king. "They have been seen near our village, sire."

Sok came out from behind the table and approached the skittish petitioner. "What do you mean they have been seen near your village?"

Arthur considered putting Sok back in his place, but decided to let the elf handle it. It was the last petition of the day and though he knew that the Fae were supposed to stay in Braydon Wood, he didn't see the harm in them exploring a bit more of Epoh.

"A group of them... Four or five, though there could be more. It's hard to tell with them sometimes... have been seen in the fields. We've moved all the children into the lodge and we've set up watches to keep an eye on them. They haven't come into the village proper yet, but..."

Sok spun around to face Arthur. "Arthur, you have to do something!" he shouted.

Ned Krats was shocked by the familiarity toward the king that Sok had just exhibited. His eyes darted back and forth between the elf and king while he waited for Arthur to reprimand his advisor.

"Why have you moved the children to the lodge?" Arthur asked, focusing on this anomalous reaction.

"Why have they moved the children to the lodge?" Sok spat. "Why do you think they moved the children to the lodge? To keep them from being stolen, that's why!"

Ah. Must be the old changeling trick. Arthur had no idea what he was supposed to do about this. Strictly speaking, this was Harpur's purview. But of course, Harpur was in no position to exercise his authority over the Fae and dispatch them back to the Wood. And there was another two days before Karrys Evergreen came to claim the kingdom and Arthur put the last part of Harpur's plan into action. "Okay, calm down," he said lamely.

"I will not calm down!" Sok yelled. "The Fae are out of their territory. That is not something one should be calm about, Arthur."

"Mr. Krats, may I have a minute alone with my advisor?" Arthur asked the puzzled man.

"Of course." Ned Krats bowed. "I'll just wait outside, then?"

"If you don't mind," Arthur said.

The second the door closed behind Ned Krats, Sok rounded on Arthur. "I can't believe you are just sitting there so calmly! You have to do something."

"And just what do you propose I do, Sok? I have no authority over the Fae and without Harpur to keep them in line, I don't know how I am supposed to handle this."

"Send Davynn and his men to kill them!" Sok said, pointing southward for emphasis.

"And start a war with them? I'm not going to do that."

"They started it! They came out of their territory." Sok was furious.

"Okay, true enough. I will send Davynn and his men to protect the village. But I will not order them to kill the Fae unless the Fae attack first."

Sok glared at Arthur. "That's not good enough. If you won't deal with this, I will go to my people and they will."

A sudden fit of desperation flooded Arthur with an anger equal to the elf's. "You will do no such thing, Sok. I will not give the elves permission to slaughter the Fae on human land."

"I can't believe you would betray me like this," Sok said. Then he turned and walked out of the hall.

"Sok, please! Come back here!" Arthur shouted. But the elf was gone.

He ripped off his royal robe and tossed it along with the crown onto the throne and ran to the door leading to the kitchens. "Tell the petitioner that I'm handling things," he yelled to the guards at the main door and then dashed into the hallway toward the council chambers.

Hiro and Bon were sitting at the round table, still talking about anti-gravity propulsion systems. "Did Sok come through here?" he barked.

"No. We haven't seen him? How was court?" Hiro answered.

"Terrible!" Arthur snapped. "Where's Davynn?"

"He and Anayah went for a walk in Braydon Wood," Hiro replied. "What happened?"

"No time," Arthur said. Then he snapped his fingers and disappeared in puff of golden smoke, leaving the android and the Krist to wonder what was going on. Again.

He had never zapped himself anywhere before, so when he landed in the gardens surrounding the Healing Guild House, just as he intended, he couldn't help but be pleased with his efforts. Looking around, he saw four elves tending to the gardens with rakes and hoes and earth-caked hands. But he didn't see Elder Dhonna anywhere. "Where is your guild master?" he asked the closest elf.

The elf pointed at the guild house. "She in there, but..."

Arthur didn't wait for the elf to finish. He ran to the door and rushed through it. Elder Dhonna was instructing three other elves on the use of various herbs in healing and she did not look pleased with Arthur's interruption.

"Arthur, I'm busy," she said. "You can't just burst in here whenever you want. I have..."

"Class dismissed," Arthur ordered, pointing back at the door.

The three students all looked at Elder Dhonna for direction. Seeing Arthur's obvious distress, she nodded toward the door and shooed them out. "Arthur, what is this about? What happened?"

He told her what happened in court and of Sok's accusation of betrayal. "You've got to help me, Elder Dhonna. You have to stop Sok from starting a war with Fae."

The guild master was as horrified as Sok had been to learn that the Fae had crossed the borders of their territory. But she understood Arthur's position. "I will try to convince the council to keep the warriors in the Wood, but honestly, Arthur, I'm not sure they will do that. Once they learn that the Fae have crossed the border, they will hunt them down."

"But the Fae are on human lands," Arthur argued. "The elves can do what they want in Braydon Wood, but I can't have the elves killing the Fae on human lands. At least not without knowing why they are there and what they want."

"I will do my best," Elder Dhonna promised. "What do you plan to do?"

"I'm going to send Davynn and some men to the village to protect it. Hopefully, Davynn will be able to talk to the Fae. Maybe he can negotiate with them. Elder Dhonna, we can't have a war. Not now. Not when we are so close to seeing Harpur's plan through."

"Right!" Elder Dhonna said. "Where is Sok now?"

"I assume he's on his way here." Arthur's desperation was palpable.

"We don't have much time, then," Elder Dhonna said. "I will gather the Elders and tell them what's happened. Hopefully, I can get them to listen to reason."

"I'm going to go find Davynn so he can get his men ready. Between Anayah and me, we can zap them to the village and make sure they are there before the elves arrive," Arthur strategized out loud.

Elder Dhonna almost didn't say what she said next. It felt like such a betrayal of her people. "Send the Drengrokil with them. Their presence might be enough to keep the elven warriors from attacking outright."

"Good idea," Arthur said. "Thank you Elder Dhonna. Thank you so much."

"Don't thank me yet, Arthur," the worried guild master said. "But no matter what happens, you and I have to be at the lair tomorrow night."

"I know." Arthur took a deep breath. "Good luck."

"You too."

Arthur zapped himself out of the guild house.

Davynn and Anayah were walking arm in arm through Braydon Wood. They had taken the path to the stone structure the elves had erected around the Boundary it housed to stop unauthorized Bounding between Epoh and Earth. The Boundary led to a rooftop on the corner of Whyte Avenue and 104 Street in Edmonton, Alberta. This was where Harpur had first met Arthur and discovered his latent magical abilities. More than a decade had passed since that fateful day when Arthur had bumped into a woman as he was leaving the comic book store where he worked. Their collision had caused her to drop her coffee cup and Arthur had inadvertently used his magic to keep it from hitting the sidewalk. If Harpur hadn't been there to witness it, Arthur might never have become the king of Epoh. And Harpur might not ever have lost his own magic.

Anayah looked at the Boundary House. It's simple, but elegant, construction complemented the landscape rather beautifully, she thought. "Have you ever Bounded?" she asked the handsome knight.

Davynn shook his head. "Not worth the risk of being crushed or torn apart."

Anayah agreed. Bounding was not without its hazards. "I wish you could see it."

"I've seen the Boundary. Many times," Davynn replied, missing her meaning.

"I mean Whyte Avenue. It's really quite an extraordinary place," she said wistfully.

Based on the stories Arthur had told him about Whyte Avenue, Davynn was quite certain that he wasn't ready for that kind of excitement. But he didn't share that with the gorgeous, ginger witch at his side. Instead, he turned to face her. "Perhaps one day we will find a way to go there."

Their eyes met and they leaned in for their first kiss...

"Crap!"

The kiss went unfinished. Davynn and Anayah, lips still puckered, turn their heads and looked up at the roof of the Boundary House.

"Sorry for the interruption," Arthur said. "I don't suppose the elves left a ladder somewhere."

"Um... Why don't you just zap yourself down?" Davynn suggested.

"Of course," Arthur said. "Don't know why I didn't think of that." He snapped his fingers and zapped himself to the ground. "Wow! This zapping thing sure does come in handy. Wish I knew I could do it when I was stuck in that tree..."

"Arthur, why are you here?" Anayah asked, clearly annoyed by his intrusion.

"Yes, that," Arthur said. "Davynn, you have to come with me right now. The Fae have come out of their territory and Sok is sending the elven warriors to hunt them down and kill them."

"The Fae have crossed the river?" Davynn asked. "They're in elven territory?"

"No. Well, maybe. I don't know if they are in elven territory. But they have been seen near a village at the end of the Colwygshire Road. Sok freaked out when he found out and accused me of betraying him when I refused to send guards to kill them and now, he's on his way to meet with the Elders to get them to send their warriors to go and kill the Fae. We have to get you and your men there first to find out why the Fae are there and stop a war between them and the elves." Arthur ran out of breath.

"It's a three-day ride," Davynn said. "If you can zap a few of us there to help the villagers and reconnoiter the situation, we'll have an advantage over the elves when they arrive. We can dispatch the rest of our troops to take the road and meet us there."

Arthur, relieved that Davynn was taking over, raised his hand to zap them back to the castle.

"Wait!" Davynn said.

Arthur paused. "What now?"

Davynn turned to Anayah. He placed his hands on either side of her face, bent down and kissed her. "I don't know when I'll get another chance to do that."

"Can we go now?" Arthur said. He snapped his fingers and disappeared.

"I'm guessing he needs a little more zapping practice," Davynn said after the golden smoke cleared and he found himself and Anayah still in the same spot by the Boundary House.

"I'm guessing he needs a lot more zapping practice," Anayah said, taking Davynn's hand. She was about to snap her own fingers when Davynn stopped her.

Anayah looked at him and then smiled. It was Davynn's chance to kiss her again.

Arthur appeared in the Drengrokil camp and looked around. "Where are they?"

"Where are who?" Frode asked. He was sitting on a stump by the firepit, sharpening his sword.

"I must have done something wrong." He snapped his fingers and disappeared again.

Frode went back to sharpening his sword.

This time, he landed on the ground next to the Boundary House, but Davynn and Anayah were no longer there. "Orhowyn's... Damn it!" He zapped himself back to the council chambers and was relieved to find Davynn and Anayah standing next to the round table waiting for him.

"What happened? Why didn't you come with me?" Arthur asked.

"You didn't take us with you," Anayah replied. "Where did you go?"

"I went to the Drengrokil camp. Elder Dhonna thought they might intimidate the elves and keep them from killing the Fae." Arthur explained. "Let's go."

Hiro and Bon were at the table listening to the exchange between the king, the knight and the witch. At the mention of elves killing the Fae, Hiro spoke up, "Would it do me any good to ask why the elves are killing the Fae?"

"I'll tell you later," Arthur said. For the sixth time that day, he prepared to zap himself to a new location.

"Let me do it," Anayah intervened. "Where do you want us to go?"

"The Drengrokil camp." Arthur relaxed his hand and allowed the more experienced zapper to zap them all to the same place.

When they appeared in the camp, Frode was holding his long and lethal sword out in front of himself as he eye-balled the freshly honed edge. The tip was less than an inch from Arthur's belly, which he sucked in with a short yelp.

Frode lowered the weapon and looked at the new arrivals to his camp. "You found who you were looking for?"

"Yes," Arthur said, happy to see the sword being retracted to a safer distance from his body. "Frode, we need your help."

"What sort of help you need?" Frode asked.

Arthur explained what was happening and what he wanted the Drengrokil to do. Frode didn't ask questions; he stood and immediately ordered his men to break camp.

"This won't take but a minute," Anayah assured Arthur.

He and Davynn watched in awe as each of the Drengrokil worked like a well-oiled machine to dismantle the tents and convert them into efficiently packed packs that they strapped to their backs.

"Wow!" Davynn said. "I'm going to have to get them to teach my men how to do that."

"Drengrokil ready to protect village and frighten murderous elves," Frode announced as he lifted his own backpack tent onto his back.

"I need to get a few of my own men together first," Davynn said.

"We will wait," Frode said.

"Anayah, why don't you show these gentlemen to Skull's Keep? I'll go with Davynn to the barracks and when the men are ready, we'll come get you there," Arthur suggested.

Anayah looked at him. "I don't think they'll fit in Skull's Keep," she said. She was only partly joking.

"They'll fit," Arthur said.

"And who's going to pay?" Anayah asked.

"Just put whatever they order on the castle account." He hated to admit it, but that account did have its useful side. Then he and Davynn ran for the barracks.

"Come on, boys. I think I know the way, but if we get lost, it's not my fault." She led the small mountains toward the north gate and into the maze of streets of the city.

Sok paced back and forth in front of the closed Elders' chamber's doors. When he'd arrived to find the Elders already in session, he realized that Arthur must have zapped himself to Braydon Wood and warned them about the Fae. He imagined that Arthur was inside the chambers with the Elders, begging them not to kill the elementals. And he suspected that

Arthur would refrain from telling them that Harpur was dead unless he was given no other choice. *Well, they'll be hearing it from me!* Sok vowed.

At long last, the door to the Elders' chambers opened and an elf named Elder Parm, master of the weaving guild stepped out. "We are ready for you, Sok," she said.

The former advisor to the king of Epoh, for that is how Sok thought of himself in that moment, tugged at the hem of his leaf-green vest to straighten it and tossed his long, silvery locks over his shoulders. He entered the Elders' chambers and was taken aback not to see Arthur there as he bowed to the twelve guild masters and the senior master who were seated on cushions arranged in a line on a dais at the back of the room. As was customary, Sok lowered himself to his knees and sat with his feet pointing away from his back. It was considered disrespectful for petitioners before the Elders to sit cross-legged. He waited for the senior Elder to invite him to speak.

Elder Dhonna was the fourth elder from the left. Sok looked at her, but he could not read her expression. Like all of the Elders, she simply looked impassively back at him.

"Silkhar Ornathan Kluupentarajhar, commonly known as Sok, what have you come before your Elders to ask?" the senior Elder, Jona asked.

Sok knew very well that the Elders knew very well why he was there and this extreme formality did not bode well for him. Unless Arthur hadn't gotten there first and they really didn't know what had happened. He looked at Elder Dhonna again, hoping for any sign that would confirm it one way or the other, but she gave nothing away at all. Fueled by his anger at Arthur for not doing something, he decided to throw caution to the wind.

"Harpur Diggins is dead."

The Elders stared back at him with impassive expressions. Except for Elder Dhonna. The angry look she gave him punctured his confidence like a pin through a balloon. He hadn't considered how his actions might affect her or how much seeing her disapproval would hurt. All he'd thought about was the Fae's audacity and how Arthur had betrayed him. But he'd played his hand and he had to see the game through to its end.

"Harpur Diggins was challenged and lost to a teal dragon named Karrys Evergreen six days ago," Sok continued. "She has not yet claimed her inheritance. Harpur's last request was that she was not to burn his body or enter his lair for eight days after the challenge if he lost. But that is not the only reason I'm here.

"The Fae have violated the conditions Harpur imposed on them and have been seen outside their territory by humans near the base of the mountains at the end of Colwygshire Road. Without Harpur here to control them, we elves must act swiftly to ensure that more don't cross the borders or invade elven territory."

"We are aware," Jona said calmly, almost disinterestedly. "It is our understanding that King Arthur is addressing the situation with the Fae on the lands he governs. You are his senior advisor. It seems to me that you should be there advising him, not here advising us."

The implication was that Sok's status as an elf had somehow been diminished by his service to the human king. The realization stung like a slap to the face and he suddenly felt very alone, forsaken by both his friend and his people. He looked again at Elder Dhonna, who shook her head, warning him to tread carefully. But all Sok saw was another betrayal.

Against protocol, he stood up without being dismissed and stared at each of the Elders before him. His heart was pounding and he vibrated with anger. "You will sit here then and do nothing while our enemy mocks us? If the Fae have crossed the Colwygshire Road, they could just as easily have crossed the river into Braydon Wood. Will you not at least send warriors to protect the forest?"

Senior Elder Jona stood as well. He stepped down from the dais and approached the errant elf. The regal elf's emerald eyes flashed with a sorrowful anger that Sok had never seen before. "The Fae are not your worst enemy, Sok," he said. "Your pride is by far the biggest foe that you face. Perhaps a few days in the cell will improve your attitude. Guards! Take him away."

Sok's own emerald eyes widened in fear and shock as he watched Senior Elder Jona turn his back and walk to the dais. "Father, no!" he begged as two warrior elves took him by the arms and dragged him toward the door. "Don't do this. Elder Dhonna, please! Don't let him do this. Father!"

Senior Elder Jona stood silently for a moment after the door closed again. He did not sit back down. "The warriors are ready?" he addressed Bele, the master of the warriors.

"They are preparing even now," Bele replied. "We will begin the march south before mid-afternoon."

Senior Elder Jona nodded. Then he turned to Elder Dhonna. "Have we done the right thing?"

He was, of course, referring to putting Sok in the cell. "The cell is the safest place for Sok right now. I'm afraid if you don't keep him there until this is over, he'll do something foolish."

Elder Dhonna hated herself for having suggested locking Sok up. The cell, an enchanted room that effectively cut elves in its confines from their connection to the forest was reserved as punishment for the worst crimes an elf could commit. And it hadn't been used for a very long time; nothing was worth the pain of being disconnected from the natural world to an elf.

"So be it," Senior Elder Jona said. "I wish I knew what prompted the Fae to do this. What do they want?"

"Sir Davynn and the Drengrokil are going to try to find out," Elder Dhonna said. "The Fae may not have sinister intentions."

"Your optimism is amusing," Senior Elder Jona said with a derisive grunt. "The elementals are sinister creatures. They are not looking to make friends, I assure you. When do you return to Harpur's lair?"

"Arthur and I will go there tomorrow," Elder Dhonna said. "We will cast the spell before Karrys returns the following day."

Senior Elder Jona nodded. "Tell me, Elder Dhonna, what made Harpur Diggins want to go through with such a strange plan?"

Elder Dhonna shook her head. "He'd laid the groundwork for the plan a long time before Karrys Evergreen issued the challenge. When she did, he made his peace with it and decided to go forward anyway."

"I see," Senior Elder Jona said. "All we can do then is to hope that it works. If it doesn't, it is possible we will be going to war with the Fae."

Elder Dhonna left the Elder's chambers feeling utterly worn out under the weight of her guilt. She tried to convince herself that leaving Sok in the cell was for his own good. He was angry and that, combined with his impetuous nature was a dangerous thing. His hatred for the Fae, notwithstanding. She would have to deal with him later. Right then, she needed to get to Colwygshire and talk to Arthur and the quickest way to do that was to use dragonfoil ash and zap herself there.

She returned to the guild house and quickly gave instructions to her students and the other members of the Healing Guild. There was so much that needed her attention in the gardens, but Harpur's plan had to come first. It was the only chance they had of avoiding a war with the Fae. Senior Elder Jona had been reluctant to wait for her and Arthur to finish what they had started for Harpur. She had been forced to tell him what the plan was as well and now he, Frode and Arthur were all privy to it. But she had seen no other way to stop Senior Elder Jona from making a rash decision and potentially doing what Sok wanted him to do; kill Faefolk. Not that a few dead Fae would have bothered her much. Her disdain for the elementals was a strong as Sok's, but they had only been seen on human lands and if the elves attacked them there, the Fae would retaliate. War would be inevitable. And the cost to the humans, if a war did break out, would be too high.

She gathered her satchel, somewhat lighter now that she had stowed the treasures from Harpur's hoard in her tree house, and packed a pouch of dragonfoil ash into it. Then she headed out into the forest, away from the elven city and any prying eyes. Under the circumstances, she didn't think the Council of Elders would hold using the dragonfoil ash against her, but with emotions running as high as they were, she thought it best not to test that theory.

She arrived at a small clearing where she was far enough away from the city to feel safe and stopped to prepare the dragonfoil ash. It was a simple enough spell, she had only to recite a short incantation, then throw the ash into the air and let it fall back down onto her. The last time she had done this; she had used too much dragonfoil ash and it had essentially exploded when the spell was activated. She had arrived at her destination, Harpur's lair, covered in soot and dazed by the impact. This time, she measured out a third less and hoped it was enough to get all of her to the castle.

"Nestiandito veriar!"

Elder Dhonna tossed the ash into the air and stepped under the dusty, grey cloud. She felt a tingling sensation as the falling ash made contact with her body and then there was a bright purple-blue flash and she was standing in the council chambers blinking away the afterimage from the flare.

"Elder Dhonna?" Arthur said looking up at the unexpected new arrival. "Where did you come from?"

He and Anayah were catching Hiro and Bon up on what was happening with the Fae.

The elf patted her head to make sure her hair wasn't on fire and checked the rest of herself out to make sure she was all there. "Well, I think I've finally figured this dragonfoil zapping thing out." She seemed quite pleased with herself, but quickly put her pride aside and became just as serious. "How are things going here?" she asked.

Arthur got up and pulled a chair out for Elder Dhonna. As she took her seat, he brushed a bit of smoldering ash from her shoulder. "Oh, my!" she exclaimed. "I guess I haven't figured it out exactly. Thank you, Arthur."

"You can zap yourself places with dragonfoil ash?" Anayah asked, impressed.

"Yes, but don't tell Sok. Elves are not supposed to use it to enhance their magic and, as an Elder, I should be setting a better example." Elder Dhonna double checked her shoulder to be sure there were no other smoldering bits of ash anywhere.

"So, you saw Sok, then?" Arthur asked. "How is he?"

"I would imagine that he's not too happy at the moment," Elder Dhonna began. She went on to recount what had happened with the Elders. Tears welled up in her eyes when she told them where Sok was and why. "I feel terrible doing that to him. But it was the only thing I could think of to keep him from doing something stupid. He was just so angry."

"Poor Sok," Arthur said. "Do you think he will ever forgive me?"

"I think that after this, he may need a little time." Elder Dhonna wouldn't make another promise she couldn't keep. "I wonder if he will ever forgive me or his father."

"His father?" Hiro asked.

"Senior Elder Jona is Sok's father. He's the one that sent Sok to the cell," Elder Dhonna explained. *At my suggestion.*

"Really?" Arthur was shocked. "Sok never mentioned that. Come to think of it, Sok never spoke of his family."

"Family is not the same in elven culture as it is for humans," Elder Dhonna said. "We consider all elves to be our family. We raise our children communally. Who our fathers are or who actually birthed us isn't all that important. And Sok never used his lineage to gain advantage. Today was the first time since was a very young elfling that I heard him call Senior Elder Jona Father. It nearly broke my heart to see how desperate he was." She wiped another tear from the corner of her eye.

"Well, we'll get him out of the cell as soon as we can," Arthur assured the guild master. "We'll fix this."

The elf sniffled and forced a smile. "Thank you. I know you will do everything you can. So, how are things going here?" She asked again.

"Anayah and I zapped Davynn, all nine Drengrokil and a dozen other guards to the village. Davynn is going to try to talk to the Fae and find out why they have come out of their territory. Another two hundred guards are marching south today. Hopefully, they won't be needed," Arthur said.

"They will be marching with the elves," Elder Dhonna said. "Five hundred warriors will be marching south as well. They will take the Colwygshire Road to the end, but they will stay in Braydon Wood once they are there. Another one hundred warriors have been sent to patrol the elven side of the river. Jona has ordered them to kill any Fae that cross the river into elven territory. They will not ask questions."

Arthur blew out a heavy sigh through puffed cheeks. "The good news is time is on our side. It will take three days for the guards and the warriors to get to the village."

"And Karrys claims Epoh as her own in two days," Hiro said. "Do we just sit tight and hope that her first act as ruling dragon is to chase the Fae back into their territory and prevent a war?"

"Something like that," Arthur said. He looked at Elder Dhonna. "I'm going to go to the lair tomorrow and wait for her. I will tell her what's happening and ask her for her help."

Elder Dhonna nodded at him. They hadn't come up with an excuse to go to the lair. The Fae had unwittingly provided them with a perfectly plausible pretext.

"I'm going with you," Anayah announced.

"Me too!" Hiro said. "Bon? Do you want to come with us?"

"No!" Arthur shouted a little too vehemently. He cleared his throat and started again. "No, I have a better idea. Hiro, you need to go to the village. The Drengrokil are going to eat a lot and you and your magic satchel can feed them and Davynn's men without having to deplete any of the villager's resources. Bon can help keep watch at night. Anayah, you should go with them."

"Why?"

"You can be our messenger," Arthur said. "If Davynn needs to get any information to me, you can zap back and forth."

"When did you get so good at being a king?" Anayah asked.

"This morning. Right after my best friend accused me of betraying him and quit his job as my senior advisor."

Now that everyone was out of his way and had a job to do, Arthur had to go and tell his beloved wife what was going on. Elder Dhonna accompanied him for moral support. And to see the twins.

They entered the conservatory to find Alex sitting on a stool in front of an easel working on her macramé project. Two ladies in waiting were standing next to her watching the complicated knotwork progress while Alex explained the technique to them. Hart and Meg were nowhere to be seen.

Arthur and Elder Dhonna approached the lesson in progress. Arthur put his hands on Alex's shoulders and kissed the top of her head. "Oh, wow! That's really starting to look... like something."

Alex rolled her eyes. "Elder Dhonna, how lovely to see you." Alex finished the knot she was working on and rose to greet the guild master.

The ladies in waiting curtsied for Arthur and then meandered away from the easel.

"Where are the twins?" Arthur asked after Alex and Elder Dhonna had finished exchanging air kisses.

"The wet nurses are feeding them," she said, waving a hand toward the closed bedroom door. "They just woke up."

"And Alma, I take it, is supervising," Arthur probed.

"Alma quit," Alex said and broke out into a huge grin.

"Aw, that's too bad," Arthur mocked. "I'm going to miss the cranky old bat."

Alex giggled. "I'm not!"

"So, what prompted this? Why did she quit?" Arthur moved to the table by the window and poured three cups of ale. He served two to Alex and Elder Dhonna and, taking the third for himself, herded the two women to the sitting group in the middle of the room.

"She said that she felt she could not do her job properly and that she was taking a position with another family in the city. I told her we would pay her for the full moon cycle." Alex held her cup out for Arthur to clink with hers.

"I have no problem with that!" Arthur sipped his ale.

A maid arrived with a tray of pastries. She put it down on the table next to Alex and bobbed a curtsy. "There's a gentleman here to see you, m' lady. Shall I show him in?"

Arthur looked at his wife. "A gentleman caller to see you? Who might that be?"

Alex shrugged. "Yes, please," she said to the maid.

A minute later a tall, sandy-haired man walked in pushing an odd-looking cart in front of him. Arthur and Alex exchanged wondering looks and then got up to go and see what it was.

"The elf, Sok, ordered this for you, your majesties," the man said. "He told me to deliver it here to the conservatory the moment it was ready." He waited for the king or queen to say something. "He called it a stroller. He said you would know what to do with it."

"Oh, Arthur!" Alex gushed. "This is wonderful. A little boxy, but it will work perfectly. I can't wait to take Hart and Meg out for a walk in it."

She examined the stroller, which consisted of a large wooden box attached to an iron frame with four wheels and a handle. Arthur never would have guessed that it was designed to carry babies if the man hadn't told him. But he was deeply touched by the gesture.

"Oh, Sok," Arthur whispered, closing his eyes and covering his mouth with his hand.

"Don't you like it, sire?" the man asked.

Arthur swallowed the lump in his throat. "It's really is amazing. Thank you... Um... what is your name?"

"Barger, sire."

"Well, Barger, how can we thank you?"

"You could pay me, sire," Barger said. "The elf said he would pay me when I delivered it, but I've been made to understand that he is not in the castle today."

"Uh, no, he is not," Arthur confirmed. "Come with me and I will find someone who can settle your account for you."

He led Barger out of the conservatory, leaving Alex to explain to Elder Dhonna just what a stroller was, and headed to the council chambers. Normally, he would get Sok to handle this sort of thing, but Sok was not at his disposal anymore. *Who else knows how to look after the accounts?*

He told Barger to take a seat at the round table while he looked for someone to pay him. "Would you like me to get you an ale while you wait?"

"You, sire?" Barger asked. "Shouldn't a servant do that?"

"I can handle it," Arthur said.

Barger didn't know how to respond. "Just my coin, sire."

Ale would have been easier. Arthur knew where to get that. "I'll be right back. Wait here."

Arthur went out into the foyer and haled a guard who was leaning on a pillar a few feet away from the council chamber doors. "Have you seen Berryl anywhere? Or any of the council members?"

"No, sire," the guard answered. "Would you like me to send someone to look for him? Uh... Them?"

"I don't suppose you have any coins on you?" Arthur asked.

"Coins, sire?" The guard was confused.

"Those little gold discs you get for doing your job." Arthur had no idea how the guards and servants were paid.

"I know what coins are, sire. May I ask why the king is in need of them?"

"Do you have any coins or not?" Arthur snapped.

"I have a few, sire," the guard said hesitantly.

"Great. Give them to me."

The guard looked worried. "But, sire, if I give you the coins I have, how will I pay for my ale at Skull's Keep tonight?"

"Just charge it to the castle account," Arthur said.

"Really, sire? I can do that?"

"Yes, yes. Just give me your coins."

The guard handed Arthur twelve coins from the pouch attached to his belt.

"How much ale were you planning on drinking?" Arthur asked as he counted the coins.

"Enough, sire,"

Arthur decided that was actually a reasonable answer. "Thank you... What's your name?"

"Um... Bobbit, sire."

"Well, thank you, Bobbit. You're a good man."

On his way back to the council chambers, Arthur realized that he didn't know how much Sok owed Barger for the stroller. He hoped that twelve coins was enough. "Here you go," he said as he entered the room and held out the coins. "I trust this will be enough."

Barger took the coins from the king and counted them. "This will do quite nicely," he said. "Thank you, sire." He stood up, bowed and hustled out of the room.

Too late, Arthur got the feeling that he'd just been duped. But he had bigger things to worry about. Like telling Alex that Sok had quit and was now imprisoned in a cell in Braydon wood, and there were four or five rogue Faefolk wandering about in a southern village, and some eight hundred guards and elven warriors were marching south to stop them, and he had to leave her again to go back to Harpur's lair, because if he didn't there was going to be a war.

I wonder if Bon knows how to make whiskey. I could really use some whiskey for times like this.

He returned to the conservatory to find Alex on the sofa weeping against Elder Dhonna's shoulder.

"Alex? Honey, what's wrong?" he asked, sitting down next to his wife.

Alex flipped from Elder Dhonna's shoulder to Arthur's. "Oh, Arthur! What are we going to do?"

"What did you say to her?" Arthur mouthed to the elf. A tendril of Alex's unruly curls snaked its way into his mouth and he tried to flick it back out with his tongue.

"I told her everything," Elder Dhonna said, dabbing at the tear stain on her caftan with a napkin.

"Everything, everything?" Arthur asked.

Elder Dhonna shook her head no. "Everything."

Arthur wasn't sure what that meant. "There, there, sweety. It's okay." He patted his wife's back. "Why don't you go and lie down for a while. Elder Dhonna and I need to talk a few things over." He coaxed Alex up off the sofa and led her into the bedroom. He handed her off to the ladies in waiting who had drifted in there to chat with the wet nurses.

"Are you insane?" Arthur asked the elf as he pulled the door closed again.

"She kept asking about Sok!" Elder Dhonna defended herself. "She was going to send someone to look for him so she could thank him for the stroller. Which is rather clever, by the way. It was just easier to tell her the truth."

"You didn't tell her about Harpur's plan, did you?"

"Of course not!" Elder Dhonna was insulted. "Too many people know already."

"So, by everything you meant everything but that." Arthur realized that Elder Dhonna had wanted to stop Alex from asking any further questions. "Who else knows about it?"

"You, me and Senior Elder Jona." She left out Frode.

"That's only three people," Arthur said.

"It's three people too many," Elder Dhonna replied. This time she was including Frode.

"You don't trust me to keep the secret?"

I don't trust myself. "It's a heavy secret, Arthur."

Arthur couldn't argue with that. "I wish there was a way to get Karrys to the lair sooner."

"What good would that do?"

"The sooner she gets there, the sooner we find out if Harpur's plan will work. If it doesn't work, we'd have more time to figure out what to do about the Fae."

"Karrys will not dishonour herself by claiming Epoh sooner than she agreed to. We will just have to be patient."

"I wish I could go and see Sok," Arthur said. "I don't know how I'm going to fix things with him. Why do the elves hate the Fae so much?"

Elder Dhonna sighed. "The Fae are not natural beings. They are reckless and greedy and have no conscience. They have no real reverence for the land, the trees."

Arthur couldn't believe that the Fae couldn't be redeemed. Admittedly, his limited experience with them had not been overly encouraging, but he couldn't help feeling that the prejudice against them was not completely justified and it bothered him that the elves that he admired so much bore such deep animosity toward another race.

"Harpur must have seen some good in them. Why else would he allow them to live in Epoh?" he asked.

"You're right," Elder Dhonna said, "Harpur adored the Fae. And the Fae respected Harpur. They are grateful to him for allowing them to live in Braydon Wood, even under the strict conditions that he imposed on them. Harpur believed that the Fae were special, that they were created to bring joy and beauty to the world."

"So, what went wrong? How did they become reckless, greedy, conscienceless abusers of the land?" Arthur was intrigued.

"There is a legend," Elder Dhonna began as she settled more comfortably on the sofa, "that long ago, a young Fae girl fell in love with a prince, but the prince's father, the king, forbade his son to marry her. The prince ran away to the Fae Lands to be with the Fae girl and the king invaded the Fae Lands to get him back. When the prince saw how viciously the Fae defended themselves, he became disenchanted with them. He begged his love to make the Fae stop, but she refused, saying it was the king who invaded their land and they would not stop until every human was dead or the king retreated. Knowing his father would not stop until he returned home, the prince stole away to find the king and beg him to stop.

"The king agreed to withdraw his army from the Fae Lands if his son would kill the Fae girl. The prince, of course, was horrified, but ultimately chose to agree to his father's terms. He returned to the Fae girl and poisoned her, then took her body back to his father to prove he had done what was asked of him. The king, in turn, took the Fae girl's body to the battle field and threw it down before the Fae queen, saying that the war was ended now that his son had chosen to be loyal to him.

"The Fae queen was incensed by the prince's betrayal and consumed the body of the Fae girl..."

"She ate the Fae girl? Gross!" Arthur interjected.

"The legend says the Fae queen consumed the body. Make of that what you will." Elder Dhonna continued, "By consuming the body of the Fae girl, the Fae queen was also poisoned, but it didn't kill her. It only corrupted her. She went on to remake the Fae, infusing her corruption into them. Over time the poison spread and every new Fae is infected by it."

"That's just a fairytale, right?" Arthur said. "It didn't really happen."

"It is a legend," Elder Dhonna corrected, "and every legend springs from a truth. Stories are no less living things than you or I. They evolve to fit the time and culture in which they are told. We may never know exactly how or why the Fae became what they are, but I believe the real poison in the story is the betrayal itself. When we hurt the people we love, we poison them and if we do not make amends, that poison spreads."

"I didn't mean to hurt Sok," Arthur said.

"The poison was already inside Sok," Elder Dhonna said. "As it is in all of us elves. The poison we suffer from is different; it's the poison of conditioning. Sok is not angry with you, Arthur. He's angry because he's been told he's supposed to be angry. You just happen to be the catalyst that brought his anger to surface."

"Do you hate the Fae?"

"I cannot say that I would be sorry to see them banished from Epoh," Elder Dhonna admitted.

"What would Harpur do if he was here?"

"He would do whatever he had to do to keep the peace," the guild master said. "It was his biggest fault."

"What do you mean?"

"Conflict is not entirely a bad thing, Arthur. It spurs growth and expands minds. When humans and elves and dwarves and even the Fae are denied the ability to assert their differences, they are also denied their ability to find acceptance. They cannot learn from one another. They cannot grow. Real peace will only ever be obtained through resolving conflict." Elder Dhonna said.

"Are you saying you want a war?" Arthur was shocked.

"Not at all," Elder Dhonna said. "That would be devastating. What I'm saying is if Harpur hadn't designed Epoh to work the way it does, we probably wouldn't be facing a war. By limiting the interaction between the different races, he denied us the ability to collaborate. We have been trained not to question, not to be curious about one another. Follow the rules and all will be well. If Harpur were here, he would stop whatever might happen from happening and we would carry on, never getting the chance to learn from it."

Arthur took a minute to digest what Elder Dhonna was saying. "But if you and I succeed tomorrow, won't Karrys do just that?"

"If we succeed tomorrow, war will be averted, yes," Elder Dhonna said. "But maybe we will also have a chance to facilitate some positive change as well.

"What are you proposing?"

"I plan to have a long talk with our new dragon lady when this is all over."

Davynn was nervous. Though he'd spent his entire career in the guard training for just such an eventuality, the reality of a potential war was far more daunting than he had ever expected. The fact that he never actually expected to have to fight was probably the biggest contributing factor to the overwhelming sense of doubt he now faced. If he was honest with himself, he'd joined the guard precisely because it was relatively safe. The closest he'd come to battle was when Edlyngton Bloomregaard had attempted to usurp the crown and he had never even had to draw his sword. Now, he wondered if he would be able to draw it against the elves to protect the Fae. Or, if it came to it, what good would his sword do against Fae magic? *I don't even know who my enemy really is.* He could sense the same trepidation in the twelve men that had come with him and the Drengrokil to protect the village until the rest of the guards arrived. He needed to keep their courage up. While he hoped for a miracle.

After Frode and his men had set up their camp in an open pasture on the west side of the village, a process that took the efficient Drengrokil all of a few minutes, Davynn sought the far more experienced warriors' advice and counsel.

"How do we approach the Fae to find out what they want?" Davynn asked.

That the Fae had allowed themselves to be seen was the one thing the knight saw as working in his favour. Had they simply wanted to steal children, they would not have been obvious about it. They would have come in the night, done the deed and disappeared back into the Fae Lands without anyone being the wiser until they awoke to find a child gone. According to Ned Krats, who they had zapped back to the village with them, the Fae had been seen watching the village from the western edge of the pasture that was now dominated by nine red and yellow-striped tents. They showed up in the early morning, watched the village until mid-morning and then were gone again. Since the first sighting, the children had been kept together in the village lodge and supervised at all times, and watches had been set day and night to keep an eye open for the Fae's return. It was proving disruptive to the spring ploughing and planting because it meant that there were fewer people to do the work.

Frode looked at the nervous knight. "Stand near where they have been seen. When they come close, ask them."

"Just like that?" Davynn knew he was overcomplicating things, but he was afraid of missing something.

"Only reason Faefolk show themselves is for attention," Frode said.

"Have you ever fought the Fae before?" Davynn asked.

"No need," Frode said. "Give them what they want, they go away again."

"What do they want?" Davynn asked.

It was a rhetorical question, but Frode answered anyway. "My guess is Fae want gold."

Davynn froze. *And tell Harpur Diggins that the queen awaits her gold.* It was the last thing the Fae creature had said to Arthur when they had retrieved the Amber Chalice. He spun on his heels and ran toward the lodge to find Anayah.

The lodge, situated in the center of the village, was the largest building and served as a gathering place where the villagers celebrated births and marriages, where funerals were conducted and where the village Lord came to collect taxes and dispense justice in the name of the king. It was the heart of the community, a symbol of connection, of protection, of belonging.

Now, it served as a hostel for the fifteen children, the youngest of which was still in swaddling. The oldest child was a boy of about ten, who did not believe that he belonged there and was vehemently voicing his opposition to having to remain in custody with the other boys and girls.

A tired and worried woman was standing next to Anayah, listening to the boy's latest attempt to regain his freedom. "I can protect myself!" he said, brandishing an imaginary sword. "No scum Fae is going to take me!"

"First of all, young man," Anayah admonished, "the Fae are not scum. Second, while I can see that you have mastered the invisible sword, it's going to take something far more substantial than that to protect yourself from Fae magic."

"Then give me a real sword!" the boy shouted. "I'll kill them all!"

Davynn was horrified. "Is this what you teach your children?" he asked the tired, worried woman. "To hate other races?"

The woman blanched and shook her head. "He's just trying to be brave," she said. "He's just a boy."

"A boy who needs to learn the value of life!" Davynn snarled, his fury fueled by his own fear. "Anayah, may I have a word with you?"

Anayah was as taken aback by Davynn's reaction as Davynn was to the boy's. She took his arm and led him out of the lodge.

"What in Harpur's name has gotten into you?" she asked when they were outside again.

"That is unacceptable!" Davynn snapped, pointing back at the lodge. "He's just a boy..."

"And one day he will be a man. Do you want this boy to grow into a man who may have children of his own or seek entry into the guard with an attitude like that?" Davynn asked.

"No, but..."

"There are no buts, Anayah!" Davynn said. "Where does this hatred come from? How is it allowed to infect our children?"

Anayah looked at the incensed knight. "You don't like the Fae either," she challenged.

Davynn frowned. "I don't hate them. I don't wish them any ill. I don't want to kill them. Harpur has put systems in place to..."

"...insulate you from them. As long as the Fae stay in the Fae Lands, they are no problem. But the moment they step across an imaginary line on the ground, they are a threat. Call out the guards; the Fae are on the loose!"

"I'm protecting my people."

Anayah crossed her arms and cocked her head to one side. "From what, exactly?"

Davynn's frown deepened. He had been told all his life that it was best to leave the Fae alone. They were tricksters, undisciplined and chaotic to be sure. *But are they truly malevolent?* Still, a boy of ten should not want to kill anyone!

"I think I know what the Fae want," he said, opting to sort out his own feelings about it all later.

"Oh?" Anayah prompted.

"They want gold." Davynn stood with his hands on his hips. He was trying to figure out how to get it for them.

"And?" Anayah prompted further.

Davynn eyes drifted westward in the direction of the Fae Lands. He told Anayah what the Fae creature said to Arthur about the queen awaiting her gold. "Harpur must have promised to pay them in gold for guarding the chalice and now they want it."

"But Harpur's dead," Anayah continued his thought, "and can't pay them."

"Right," Davynn said. "And I don't think I want to be the one to tell them that."

"Does it matter where the gold comes from?" Anayah asked.

"What are you thinking?"

"I could conjure some."

Davynn shook his head. "Can you conjure it right from Harpur's hoard?"

"That's not how it works," Anayah said. "The magic finds the gold. I can't tell it where to get the gold from. It's not like zapping something from one place to another. But why does it matter?"

"Because what if the gold you conjure comes from the dwarves? They keep very close tabs on their gold and if any goes missing, we might not just have a war with the Fae on our hands. We could have the dwarves attacking as well," Davynn explained. "I think it would be best if you zapped yourself to the lair and zap back with whatever you can from there."

Davynn had a point. "How much do I bring? Shouldn't we find out if that is what the Fae actually want first?"

"Bring as much as you can," Davynn said, beginning to feel a little more confident. "If they want something else, we'll figure it out. In the meantime, we'll be prepared if that is what they do want. Maybe we can stop all hell from breaking loose."

"I'm on my way," Anayah said. "I'll stop at the castle and let Arthur know what we're planning."

"Yes," Davynn said. "Thank you. Hurry back."

Unexpectedly, Anayah planted a kiss on Davynn's mouth. Then she snapped her fingers and disappeared. He stood where he was, holding onto that kiss for as long as he could. Until his reverie was interrupted by a gruff voice.

"Witch is bringing gold?" Frode asked.

"Uh... Yeah." Davynn turned to face the Drengrokil leader. "I'm pretty sure you are right and that's all the Fae want."

Frode grunted in agreement. "Little Krist man says food is ready. Says to come fetch you."

Food sounded good to Davynn. Before he followed Frode to the Drengrokil camp to eat, he stopped and let the guards he'd posted in and around the lodge know that they would be relieved and fed soon. They had organized rotations so that between the guards and the Drengrokil there would be a continual presence at the lodge as well as watchers in the pasture. If the Fae showed up, someone would spot them, and though Davynn was almost positive that the children were not in any immediate danger, he chose to keep a vigilant eye on them until he was sure.

The Drengrokil were fascinated by Hiro's satchel. As he pulled plate after plate out of the small bag, they made a game out of it, challenging him to produce dish after dish. Not everything translated well and Hiro ended the game when one of the small mountains asked for *elvabroon*, which literally translates to elf brain. Later, Hiro would learn that elvabroon was the name of a sweet dumpling, a treat he would come to serve often, but just then he preferred to keep elf brains off of his dinner plate.

They were also curious about the hover gilly and after dinner a new game to see how many Drengrokil it could carry ensued. At first none of the big warriors were sure that it would take the weight of even one of them, but as more ale was consumed, they soon began testing its limits. In the end it was determined that the hover gilly was easily able to lift all of them. Three Drengrokil stood on its deck behind Hiro while the other six hung from its sides by their fingers. Even Frode had to get in on the fun and was deeply impressed with the strength and flexibility of the strange little craft.

As the sun set, however, Frode reined in his men and they were all business again as they took their posts and began the night watch. The villagers, content to trust the Drengrokil to keep them safe, retired to their huts and the guards not on watch settled into their bed rolls. A low fire in the center of the Drengrokil camp burned merrily as Frode, Hiro and Bon sat near it on stumps that Wolf had procured from the nearby forest.

Davynn, though, was too restless to sleep or even to sit. Anayah had still not returned and his concern was rapidly ramping up to abject hysteria as he imagined of all the horrible things that might have happened to her. So, he paced. And fretted.

"Witch will be back soon," Frode said. "Come. Sit. Drink."

"Where is she?" Davynn asked for the umpteenth time, ignoring Frode's invitation.

"Do you want me to take the hover gilly back to the castle and see if she's checked in with Arthur?" Hiro offered.

"So you can get lost too?" Davynn shot back, passing behind the Krist. "I have enough to worry about."

Frode pulled a nearby stump closer to the fire and just when Davynn turned and was about to pace back behind him, he stood up and stepped into the knight's path. "Sit!"

Davynn looked up at his hero and saw the impassible determination in the big man's face. He sat.

"Worry will not bring witch back faster," Frode said, shoving a flagon of ale into Davynn's hand. "Worry only makes you crazy in head. Crazy leader is not good leader."

Davynn had never thought of himself as a real leader and the recognition of his leadership by Frode was a compliment he took to heart. He took a drink of his ale and steeled himself to live up to Frode's assessment. But he couldn't help yelping in surprise when a large chest appeared between himself and the fire a few seconds later.

"There is note attached," Frode calmly stated the obvious.

Davynn plucked the piece of parchment from under one of the leather straps on the chest and unfolded it. He read the note out loud.

> Hope this will be enough for the Fae. Will stay at the lair until
> Arthur arrives tomorrow. Animals and carrion birds are trying to
> get at Harpur's body. Arthur is up to speed on the Fae situation.
> Will return to village as soon as possible. Anayah.

"See? No need for worry," Frode said.

"No need to worry?" Davynn said, forgetting his resolve to be stoic. "Anayah's alone on the other side of the kingdom surrounded by wild animals!"

"She's a witch," Hiro reminded the knight. "I'm sure she can take care of herself."

"Still..." Davynn mumbled, feeling a little stupid. And a lot protective. "I should be there with her."

Frode gave Davynn a sideways glance. "So witch can worry about you? Is better she use magic alone. Knight's sword only make trouble for beautiful witch."

Flooded with doubt and worry, Davynn stood up, drained his ale cup and announced, "I'm going to sleep."

Hiro watched the knight stalk away from the fire. "I think I will turn in too," he said, slipping down from his stump and whistling for the hover gilly. "Should we put that chest of gold somewhere safe?" he asked.

Frode looked at the chest and shrugged. "No one will disturb gold."

He estimated that it weighed upwards of three hundred pounds. It wasn't going anywhere.

Hiro wished Frode and Bon a good night and left them to talk about whatever an android and a Drengrokil might find to talk about. He didn't need much sleep, but he did need to rest and some time alone would provide just that. Finding a quiet spot in a copse of trees at the south end of the village, Hiro parked the hover gilly and opened his satchel. He withdrew a leather-bound journal and a quill pen and, with the aid of a small lantern, began recording his thoughts.

Once they were alone at the fire, Bon turned to Frode. "Do you think that Harpur's plan will work?"

Frode's eyes narrowed and he studied the strange being across the dancing flames. "You know what plan is?"

"I have deduced the only possible intention behind Harpur's actions," the android admitted.

"Is good plan," Frode said, not giving anything away. "Is weird plan. Great purple dragon is brave to make such plan."

"Brave?" Bon urged.

Again, Frode studied the android, trying to determine if Bon actually knew the plan, or if he was fishing for confirmation. "Great purple dragon risks everything sacred to dragons with plan. If plan works, will never go to Arachovor. If plan not work, will never go to Arachovor."

"Tell me about Arachovor," Bon said. His time on Thraeh was short and he was there to learn all he could about dragon culture.

"Is place where honourable dragons go when dead," Frode answered frankly.

"Are you saying that Harpur's plan is not honourable?"

Frode took a drink from his cup. "Honour is here." He brought his huge fist to this heart. "Not in rules of councils. Harpur Diggins' honour is in love for peoples of Epoh. Otherwise, plan would be different."

Bon took a moment to consider the enormity of the sacrifice that Harpur was making. Essentially, if Frode was right, he was forsaking his own kind along with centuries of tradition. But was it love for the people in his kingdom that drove the great purple dragon? Or was it pure vanity? Bon wondered how an android would fare in the Sands of Sancheera.

"Thank you, for the insight," he said. "I am eager to see how this all unfolds. Will you and your men be staying in Epoh?"

"Drengrokil go where need to be," Frode answered. "If need to be here, will stay here. If need to be other place, will go to other place."

It wasn't a very satisfying answer, but Bon accepted it.

They spent most of the night questioning each other. Frode wanted to learn more about androids and Bon wanted to discover all he could about dragons. So, they traded stories about their experiences and adventures until Frode announced that he was going to his tent to get some sleep. Dawn was not far off and Bon pointed this out to the big man.

"You will miss meeting the Fae when they appear."

"Only need a little sleep," Frode replied, holding his thumb and index fingers an inch or so apart. "Drengrokil brothers will wake me when sun comes up. Besides, much worse to miss food from Krist's magic satchel." He patted his stomach and lumbered off to his tent.

Bon added another log to the dwindling fire and sat in contemplation of what he had learned, most of which was still supposition. But after centuries of existing in magical worlds and recording many wonderous things, he was confident enough that his theories and deductions were an accurate beginning to understanding dragon culture on Thraeh. Time would tell, but for now he had this apparently anomalous example of dragon rebellion to observe and record.

Chapter Nineteen

Alex emerged from her room to find Arthur and Elder Dhonna still talking together on the sofa. Her red-rimmed eyes sought assurance from Arthur that a war with the Fae could be averted. The very idea of it terrified her. Epoh was supposed to be a peaceful, safe place. The ladies in waiting followed their queen out of the room, carrying the twins, both of whom were wide awake.

Arthur stood to greet his wife. He took her hands in his and kissed her forehead. "Are you feeling better?" he asked.

"Tell me it's going to be okay," Alex demanded.

Arthur couldn't make that promise. Neither could he stand to see Alex upset. "We are doing everything we can."

He could see that this was not what she wanted to hear. It wasn't what he wanted to tell her either. But until he and Elder Dhonna could get back to the lair and cast the spell, he couldn't say one way or the other how things might turn out. No one knew what the Fae wanted yet. If they had any ill intentions and decided to act on them before they knew if Harpur's plan would work, there could be bloodshed. Seeing the fright in her eyes reminded him how heavy the secret he was keeping from her really was.

Elder Dhonna approached the ladies in waiting and asked if she could hold one of the babies. Little Meg was transferred into the elf's arms and, like Sok had done, Elder Dhonna began softly singing an elven lullaby to her.

Arthur took Hart from the other lady in waiting. Cradling the prince in one arm, he took Alex's hand and led her back toward the sofa. Then he spotted the stroller parked on the other side of the room near the door.

"We have some time before supper. Why don't we try this contraption out and take Hart and Meg for a walk?" he suggested, hoping it would distract Alex from her fretting.

"You can't just take them out," one of the ladies in waiting said. She was shocked by the king's proposal.

"Oh? Why not?" Arthur asked, continuing to head toward the stroller.

"They haven't been presented yet," the other lady in waiting said.

Arthur rolled his eyes. "Alex, do you care if anyone sees the twins before they've been *presented*?" He infused the last word with sarcasm.

"Not particularly," Alex answered.

"Neither do I," Arthur said. "Looks like we'll need a blanket or something to pad the box."

Alex shooed the scandalized ladies in waiting off to find blankets. "Elder Dhonna, will you join us?"

"And be seen in public with unpresented heirs to the throne?" the elf said in mock horror. "I wouldn't miss it for the world!"

Both of the ladies in waiting pursed their lips, but said nothing.

Getting the twins ready for their first outing turned out to be something of a process. The stroller was not equipped with a shade hood, so Arthur had to rig one up. He sent one of the ladies in waiting to the armory for arrows while he went to Hiro's laboratory in search of a hammer and a saw. When the bewildered lady in waiting returned with the weapons, Arthur sawed the fletching off the ends of four of them and then hammered the arrow tips into the sides of the box. Then he draped another blanket over the ends of the arrows to form the shade hood. With a flourish of his hands, he presented the rather ingenious results to his intrigued audience.

"I'm going to call you MacGyver from now on," Alex said, somewhat cheered by her husband's inventive efforts.

"MacGyver?" Elder Dhonna asked, puzzled.

"It's a private joke," Arthur said, brushing off the complications of trying to explain television to the guild master.

When they were finally ready to leave, one of the ladies in waiting piped up, "Shall I arrange for guards to accompany you?"

Arthur had been anticipating this. He sighed heavily. "We'll grab a couple on our way out. I'm sure there are a few loafing around the castle with nothing else to do."

Alex had the honour of pushing the stroller, which, in spite of its ungainly appearance, maneuvered smoothly. They made their way through the halls toward the castle foyer where Arthur engaged two of the loafing guards to carry the stroller down the steps onto the cobblestone drive that separated the castle from the ornamental gardens, a lush expanse of lawn dissected by a meandering path through flower beds and flowering trees. It was still too early in the season for the blossoms to be out, but the budding leaves provided verdant cheer to the landscape assisted by the warm afternoon sun. When they reached the path, Arthur told the guards to wait for them there. He had no intention of strolling through the gardens with a guard detail dogging them.

People stopped and stared at the queen pushing the strange cart. It had become routine to see the king out and about in the city, but Queen Alex was a much rarer sight. Necks craned and eyes bulged. As they began to realize that the twins were the cargo, the gossip started to flow. Soon the garden perimeter was bordered by a crowd that gathered as if to watch a holiday parade. Arthur and Alex waved and smiled.

"Next time, I'll have to bring candy to throw at them," Arthur quipped.

"Why would you throw candy at people?" Elder Dhonna asked.

This time Arthur explained the Earth tradition.

"How odd," the elf said.

"I miss parades," Alex said. "I think we should have one before the presentation of the twins."

"Who's going to organize it?" Without Sok, Arthur was at a loss as to how to make things happen in Colwygshire.

"I will," Alex said. "How hard can it be?"

If it kept her distracted from a pending war with the Fae and a desire to view Harpur's body, Arthur was all for it. "I'm sure you will do a fantastic job."

"We can make it an annual event," Alex said. Then she remembered the uncertain times they were living in. "Do you think we will still be here next spring?"

Arthur struggled with how to respond. His hesitation set off alarm bells in his wife.

"Arthur? Do you think we still be here next spring?"

Arthur shot a worried glance at Elder Dhonna, pleading for her reassurance.

"Please don't worry, Alex," the guild master said, laying a hand on Alex's arm. "Everything is going to be alright."

Arthur felt terrible. He hated seeing his wife like this and he knew that the tiny bundles in the make-shift stroller were the focus of her deepest fears. They were his too. He wrapped his arm around Alex's shoulders and looked at the twins. The motion of the stroller had lulled them both to sleep and their peaceful little faces tugged at his heart.

They had reached the far end of the garden path and were turning around to return to the castle when a plume of red smoke erupted in front of them. Anayah stepped out of the fume and smiled.

"Oh! A stroller, how marvelous." She peeked under the sun shade at the sleeping twins. "I wish I had thought of that as a gift. Where did you get it?"

Arthur, anticipating news from the front, frantically tried to think of a way to separate Anayah from Alex to hear it. He didn't want Alex to learn of any bad news. "Sok commissioned it for us," he said, hoping to catch her eye before she said anything she shouldn't.

"Where is the elf, anyway?" Anayah asked as she straightened up again. "He'll want to hear this too."

"Hear what?" Alex asked.

Arthur was shaking his head behind Alex, but Anayah didn't pay any attention. "Davynn figured out what the Fae want. It seems that Harpur must have promised them gold in exchange for guarding the Amber Chalice and I'm on my way to the lair to get it for them."

Well, that isn't so bad. "That's all they want?" he asked.

"Anayah, you can't just walk into the lair and take Harpur's gold," Elder Dhonna said.

"Well, neither can he," Anayah responded. "But if it will appease the Fae and end this before it escalates, I'm willing to take the risk."

Elder Dhonna frowned. Stealing from a dragon was just not done. Even if the dragon was dead. She understood why Anayah was doing this, but it didn't sit well with her to know that it was Harpur's gold that was being pilfered.

"What are you waiting for?" Alex chirped. This was obviously the best news she could have hoped for. "Go and get the Fae their gold!"

"Harpur would not be pleased," Elder Dhonna insisted.

"Harpur will never know," Anayah said. She turned to Arthur. "You'll tell Sok? He'll be relieved to know that the Fae are not up to no good."

"But Sok's in..." Alex began.

"We'll let Sok know," Arthur interrupted, clamping his hands around Alex's upper arms. "I'm sure he will be relieved when he finds out."

"Great!" Anayah stepped away from the stroller. "Hopefully, we'll all be back at the castle tomorrow and everything can get back to normal." She snapped her fingers and zapped herself to the lair.

"She really shouldn't be taking anything from the lair," Elder Dhonna said.

"Why didn't you tell her that Sok is in prison?" Alex asked.

Arthur looked at his wife. He couldn't remember who knew what about anything and again he felt the weight of it all settle in the pit of his stomach. "No need to upset anyone else," he said. "We should probably get back. It's time to get ready for supper. Elder Dhonna, will you join us in the great hall? It will be nice to have some company at the head table."

The guild master declined the invitation. "Thank you, but I will go back to Braydon Wood. I will meet you there tomorrow."

"What are you doing tomorrow?" Alex asked as they started walking again.

"Uh... I have to go to the lair and talk to Karrys when she arrives. Let her know what is happening and find out what her intentions are for the kingdom." Arthur decided it was easier to tell Alex this half-truth. He knew it would remind her that their troubles did not end with the Fae getting their gold, but he didn't have the energy to come up with an outright lie that he would have to remember later.

Then a thought occurred to him. "Elder Dhonna, can you get us into the Boundary House?"

"Why?" the elf and the queen asked together.

Arthur suddenly felt unsure and regretted asking. "I'm just curious."

Both women saw right through that.

"You're not thinking of sending me and the twins to Earth, are you?" Alex was appalled.

"Only if it becomes too dangerous for you to stay here." He'd crossed the Rubicon.

"I'm not leaving you!" Alex stated firmly.

"It wouldn't be for long," Arthur bargained. "Just until we know the Fae are not going to be a problem and we know what Karrys intends. If things go sideways here, I will join you there."

"You would abandon your throne?" Elder Dhonna was as appalled as Alex. "Your people?"

Would I? Arthur didn't know how to answer that question. It was fun living in Epoh and being the king, more or less, while Harpur was alive and he didn't have to do much. But these last few days had been hard and the reality of having to be a real king with real king problems wasn't so fun. He had Meg and Hart to think about now and returning to Earth, to his beloved Whyte Avenue, seemed a lot safer than dealing with a new dragon ruler or unpredictable elementals. With his magic, he wouldn't have to work; he could get a big house for him and Alex and the twins. The fantasy continued to play itself out idyllically in his head as he walked. No more crown. No more court. Life would be good.

"Arthur, answer Elder Dhonna's question!" Alex demanded.

Arthur looked at his wife and then at the guild master. All he saw was more worry in Alex's eyes and... *Is that anger?* ... in Elder Dhonna's. "Forgive me," he said. "I was just having a moment. Of course, I wouldn't abandon Epoh." *Would I?*

Alex and Elder Dhonna both looked dubious. But they decided to accept Arthur's back peddling. For the moment.

When they reached the top of the gardens, Elder Dhonna stopped and turned to Arthur. "I will see you in the morning?"

"I will be there," Arthur assured her.

The elf studied the king for any sign of duplicity. The fact that there was no way Arthur could enter the Boundary House without the help of the elves was little reassurance. She considered staying at the castle to make sure he would follow through with the plan, but chose instead to trust him. "Don't forget the chalice," she said and then walked away.

"She doesn't look too happy with you," Alex observed.

Arthur didn't respond. He motioned for the guards to help lift the stroller back up the steps and wrapped his arm around Alex's waist. "I wonder what Finch has cooked up for supper tonight," he deflected.

"I hope it isn't venison again," Alex said. "I'm surprised there are any deer left in the forest; we've had it so often lately."

"You know you are supposed to tell the castle staff what to do?"

"Have you ever tried to give Finch directions?"

The king and queen of Epoh ate venison for supper that night.

Sok sat cross-legged on a low bench against the wall of the elven cell and stared at nothing. The moment the warriors had closed the door on him, his connection to the natural word was severed, leaving him in a mild state of shock. He couldn't even sense the walls that imprisoned him, though he could see they were made of wood. He could see his feet were touching the floor, but he couldn't feel it. It was as if the space he was in was a vacuum. Even the few steps he had to take to reach the bench left him disoriented, unable to tell up from down. Sitting still was the only way to keep his stomach from flopping around. But it was the utter and absolute silence that was the most disturbing. No sound penetrated the walls of the cell; all he could hear was the pounding of his heart and his gasping breaths.

He knew why he had been put there. Senior Elder Jona wanted to keep him from interfering with the Fae. What he couldn't understand was why. He'd fully expected the Elders to be as incensed as he was at the elementals' impudent breach of the conditions they were supposed to abide by. As far as Sok was concerned, there was no excuse for them to leave their territory and the only acceptable response should have been to hunt the offenders down and kill them. Without Harpur to intervene, it was up to the elves to keep them in line. No matter whose territory they had invaded.

And Arthur! His response was beyond intolerable. As if the elves needed his permission to handle the situation the way it should be handled. *When did he become so political?*

Sok kept rolling the events of the past fortnight over and over in his head. He understood that there was a connection between Harpur's death and the actions of the Fae, but he couldn't make the pieces fit. The Fae couldn't possibly know that Harpur was dead, so their bold exodus out of their assigned territory could not have been due to a lack of fear of reprisal from him. Even if they had somehow found out that Epoh's ruling dragon was deceased, it would be stupid, even for the Fae, to risk the wrath of the new heir, who could quite easily interpret their actions as hostile. If the Fae couldn't follow Harpur's rules, why would Karrys expect them to follow her rules. *The bloody fools are going to get us all banished from the kingdom!*

As the hours passed, Sok's anger with Arthur began to shift to Harpur. All of this was the dragon's fault. *If he had only trusted us and told us what he was up to instead of keeping everything a deep, dark secret, maybe we could have helped him. Maybe we could have prevented the Fae from daring to show themselves outside of their territory.* He went over everything. The Amber Chalice. The missing page from the spell book. Harpur's insistence on accepting the challenge.

Then Sok remembered Morgaine Fayle. It was her appearance that had set everything in motion. *Who is she and what does she have to do with all of this?*

Suddenly, it all clicked and the pieces fell into place.

"No," Sok said aloud. "It couldn't be. Harpur wouldn't do anything as weird as... Why that wily old dragon!"

Sok jumped up off of the bench and instantly felt the eerie sensation of not standing on solid ground. He took a minute to let the disorientation pass and then ran to the door.

"Hello!" he shouted, pounding his fists on the wood. "Hello! I need to talk to Elder Dhonna! Please! Someone get Elder Dhonna for me."

He had no idea if anyone could hear him. His voice echoed around the cell and it felt like his fists were bouncing off a cushion, but he kept yelling and pounding until a small slot opened and two annoyed, gray eyes glowered through it at him.

"Be quiet!" The slot closed again.

For the brief second that the slot had been opened, Sok felt the energy of the natural world seep through. He breathed it in and let it wash over him. Then he started yelling and pounding again.

"Please!" he shouted. "It's important! I need to speak to Elder Dhonna right now."

The slot opened again. "You can speak to Elder Dhonna when Senior Elder Jona releases you. Until then, keep quiet."

Sok stuck his hand through the slot so the elf on the other side of the door couldn't close it. "And I told you it's important. I'm not going to stop until I see Elder Dhonna! For Harp... Orhowyn's sake, find her and bring her to me!" At the last second, he remembered that no one else was supposed to know Harpur was dead yet.

"Get your hand back inside," the elf snapped. "Do you know how much trouble I will be in if I leave my post? They will throw me in there with you!" He tried to pry Sok's fingers from the edge of the slot.

"You're going to be in a lot more trouble if you don't get Elder Dhonna for me," Sok threatened. He gripped the opening with both hands and held on for dear life.

The natural energy flowing in through the narrow opening gave Sok the strength he needed to hold on. He pushed his face as close to the slot as he could and breathed it in in great gasping gulps. Another passing elf heard the kerfuffle and stopped to find out what was going on.

"The prisoner won't let go of the door," the elf on guard said. "He's demanding to see Elder Dhonna."

Sok couldn't see either of the elves, but he sensed the other elf's hesitation. "Is there a reason why he shouldn't talk to Elder Dhonna?"

"He's in the cell for a reason. This isn't a social hall," the guard said, still trying to pry Sok's fingers free. "And I have to get this slot closed before..."

Sok heard and felt a rumble rock the cell. Still gripping the slot, he looked around. The magic that was holding the cell together and blocking the natural energy was beginning to crumble. Visible cracks in the otherwise invisible shield spider-webbed all around him. He realized that the energy from outside the cell was counteracting the magic inside and quickly adjusted his grip to open the slot as wide as it would go, letting in as much natural energy as he could.

The rumbling and shaking intensified as more and more energy poured into the cell. The panicking guard stopped trying to stop Sok from destroying the prison chamber and backed away. "Get some help!" he shouted at the other elf. "The prisoner is going to escape."

Sok held on with every ounce of strength he had. He leaned away from the door to allow the air from outside to flow in and squeezed his eyes shut. "Harpur, get me out of this in one piece and I swear I will keep your secret forever!"

Without warning, Sok was thrown forward into the door as the magic that was holding him prisoner exploded around him. The door burst outward, dragging Sok with it and the next thing he knew, he was lying face down on the ground amid a pile of splintered wood. He pushed himself up and shook off the jolt from the impact. Coming to his feet, he looked at the wide-eyed guard. "Thanks!" he blurted and then ran off into the forest.

Behind him, he heard the guard call out, "Your hair!"

But Sok didn't have time to find out what the guard meant. He had intended to head west, skirting the elven city until he came to the Healing Guild House where he thought Elder Dhonna might be. But he realized that the guard would report he had asked to speak to the Healing Guild Master and would look for him wherever she was first. So, he turned eastward instead and made his way in the opposite direction around the city through Braydon Wood.

If he couldn't go to Elder Dhonna, he would go to Arthur. And beg for forgiveness.

Avoiding the paths through Braydon Wood slowed Sok's progress, but eventually he came out on the east side of Colwygshire a short distance from the east gate. The sun had long since set and the open space between the forest and the city wall was unoccupied, as he'd expected; there was little reason for anyone to be out there at this time of day. He ran to the gate and stopped in the shadows before haling the guards. They were just about to close it for the night.

"What were you doing out there?" one of the guards asked. "Thought you'd be heading south with armies to deal with the Fae that's wandering about down there."

Sok couldn't hid his surprise. *They've sent armies to deal with the Fae? Maybe Arthur changed his mind.* He quickly recovered, thankful for the shadows. "Yes, that was the plan, but I had something else I had to look into first. I trust the king has gone with them?"

"No, sir," the guard said, "his majesty is still here in the castle. Spent the afternoon with the queen pushing the prince and princess around the gardens in a fancy cart. Never thought he was a coward, but..."

"I'm sure cowardice is not the reason King Arthur has stayed behind," Sok snarled as he suppressed his delight in learning that the stroller had been well received. "Mind your manners, or I'll report your treasonous gossip to Sir Davynn forthwith!"

"Treason?" The guard looked horrified. "No, Mister Sok. That's not at all what I meant. I just..."

"I know what you meant," Sok hissed. "Don't ever let me hear you call our king a coward again!"

"Yes, sir... I mean no, sir. I mean..."

"Never mind!" Sok marched through the gate past the repentant guard and continued to the castle. "Unbelievable," he muttered, forgetting he'd attached the same moniker to Arthur several times earlier that day.

"Like your hair," the guard said to his back.

He took a slightly circuitous route to the castle, one that brought him to Skull's Keep. He ducked inside to grab a sandwich, knowing that the kitchens in the castle would already be shut down for the day, and found a group of guards well into their cups singing a traditional folk song off key and barely recognizable through the slurring of the lyrics.

"What's going on there?" he asked the barmaid.

The harried young woman looked at Sok. It took a few seconds before she recognized him. "They've been in here since just after supper, sir. Said the king gave them permission to use the castle account for their ale tonight."

"What?" Sok bellowed. "Which one of them told you that?"

"I believe it was Bobbit, sir," the maid said.

"Make me a sandwich," he ordered. "I'll be taking it with me."

The barmaid nodded and turned to prepare the elf's food.

Sok approached the table of revelers and waited for the butchered song to end. "Which one of you is Bobbit?" he demanded.

Twelve bleary eyes found their way to Sok's angry face. "He is," they all said, pointing at each other, then laughing.

Sok waited for the laughter to abate. "One more time," he said, "which of you is Bobbit?"

It slowly sank in that Sok was in no mood for their drunken humour.

"I'm Bobbit," one of them finally slurred. "Wha' can I do fer ya?"

"You can tell me why you are charging your ale to the castle account." Sok stared at Bobbit.

"His mad-jest-y tol' me I could."

"Why would King Arthur tell you to do that?"

"I gave him shum coins and 'e said I could use the cashtle account tonigh'." Bobbit said.

Sok couldn't imagine why the guard would give Arthur coins. "How many coins did you give him?"

"Twelve." Bobbit held up his fingers as if to demonstrate how much that was, but couldn't figure out how to make twelve out of the ten digits at his disposal.

"And why did you give him twelve coins?"

"Dunno." Bobbit shook his head back and forth.

Sok pinched the bridge of his nose. It was clear that much more than twelve coins' worth of ale had been consumed. "How much have you charged to the account?"

"Sixty-two," the barmaid said, bringing Sok's sandwich to the table.

"Sixty-two!" Sok screeched. The other patrons in the pub all went silent and looked toward the apoplectic elf.

"So far," the barmaid confirmed.

Sok glared at the guards, whose heads were all hung in shame. "The party is over, lads. Get yourselves back to the barracks right now. I will deal with you in the morning."

Chair legs scraped across the floor as the rapidly sobering guards scrambled to get up and leave as quickly as possible. Sok watched them go. Then he snatched the sandwich out of the barmaid's hand and started to follow them.

"That will be one coin, six pence," she called after him.

"Put it on the castle account!"

Sok tore into his sandwich as he stalked the quiet streets on his way to the castle. Buoyed by the epiphany he'd had in the cell and annoyed by the incident in Skull's Keep, his emotions waffled between excitement and frustration. With each bite of the sandwich, however, he settled into his usual state of calm, only wondering once what Senior Elder Jona would do to him for destroying the cell the way he had. *Should have designed it better*, he thought as he popped the final bit of crust into his mouth and sprinted up the steps to the castle.

The half-dozen guards stationed in the foyer actually appeared to be on watch when he entered, a pleasant surprise he acknowledged with a nod to each of them, which was returned with bewildered frowns. He crossed the foyer and entered the council chambers. As he expected, it was dark and empty, but he'd hoped a tray of pastries might have been forgotten on the round table. The only thing on it was Arthur's coronet. The elf sighed. He picked it up on his way past and exited through the back doors. From there he took the stairs up to the fourth floor and traversed the hallway to Arthur's private chambers.

"Is he in?" he asked the guards at the door.

"Who wants to know?" the guard on the right asked suspiciously.

"I do!" Sok said. "Now open the door or I'll have you both flogged for insubordination."

If the guards didn't recognize the hair, they recognized the threat. They exchanged glances and then shrugged.

"Came up just a few minutes ago," the guard on the left said while the guard on the right knocked on the polished oak portal.

A minute later the door opened and Arthur stood there, astonished to see Sok.

"What are you wearing?" Sok said, pushing the coronet into Arthur's hand and entering the room as if nothing had happened between them.

"A night shirt," Arthur answered simply, unsure how to behave. "What happened to your hair?"

Sok walked over to a small table next to the door, above which a mirror hung. "Ack!" he yelped, looking at himself. "My hair!"

"You look like Jareth, the goblin king," Arthur said.

"Is that something from Earth?" Sok fluffed up what remained of his silver locks with his fingers trying to come to terms with the loss of his long, silvery hair.

"Yes, goblin kings are something from Earth. What are you doing here? How did you get out of the cell?"

Sok sighed and turned away from the offending mirror. "Long story. Suffice it to say that I found a design flaw in the construction. I assume that Elder Dhonna told you my father locked me in the cell?"

"She did." Arthur scratched his head. "You escaped?"

"That's not important right now." Sok said. He was looking for something in the room.

"What are you looking for?"

"Something to eat."

"There's a few pieces of cake on the..." Sok had already seen the tray on a table behind the sofa. "So, escaping from elf prison isn't important, but cake is?"

"Cake is always important," Sok said. He chose the biggest piece from the tray and sat down on the sofa to eat it. "I know what Harpur's plan is."

Arthur scratched his head again. It was great to have Sok back and it was even greater that he didn't seem interested in talking about what had happened in the great hall during court, but Arthur felt like he needed to tread carefully after that little bombshell.

"Oh?" he said. "And what is Harpur's plan?"

Sok chuckled. "Can't tell you. It's a secret. Don't you have a robe or something you can put on over that thing?"

Arthur looked down at his royal-blue, flannel night shirt. He did have a robe. But maybe the elf wouldn't stay too long if he didn't put it on. In the meantime, a piece of cake sounded like a good idea. He helped himself and then sat down in a chair across from Sok. "If it helps, I know what Harpur's plan is too."

"Do you now?" Sok seemed surprised. "How did you figure it out?"

"It's kind of obvious if you really think about it." Arthur took a bite of cake.

"What's your favourite part of the plan?" Sok asked casually.

"Oh, no, you don't!" Arthur said around a mouthful of cake. "You're not going to get me to tell you what I know when I don't know what you know. For all I know, you don't know anything and, as you said, it's a secret."

Sok frowned. He hadn't expected Arthur to be so clever. "Very well. We'll just have to both know what we know and not know if each other really knows what we claim we know."

"I don't claim to know. I know," Arthur said.

"I know you think you know," Sok said, "but I'll bet I know some things you don't know."

"Like what?"

"That's for me to know." Sok devoured the last of his cake.

What Arthur did know was that he knew some things that Sok didn't know. But it was time to address the real elephant in the room. He leaned forward and rested his elbows on his knees. "Sok, about this morning..."

"Fire off a dragon's back," Sok interjected. Then, seeing the look of disappointment on Arthur's face, he found the courage to do what he needed to do. "I'm sorry for the way I behaved. I let my hatred for the Fae get in the way. I hope you will forgive me."

Arthur was touched. He heard nothing but sincerity in Sok's apology and he wanted to respond in kind. "There's nothing to forgive you for," Arthur said. "We all have things that trigger us. It's me who needs to be forgiven. I should have been more sensitive to how you were affected by Ned Krats' news."

Sok smiled. "I guess we're both a couple of prats."

"We have our moments, that's for sure," Arthur said. "But you will be happy to know that the situation with the Fae is being handled."

"I understand that an army has been dispatched." Sok didn't want to appear too gleeful about this, but he couldn't keep all of the delight he felt out of his voice.

"Yes, two hundred guards from the castle and five hundred elven warriors are marching to the village," Arthur admitted. "But we are relatively sure that they will be recalled tomorrow."

"You're sending gold to the Fae?" Sok asked.

"How did you know?"

"It would make sense," Sok said. "They must have approached the village because they hadn't heard from Harpur and they wanted whatever he had promised them for guarding the Amber Chalice."

Arthur couldn't help being impressed. *Maybe he does know everything.* "How did you figure it out?"

"Pretty much all one can do in an elven prison cell is think," Sok said, sounding like he'd served decades of hard time.

"You were there for half a day," Arthur scoffed. "Which reminds me, how did you get out?"

"I blew up the cell with natural energy," Sok said as if it should have been obvious. "Simple really."

"Well, I'm glad you're back," Arthur said. "And I'm glad things are good between us. Things are good, aren't they?"

"That depends," Sok said, leaning back on the sofa and frowning at Arthur.

"On...?" Arthur couldn't think of anything else he might have done to upset his friend.

"On why you told Bobbit he could charge ale to the castle account at Skull's Keep."

"How in Harpur's hoard did you find out about that?" It was the last thing Arthur expected to be challenged on that night.

"I stopped there for a sandwich on my way back from Braydon Wood and Bobbit and a bunch of his pals were getting quite drunk. All on the castle's gold."

"Well, how drunk could a bunch of them get on twelve coins?" Arthur asked, not seeing the harm.

"It was sixty-two coins," Sok said.

"What? Bobbit only lent me twelve coins!"

"Just why did you have to borrow coins from a guard in the first place?" Sok asked.

"A guy named Barger delivered the stroller you commissioned. Nice gift, by the way. Alex loved it" Arthur began.

"And you didn't know how to pay him, so you borrowed coins from Bobbit. Why did you borrow twelve? The deal I made with Barger for the stroller was for eight."

"I knew that guy was swindling me!" Arthur said with disgust.

Sok rolled his eyes and sighed. "I'm not gone a full day and already you've run up a deficit of fifty-six pieces of gold. I can't imagine what would have happened if I'd been locked up for a full term."

"How long is a full term?"

"Eleven days," Sok said with a shudder. "No elf can survive in the cell much beyond that."

Arthur couldn't imagine what it must have been like for Sok. "I guess you're a fugitive now, hey?"

Sok nodded. "Senior Elder Jona won't be happy with me, but I'm hoping that once Harpur's plan is completed, Elder Dhonna will back me up with the Elders. So, I'm asking for sanctuary until all this is sorted out."

"It depends." Arthur looked slyly at the elf.

"On what?"

"On whether or not we're good," Arthur said.

Sok rolled his eyes again. "We're good, Arthur."

"Then, by the power invested in me as king of Epoh, I hereby grant you sanctuary."

Sok planted his chin in his palm and shook his head. It was good to be back.

Chapter Twenty

Elder Dhonna was late to meet Arthur in Braydon Wood. After Sok's dramatic escape from the cell, the previous day, the Elder's had been in constant consultation, which consisted mostly of listening to Senior Elder Jona rant about his wayward and rebellious son and all the un-elvenly things he was going to do to Sok when he got his hands on him. There was a brief discussion about reconstructing the cell, but, in all honesty, not one of the Elders actually wanted to see that happen, and so that was tabled to a later date.

They hadn't been dismissed until late in the night after the search party had reported that they hadn't found Sok anywhere, but would continue the search again in the morning. Senior Elder Jona grudgingly conceded to the wisdom of that and ordered the other Elders to return at dawn.

"No one is to come in or go out of the city until that boy is found!"

His last words to the Elders left Elder Dhonna with a bit of a dilemma. If she couldn't leave, she couldn't meet Arthur. And if she couldn't meet Arthur, they couldn't go to Harpur's lair. The fact that Sok had asked to speak to her had, for some time, put her under suspicion of collusion. It had taken quite a bit to convince Senior Elder Jona that she had no idea why Sok had asked for her. She didn't know if Sok knew how exposure to natural energy would affect the cell, but she suspected he'd stumbled on it accidentally when he demanded to speak to her. But Senior Elder Jona was not entirely convinced and ordered her to stay in the Braydon Wood city along with all of the other Elders. She tried reminding him of Harpur's plan and the part she was to play in seeing it through. Even that did not exempt her from the lockdown, such was the depth of Senior Elder Jona's fury with Sok. She could see no other option but to defy the order and go anyway.

The problem was that when she woke up that morning, two warriors had been posted outside her treehouse door to keep an eye on her. She looked at the strapping young warriors and pasted a smile on her face to hide her dismay. "I do know the way to the council chambers," she said to them.

"This gives us no pleasure, Elder Dhonna," replied the taller of the two warriors, a young elf named Cam, who had emerald eyes and long silver hair like Sok's. "Senior Elder Jona insisted."

"Very well," Elder Dhonna said with a sigh of resignation. "But first I must stop at the guild house to collect a few things."

"Our orders were to bring you straight to the council chambers," Will, the other warrior said.

"It will only take a minute and I do need to get my things from the guild house. I'm sure you can appreciate that as Healing Guild Master, it would be unseemly for me to be without my medicines," she argued.

Cam made the decision for both warriors. "Let's hurry then," he said. "The sun is almost up and Senior Elder Jona will be waiting."

They took the overhead bridges that linked the trees throughout the elven city to the guild house and descended the ladder to the ground. Elder Dhonna ran up the path and into the guild house ahead of her escorts. Her plan was simple, albeit desperate. If Senior Elder Jona could not be convinced to let her go to Harpur's lair, she would use the dragonfoil ash and zap herself out of the council chambers without his permission. *At least he won't be able to throw me in the cell for it.*

When they reached the council chambers, Cam held the door open for Elder Dhonna. "We will be waiting for you out here," he said.

"Hopefully, not for long," Elder Dhonna replied, then entered the chambers.

All of the Elders were already assembled, except for Bele, who had marched south with the warrior army. Senior Elder Jona looked up from his seat on the dais and eyed the tardy guild master. "I was beginning to think we would have to send out a search party for you as well."

"Nonsense," Elder Dhonna said as she crossed the room and took her place on the platform. "But I do not see the point in keeping the Elders here when we all have work to do. We could convene when Sok is found."

"And when do you think that will be?" Senior Elder Jona countered.

"I suspect that it will be whenever Sok is ready to be found, Senior Elder Jona. You know your son as well as any of us and he has probably sought sanctuary in the castle at Colwygshire. This..." she swept her hand across the room to indicate the unwarranted gathering of the Elders, "...is a waste of our time. What purpose is there in keeping us away from our guilds when there is nothing we can do until Sok decides to come back on his own?"

"You told me yourself that Sok had a falling out with the human king. Why would you now suggest that he would seek sanctuary at the castle?" Senior Elder Jona looked stricken. He'd taken some measure of comfort in learning that Sok and Arthur had argued and hoped that it meant that Sok would return to Braydon Wood to take his proper place in one of the guilds.

"May we speak privately?" Elder Dhonna asked.

Senior Elder Jona hesitated. He knew he had been rash in his decision-making since Sok's escape, spurred by frustration with the young elf. Rather than think things through and listening to his council of Elders, he'd lashed out, trying to exert some control over his uncontrollable offspring. "Council is adjourned until further notice," he said. "But no one is to leave the city!"

Elder Dhonna bit her lip to keep from groaning. It was a partial win, but she needed him to lift the curfew. When the others, who had not needed to be told twice that they could leave, had cleared the room, she turned to the senior elder. "I believe that Sok has figured out Harpur's plan and has gone to the castle to help." She watched Senior Elder Jona process her words.

"Why does that boy insist on living with the humans? Why can't he just stay here and be a proper elf?" Senior Elder Jona spat out.

"Sok is a complicated elf, to be sure," Elder Dhonna said. "But he's also a good elf. No one can say why his heart has led him to do what he does, but he does it well. He's very good at his job. You should be proud of him."

"That's just it," the senior elder said. "I am proud of him. He's smart and resourceful. He's..."

"Everything you wanted to be?" Elder Dhonna finished for him.

Senior Elder Jona didn't respond.

"Let me go to the castle and see if he's there. He asked to talk to me when he was in the cell. Let me find out what he wants."

"You'll come right back whether he's there or not?"

"I know he's there." Elder Dhonna would not commit to returning until she and Arthur finished what Harpur asked them to do.

"You may go," Senior Elder Jona said gruffly. He considered stipulating strict conditions, but he knew in his heart that the Healing Guild Master would not comply. There was no point in putting either of them in the position of having to deal with the consequences of their actions.

"Thank you, Senior Elder Jona." Elder Dhonna jumped up. Glad that she didn't have to resort to using the dragonfoil ash in front of him, she took her leave as well. When she reached the door. she turned back to the troubled senior elder. "Can I relieve Cam and Will of their duty?"

"Yes, yes," Senior Elder Jona waved her away.

Elder Dhonna did not leave the city through the main gate at the road to Colwygshire. Instead, she made her way to the western edge of the elven metropolis and slipped into the forest behind a ground-level grain storage bin. From there she followed a path to the place where she was to meet Arthur. It came as no surprise to find him *and* Sok waiting for her.

"That cloak isn't going to fool anyone," she said to the fugitive elf as she entered the clearing and then gasped when Sok lowered the hood. "What happened to your hair?"

Sok's hand went involuntarily to the shock of silvery spikes on his head. "Singed it blowing up the cell."

"Singed is a bit of an understatement," Elder Dhonna said. "Let's get going. I'm not sure if the search party is still looking for you."

"Aren't you going to ask why he's here?" Arthur inquired grumpily. It was clear he was hoping Elder Dhonna would not allow Sok to accompany them.

"I know why he's here," Elder Dhonna said. "He's figured out Harpur's plan and he intends to be there when we cast the spell. I'm not going to waste my breath arguing with him. At least if he's with us, we'll know what he's up to."

"But he's not supposed to know what we're doing," Arthur complained. "We're all going to get in trouble if he comes with us."

"We'll deal with that later," the guild master said. "Now, can you zap all three of us to the lair, or do I have to get out the dragonfoil ash?"

A huge grin broke open across Sok's face. "Told you!"

"Hold onto my arms," Arthur said and the moment he felt their grip on his shirt, he zapped them to the lair.

They landed a few feet from the entrance to the lair in Arthur's increasingly familiar cloud of golden-yellow smoke and waited for it to dissipate. A few seconds later, they were looking at Anayah who was dozing on the boulder next to the lair. Her head snapped up and her eyes blinked at them several times. She raised her hands to throw a magical shock at them, but stopped just in time as recognition finally penetrated the fog in her over-tired brain.

"Good, you're finally here," she said. "I thought you were the bear."

Arthur's head swiveled back and forth, looking for a lurking bruin. "What bear?"

Anayah yawned. "Scavengers have been trying to get to Harpur's body. I've been up all night scaring them away. There's one rather persistent bear that keeps coming back, though."

Arthur, Sok and Elder Dhonna all turned to look across the meadow at Harpur's body. For having been dead seven days, it looked remarkably devoid of signs of decay, though the sickly sweet and pungent aroma of rotting flesh could still be detected on the westerly breeze. The only other concession to death that was apparent was the loss of the glossy sheen in Harpur's scales. They were now a dull, purple-gray. Three buzzards circled above the meadow and the surrounding trees were filled with scolding worcs.

Arthur gagged. He pulled the neck of his tunic over his mouth and nose. "How bad is it over there?"

"Not bad," Anayah said, "other than the smell. His scales are keeping the animals from..."

Arthur didn't need any graphic details. "I get the picture. You should get some rest. You look like a zombie."

"What's a zombie?" Sok asked.

"They are dead people who have come back to life and eat the brains of living people," Arthur explained.

Sok flashed back to the night he'd spent in Harpur's lair on Earth. Harpur had been channel surfing and had stopped on a show with just such creatures lurching across the screen. "Like those things in the moving picture on Harpur's wall back on Whyte Avenue! How did you ever survive in a world with those things around?" Sok mimicked the movements of the walking dead.

"They aren't real," Arthur said. "They're fictional creatures."

"But I saw them," Sok insisted. His fingers were contorted to look like claws and he snarled to add to the effect.

"Didn't I explain to you how television and movies worked? It's all just pretend. What you saw were real people wearing makeup and costumes pretending to be zombies." Arthur pushed Sok's hands down.

"They looked real," Sok mumbled.

"I think we're getting a little off track here," Anayah interjected with another yawn. "You'll want to keep an eye out for the bear. He seems determined. I've been frightening him away with loud bangs and shocks. Couldn't bring myself to kill him, but a few of the worcs didn't fare so well."

Arthur noticed several dead black birds lying in the grass around Harpur's body. He didn't treasure the idea of picking off birds or shocking bears all day. "Can I just put a forcefield around Harpur to keep the animals away?"

"Good idea," Elder Dhonna said. "But you will have to lift it when we..."

Anayah was too tired to be curious about what the guild master had left unsaid. "You do whatever you think is best. I'm going to the village to get some sleep. If there's any news, I'll come back later and catch you up." She raised her hand to zap herself away, then stopped. "Wait. Why are you here?" she asked Sok.

Arthur, Sok and Elder Dhonna all froze. They hadn't actually been expecting Anayah to be at the lair and it hadn't occurred to them that they might need to prepare a plausible explanation for Sok's presence. Elder Dhonna finally took the lead with the truth.

"Sok figured out what Harpur's plan is," she said. "He's also a fugitive, so we brought him along to keep him safe."

Anayah's sleep-deprived brain struggled to form the many questions Elder Dhonna's paradoxically vague elucidation raised. "You know what? I'm just going to go to the village now. Someone will tell me all the details sooner or later. Good luck with whatever you are all doing here." She snapped her fingers and was gone.

"I can't believe she accepted that," Arthur said.

"Bear!" Sok shouted, pointing past Harpur's body.

A large, brown bear stood at the head of the trail on the west side of the meadow leading down into the valley below the lair. It snouted the air, sniffing for danger before taking a few tentative steps toward the feast that lay just a few more steps away. Then it stopped and snouted the air again, obviously scenting the new presence of Arthur, Sok and Elder Dhonna standing near the entrance to the lair.

When it raised itself up on two legs to its full height and roared, Arthur jumped back and prepared to run into the bush. But Sok grabbed his arm and held him in place. "Do something," the elf whispered.

"Do what?"

The bear dropped back down onto all fours and looked at Harpur's body. It seemed to Arthur that it must have recently come out of hibernation and was looking to break its long winter fast on a tasty bit of dragon. But Anayah's shocks had made it cautious and now there was a small herd of fresh prey only thirty yards away. It swung its big head back toward Arthur, Sok and Elder Dhonna and appeared to have made up its mind. With a great lunge, the bear sprang forward and ran straight toward the quivering trio.

"Anything!" Sok yelled as he jumped behind Arthur and pushed him toward the bear. "Kill it if you have to!"

"I can't kill... Oh, crap!"

The bear was moving fast and Arthur had only seconds to do something before it would be upon them. He raised his hands and closed his eyes and started waving his arms about.

The bear stopped less than three feet away from Arthur's thrashing limbs as if it had crashed into a brick wall. An alarmed and puzzled expression contorted its face as its entire body began to repeatedly stretch and contort like a rubber Gumby doll being abused by a toddler. Then it started spinning in the air, rolling sideways at a dizzying speed until it finally expanded to three times its normal size and then shrank to the size of a mouse, at which point it dropped to the ground where it lay dazed and confused in deep shock.

"Sire, you shrank the bear!" Sok exclaimed in fascinated horror as he reached around the king and stilled his spastic arms.

Arthur opened his eyes again. It took him a minute to locate the tiny bruin laying in the grass. "That's not exactly what I intended," he said shakily as he leaned over to look at the result of his magical misfire.

Sok and Elder Dhonna stepped closer and bent down to examine the pathetic little thing with him.

"What did you intend to do to it?" Elder Dhonna asked.

"At first, I was going to zap it to the Fae Lands. But then I thought that might not be a good idea and I was going to zap it to the western mountains. But then I realized that I might zap it into a tree or a rock and that just seemed cruel. So, I tried to turn it into a teddy bear...," Arthur explained.

Sok and Elder Dhonna swiveled their heads to look at the shaken wizard-king. "A teddy bear?" they asked in unison.

"It's a stuffed toy. Kids love them," Arthur said.

Neither of the elves could imagine a child playing with a taxidermized bear. Both of them opted not to pursue the bizarre Earth practice of letting children play with dead animals.

"What should we do with it?" Arthur asked.

The little bear was recovering from its ordeal. It stood up and shook its head, emitting a tiny, frightened growl as it looked up at the monstrous beings it had planned to eat just a few minutes earlier.

"It's harmless now," Sok said. "Just leave it."

"But how's it going to eat?" Arthur asked. "It can't hunt like that."

"The magic will wear off eventually," Elder Dhonna said. "And bears are omnivorous. It will figure out to eat leaves and fallen berries in the meantime."

They watched the bear turn and try to run away through the thick grass, stumbling and falling as it learned how to navigate the world in its new and unfamiliar state.

"Poor little guy," Arthur said, straightening up again. Another waft of putrefaction caused him to cover his mouth and nose again.

"That poor little guy wanted to eat you," Sok reminded him.

Elder Dhonna reached into her satchel and pulled out a small jar. "Rub a bit of this under your nose," she said handing it to Arthur. "It will help with the smell. Which isn't going to get any better as the day warms up."

Arthur opened the jar and smelled the jelly-like contents. "Whoa! That smells worse than Harpur."

"Use it or don't," Elder Dhonna said. "But you will need your hands free to cast the spell."

Arthur winced as he rubbed a small amount of the unguent under his nose. The strong odor of kerosene with flowery undertones and a citrusy top note caused his eyes to water and he spent the next few minutes blinking tears away. He handed the jar to Elder Dhonna, who stashed it back in her satchel. "Aren't you going to use some?" he asked.

"I'm good," Sok said.

"No need," Elder Dhonna said. "Shall we go inside and get things ready?"

Arthur and Sok followed the guild master into the lair. Nothing, save for the gold that Anayah had taken for the Fae, had changed. Yet the cavern felt oddly deserted and forsaken. "I don't feel Harpur here anymore," Arthur observed out loud. "I really do miss him."

"We all do," Elder Dhonna said. She moved to the broken stalagmite and began emptying vials and packets onto its surface. "Put the chalice on the stalagmite," she directed.

Arthur opened a pouch that was hanging from his belt and removed the Amber Chalice. He set it down on the stalagmite amid the potions. "What's that for?" he asked, pointing to a slim dagger Elder Dhonna laid down next to the chalice.

"What do you think it's for?" the guild master replied as Arthur squeezed his hands into fists. "Have you memorized the spell?"

"I think so," Arthur said. He patted his coat pocket. "But I brought it along, just in case."

Elder Dhonna sighed. "Why don't you go somewhere and practice reciting it. I still have to get the *icky* part ready." She reached into her satchel again. This time she withdrew a small sack. Something was wriggling inside it.

"That's not a snake, is it?" Arthur croaked.

"Arthur, just go outside and practice the spell."

"But it's alive!"

Sok stepped closer to get a better look at what was going on. "It won't be for long," he said.

"You're just going to murder an innocent snake? How can you guys be so cavaliere about stuff like this?" Arthur was horrorstruck.

"I take no pleasure in this, but I can assure you that the snake won't suffer." Elder Dhonna said.

Sok took Arthur by the arm and guided him out of the lair. "Some magic is messy, Arthur," he said.

"It's disgusting," Arthur said. "I don't like this one bit."

"That's a good thing," Sok said. "This is dark magic and you don't want to mess with it. But Harpur asked you to do this for him. It's a one-time thing and once this is over, you will never have to cast such a spell ever again."

"I don't intend to." Arthur slumped down onto the boulder next to the entrance.

"What part of the snake is Elder Dhonna harvesting for you?" Sok asked, taking a seat next to the troubled king.

"An eye."

"Interesting," Sok said. "A single snake's eye symbolizes recovered memories of the past." He seemed to be recalling a past memory of his own. "So Harpur did tear that page out of the spell book. He lied to me."

"Actually, I think Elder Dhonna did that." Arthur corrected the elf.

"Ah, of course," Sok said. "I should have realized that. Look, Arthur, don't worry about the snake."

"It just seems so cruel," Arthur said.

"If it helps, Elder Dhonna will use the rest of it for medicines. It isn't dying in vain."

Arthur sighed. "It shouldn't have to die at all."

"Neither should have Harpur," Sok said. "But there he is. And he needs you to... What's that thing you say all the time? ...suck it up?"

Arthur chuckled in spite of himself. "You're right. I need to suck it up."

He pulled the torn page from the spell book out of his pocket and unfolded it. All he had to do was say the words. And mix a potion in the chalice. *I hope Elder Dhonna brought something to scoop the snake eye up with*. He shuddered at the thought of having to touch it himself.

The ointment on his upper lip had started to cause his skin to tingle. He wanted to rub it off, but refrained from doing so. Sok watched in amusement as Arthur's mouth and nose performed a complicated dance on his face, bobbing and twisting to relieve the irritation.

"Can I make a suggestion?" Sok said.

"What's that?" Arthur did not look up from the page.

"Conjure a scarf to wrap around your face. If you keep making faces like that, you're going to ruin the spell."

Arthur thought that was a good idea. He dragged his sleeve across his face to remove the irksome ointment and snapped his fingers to summon a scarf. A long, wide ribbon of pale pink cloth appeared in his hands. It was embroidered with delicate periwinkle flowers. "I'm beginning to think that magic has a mind of its own. And a decidedly sarcastic sense of humour." He wrapped the feminine accessory around his face and tied it at the nape of his neck.

"Now you're getting it!" Sok said, clapping him on the shoulder. "With practice, you'll master your magic and maybe next time you can go for basic black." He did not tell Arthur that the ointment had left his upper lip bright red.

Arthur returned to studying the spell.

A while later, Elder Dhonna emerged from the lair and stared at Sok until he relinquished his seat on the boulder. She sat down next to Arthur while the younger elf inspected the grass a few feet away.

"What are you looking for?" Arthur asked.

"I don't want to sit on the bear," Sok said.

"It went the other way," Elder Dhonna pointed out.

"I know. I'm just being careful. Arthur doesn't need another thing to be upset about today."

"That's very considerate of you," Arthur said. "I'm sure the bear appreciates it too."

As soon as Sok sat down and got comfortable, Elder Dhonna turned to Arthur. "Everything is ready in there. Do you want me to explain all the ingredients to you?"

"Now?" Arthur asked. Things were starting to get real for him.

"Best to get it done while things are still fresh," Elder Dhonna said.

Arthur grimaced. "Do I have to touch the eye?"

"It's not that bad," Elder Dhonna said. "Just pick it up and drop it in the chalice." She patted his knee and stood up to go back inside.

Sok leaned back to allow the guild master to step past him. "It's just an eye, Arthur. It's not like you have to touch a naval or anything really gross."

Arthur stared in bemusement at his friend. "What is so gross about a navel?"

Sok convulsed in revulsion. "Don't even talk about them to me."

"You brought it up!"

"Yeah, and I'm sorry I did." He shuddered again.

Arthur left Sok in the grass and followed Elder Dhonna inside. Everything on the stalagmite looked benign enough. Except, of course, for the serpent's optical orb. And the razor-sharp dagger.

"Everything is laid out in the order you need to add them." Elder Dhonna explained. "When you have added everything else, slice your palm..."

"I thought you said I could just prick my finger!"

"Harpur's broken wing, Arthur! It's a little cut. You have two natural healers here with you. And one of them is a guild master!" Elder Dhonna scolded. "Do you want me to put some numbing cream on your hand so you won't feel it?"

"That would be nice. Thank you." Arthur held out his palm.

Elder Dhonna rummaged in her satchel for the numbing cream. "There!" she said after she smeared a small amount on his hand. "Just don't cut too deep. You won't be able to feel your palm for most of the day."

Arthur flexed his hand. It was as if his fingers had been detached from his hand and were operating independently. "Creepy," he mumbled.

Elder Dhonna stalked away, muttering something about a big baby. Arthur made a face at her back and then turned his attention to the ingredients on the stalagmite.

There were two vials of liquid—one green and one clear—a packet of powder, the snake's eye and what looked like a small lump of coal. He reached for the first vial and poured it into the chalice. *One down.* Then he poured in the contents of the second vial. *So far, so good.* When he dumped the packet of powder into the liquid, it began to bubble and froth, not violently, but enough to make Arthur refrain from leaning over it. *I hope that's normal.*

It was time for the eyeball. Arthur reached down to pick it up, but his extended fingers refused to close around it. He closed his eyes, thinking that doing it blind might help. Then realized that he could knock over the chalice and spill the potion. *It's just an eyeball, Arthur. You can do this.* He tried again, reaching down and bringing his thumb and index finger to either side of the small orb, but could not bring himself to touch it.

"Elder Dhonna?" he called out.

"Are you done?" she called back.

"Not quite. I'm just wondering if I can move the snake's eye with magic instead of touching it."

Arthur sensed the eye rolling that had to be happening outside the lair.

"Yes, that's fine," Elder Dhonna called back. "Just stop the magic before it goes into the cup. Let it drop in."

Arthur breathed a sigh of relief. Carefully, he raised the eyeball up off the stalagmite and moved it over the chalice. Then he let it fall into the frothing potion with a satisfying plop. That done, he picked up the final ingredient, the little stone that looked like a lump of coal, and tossed it into the chalice. Instantly, the bubbling stopped and the potion settled. It looked like an ordinary cup of water. Even the snake's eye and the lump of coal had instantly dissolved.

"Weird," Arthur said out loud as he picked up the chalice and the dagger and carried them to the entrance of the lair. "All done," he said proudly and held the cup out for Elder Dhonna to inspect his work.

"That looks perfect," she said. "Now you can finish the spell."

Arthur turned and looked across the meadow at Harpur's body. He squeezed his numb hand around the dagger hilt and steeled himself for the final step. As he approached Harpur he heard the buzzing of flies and he realized that not all of the dragon's body was invulnerable to the process of decomposition. The scarf around his face failed to filter out all of the smell and he wished he had stuck with Elder Dhonna's ointment. Irritating as it was, it worked. Breathing through his mouth helped some, but the stench still found its way to his olfactory senses and he gagged involuntarily. When he reached Harpur's head, it was all he could do not to drop the chalice and vomit.

Harpur's black and swollen tongue lolled out of his open mouth, crawling with maggots. The larvae swarmed in and out of his empty eye sockets and nostrils. Arthur swallowed his bile and forced himself to kneel down next to his friend's writhing head. Tears filled his eyes and he had to blink them away to find a flat spot on the ground to safely put the chalice down. He could feel Sok and Elder Dhonna watching him from across the meadow and he was determined to do this right. His magic was the only chance they had to successfully accomplish Harpur's plan. *The faster you get this done, the faster you can get away again* Arthur told himself.

He transferred the dagger to his right and aimed the point at the fleshy mound under his thumb. Again, his muscles refused to do his mind's bidding and the sharp blade simply hung in the air glistening with menace. *You won't even feel it, Arthur. Just a quick poke and it will be over.*

Arthur watched the knife point inch closer to his palm. In spite of the cool morning air, beads of sweat formed on his brow and his jaw clenched in anticipation of the imminent wound he was about to inflict upon himself. He finally made himself push the dagger into his palm and to his great relief, the numbing cream did its job. He felt nothing as his blood welled up around the knife point and began to run across his skin toward his wrist. Dropping the dagger, he reached for the chalice and began to recite the incantation he'd memorized.

"By flame and bone, by breath and scale,
Let spirit rise where flesh must pale.
From vessel worn to vessel new,
Pass through fire, and be made true.
Let no shadow break this path,
Let no malice stir its wrath.
Bound by stars and stone and sky,
Let soul take wing, but not to die.
Heart to heart, and mind to mind,
Old self leave, and new self find.
As name remains, let form be changed—

So speaks the will, so be arranged."

Across the meadow, Sok and Elder Dhonna held their breath and watched with rapt attention. They heard Arthur's voice crescendo as he spoke the words, infusing them with focused intention, and when the last syllables reached their ears – *Urscalla, urscalla, urscalla!* – the tension in their bodies released like a fat lady's corset stays tearing free.

Arthur wrung a few drops of his blood into the chalice. As the vital plasma joined the potion, it once again began to bubble and a purple-red mist rose up from the spumy concoction. He had only a few seconds to complete the final step of the spell; it had to be done while the potion was actively foaming. He reached forward and poured the contents of the chalice into Harpur's ear.

Even though he knew the results of his magic would not be known until the next day, the anticlimax left him feeling more than a little disappointed. Subconsciously, he had hoped that the potion would work immediately. But nothing had obviously changed. The maggots continued to crawl in and out of Harpur's vulnerable orifices and the reek of decay continued to waft on the breeze. Arthur sighed and stood up.

As he bent down to pick up the dagger, two shadows fell across the ground in front of him. He looked up to see Jack and Diane standing on the other side of Harpur's body, smiling broadly. They were still dressed as pirates.

"Where did you come from?" Arthur asked. "And where did you go?"

"We've been with you all along," Diane said.

"We are never far away," Jack said.

Their typical non-answer didn't surprise Arthur. "Why are you back then?"

"We've come to warn you," Jack said.

"Warn me about what?" Arthur's heart clenched with icy fear. He heard Sok and Elder Dhonna approach behind him and stepped back to get closer to them.

"Your efforts will succeed," Diane said.

"But you will not know it," Jack finished.

"What does that mean?" Sok asked, coming across the meadow to stand next to Arthur. The elf had never been a fan of Arthur's guardians, but this enigmatic warning felt like an ominous threat. "Tell us what you mean by that!"

Arthur raised his hand to quiet Sok. "It's okay," he said. "I think I know what they are talking about." As vexing as his guardians so often were, Arthur believed he was beginning to understand their subtle guidance.

"Well?" Sok said. "Are you going to tell us?"

"In time," he said with a sly smile. "Right now, there is something I need to do at the castle. I'll be back as soon as I can."

Before Sok or Elder Dhonna could say anything, Arthur zapped himself away and Jack and Diane disappeared with him.

"What in Harpur's lair was that all about?" Elder Dhonna asked.

Sok shrugged. "I don't suppose you brought anything to eat?"

Elder Dhonna shook her head in wonder. "No. I was depending on Arthur to conjure food for us. Come on, we can forage for something in the forest." She turned and walked toward the trailhead where the bear had first appeared.

Sok frowned at the guild master's back. Then he looked down at Harpur's body. "Why couldn't your legacy to the land be a pastry tree?" He ran to catch up to her.

The first Fae to show up in the pasture near the village was spotted just after dawn. Following instructions, one of the guards on duty slipped away quietly to alert Davynn and Frode, who were just about to be served their breakfasts by Hiro, who was just reaching into his magic satchel.

"The Fae have been seen, Sir Davynn," the guard said.

Davynn looked at the Krist with chagrin. "Just some jamba for now." He stood up, accepted a steaming cup of the hot nectar from Hiro and waited for Frode to do the same before following the guard back to the edge of the pasture.

"How many Fae?" Frode asked the guard as they trudge through the due-kissed grass.

"Just one so far," he replied. "It's right over there."

The guard pointed to a small bush that was growing in the south-west corner of the pasture. Davynn recognized the creature right away. It was the same one he and Arthur had encountered in the Fae Lands. The knight scanned the pasture for signs of other Faefolk and spotted two others by a fence post a short distance away from the first one.

"I see three," he whispered to Frode.

"More are in bushes behind them." Frode nodded to a clump of trees about ten yards further west.

Davynn turned to the guard that had alerted them to the Fae's presence. "Get the rest of the guards and Drengrokil ready. Have them wait on the other side of the tents." Davynn felt for his sword hilt. Despite its uselessness against Fae magic, it gave him comfort to know it was there. He looked up at Frode. "Ready?"

"Is good a time as any," the big man said and together they walked forward into the pasture.

They had only taken a few steps when the Fae creature in the south-west corner stepped out and away from the bush. The others, Davynn noted, all seemed to melt deeper into the cover of their respective hiding places. "I don't like that," Davynn observed.

"Is just caution. Fae will move closer to protect leader." Frode seemed unconcerned.

Davynn knew what the Fae were capable of. Frode's blasé attitude gave him little comfort. All he could do was hope that they were right and all the Fae wanted was gold. And that they had enough gold to cover Harpur's debt to them if that was indeed the case. What worried him most was that gold gave Fae strength. The more they had, the stronger their magic was. If giving them the gold would make them go back to their own territory and stay there, he was all for it. *But what if they know Harpur is dead and are planning on using the gold to build their magic to turn it against the other races?*

The knight and the Drengrokil leader stopped when they were a dozen paces from the Fae creature. It stopped as well and crossed its twig arms across its charred-log body.

"Where is our dragon lord, Harpur Diggins?" it rasped.

"Hale and greetings, good Faefellow," Davynn said politely. He even bowed to show his good intentions. "Harpur Diggins has important business in the north. He has sent me to see what brings you out of your territory."

The Fae creature narrowed its eyes. "Harpur Diggins knows what we want. We want what he promised the queen."

"Of course," Davynn said, relieved that the Fae creature was buying the ruse. "You want gold. We have that."

The creature looked around the pasture and toward the Drengrokil tents. "I see no gold. Where is it?"

"We will bring it to you," Davynn said. "But first we need your assurance that you will return to your territory and leave the good people of this village unharmed."

"Show me the gold. Only then I will give you my assurance," The Fae creature snarled.

The last thing Davynn needed was a stand-off with the Fae. The longer it took to get them back into their territory, the closer the elven and human armies got. There was still time, but Davynn wanted this wrapped up long before the elven warriors could arrive.

"Harpur is not happy that you have encroached on human territory," Davynn said, hoping the veiled threat would make the creature think twice.

"Then Harpur Diggins should tell us that himself," the Fae creature said. "We have been calling him and he does not respond."

"I told you," Davynn said, "he has important business in the north and cannot come at this time. I am his emissary and I have his authority to deliver your gold as soon as I have your pledge that you will return to your own territory and remain there."

The Fae creature unfolded its arms. "As you wish. If you give us all the gold that Harpur Diggins promised us, we will return to the Fae Lands. If you don't, we will start taking children; one each day until we are paid in full."

Frode raised a hand to signal his men. A few minutes later two of the Drengrokil warriors approached carrying the chest of gold Anayah had sent from Harpur's lair. They set it down half way between the Fae creature and Davynn and Frode. One of them undid the straps and flipped the lid back to reveal the treasure inside.

"What is this?" the Fae creature spat.

"It's your gold," Davynn said.

"Where is the rest of it?"

"This is what Harpur sent. Take it or leave it; it makes no difference to me." Davynn had the eerie feeling that his bluff was about to be called.

"It's been many years since I was last in our dragon lord's lair," the Fae said, "but I cannot imagine that since that time, Harpur Diggins' hoard has been reduced to two chests of gold."

"What are you talking about?" Davynn was nonplussed. "Harpur Diggins has one of the largest dragon hoards on Thraeh. This is but a trifling amount of what he keeps in his lair."

"And half of it belongs to the Fae!"

"Half!" Davynn nearly choked on the word. "Have you mud for brains? The Fae are not getting half of Harpur's hoard!"

"What I have," the Fae creature said, reaching into a hidden compartment under the bark on its body and pulling out a scroll, "is a contract that says if Harpur Diggins does not deliver three chests of gold within three days of retrieving that poisonous chalice from our lands, we are entitled to half of his hoard."

Davynn felt like he'd been punched in the stomach. He couldn't breathe.

Frode walked toward the Fae creature to get the contract, but it jumped out of his reach and stuffed the scroll back under its bark. "Stay away! I'll set my warriors on you if you try to touch me again."

Frode slowly lifted his long, curved sword and pointed it at the Fae. "And I will fry Fae where it stands if not get contract."

The Fae creature's eyes focused on the business end of the weapon as red bolts of lightning-like sparks crackled from its point. It pulled out the scroll and held it at arm's length for Frode to take. "Fine," it hissed. "It's all in there."

Frode jabbed his sword a couple of inches closer to the Fae creature and then unrolled the scroll. He ran his own eyes down the length of parchment and then turned back to the tormented knight. "Is fake," he said, handing the scroll to Davvyn. "Is only hoax. Fae try to steal gold from dragon. Drengrokil kill them now, yes?"

"What?" Davynn asked, trying to recover from the shock. "No! No killing." His brain was scrambling to find perspective. "Are you sure the contract is a forgery?" He asked, walking to the discarded scroll and picking it up.

"Fae spell Harpur Diggins name wrong," Frode said. "No dragon spell name wrong on contract. Is forgery for sure."

Davynn searched the document for the signature below the scrawled and nearly illegible terms. There it was, proof of the fraud the Fae had attempted to perpetrate. H-A-R-P-R D-Y-G-Y-N-Z. "Unbelievable!" He wheeled on the Fae creature. "When Harpur hears about this, you will be answering to him."

"You can't blame us for trying," the Fae creature said. "We've had that precious thing of his poisoning our lands for centuries. And he did promise us gold for keeping it." His eyes darted back and forth between the chest of gold and Frode's electric sword.

"How much gold did he promise you?" Davynn demanded. Anger had replaced the trauma. "And don't bother lying to me."

The Fae scowled. "One hundred gold coins," it said.

"Then that is what you shall get." Davynn began counting out one hundred coins from the chest. He threw them toward the thieving Fae creature who clambered to pick them up and shove them into the compartment in his body. When he had counted the coins, he spun back toward the Fae. "There are five hundred elven warriors marching this way right now and they are itching to reduce the Fae population in Epoh by as many as they can. I suggest you and your friends return to the Fae Lands and hide. I am not responsible for what they might do when they get here."

The Fae creature picked up the last of the coins and then stared at Davynn. "What happened to our dragon lord?" It asked.

"I told you, Harpur has important business to attend to in the north." Davynn reiterated.

"Then why did he send so much more gold than what he promised the queen? Harpur Diggins would never part with more than he owed. What has happened to him?"

Davynn glanced at Frode and nodded his head slightly. The Drengrokil lifted his sword and stepped closer to the creature. "Is not Fae's place to question dragon lord."

The creature backed away from the red sparks arcing off the sharp point of the sword aimed at its heart, then turned and ran toward Braydon Wood. It whistled as it sprinted for the safety of the forest and Davynn watched in alarm as dozens of Faefolk rose from the ground and followed their spokesman into the trees.

"Harpur's amethyst ascot! Did you know there were that many of them out there?" he asked Frode.

"Only suspected," Frode said. "What will you do with forged contract?"

"I'm going to hang onto it for the time being," the knight said, rolling the parchment back up. "I'm sure Sok will want to add it to the archives in Colwygshire. But we better go tell the villagers that they can let their children out of the lodge again."

"Villagers know," Frode said.

Davynn turned toward the tents to see the villagers cheering and hugging each other next to the tattered shelters. "Then let's go see what Hiro has for breakfast."

While the two Drengrokil that had hauled the chest of gold out to the pasture hauled it back to the camp, Davynn and Frode accepted the accolades of the villagers and assured them that the Fae would not be bothering them again any time soon. By the time they made it to the center of the Drengrokil camp, children were running all over the village, screaming in delight at their new-found freedom. The young boy who had insisted on being allowed to fight the Fae came up to Davynn and tapped him on the shoulder.

"I'm sorry for the way I behaved last night, Sir Davynn," he said.

Davynn saw nothing but contrition in the lad's face. "Thank you, for that," he said. "It takes a big man to admit his mistakes. The Fae can be treacherous and mean, but we can't condemn anyone until we are sure they have done something wrong and we haven't wronged them first. Do you understand?"

"I do, Sir Davynn," the boy said. "Thank you for helping our village. I want to be a guard just like you when I grow up."

Davynn smiled. "And a fine guard you will make... What is your name, boy?"

"Eowyn, sir. Eowyn Hunter."

"Well, Eowyn Hunter, I will be waiting for you to come and join us in Colwygshire someday. Would you like to join the Drengrokil and the other guards for breakfast?"

"I have to go and do my lessons now," Eowyn said. "Mama and Papa say that I can't be a guard unless I do good at my lessons."

"Your mama and papa are very wise," Davynn replied with a smile.

The boy ran off and Davynn welcomed a heaping plate of pancakes and eggs handed to him by Bon. The android congratulated him and Frode on their masterful skill in handling the Fae.

"I don't know about masterful," Davynn said. "My heart nearly stopped when that creature told me Harpur had promised the Fae half of his hoard."

"Perhaps after everyone has finished their breakfast, Hiro and I can take the hover gilly and meet the armies. We can let them know that the situation has been handled," Bon suggested.

"Nah," Davynn said. "Let them march for another day. The exercise will do them good. Besides, if Anayah doesn't get back here soon, we'll need the hover gilly to ferry us back to the castle."

"Speaking of devil," Frode said as a plume of red smoke erupted next to the chest of gold.

Anayah collapsed onto the chest. "Where can I sleep?" she mumbled.

Davynn looked at the exhausted witch with deep concern. "Anayah, are you okay?"

"I will be when I get some sleep." She yawned.

Davynn put his plate down on an empty stump and went to sit next to Anayah. The tired witch slumped against him and yawned again.

"Witch can sleep in tent," Frode said. He stood, scooped Anayah into his arms and carried her to his tent.

Bon picked up Davynn's plate and handed it to him. "I wonder what happened to her last night?"

"She did say that she was keeping animals away from Harpur's body. She must have been up all night guarding him." Davynn speculated.

"Oh, to be a fly on the wall at the lair," Hiro giggled. "Arthur must be in a tizzy up there surrounded by wild animals."

Davynn couldn't help but laugh. "I'm sure Elder Dhonna has her hands full keeping him focused. I just hope there are no bears around."

Frode returned and sat down on his stump. "By noon, witch good as new."

"I guess we're stuck here until she wakes up," Davynn said.

"Worse places to be," Frode said.

"I still think Hiro and I should go and turn the armies around," Bon said as he passed the last of the breakfast dishes to the Krist to put away.

"Why are you so bent on doing that?" Davynn asked. "I could use another cup of jamba, Hiro."

The Krist was happy to oblige and offered more to Frode as well.

"It just seems pointless to let them keep marching when there is no reason for them to be marching," Bon said.

Davynn looked at Frode. "I think they could use the exercise. What do you think?"

"Is good for armies to march." Frode agreed with Davynn. "Builds stamina."

Bon's face remained passive, but Davynn detected disappointment in the android's circuitry. "Tell you what, Bon, when Anayah wakes up and we start zapping back to the castle, you and Hiro can take a few of the Drengrokil and stop on your way back to let the armies know that they can return home. I'm sure Frode's men will love experiencing time bending in that thing."

Bon nodded. Telling the armies they could go home was not his ultimate goal. He had hoped to sneak away to the lair and check on Arthur and Elder Dhonna. He really wanted to find out if his deductions about Harpur's plan were accurate. Having two or three Drengrokil with them would curtail this covert mission, but perhaps he could convince the Drengrokil to march back to Colwygshire with the armies.

By noon, the Fae's clumsy attempt to defraud their dragon lord out of half of his treasure became a laughable tale destined to be embellished and retold by bards and minstrels throughout the kingdom. Already, the villagers were threading exaggerated elements of heroism into the narrative, embroidering it with accounts of nearly-snatched children and upgrading the sparks in Frode's sword to full-scale dragon fire that had sent the Fae spokesman running into Braydon Wood with its bottom aflame.

Davynn was relieved when Anayah finally emerged from Frode's tent, rested and ready to zap them all back to the castle. After the Drengrokil broke camp, it was determined that only two or three of them could fit safely on the hover gilly with their packs on, and so Frode decided that none of them would have the pleasure of time bending with the Krist and the android.

"Another time, perhaps," Bon said and Davynn thought he was just a bit too happy about the outcome.

While Anayah zapped the guards and Drengrokil back to Colwygshire in groups of three or four at a time, Davynn filled her in on the morning's events. Mostly without any aggrandizement, but with some downplay on his own perceived incompetence. When Davynn, Anayah, Frode and the gold were all that remained, Anayah wrote out another note of explanation and attached it to the straps on the chest. Then she zapped it back to the lair and, in a final puff of red smoke, she, the knight and the last small mountain vanished from the village.

Chapter Twenty-one

Arthur had landed in his private chambers and quietly tip-toed to the door to see if he could detect the presence of any guards. Low voices drifted through the heavy oak barrier and so he carefully engaged the latch to lock the door. No one could know he was there, not even his lovely queen, whom he dearly wished he could see, and certainly not the guards outside his rooms.

Once the door was secure, Arthur went to his writing desk and sat down. He prepared a stack of parchment, laying it out next to the ink-stained blotter in the middle of his desk. He opened the ink well and then reached for the quill that was supposed to be in the stand beside the ink. The quill was not there.

"Bloody elf!" he mumbled, certain that Sok was to blame for the missing biro. "Always taking my pens."

A quick rifle through the clutter on the desk yielded nothing and so, Arthur conjured a quill and dipped it into the ink. For the next several hours, he filled page after page with writing that grew progressively less legible as his hand grew increasingly cramped and sore. But he was determined to finish the missive and get back to the lair as soon as possible. One by one, he laid the finished, numbered pages out on the floor to dry so he wouldn't smudge a single precious word he'd recorded. By the time he was done, the detailed prose he'd started out with had deteriorated into bullet points and his hand and shirt were smeared with ink stains.

Hoping that he hadn't left anything important out, he gathered the dried pages and folded them in half. Then he plucked a book at random from a shelf next to the writing desk and tucked the folded pages inside it. He then stowed the book along with the chalice, which he'd brought with him from the lair, in the vault in his bed chamber. Before he closed the door, he pulled Harpur's life book out and carried it to the bed. Flipping to the last page, he was disappointed to see that nothing new had been added. Not knowing if that was a good thing or a bad thing, he closed the heavy book and returned it to its safe hiding place.

He had just closed the vault again when he heard the outside door to his private chambers rattle. Rather than wait to see who might be trying to gain entrance to his rooms, he snapped his fingers and zapped himself back to the lair.

Elder Dhonna was sitting on the boulder and Sok was sitting on a chest. They were eating mushrooms and roots and Sok did not look pleased.

"It's about time you came back," Sok said, tossing his foraged repast over his shoulder. "Can you conjure up something proper to eat?"

Arthur looked at the mushrooms and roots on the ground behind the elf. "Isn't that what elves are supposed to eat?"

Elder Dhonna laughed. "He's been spoiled in that castle of yours," she said. "He's forgotten what being an elf means."

"That's not true!" Sok said. "I just have a more refined appetite than most elves. Arthur, a pastry, a sandwich, anything that doesn't have dirt stuck to it? Please?"

Arthur conjured up some bread and cheese and a few pastries and set them down on the chest next to Sok to be devoured. "What's in the chest?" he asked.

Sok handed him a note.

"Well, that's a relief!" Arthur said after he read the brief message from Anayah explaining that the Fae had been paid in full and what was left in the chest needed to be returned to Harpur's hoard. "I hope someone tells the armies that their services are no longer needed."

"I'm sure Davynn will turn them around," Elder Dhonna said. Then she shot a sideways glance at Arthur. "Did you do what you needed to do at the castle?"

"I did," Arthur said. He reached for one of the pastries and took a bite.

"And what did you need to do?" Sok took a more direct approach on the path of curiosity.

"I can't tell you," Arthur said. "At least not right now."

"When can you tell us?" Sok asked.

"It's hard to say." Arthur looked up into the distance, thinking about how best to answer the question. "It depends on what I know after Karrys gets here tomorrow."

"You're beginning to sound like your guardians," Sok said with a scowl. "Where are the pirates anyway?"

"I suspect they are wherever they go when they aren't here with me." Arthur smiled at Sok's eye roll. "So, what did you two do all day?"

"Mostly we walked through Braydon Wood picking mushrooms for dinner," Sok said.

"Stop complaining," Elder Dhonna scolded. "You enjoyed yourself."

Sok nodded. "I must admit that being in the forest was much more pleasant than being in the cell. I'm not looking forward to facing Senior Elder Jona about that."

"At least he can't lock you back up," Arthur said. "Maybe I should offer him the use of the dungeons until the cell can be rebuilt."

"You wouldn't!" Sok nearly choked on his bread and cheese.

Arthur laughed. "Don't worry, Sok. I granted you sanctuary, remember?"

The evening air began to take on a chill and the three of them moved into the lair to escape the cold spring breeze that was blowing in from the north-east. They settled on the floor at the back of the cave and Arthur conjured hot jamba to warm their bones. For a long while, they sat in companionable silence, each of them lost in their own thoughts.

"You did well today, Arthur," Elder Dhonna finally said.

The lair was dark. Arthur considered conjuring some candles, but the darkness felt appropriate. "I guess we'll find out tomorrow just how well I did do," he said.

"I wonder what Jack and Diane meant when they said your efforts will succeed, but you will never know," Sok said. "You don't think they meant that something is going to happen to you?"

Something is going to happen to all of us, Arthur thought to himself. He was doubly glad for the darkness; it hid his rueful knowing smile. "Like what?"

"Like maybe..." Sok couldn't bring himself to say it out loud.

"Sok!" Elder Dhonna admonished the young elf. "The guardians would never tell Arthur that he was going to die."

Die! That hadn't occurred to Arthur. He sat up straight and peered into the darkness in Sok's direction. "Why would you think that's what they meant?"

"What else could they have meant?"

"Lots of things," Arthur said with an edge of desperation. *Was I wrong?*

"Such as?"

The sly tone in Sok's voice gave Arthur pause. "Nice try! I'm not going to tell you what I was doing today, so stop trying to pry it out of me."

Sok did not respond and another silence fell over the lair. This one, not so companionable. Sok and Elder Dhonna soon drifted off to sleep, but poor Arthur was plagued by dark thoughts. *Is this my last night on Thraeh? Will I ever see Alex and the twins again? Bloody elf! Bloody guardians!* He tried to close his eyes and lose himself in unconsciousness, but Sok's suggestion of a less than optimum outcome for him would not let him rest until the wee hours of the night when sheer exhaustion finally won. Still, he rose before the others, abandoning his restive repose just before dawn.

Arthur sat down on the chest that they had left outside the lair and shivered slightly in the early-morning chill. In the pre-dawn twilight, Harpur's body looked smaller, as if it was shrinking away from the fate that awaited it, and Arthur wondered once again if a similar fate was awaiting him. He shivered a second time, though this time it was not the cold that sent the tremor up his spine. He had been so sure that he had interpreted Jack and Diane's warning correctly and had done the right thing in going back to the castle. If he was wrong, no one might ever know what had happened. Only he and Harpur knew how to open the vault in his chambers. Even if the guardians were right about their efforts being successful, would things be like they were before Harpur was challenged? It seemed unlikely. Especially if he had interpreted Jack and Diane's warning correctly.

Another thought occurred to Arthur. *Who will become king if I do die?*

Meg, who was the first in line for the throne, was just an infant and, though he was perfectly capable, Sok was an elf. And an elf could not be king of Epoh. *Davynn, perhaps?* Davynn would make a good king.

Alas, it was not up to Arthur. Though it was most likely a regent would be appointed, it would be many years before Meg—or Hart—could wear the crown.

The crown.

"Where did I leave it this time?" Arthur wondered aloud. Suddenly, and for the first time, he wanted to feel the weight of it on his head.

He pictured the diadem in his mind, sitting on his head, sparkling in the new light of the new day. He closed his eyes and felt it materialize around his skull. Usually, it felt like a heavy ring of metal digging into his skin. But this time it felt as if it had been molded to fit perfectly. He reached up to touch it, to be sure it was really there, then, satisfied, he stood up and walked toward Harpur's body to say his final good byes.

A short while later, Sok came up behind him. "Is that a crown on your head?"

Arthur turned to elf. "Isn't that where my crown is supposed to be?"

"No need to get snippy," Sok said. He bent down and picked one of the purple and teal flowers growing next to Harpur's body. "When do you think she'll get here?" He was referring to Karrys Evergreen.

"Real soon," Elder Dhonna's voice replied. She was walking across the meadow toward them, pointing at the sky to the south.

Arthur and Sok followed her finger and saw the distant shape of a dragon flying over Braydon Wood. They both inhaled deeply and released their breath in great sighs of resignation. Elder Dhonna joined them on Arthur's left. He wrapped his arm around her shoulders in a gesture of comfort and all three watched as Karrys Evergreen approached and landed in the meadow at the tip of Harpur's tail.

The teal dragon turned her good right eye to the three friends. "What are you doing here?" she hissed.

"We've just come to pay our final respects," Elder Dhonna said.

"Well, pay them and be gone," Karrys said. "Epoh is mine now and I don't want you lot hanging around my lair." She turned her huge head back toward the entrance to the lair and spotted the chest. "Planning on making off with some of my treasure?"

"Actually, we were returning it to the lair," Arthur said.

Karrys lowered her great head and eyed them suspiciously. "Someone tried to steal from me?" she asked.

"Not exactly," Sok said, wondering if this would be the end for all of them and not just Arthur. "It turned out Harpur owed a debt to the Fae and we needed to be sure we had enough to cover it. We didn't want his obligations to run over into your reign, so we dealt with it for you. You're welcome."

Karrys withdrew her head again. A puff of blue-green smoke escaped her nostrils. "I see. How considerate. Now leave. I'm sure you do not want to see the final minutes of your friend's existence in this world."

Arthur, Sok and Elder Dhonna all looked at each other.

"Of course," Elder Dhonna said. "We will leave you to it. Welcome to Epoh."

They walked past Karrys toward the trail head on the eastern edge of the meadow. Without looking back, they walked down the path until they reached the fork leading to the paddock. There, Elder Dhonna stopped and turned to Arthur.

"Do you know the little copse of trees above the lair?" she asked.

"Just to the right of the entrance, about fifty feet up the mountain?"

"That's the one. Zap us all there."

Arthur didn't hesitate. As soon as Sok and Elder Dhonna got grips on his shirt, he snapped his fingers, bringing them all to a flat spot just behind the copse. Elder Dhonna held her finger up to her lips to remind Arthur and Sok to be quiet and then led them forward into the cover of the trees.

From there, they had a good view of the meadow. Karrys had moved to the north side of Harpur's body, putting the three voyeurs behind her and to her left, well out of sight. She appeared to be examining the corpse. For what, none of them could guess, but Arthur dearly hoped that she did not sense the magic of the potion he had poured into Harpur's ear the day before. He held his breath until, at last, the teal dragon raised her head and let loose a fierce jet of dragon fire across Harpur's cadaver. As his scales caught, a huge, purple, smokeless conflagration rose into the air. Arthur had to clamp his hand over his mouth to keep from gasping and giving their presence away.

For the next few horrible minutes, it looked as if Harpur's body was just going to burn to ash. But then Arthur did a double-take. A faint reddish-purple mist began to rise from the blackening scales. It swirled and thickened, darkening to an amethyst-coloured fog that swelled upward above the flames.

Karrys looked at the purple fog and shook her head as if to clear her vision. She backed away from the burning body, unsure of what was happening to it. She could see the body crumble and disintegrate, consumed by the flames as she had expected it to. But the inexplicable fog rising up from it left her confused, and so she did what dragons instinctively do when faced with something even remotely threatening. She attempted to burn it. The moment her enormous maw widened to release her dragon fire, the fog twisted into a thick vaporous rope and shot down her throat.

Seconds passed as the stunned teal dragon stood frozen in place, unable to reconcile the strange assault she was experiencing. Then her head began to sway back and forth and her wings slumped down at her sides. A moment later, she crashed to the ground.

Harpur's body continued to burn.

"Was that supposed to happen?" Sok asked.

He and Arthur looked at Elder Dhonna. She was as stunned as they were. "Harpur wasn't specific, but he did say that if the spell was executed properly, his spirit would separate from his body and stay bound to this world. He didn't mention anything about Karrys dropping like a stone that way."

"Huh!" Arthur grunted. "Maybe we should go down there and find out if she's still alive."

"Not until Harpur burns out completely. I can feel the heat from here," Sok said.

Arthur had forgotten that his imperviousness to heat and fire was not shared by the elves. "I can go. The heat won't bother me." He started to step out of the copse.

"Wait," Elder Dhonna said. "What if she comes to while you're down there and things didn't go according to plan?"

"Good point." Arthur stepped back into the copse. "I really don't want to find out the hard way if I can withstand dragon fire."

"If you can withstand dragonfoil fire, you can withstand dragon fire," Sok said. "But something tells me your clothes can't."

Arthur rolled his eyes at the elf. "You really ought to let that go."

"Never," said the elf, chuckling at the memory of a naked Arthur stepping out of the ashes of a dragonfoil tree. "Long live the naked king!"

Arthur thumped Sok on the shoulder. "Seriously! Let. It. Go."

"Both of you let it go," Elder Dhonna said. "Honestly, you're like a couple of adolescent elflings. I think we should all stay right here and wait until the fire goes out. If Karrys doesn't come around by then, we'll have to figure something out, but neither me nor my clothes are impervious to fire, and I have no intention of dying today."

Arthur and Sok fell silent and focused their attention on the fire that was consuming Harpur's body. The purple flames devoured it completely in what seemed like mere minutes. Even the bones were reduced to ash as if they were made of cardboard. Soon the great purple dragon was, quite literally, dust in the wind. When the last of the flames went out, Arthur, Sok and Elder Dhonna all shifted their attention to Karrys Evergreen, who remained absolutely still next to the drifting pile of ash that had been Harpur.

"Can you tell if she's breathing?" Arthur asked.

"I think you killed her," Sok said.

"I didn't kill her! If she's dead, it was all Harpur's doing." Arthur wasn't about to take the blame for killing Epoh's new ruler.

"Shh," Elder Dhonna said. "I think she's coming to."

Below them, Arthur, Sok and Elder Dhonna saw the teal dragon begin to stir. Karrys folded her wings across her back and then slowly worked her legs underneath herself so she could stand up. Her first attempt was fruitless and she collapsed back down, releasing a great gust of breath that sent a cloud of ash up into the air. For a few minutes, she laid still as she mustered her strength before finally struggling to her feet.

She looked down at the ashes and reached out with her talons to touch them. When she withdrew her talons, she stared at the gray dust that clung to them. It looked to Arthur like she didn't quite believe they were real. Then she threw her head back and let out a deafening roar followed by a long stream of dragon fire. Arthur was sure there were streaks of purple in the otherwise orange and teal flames.

"Should we go down there now?" Arthur whispered.

"Not yet." Elder Dhonna held up a hand to signal both Sok and Arthur to stay put.

For the next little while, Karrys appeared to be testing her body. She stretched and flapped her wings. She swished her tail. She ran her one good eye over every inch of herself that she could see with it. And then she strode right through the ashes to the edge of the meadow and launched into the air.

"Where is she going?" Sok was stunned.

"It worked!" Elder Dhonna shouted. "Karrys is Harpur!" The guild master burst out of the copse and ran down the mountain side to the meadow, yelling, "It worked. It really worked!"

Arthur and Sok shrugged at each other and then ran to the meadow to join the over-joyed guild master and watch the teal dragon circle and glide over Braydon Wood.

"What do we call her now?" Arthur asked.

"Harpur, of course," Sok said.

"We can't call her Harpur," Elder Dhonna said. "No one is supposed to know what he's done."

The teal dragon turned to come back to the meadow and the three ecstatic Epohians waved and shouted, welcoming back their friend.

"Orhowyn's mighty heart, that felt good," the teal dragon said after landing gracefully in the middle of the meadow. "Now what's he doing here?"

"You mean me?" Sok asked.

"Who else would I mean?"

"That's Harpur alright," Arthur said.

"I figured out what your plan was while I was locked in the cell after insisting that Senior Elder Jona send the elven warriors to the south to kill the Fae that had come out of the Fae Lands. Then I accidentally blew up the cell when I tried to get Elder Dhonna to come and get me out so I could help with the plan and now I'm a fugitive, so Arthur and Elder Dhonna brought me with them so they could keep me from getting into more trouble. I'm kind of hoping now that you're back, that you will help settle things with Senior Elder Jona for me." Sok stopped to inhale.

But before he could say anything else, Harpur turned to Elder Dhonna. "Perhaps you should explain, Bella Dhonna."

Elder Dhonna's heart lurched at hearing the familiar nickname. "This really is very weird, Harpur."

"Yes. You should experience it from my point of view," Harpur concurred, giving his new body another once over. "Speaking of points of view, what happened to my eye? The last time I saw Karrys, she had two."

"I'm afraid you did that to yourself," Elder Dhonna said. "During the challenge."

"I don't recall that part," Harpur said. He looked at the spot where the dragon skull had been and growled. *But I recall that part of the challenge.* Swinging his head back to the guild master. "It's not important. Tell me what the elf is talking about."

Elder Dhonna sat cross-legged in the grass. She had a long tale to tell and she wanted to be comfortable while she recounted the events of the previous eight days. While Sok and Arthur settled down next to her, she began at the beginning, which was, essentially, the end for Harpur and continued to where they found themselves then.

"Did I leave anything out?" she asked Arthur and Sok.

The elf and the king shook their heads. There were elements of the story that they were hearing for the first time too. Arthur did find it intriguing that she left out the part about him going back to the castle after Jack and Diane's brief visit the day before. But unless Sok decided to fill in that gap, he wasn't going to correct her. He also found it interesting that she admitted to telling Frode and Senior Elder Jona about the plan. He wasn't sure he'd have had the guts to come clean on that score either. Then again, this was Harpur – as weird as that was to accept – and Harpur would never harm Elder Dhonna.

Harpur had listened without interruption to Elder Dhonna's detailed report. When she was done, he had only one question for her. "Who else besides you three, Frode and Senior Elder Jona know about the plan?"

"No one," Elder Dhonna said. "And I only told them because I had to. I am sorry, Harpur. But I know they won't tell anyone."

"It's okay, Bella Dhonna," Harpur assured her. "I understand. Now, I do have an errand that I must see to immediately."

"What errand?" Elder Dhonna was astonished.

"Just something I need to take care of. It's nothing you need be concerned about." Harpur moved to the edge of the meadow. "I would appreciate it if you three would all stay here until I come back. I shouldn't be long."

Without waiting for their consent, Harpur leapt into the air and flew to the south-east.

"Looks like he's going to Colwygshire," Arthur observed.

"Looks like you need to conjure up some lunch for us," Sok said.

"I could sure use something to eat. But I was thinking Elder Dhonna could show us where to forage for some of those mushrooms and roots you had yesterday. They looked real tasty." Arthur winked at the guild master. He stood up and held out a hand to assist Elder Dhonna to her feet. Arm in arm, they strode toward the western-leading trailhead.

"Is this because of the naked king thing?" Sok called out as they disappeared into the trees. "Aw, come on, Arthur, I was only joking. Okay! I'll let it go. Arthur?"

As the trio left the meadow, Bon and Hiro arrived in the hover gilly. They watched Karrys Evergreen fly away and then floated over to the dwindling pile of ash that was once Harpur Diggins.

"Should we catch up to them?" Hiro asked the android.

"No," Bon replied. "I think we should return to the castle. It appears that all has gone according to plan here."

Hiro turned the hover gilly around and took them back to the castle.

Morgaine Fayle entered the elven city in Braydon Wood and made her way to the Elder's council. She was wearing a long gray cloak with the hood pulled over her head. Her long, black hair hung down over her face, covering her left eye. She kept her head down, eyes on the ground, avoiding interaction with the elves that moved about among the trees.

The doors to the Elder's council chamber stood open, a sure sign that Senior Elder Jona was not inside and Morgaine had to ask a young elf girl where he might be found.

"I haven't seen him today," the girl said. "He could be in his treehouse."

"Can you show me which one that is?" Morgaine asked as sweetly as her sultry voice would allow.

"It's this way," the girl said and headed around the Elder's council to a pathway that led to the north side of the city.

Morgaine followed the girl to a tree with a trunk a good twelve feet in diameter. Through an arched doorway set into the trunk, she could see a winding staircase leading up through the center of the tree. High above her, an elaborate treehouse supported by sprawling branches circled the trunk. On a small balcony to her right, Senior Elder Jona sat at a round table enjoying a cup of jamba. Morgaine thanked the girl for her assistance and waited until the elfling ran off again back in the direction they had come.

When she found herself alone again, Morgaine moved closer to the balcony and slipped into the bushes at the base of another large tree where she couldn't be seen by any passing elves, but where she had a clear view of the senior elder sitting directly above her. She watched for a few minutes, considering her options and then decided that there was no need to speak to him directly. The less anyone knew of her, the better. And the quicker she did what she had to do, the safer she would be. She raised her hands and waved them in Senior Elder Jona's direction, watching with satisfaction as a perplexed expression crossed his face. He seemed to be trying to recall something, some suddenly elusive memory, like a dream that refused to rise to the surface. When he shrugged it off a moment later, Morgaine Fayle slipped out of the bushes and wound her way back out of the city. She had just reached the gate opening onto the main road to Colwygshire when the young elven girl came up to her and tugged at the sleeve of her cloak.

"Did you find Senior Elder Jona, miss?" the girl asked.

Morgaine smiled down at the child. "I did. Thank you again," she said and moved quickly through the gate.

A swift glance over her shoulder showed her the girl standing and watching her walk away. Without hesitation, Morgaine turned slightly and waved her hand at the girl, who frowned, scratched her head and then ran off again. Morgaine breathed a sigh of relief and then hurried down the road to Colwygshire.

When she drew closer to the human city, she saw the red and yellow tents of the Drengrokil set up in a semi-circle a hundred feet or so north of the city walls. Nine of the huge warriors were milling about, honing swords, drinking ale and talking about their adventures with a knight and a witch. They were soon joined by a Krist and an android, who floated out of the forest and into the camp. She had come to see the Drengrokil leader and had hoped that she would be able to talk to him alone. The presence of the Epohian guests in the camp, however, caused her to change her mind. She would have to postpone meeting Frode in person to another time.

Like she had done in the elven city, she slipped unnoticed into the cover of some bushes and watched and listened to the conversation wafting out of the camp. She needed to discern which of the Drengrokil was Frode and that quickly became apparent when Anayah scolded him for making a teasingly lewd comment about her and Davynn.

"Frode is only joking, witch," the big man said. He tapped his temple. "I think witch and knight make good match."

Morgaine smiled and waved her hand. A second later, a puzzled frown clouded Frode's face and he stopped laughing.

"Frode? What is it?" Davynn asked, seeing the puzzlement in the Drengrokil's expression.

"Is nothing," Frode replied. "Is probably just too much ale." He raised his cup and drained it. His laughter returned.

Then Morgaine waved her hand again and watched as puzzled expressions briefly crossed the faces of the knight, the witch, and the Krist. She didn't realize that the puzzlement on the android's face was not due to her magic.

Morgaine watched the comradery taking place in the Drengrokil camp for a few more minutes. Part of her wanted to join them, meet the Drengrokil and drink ale. Instead, she became invisible and zapped herself into the castle. There was one more person she had to deal with before she returned to the lair.

Alex was sitting in the conservatory, happily working on her macramé project at the easel. The twins were sleeping in the stroller next to her and Morgaine carefully approached to take a peek at them. *Be happy, little ones,* she thought. Then she raised her hand and waved it at Alex. For a moment, the queen stopped working the cords and blinked her eyes in momentary confusion. Then she shook her head and returned her attention to her work.

Harpur took his time returning to the lair. He knew he had to get back there and finish what he'd started, but flying again felt so good. His new body was strong and agile and, even though it was weird, he was adjusting to it quickly. The only downside to being in Karrys' body was the missing left eye. He had a tendency to pull to the right when he was flying and he had to compensate by turning his head slightly to the left. Thus, his peripheral vision was narrowed, but he didn't mind. He could fly. Nothing was better than that after so many months being stuck in his human form. But now, it was time to get back to the business of being a real dragon.

He swooped and circled over Braydon Wood, not caring if he was seen. Soon enough, all of Epoh would know a new dragon ruled the kingdom. Karrys Evergreen would now take her rightful place as the dragon lord—Harpur couldn't quite bring himself to think of himself as a lady—and reign in Harpur's stead as protector of the kingdom. Nothing would change. Much.

When he finally landed in the meadow, Arthur, Sok and Elder Dhonna were once again seated by the entrance to the lair awaiting his return. He eyed them thoughtfully as he approached them, ruefully absorbing the great smiles on their faces, knowing it was the last time any of them would greet him as anyone other than Karrys Evergreen. *This really is very weird,* he thought.

"I see you haven't finished returning my gold to my hoard," he said, glowering at the chest that Sok was sitting on.

"It's heavy," Sok said.

Harpur looked at Arthur. "After all the feats of magic you have accomplished in recent days, you couldn't see this properly stowed where it belongs?"

Arthur opened and closed his mouth several times while he searched for a reasonable answer. "Um... It made a good seat. I was going to put it back when... Everything got wrapped up here."

"Hmm... Indeed," Harpur said.

"We were just about to have some supper," Sok said. "Why don't you transform and join us?"

Harpur snapped his head around to look at the elf. "I won't be doing that any more than absolutely necessary from now on. But you three go ahead. I think I will hunt for my dinner tonight."

Arthur, Sok and Elder Dhonna were all a little taken aback. They had expected Harpur to celebrate with them.

"Where will you hunt tonight?" Elder Dhonna asked. Harpur was behaving strangely, but she put it down to being in a new body and needing to adjust.

"There is a bear den a few miles to the west," Harpur said, imagining nicely crisped bear meat.

"If it's the one that was around here yesterday, don't bother," Sok advised. "It wouldn't even make a good snack for you."

"Ah, yes," Harpur said, recalling Arthur's peculiar solution to that problem. "I'm sure I will find something tasty somewhere."

"You know," Sok said, "we would really love it if you would join us one more time. We've missed you and we went through a lot to bring you back."

Harpur backed away from the trio and stretched his wings out. For a moment, they all thought he was going to fly away again, but he simply laid down, crossing his left front foot over his right. "I will not transform," he said quietly, "but I will sit with you for a while."

Arthur stared at Harpur's left foot. One of the talons was mottled with a dark streak running through it from quick to tip. It reminded him of something, but he couldn't quite grasp what it was. He studied the teal dragon, looking for some other clue that would open his memory bank and let out whatever was bothering him. The shiny scales, glistening in the late afternoon light tugged at his memory as well. There was something about Karrys that felt oddly familiar to him.

Sok kicked Arthur's shin, bringing him abruptly out of his reverie. "You're not in court, Arthur. Pay attention. As I was saying..."

"That's it! Court!" Arthur stood up and walked over to Harpur. "You're Morgaine Fayle, aren't you?"

"Only when I have to be," Harpur said.

"But why use a different name? Why didn't she just call herself Karrys Evergreen?"

Harpur had access to all of Karrys' memories as well as his own. He sifted through them for an answer for him. "It seemed prudent to her at the time to use an alias."

"But why Morgaine Fayle?"

"If you are thinking that Karrys chose that name in legendary irony, you are wrong," Harpur said. "Morgaine Fayle is simply a name that appeals to her. Don't read anything into it."

"Well, you have to admit that it is odd," Arthur said.

"You're odd, Arthur," Sok called over from his seat on the chest. "As I was saying, how about some of that lasagna stuff that Hiro said was popular on Earth?"

"I don't know how to make lasagna!" Arthur retorted. "Here, have some meat and cheese." He conjured a plate full of meat and cheese for Sok.

"I assure you that you have nothing to fear from Karrys Evergreen," Harpur said.

Arthur wanted to believe that. But Harpur's words in Karrys' voice were hard to reconcile. "Is this always going to be so weird?" he asked the dragon.

Harpur thought about it for a minute. "I don't expect it will weird for very long," he said.

Arthur heard something in Harpur's tone that reminded him of the pages he'd written out the day before. Knowing they were safely hidden in his chambers gave him some comfort. *Don't bet on it, dragon!*

He returned to his seat next to Elder Dhonna on the boulder and helped himself to some of the meat and cheese from Sok's plate. Elder Dhonna was munching on the leftover roots and mushrooms they had foraged and seemed quite content to make that her supper, though she did ask for some ale.

"It's a celebration, after all!" she said, accepting the cup from Arthur with a broad smile.

It was indeed a celebration. Of sorts. They spent what remained of the daylight chatting and laughing and recalling the events that had led up to that moment. Harpur contributed little, preferring to listen for any tidbits of information that Elder Dhonna might have left out of her earlier account. But when the sun dipped behind the western mountains, he decided that it was time to end the festivities.

"It's getting dark," Harpur said. "You should get back to the castle."

"Aren't you coming with us?" Arthur asked.

"No, Arthur," Harpur said. "I will be staying here at my lair from now on."

"Why?" Arthur didn't like the sound of that.

"Karrys Evergreen will not rule Epoh the same way Harpur Diggins did," Harpur said. "If we are to keep what happened here a secret, it would not do for me to act the same way that I did before."

"But..." Sok began.

"Do not worry about things in Epoh. Nothing will change. Much. I will be available to you when you need me and I will drop in to check on you from time to time. But you must go back and announce that Harpur Diggins has been defeated and that Karrys Evergreen is the new ruler. Assure your people that they are safe and will be protected as they always have been." Harpur stood up and stretched his wings again.

"What do you mean by nothing will change much?" Elder Dhonna asked.

"I will be making a few necessary changes to how things work," Harpur explained. "The Fae will be moved farther to the west and given a new territory where they are less likely to bother anyone. Their portion of Braydon Wood will be returned to the elves. Other than that, you may expect life in Epoh to carry on the way it always has."

Elder Dhonna cleared her throat. "May I make another suggestion?"

"What is that, Bella Dhonna?"

"First, you need to stop calling me that. At least when there are others around." Elder Dhonna pointed out the danger the term of endearment posed.

"I will exercise great caution in the future," Harpur assured her.

"Second, allow the races to live as they please, where they please. The ruckus over the Fae demonstrates how keeping us separate fuels our fear for one another." The guild master looked Harpur directly in the eye.

"I will take that under advisement," Harpur said. "But right now, I am hungry and I wish to hunt."

Arthur, Sok and Elder Dhonna all stood and prepared to zap to Colwygshire. Suddenly, they all felt the finality their departure represented. They had just gotten their friend back and now he was sending them away.

"Good bye, Harpur," Elder Dhonna said.

"Good bye, Bella Dhonna," Harpur said. Then he raised one front foot and waved it toward his friends.

For a moment Arthur couldn't remember what he was doing. Then he remembered he was zapping himself and the elves back to Colwygshire. "Well, it was nice meeting you officially, Karrys Evergreen. On behalf of the peoples of Epoh, I thank you for allowing us to stay here under your protection."

"You are very welcome, King Arthur," Karrys replied. Then she turned to the guild master. "Elder Dhonna, I apologize for the way I treated you in Andonsheer. I do hope that you will forgive me."

Elder Dhonna's eyebrows shot up. "Of course," she said. "I'm just happy that things turned out well for everyone."

"And young Sok," Karrys said to the elf, "be good."

"I'm always good!"

Before Sok could damage the peaceful accord he believed they had established with Karrys Evergreen, Arthur snapped his fingers and zapped them away.

When they were gone, a single dragon tear slid across the teal dragon's snout and fell to the grass. Then Karrys Evergreen launched herself into the night sky and went in search of a proper dragon feast.

Chapter Twenty-two

Weeks of planning went into the presentation ceremony for Prince Hart and Princess Meg. Queen Alex insisted on having a parade and was delighted by the inventive floats and costumes the citizens of Colwygshire put together for the auspicious occasion. The staging grounds had been set up outside the north gate of the city from which the parade wound its way through the tangled streets to the castle and then to the main gate where the route turned south and ended in the open fields outside of Colwygshire.

With Sok as the Parade Marshal leading dozens of cheerfully decorated carts and wagons pulled by horses, goats and donkeys the spectacle that passed the castle balcony overlooking the gardens brought tears of joy to Alex's eyes. Jugglers and musicians gamboled and sang their way along with the floats. Even the Drengrokil took part, carrying an open litter on their shoulders upon which eight scantily-clad women danced while Olly, Versifier to the Court, played lively jigs on his lyre.

Preparations for the event had provided the perfect distraction from the news of Harpur Diggins' defeat by Karrys Evergreen. Though she was often seen circling high above Braydon Wood, she never came close to the city or interfered with life in Epoh. For Arthur, her early morning flights were a reminder of how much he missed Harpur. Every time he saw her, he felt like he should remember something important, but whatever it was remained elusive, locked away in the unreachable depths of his mind.

When the last float in the longest parade Arthur had ever seen finally passed the balcony, he and Alex made their way with the twins down to the front of the castle and climbed into the royal coach to be taken to the festival grounds outside the city. They were followed by an open wagon that carried the twins' new governesses, also twins, who were the antithesis of the stern Alma, all the accoutrements the babies might need during the day, two wet nurses and the upgraded stroller with its new, retractable shade hood. Davynn, Anayah, Hiro and Bon completed the royal convoy in the hover gilly.

The weather was perfect, warm, but not hot, as if nature was giving its blessing to the festivities. As Arthur and Alex's coach pulled up to an enormous tent, Alex gushed at the mountain of gifts piled onto and around a table next to the dais under the tent where a matching pair of thrones waited for them.

"Best baby shower ever!" Alex squealed in delight.

"We're going to be here all night," Arthur grumbled.

"Oh, stop it," Alex said. "This is wonderful."

Arthur alighted from the coach with Hart in his arm and assisted Alex, holding Meg, down to the red carpet that led to the dais. The king and queen, prince and princess made their way to the thrones as hundreds of guests thronged around the tent hoping to get close to enough to see the wee ones in person. But guards maintained a tight perimeter around the tent and only the occupants of the wagon and the hover gilly and a small handful of special guests were permitted to enter.

While Arthur and Alex stood before their thrones, waving at their loyal subjects, Sok was directing a footman to place a slightly plainer, slightly smaller version of their thrones on the dais next to Arthur's.

"What are you doing?" Arthur whispered to the elf.

"I thought it would be best if I was close by," Sok said, sitting down and smiling, then jumping back up when he remembered that he had to wait for Arthur and Alex to sit first.

Arthur shook his head and resumed waving while he waited for the governesses to finish setting up the area for the twins on the opposite side of the dais. When they were done, Arthur and Alex handed the twins over and finally sat down.

Through the speeches that followed, Arthur felt like he was in court. For the most part he tuned out and stared at the empty chair that had been reserved for the conspicuously absent Harpur Diggins, an homage to the great purple dragon to whom he owed so much and missed terribly. Sok's long-winded and unscheduled speech preceded lunch and only ended when Finch, the castle's cantankerous head house-keeper, stepped onto the dais and announced that the midday meal would be served forthwith.

The affronted elf, rallied by adding, "We have prepared something special for you. Thank you all for sharing in this glorious day of celebration with us." As if he was responsible for it all.

A table was brought in for the king and queen and placed in front of them. Footmen deftly arranged two place settings for the royal couple while Finch pulled a protesting Sok by the ear off the dais and down to his place at table next to Harpur's empty chair.

"I told you there would be no last-minute changes to the itinerary, you cheeky sod," Finch reprimanded. "Now, stay where you're put!"

To Arthur's surprise, Sok actually stayed put. For a while.

After lunch, a veritable smorgasbord of Earth cuisine that included rather authentic hamburgers, pasta salad, fruit salad, chilli and—to Arthur's amazement—ice cream with nuts and chocolate sauce, Sok reasserted himself into the proceedings by personally escorting Lissa Olive Valentina Evern and her nervous and giddy parents to the dais.

The little girl who had made the rag doll for Meg, walked proudly up to Arthur and Alex and executed a perfect curtsy. She held out another rag doll, shaped like a dragon. In the center of the purple, home-spun body, was a large orange heart. Arthur clasped his hand over his mouth and fought back the tears that threatened to spill out of his eyes.

"Would you like to give it to Hart yourself?" Alex asked, seeing how overcome her husband was.

"Oh, yes!" Lissa beamed. "I would like that very much."

Alex signaled to the governesses to bring Hart and Meg to the dais. Then she led Lissa by the hand to Sok's impromptu throne and helped her get seated. When the girl was settled, one of the governesses stepped forward and put Hart in her arms. The little girl's smile fairly outshone the sun that day. She held the rag doll dragon up for Hart to look at and was rewarded with a toothless baby grin.

"I wish I had a camera," Alex said.

Arthur was too choked up to respond.

Lissa's father stepped closer to Arthur and leaned over to whisper, "She will never forget this, your majesty. Thank you."

"You are welcome," Arthur croaked.

The two men stood side by side, sniffling while Lissa was given a turn holding Meg and the first rag doll she had made and given to Arthur in the market the day the twins were born. It was the highlight of Arthur's day too.

With the last of the ceremony portion of the day complete, Arthur and Alex set to opening the gifts while the scheduled entertainment commenced. Music and dancing and laughter filled the air. And ale and cider and wine filled the bellies of the hundreds of Epohians that had joined the celebration. Virtually everyone in the kingdom had received an invitation.

Hours later, an exhausted Alex opened the last gift.

"A comic book?" She was astounded as she thumbed through the pages of the home-made graphic biography of her and Arthur's life in Epoh. It was stunningly illustrated and the cover showed a portrait of Hart and Meg in their stroller.

Hiro glided up to the table on his hover gilly with Bon. "That is from Bon and me," he said. "We wanted the little ones to know the story of your lives in the kingdom."

"But a comic book?" Alex asked. "How do you know about comic books?"

"Arthur told us about them," Hiro explained. "And Anayah helped us put this one together."

Alex handed the book to Arthur, who started sobbing afresh. It had been a long time since he'd held a comic book in his hands.

"Do you not like it?" Hiro asked, alarmed by Arthur's emotional reaction.

"It's the most wonderful gift anyone could have given us," Arthur blubbered.

"Arthur used to work at a comic book store," Alex explained quietly to the Krist. "He collected comic books. This has more meaning for him than you could ever know."

"They have stores that sell these things?" Hiro asked, intrigued.

"On Earth they are quite popular. They even have conventions to celebrate the characters," Alex said.

"That's amazing," Hiro replied. "They must be very valuable; it takes a long time to draw and write one. I can't imagine there are more than a few at a time in the stores, though. How do they stay in business?"

Anayah came to Alex's rescue. "One day I will tell you all about printing presses, Hiro. But that's a conversation for another time."

Suddenly Bon excused himself and melted into the crowd outside the tent. No one paid much attention, assuming the android had seen something of interest and had gone off to investigate. Which is precisely what had happened. While Arthur and Alex, Davynn and Anayah, and Hiro and Sok all pitched in to load gifts and governesses, babies and stroller and an emotionally drained king and his queen into the appropriate cart, wagon and coach, Bon was following a guest through the throng of revelers toward the Colwygshire Road.

The guest in question was a woman dressed immaculately in a teal tuxedo jacket with tails over black trousers. A cream-coloured ascot was tied neatly at her throat and pinned in place with a teal sapphire brooch. Her raven-coloured hair flowed down her back from under a smart, teal top hat with a purple band. She wore a patch over her left eye and a large satchel hung from her shoulder.

Bon caught up to her just as she reached the western side of the road and fell in step beside her. "Morgaine Fayle, I presume," the android said.

The woman stopped and turned to look at Bon with curiosity equal to his own.

"Or should I say Harpur Diggins?"

Morgaine Fayle started walking again and Bon fell in step at her side. "I thought I had wiped your memory too."

"My mind doesn't work like the others," Bon admitted. "If it makes you feel better, I won't say a word to anyone."

"I'm relatively sure you won't. What gave me away?"

They reached the woods and Morgaine continued into the trees. Bon wondered where Morgaine Fayle was going and since she did not protest his company, he continued to follow her.

"Your attire. The top hat, in particular," Bon said. "May I ask why you did it?"

"Hmm... I suppose that was a bit risky." Morgaine removed the hat from her head and looked at it. "Perhaps I will switch to a bowler in the future. As for why I did it, I wanted to fly. I wanted to wield magic, hunt for meat, breathe fire. I wanted to be a dragon again. But mostly, I needed to keep Arthur and his family safe." Morgaine delivered her forthright reply with sincerity.

"Safe from what?"

"Himself?" Morgaine laughed. "I'm sorry. That wasn't fair. Arthur is far more resourceful than many would believe. But in a way it's true. I have grown very fond of him over the years. Perhaps I'm also growing sentimental in my old age. But I knew it was only a matter of time before I would be challenged and lose. And I just could not leave him to the whims of another dragon."

"Do you think that Karrys posed a danger to Arthur?"

"Not as such. She intended to let things continue as they were..." Morgaine paused, "...for the most part."

"Care to share what changes she did intend?"

"I do not," Morgaine stopped and turned to face the android. "Bon, I appreciate you telling me that you know who I am. I'm not sure why you did that, but it speaks to your integrity. Unless you have a death wish. You will keep my secret, won't you?"

"I have no intention of revealing what I know to anyone," Bon replied. "And since I am not programmed to lie, you may trust me completely. May I ask what you have in your satchel?"

"Are all androids as incorrigible as you?" Morgaine asked by way of deflecting.

"I would hope so," Bon said. "Though I prefer to think of myself as tenacious."

"Well, if you must know," Morgaine said conspiratorially, "my satchel contains proof of Arthur's resourcefulness. For his own protection, however, I will be keeping it somewhere safe. Now, I'm afraid I must be leaving. Perhaps we can arrange to get together at the lair soon. I would enjoy some stimulating conversation."

"I would enjoy that as well," Bon said. "You will send word when you are available?"

"I will, indeed," Morgaine said. Then she walked deeper into Braydon Wood and was gone.

Bon returned to the field outside of the city to find that Arthur and Alex had already left for the castle along with the twins. Sok, Anayah, Davynn and Hiro were about to go and join the party that was in full swing around a huge bon fire a little farther to the south of the tent.

"Where did you get to?" Anayah asked as they began making their way to the bon fire.

"I went for a short walk in forest," Bon replied. The truth, if only part of it.

"I see Karrys has come to check out the festivities," Hiro said pointing to the western sky above Braydon Wood.

They all stopped walking and turned their gazes skyward. Karrys Evergreen looked like a teal jewel circling high above the trees.

"Harpur used to do that," Sok said, "before he went to Earth to watch over Arthur."

"I miss those days on Whyte Avenue." Anayah sighed.

Davynn wrapped his arm around her waist and gave her a little squeeze. "Would you rather be there then, or here now?" he teased.

Anayah smiled ruefully and, slipping her own arm around the knight's back, leaned in to give him a peck on the cheek. "Here now."

"I miss him too," Davynn said.

Karrys circled one more time and then changed directions, flying north-west toward her lair.

They started walking again, navigating the crowd of townsfolk and villagers that had gathered to officially welcome Hart and Meg to the royal family.

"I wonder why Elder Dhonna did not attend the presentation," Bon said as they reached the bon fire.

"Why would she attend?" Sok asked.

Realizing the scope of Harpur's memory wipe, Bon also realized that he would have to be careful about what he said from then on. Sorting out what was remembered and by whom was going to be something of a challenge.

"No reason," Bon said. "I thought perhaps she might be interested in meeting the prince and princess."

"She has more important things to do," Sok said. "A few weeks ago, the elven prison cell blew up and now the Council of Elders is trying to decide whether or not to reconstruct it."

Harpur has been busy, Bon thought to himself. "Ah, here comes Frode."

The appearance of the Drengrokil leader was a welcome distraction for the android.

"Is good party," Frode said. "Nice way for Drengrokil to end time in Epoh."

"Are you leaving us, then?" Davynn asked, disappointed to learn that his hero would not be staying in Epoh.

"Drengrokil are returning to Andonsheer," Frode explained. "Turns out Karrys Evergreen is not dragon that kill my men, so no need to stay and kill *her*."

Very busy, indeed! Bon thought. How the dragon had managed to alter the minds of so many people was beyond his comprehension. More than ever, he was looking forward to sitting down with Karrys and having a good long talk.

Just then little Lissa emerged from the crowd and latched onto Frode's big hand. Her face was aglow with delight as she smiled up at the small mountain of a man. "Mr. Frode, sir?" she said. "Will you come dance with me?"

"Is my honour," Frode said, bowing gallantly.

As the bizarrely mismatched couple joined the other dancers, Lissa's panting father ran up to the group of friends. "Have you seen my daughter?" he asked, scanning the crowd.

Anayah pointed to the writhing throng of dancers on the other side of the bon fire. They all watched as Frode hopped and bobbed and twirled to the music with the tiny girl squealing merrily in his arms. Lissa's father didn't know whether to be horrified or happy.

"She's in safe hands," Anayah assured the child's doting poppa.

The celebrations continued on into the night. The people of Epoh all felt safe and protected as they danced and sang and drank the evening away. When the last of the revelers finally returned to their homes, Sok, Anayah, Davynn, Hiro, Frode and Bon found themselves sitting on chairs from the royal tent, staring up at the star-dappled sky.

"That's odd," Sok said.

"What's odd?" Davynn asked.

"Draconis Major. Some of the stars are still purple." Sok pointed to the constellation in the north sky.

"Hmm..." Hiro peered at the group of nine stars. "The stars are all changing from teal to purple and back again. Why are they doing that?"

"Perhaps it takes some time for the stars to completely change after a new ruling dragon takes over a kingdom," Bon said. He made a mental note to apprise Karrys of the phenomenon as soon as possible.

"I don't think that's how it's supposed to work," Sok said. "I will have to look it up. By the way, Davynn, I've been meaning to ask you about that scroll you gave me with Harpur's misspelled signature on it. Where did you get it?"

The knight frowned, trying to recall where it had come from. "I don't remember where I found it. Or when. I must have tossed it in my room and forgot about it until it showed up again a few weeks ago. Is it important?"

"Probably not." Sok turned his gaze back to the changing stars of Draconis Major. *Something's not right. I need to talk to Arthur.*

"Speaking of strange things showing up out of nowhere," Hiro interjected. "There is a bunch of unfamiliar leaves in my laboratory. I have no idea what they are or where they came from."

"Show them to Elder Dhonna sometime," Anayah suggested. "She might be able to help you identify them."

"Yes. Good idea." Hiro stretched and whistled for his hover gilly. He'd parked it behind the royal tent earlier in the day and it was from there that it floated over to him. "I think I am ready to head back to the castle now. Bon? Do you want to ride with me?"

What Bon wanted was to be zapped to Karrys' lair and warn her about the constellation. But he couldn't make that request without raising questions he could not answer, so instead, he climbed onto the hover gilly. He would have to find a way to contact Karrys without the others knowing.

"Anyone else?" Hiro asked with a giggle.

"I'd like to walk," Davynn said, looking at Anayah for approval.

"Me too," the witch said, smiling at the knight.

"I'll ride with you," Sok said, climbing aboard next to Bon.

"Wolf is passed out in bushes," Frode said, standing up and turning toward a clump of small trees near the royal tent. "I will drag him back to camp."

As they went their separate ways, Arthur was standing on the balcony outside his private chambers. After Alex and the twins had gone to sleep, he was feeling restless, so he had come up to his rooms to have a nightcap and try to relax. It had been quite a day. The presentation of Prince Hart and Princess Meg, had gone off without a hitch and it had been so good to see Alex enjoying herself. The parade, the ceremony, Lissa beaming as she held the twins, the fine dinner, the wonderful entertainment... It had all added up to the perfect day.

But something kept nagging at him. For weeks he'd had the feeling that he had forgotten something. Something important. He was sure it had something to do with Harpur leaving court early the day the twins were born, but now that Harpur was dead, he couldn't ask the dragon what that was about. He couldn't stop thinking about it either. Nor could he shake the notion that he needed to figure out what it was. Before it drove him completely crazy.

A knock on his door drew his attention away from his tormented thoughts.

"Come in, Sok," Arthur called from the balcony. He'd seen the elf approach the castle on the hover gilly with Bon and Hiro. It was a short mental leap to assume it was the elf come to visit in spite of the late hour.

"Oh, good," Sok said, joining Arthur on the balcony, "you're still awake."

"I am," Arthur said. "What brings you up here this late at night?"

"I wanted to show you something," Sok pointed up at the night sky.

"What am I looking at?" Arthur asked.

"Draconis Major," Sok said. "Its stars are supposed to appear the colour of the ruling dragon in the kingdom from where it's viewed. But our Draconis Major is both purple and teal."

Arthur wasn't sure exactly where Draconis Major was. He scanned the sky until he noticed a star that seemed to twinkle purple and blueish-green. "I take it that has some significance?"

"It definitely isn't normal," Sok said. "I'm not completely sure, but I think the stars are supposed to change colour as soon as a new dragon inherits a kingdom."

"Hmm..." Arthur grunted. "What do you think it means?"

"I think it means I will be doing some research. Hopefully, it's nothing."

"Let's go with that for now." Arthur yawned.

"Yeah," Sok said. "Forget I mentioned it. Good night, Arthur."

"Good night, Sok."

Chapter Twenty-three

The morning after the presentation of Prince Hart and Princess Meg to the people of Epoh, Harpur Diggins woke up atop his hoard of treasure and looked around his lair. He breathed in the smell of the golden bed he laid upon and smiled. It was good to be back. Even if it was still a little weird to be in Karrys Evergreen's body.

He slithered down to the ground and outside onto the meadow that stretched out in front of his lair. It was awash with purple and teal flowers, his legacy to the land after his *defeat* by the younger, stronger, teal dragon. He stretched his wings, flapping them a few times, just to feel their power. For the fun of it, he released a long jet of dragon fire into the air, effectively forcing several worcs to abruptly change course to avoid being roasted alive. The black birds scolded the dragon as they circled back around and resumed their original flight plan.

The sun was just rising in the east, brushing the sky with the first hints of pale, yellow light. Birdsong filled the air, punctuated by the chirps of hungry fledglings still in the nest and demanding to be fed. Harpur could smell a bear sow and her young south-west of the lair. He would not hunt her, though. She had future meals to raise for him first. No, he would find plenty of elk on his way to Averborn. One or two of them would sate his appetite quite nicely.

He scanned the meadow from east to west with his one good eye. It was still odd not to see the dragon skull at the edge of the drop off to the valley. Not seeing it reminded him of how he had died, pierced through the heart as he fell onto the skull's horn. Karrys had nearly forfeited her victory over him because of that. Technically, she had not delivered the death-blow, but the legacy flowers had convinced her that she was the rightful heir to the kingdom and he was thankful that they had appeared so quickly. A few more days and the Dragon Council could have ruled against Karrys, leaving Epoh to Harpur's sons, Framanjesk and Phiercesten. And Harpur actually, very dead.

In the intervening weeks since Arthur had cast the spell that allowed him to take over Karrys Evergreen's body, he had worried about Framanjesk and Phiercesten revealing what he had done. When they had showed up unexpectedly at the challenge, Harpur had been caught off guard. He hadn't anticipated that they might want Epoh for themselves, so he did the only thing he could think of and promised them that they would be inducted into the Order of the Winter Dragons at Averborn on the summer solstice. *Scalla ap Averborn.* Come to Averborn on the solstice.

The only reason a dragon would ever go to Averborn was to participate in the Order of Winter Dragons. This rare privilege was not something he had intended to bestow upon his sons. Not that they weren't worthy of it. Being a member of the Order of the Winter Dragons was an honour Harpur had fought for in his own youth and, while Framanjesk and Phiercesten were legacies of that honour, Harpur believed they should earn it as he had done. If they wished to.

But it did seem that the young dragons had heeded his wish and were at least willing to see how he would induct them after he was dead. He assumed that they assumed that Harpur had made arrangements prior to the challenge. It was still possible that they had not deduced what Harpur had done and had accepted it as their father's last wish instead of pursuing their right to challenge Karrys for Epoh. So much could yet go wrong. But Harpur had to hold onto the hope that Framanjesk and Phiercesten wanted the Order of the Winter Dragon more than they wanted Epoh. It had been weeks since he had fallen to Karrys Evergreen after all, and no dragon had shown up to denounce him, neither had his sons come to challenge *her*.

I will know soon enough, Harpur thought as he launched Karrys' body into the air and flew north to Averborn. Just as Elder Dhonna had seen in her dream, a vast tundra opened up before Harper when he crossed the northern mountains and, as he sailed over it, he spotted his breakfast grazing amid the golden rocks that peppered the land. A few minutes later, Harpur was on the ground, about to devour a young elk that had foolishly veered away from its small herd when he had made his intentions known. Before he tore into its crispy flesh, he silently thanked the land for providing for him, a ritual he repeated after the last of the carcass disappeared into his gullet. Then, sated and eager to complete his task, Harpur continued his journey to Averborn.

When he arrived at the pool in the center of the labyrinth, Phiercesten and Framanjesk were waiting for him. The young dragons watched the teal dragon approach from outside the ring of seven golden standing stones surrounding the pool, curious to hear what she had to say. When Karrys landed a respectful distance from the sacred pool, the brothers approached her cautiously.

"Welcome, Karrys Evergreen," Phiercesten said. His purple scales with their iridescent emerald sheen glittered in the early morning light.

Next to him, Framanjesk offered no greeting and Harpur got the feeling that he was being sized up for battle. Had he been in his own body, he would have scoffed at the brazen youth, but Karrys' smaller physique would make victory over the emerald dragon before him difficult. Though he was still adjusting to the abrupt gender change, he wanted to keep this vessel healthy. He turned so that he could better keep an eye on Framanjesk and reminded himself that neither of them knew who he really was.

"Hale, Phiercesten and Framanjesk, sons of Xzynthyrius Dreamfinder." Harpur's real name felt awkward on his tongue. "I have come to honour your father's request that you be inducted into the Order of the Winter Dragons. As part of the terms of the challenge in which he fell to me, Xzynthyrius asked that I present you with his medallion of membership, which will ensure your induction into the Order of the Winter Dragons on this day. As his recognized legatees, it is your right to accept your place within the Order. May you both serve the Winter Dragons with the same honour as Xzynthyrius Dreamfinder once did."

"It cannot be that simple," Phiercesten said.

"I am only doing what Harpur asked of me," Harpur said. "He assured me that you only need to accept the medallion. If you do not wish to, that is your right as well."

Phiercesten and Framanjesk looked at each other, then they looked back at Karrys. "Where is this medallion?" Framanjesk asked.

Harpur waved his talons and a large, gold medallion appeared, suspended in the air between him and his sons. He backed away, careful not to disturb any of the stones that lined the path of the enormous labyrinth surrounding the pool. "It is yours if you want it," he said.

"And if we don't?" Phiercesten probed.

"Then drop it in the pool and leave this place," Harpur said.

"You seem to know a lot about how things work in the Order," Framanjesk said.

"As I told you," Harpur replied, "I am only doing as Harpur asked. Beyond this I know nothing about the Winter Dragons other than they exist as a benevolent order of wizardry. Take it, or don't. It makes no difference to me. I have fulfilled my agreement with Harpur in meeting you here and presenting you with the opportunity that he wished you to have. Now, I will take my leave."

Before either of his sons could say anything more, Harpur leapt into the air and turned back toward Epoh. He felt the eyes of Phiercesten and Framanjesk watching him, but he did not look back. A pang of sorrow stabbed at his heart as the distance grew between him and Averborn. This was one more part of his life as Harpur Diggins that he was leaving behind. First, he had cut off all ties with his friends in Colwygshire, erasing their memories of the events surrounding his death. Now, he had forfeited his place in the Order of the Winter Dragons. Not that that was such a big deal. The Order had been fun when he was younger, but as he had advanced in age and skill, wowing other dragons with feats of magic, just for the opportunity to openly practice it, had lost its appeal. Still, he had earned it and it had been a great honour.

There were a few more things he had left to do before Harpur Diggins could truly be put to rest. He returned to his lair and breathed a sigh of relief over having dealt with Phiercesten and Framanjesk. He had half expected them to challenge him further, possibly even follow him back from Averborn. But it seemed they had accepted that their father was dead and that Karrys Evergreen was the rightful ruler of Epoh. Should either of them ever decide to challenge him for the kingdom, he would decide how to deal with it. For now, though, these other things required his immediate attention; unanticipated details that he had to clean up before they could become insolvable problems. Bon, for instance.

The android was a threat. As the only being in Epoh who knew his secret, Bon had to be destroyed. Harpur had thought of little else since he, in his guise as Morgaine Fayle, had met the android at the presentation festivities and learned that he possessed knowledge Harpur could not afford to allow him to possess. As much as he hated the idea, the only solution that assured Harpur's secret would be kept, was having Bon disappear forever. Toward this eventual end, Harpur used his magic to compose a note asking Bon to meet Morgaine Fayle at the Boundary House in Braydon Wood and sent it to the android in Colwygshire.

While he waited for the appointed time to meet Bon, Harpur stretched out in the meadow to bask in the spring sun and think about another problem that was plaguing him. The book of Harpur's life was still being written and Karrys' book had not shown up. During the presentation of the twins the day before, Harpur, in his human form as Morgaine Fayle, had gone into Arthur's private chambers to retrieve the book and the Amber Chalice from the vault. He had wanted to do that sooner, but he needed to be sure that Arthur would not come in and find Morgaine stealing the contents of the vault. The presentation ceremonies had provided the perfect opportunity.

When he had opened the vault and found another book stuffed with hand-written pages documenting everything about the challenge and what he had done, Harpur didn't know whether to be deeply impressed by Arthur's ingenuity or extremely angered by it. He had taken it, along with the book of his life and the Amber Chalice, recognizable to him only by the amber stone embedded into it with the intention of taking them to the lair for safe keeping. But when he returned to the lair after leaving Bon, and discovered that his book had not ended with his death as it should have done, he realized that he had to hide it somewhere it would never be found. He also had to get Karrys' book and hide it as well. That would require a trip to the dragon compound in Andonsheer.

So many things had to be tended to if he was ever to pull off his ruse. He would always worry about being discovered, but the more he tended to now, and the faster he got it all done, the more his mind would be eased. Waiting for his meeting with Bon gave him time to fret and that stirred up his agitation to the point where he couldn't enjoy the basking any longer. He left the meadow and flew south over Braydon Wood. There was just enough time to get to Andonsheer and retrieve Karrys' life book before he met with Bon.

There were three other dragons in the compound when Harpur arrived. They greeted him as Karrys and offered their congratulations on her new rulership over Epoh. Harpur didn't recognize any of them and had to sift through Karrys' memories to identify the white, the blue and the red as the acquaintances they were to the dragon that embodied him. He accepted their accolades with as much decorum as he could muster, but it was unpleasant in the extreme having to listen to them talk about the great purple dragon's long-awaited defeat.

"If you will excuse me," Harpur finally said. "I must retrieve my life book and get back to Epoh. Xzynthyrius Dreamfinder left a huge mess that I need to clean up."

He went into the tunnel that led to the cells and followed the downward sloping corridor past them into an underground room on the north side of the compound. The room was incongruously small for its purpose of storing dragon life books and resembled a human-size library more than a depository for dragon-sized dragons. The space was designed to keep the life books of those dragons who chose to store them there safe. Since no dragon could actually enter unless they transformed, the only way to retrieve Karrys' book was by magic and Harpur stood at the entrance and called it to him. Karrys' book was somewhat smaller than Harpur's and its leather cover was ornately embossed with a pattern of leaves. Once he had it in his hands, he retreated from the tunnel and left the compound.

In the first weeks after the challenge, Harpur had ordered the Fae to relocate to the south-western edge of Braydon Wood. Their new territory was larger with a pretty lake fed by a waterfall that tumbled spectacularly down from the mountains on that side of the kingdom. The bucolic landscape pleased the Fae queen and she had offered no resistance to the change in terms, ordering her people to comply immediately.

The elves, of course, were not so enthusiastic about the new arrangement. The Elders protested Karrys' edict vehemently until she threatened to banish all elvenkind from Epoh if they did not accept her terms and agree to stay out of the new Fae Lands. It had hurt Harpur more than he wanted to admit to hear Elder Dhonna's condemnation of his wishes. Her anger was almost more than he could bear.

"You cannot do this!" Elder Dhonna had exclaimed. "The Fae will ruin the lake."

"The Fae have lordship over the waterways in Epoh. That is as Harpur decreed and this is as I decree. They will not harm it, Bel... Elder Dhonna." Harpur had almost let his pet name for the guild master slip and it pained him to know that he had to stay away from her.

"This is wrong!" Elder Dhonna insisted. "You must not let this happen."

Harpur's temper, fueled by the pain of seeing his dear friend so upset, flared as the orange glow of dragon fire burned visibly under the teal scales of Karrys' body. "Then the elves are no longer welcome in Epoh! If you do not wish to live here under the terms that I have set, then leave. There is no room in my kingdom for your insolence."

The other Elders had rushed to calm Elder Dhonna and quickly agreed to the new terms. Before Harpur could say or do anything he might have come to regret, he had flown away, leaving the Elders to console his friend. It was all he could do, not to turn to the east and burn a village out of sheer frustration.

He knew that in time, the elves would adjust and come to a place of acceptance; if not forgiveness. But it was his kingdom after all and having the Fae a safer distance from the humans was in everyone's best interest. And, so, the Fae moved out of the lands they had occupied for centuries and the elves moved in to administer to the trees they had been cut off from for as many centuries. As Harpur flew over the old Fae Lands with Karrys' life book, he could see groups of elves working to heal the forest where the Fae had let it decline. Satisfied, he veered to the east and circled back northward to the Boundary. It was time to meet with Bon. He would hide the books and the chalice after he was done with the android.

Harpur landed in a clearing not far from the Boundary and transformed into Morgaine Fayle. Her ample curves filled the teal leggings and vest in ways he was sure he would never fully get used to. He could have created a more androgynous guise to transform into, but any deviation from what was normal for Karrys could potentially give him away. So, he adjusted himself as best he could and then became invisible before setting off on the short walk to the Boundary. Before he confronted Bon, he had to know that the android was alone. Harpur was almost disappointed to find the android very much unaccompanied and studying the keep surrounding the Boundary with keen interest.

From the corner of the Boundary House, Harpur watched Bon as he searched for an alternative to luring him back to the clearing and burning him to ash. He was startled when the android turned and looked directly at him.

"Ah! There you are," Bon said. "I was beginning to think that I had misunderstood your invitation."

"You can see me?" Morgaine asked.

"I can see your heat signature," Bon replied.

Feeling somewhat foolish, Harpur became visible again as the sultry, raven-haired beauty he was now. "I should have known," Morgaine hissed.

"Like you, I like to keep some of my more useful talents to myself," Bon said, looking at the large book Morgaine carried in her arms. "But I assume that you have requested to meet me so soon because you have decided to destroy me."

Morgaine tilted her head and frowned. "If there was any other way..." she began, but didn't finish.

"I believe that there is," Bon said. "Another way, that is."

"Oh?" Morgaine kept her face passive.

"I am here on Thraeh for only a short time. My mission is to study dragon culture and I have been granted a year to do that. Make me your prisoner. Keep me in your lair with you and teach me about dragons. When my time here is up, I will go on to the next world and your secret will remain safe." Bon turned his attention back to the Boundary House and the enchanted lock on the door.

"That is an intriguing proposal," Morgaine said, folding her arms and leaning against the Boundary House. "I dare say, though, that it would not make me any more popular with our friends in Colwygshire."

"Is it your aim to be popular?" Bon asked.

Morgaine couldn't help herself and she laughed. "No, I suppose it is not. What happens when they attempt to rescue you? They will try."

Bon looked over at Morgaine. "Will they? You didn't wipe the knowledge of dragon magic from their memories. If you make it clear to them that this is your wish and that any attempt to rescue me will result in..."

"I won't kill them."

"I was going to say banishment from the kingdom, but a good death threat is often very effective too." Bon smiled at the dragon-wizardess and refrained from pointing out that she was perfectly willing to destroy him.

"Have you met them?" Morgaine asked, incredulous. "I wouldn't get a moment's peace once they learned I was holding you prisoner."

"Then you have no choice," Bon said, looking directly at Morgaine. "You will have to destroy me. But not here, so close to the city. I assume you will want to take me back to your lair to do the deed."

Harpur's resolve had completely dissolved. The idea of destroying Bon was unconscionable. To waste this technological marvel would be unforgivable. Besides, it was only for a year. Once Bon was gone to wherever he would go to next, there would be nothing Arthur, Sok, Anayah, Hiro or Davynn could do. He would just have to make sure that Bon was warded in such a way that Anayah couldn't free him magically. And it would be nice to have some company at the lair. There was much he could learn from Bon as well.

"Very well," Morgaine said. She snapped her fingers and a warded steal cage appeared around the android. "But you really will be my prisoner. And you will remain in this cage."

Bon examined the enclosure. "I have been in worse situations."

With another snap of her fingers, Morgaine zapped herself and Bon back to the lair.

"Can you believe the gall of that dragon?" Anayah barked. For the hundredth time. "Who does she think she is anyway?"

"I believe she thinks she is the ruler of Epoh," Sok said. He turned his glazed eyes to Davynn, hoping that the knight would find a way to calm the witch down.

"I mean, why in Harpur's holy top hat, would she take Bon prisoner? It doesn't make sense." Anayah slammed her hand down on the round table in the council chambers. "We have to rescue him!"

Arthur sighed. "We've tried, Anayah. Karrys has the whole meadow warded. We can't even get close to the lair. But Bon's letter says that he's there willingly and that Karrys is treating him fairly."

It had been several days since Arthur had received the letter from Bon explaining his imprisonment in Karrys Evergreen's lair. While he didn't say why Karrys had taken him prisoner, he had been explicit in stating that he was in no danger and that they should not try to rescue him.

Of course, they *had* tried to rescue him. But Karrys had warded the entire meadow so that anyone who attempted to access it, whether magically or physically, was immediately zapped back to where they had come from. No one could get near the lair.

"I don't give a fig about what Bon said in his letter," Anayah shouted. "That arrogant she-dragon must have forced him to write what he did."

"And we were so close to figuring out the anti-gravity propulsion system for the hover gillies," Hiro mused. "Without Bon, I don't think I will be able to finish it."

Anayah shot a scathing glare in the direction of the stumped Krist.

"Maybe we can negotiate visitations," Sok suggested. "Then Hiro and Bon can work on the hover gillies and we can still get to spend some time with him."

Anayah redirected her scathing glare.

"Well, I am not about to challenge our ruling dragon over this. Whatever compelled Karrys to take Bon prisoner is not a matter I'm going to get tangled up in," Davynn folded his hands on the table and took Anayah's refreshed glower head on. "There's no point in stirring up a confrontation that could get us killed."

"Or worse," Sok said. "She could banish us from the kingdom."

"How is banishment worse than death?" Arthur asked.

"If we're dead, we won't know that we aren't in Epoh." Sok looked forlornly at the empty tray that had once held an array of pastries. "Hiro, we could use some more comfort food."

Hiro reached into his satchel and produced a platter of sandwiches. Sok volunteered to be their taste tester.

"I don't believe you people!" Anayah snapped. "I'm going to my room."

When the red smoke the witch had disappeared into cleared, the remaining four companions all breathed a sigh of relief.

"She's a feisty one," Hiro said.

"She's not going to her room, is she?" Arthur asked.

"Probably not," Davynn said.

"Who's up for rescuing the witch?" Sok took another bite of his sandwich. "Again."

The four remaining companions all breathed a sigh of frustration.

"I'll go tell Alex I'll be away for a while," Arthur said, reaching for a sandwich.

"I'll go get some horses ready for us," Davynn stood up and took two sandwiches.

"I'll go tell Berryl that he's in charge for the next few days." Sok grabbed another sandwich to take with him.

"I'll wait here until you're all ready," Hiro said, reaching over the front of his hover gilly and pulling the platter of sandwiches closer to himself.

Epilogue

Harpur stood in the meadow in front of his lair and stared up at the northern night sky. The day that he had taken Bon prisoner, he had intended to take his and Karrys' life books and the Amber Chalice to the Fae Lands for safe keeping. But when the android informed him about the anomalous colours in the constellation, Draconis Major, he changed his mind and stowed them in a remote cave in the mountains above the new Fae Lands. What was most disturbing about this was that Sok had been the one to notice it.

He had assumed that his secret would be safe with Bon imprisoned as he was, but the stars told a different story. All it would take was for another dragon to visit Epoh at night and notice the constellation. Or for Sok to do a bit of research and put two and two together. The only thing he could think of to tell them, should it ever come to it, was that Karrys had somehow ingested some of his blood during their challenge battle and his essence was within her. It was plausible. If only barely. And he chided himself for not having thought of it before he'd had Arthur resurrect him in Karrys' body. It seemed that every time he solved one problem, another one just popped up to take its place.

"Karrys Evergreen, I demand that you set Bon free this instant!"

Harpur swung his head around to look at the angry witch standing at the trailhead at the edge of the meadow. She had attempted to zap herself, Arthur, Sok, Davynn and Hiro to the lair several times, but the warding had bounced them back to the castle. Now she stood just beyond the perimeter of the warding, yelling at Karrys to free the android. Clearly, Bon's carefully crafted letter had not been enough to appease Anayah.

Rather than engage her, Harpur slithered back into the lair and warded the entrance to keep the sound of her shouting out. He hoped she would get tired and give up.

"You aren't going to harm her, are you?" Bon asked from inside his cage.

"She'll go away eventually." Harpur sighed as he climbed to the top of his hoard and curled up to sleep.

"What are you going to do about the Order of the Winter Dragons?" Bon asked.

That was yet another problem in a seemingly endless parade of problems. He'd received a message from the Order of the Winter Dragons ordering Karrys to attend an extraordinary meeting at Averborn on the next full moon.

"I haven't decided," Harpur said.

"If you go, may I come with you?" Bon asked.

"I don't think that would be wise." Harpur picked up a handful of gold and let it sift through his talons.

"I understand," Bon said.

Silence filled the lair around the trickling of water that dripped from the stalactites on the ceiling. Suddenly, Harpur leapt down from his hoard of gold and roared in furious weariness. It had only been a couple of months since the challenge and already he was exhausted by trying to keep up his ruse. He glared at Bon in the cage and his chest glowed with the orange fire in Karrys' chest. The android backed away as far as the bars that contained him would allow.

"Not like this," Bon whispered.

But Harpur did not set the android on fire. He wheeled around and burst out of the lair onto the meadow. The moment he appeared, Anayah started shouting at him again, and again the fire swelled inside of him.

"Go away, witch, and leave me alone!" he hissed at Anayah through the warding.

"I will not go away. Not until you release my friend."

Harpur roared again. Teal-black smoke billowed from his nose and mouth. But Anayah didn't move. Shaking with terror, she stood her ground and Harpur nearly lost control.

"If you will not go away," Harpur growled, "you will join him."

It was a rash and wholly perilous threat. For several long minutes, Anayah and Harpur stared at each other. And then the witch called the dragon's bluff.

"I dare you," Anayah seethed.

Having backed himself into a corner, there was nothing else he could do. Harpur waved his talons at Anayah and she was instantly confined inside a warded and sound-proof cage of her own and zapped inside the lair. Then Harpur launched himself into the night sky and flew over Epoh toward the Crysteel Sea.

Acknowledgements

My undying gratitude goes out to my editor and sister, Peggy Thiessen. I cannot thank you enough for your help in bringing this story to life.

About the Author

Saoirse Temple is the author of the *Bounders of Epoh* trilogy—*The Fire of Orhowyn*, *The Amber Chalice*, and *The Power of Averborn*—as well as the *Dear Diary Style Files*, a humorous series on writing craft. An editor and book coach by trade, she delights in helping stories find their sharpest, brightest forms.

When she isn't writing or wrangling words, Saoirse can often be found sketching dragons, dreaming up new worlds, or coaxing inspiration out of a strong cup of tea.

Discover more at: **www.saoirsetemple.com**

The custom scene break symbol used in this book was created by Saoirse Temple. Visit https://www.saoirsetemple.com/category/all-products to purchase scene break symbols for use in your publications. To order your own custom scene break symbol, contact Saoirse directly at: saoirsealtemple@gmail.com

Follow Saoirse on
Facebook: www.facebook.com/saoirsetempe[1]
Instagram: @saoirsealt

---

1.   http://www.facebook.com/saoirsetempe

www.ingramcontent.com/pod-product-compliance
Lightning Source LLC
Chambersburg PA
CBHW020926020726
47495CB00002B/369